THE GLASS CHALICE

Francis McCrickard

THAT CANYON PRESS

Seven Steps of Wisdom

To question with humility; to listen closely; to believe faithfully; to work with purpose; to hope bravely; to understand wisely; to love deeply.

Liber de numeris IV 25

Cover design by: Anna McCrickard

http://www.overlap.co.uk

That Canyon Press: thatcanyon@gmail.com

ISBN NUMBER: 9798553903497

The Glass Chalice is set in early ninth century Ireland and Egypt. Ireland had not been invaded since prehistoric times and had avoided the disruption caused in large areas of the rest of Europe by the collapse of the Roman Empire. Christianity had been established there for over three centuries and during what came to be known as the Dark Ages, Irish monasteries were sanctuaries for Christian learning and for the continuation of classical studies. Students came to them from all over Europe to receive their education.

The Irish monks themselves were great travellers. For more than two centuries before the period the story is set in, they had carried their faith and learning throughout Europe and beyond. There were important early contacts between the Christian Church in Egypt and in Ireland. Early monasticism in Ireland owed a great deal to the practices which the Desert Fathers introduced to third and fourth century Egypt.

The initial idea for the story came from a tale told of St. Patrick. It is to be found in the earliest known document that gives an account of the saint's life, a memoir written in the second half of the seventh century by Tirechan. After ordaining a certain Ailbe at Duma Graid, near Lake Kilglass, Patrick spoke of a cave in the Mountains of the Children of Ailill. Inside that cave was a stone altar with four glass chalices at its corners, evidence that Christian worship had taken place in Ireland before his arrival. Chalices of glass were used in the early Church and H.V. Morton in his book **Through the Lands of the Bible** speculates that the chalices Patrick saw came from Egypt.

To my forebears

PART ONE

CILLEBAIRRE, Ireland

The Raiders

The strangeness was close, pulling at his heart as well as his head as Ruadhan knew it would be from the excitement and the fear. He crawled into the gorse bushes before it overcame him completely.The thorns pulled at his tunic and tore his face, legs and arms viciously but he hardly felt them. When he'd crawled in far enough to be hidden, he lay as still as he could and hoped that when it started, *if* it started, it would not betray him. That it would happen was never certain. The signs couldn't be read easily. They changed their pattern: differing weaves of noises in his ears, sudden coldness, a blurring of vision, violent trembling, dizziness and a hammering in his head; sometimes, all of them. Only when the hammering was followed by *bursting*, sensations in his head like knots of wood splitting and spitting in a fire, did Ruadhan know the strangeness would lay him unconscious. At those times, Fáelcar roped and fastened him like an animal until it was over.

"He is a danger to us all!" Fáelcar raged, "And to himself, not that that matters much." His kicking and punching and roaring were worse than any beast, Fáelcar said. Ruadhan remembered nothing of any of it after the *bursting*. He would not have let anyone rope him.

The crowd of strangers bristled with swords and axes on the slope below him. They were arguing in words he did not understand. Northmen, *Finngaill*, the fierce invaders from across the sea; it had to be them. They arrived like a summer storm and rapidly soaked the land in blood. They wanted a vantage point to survey the land ahead of them and had chosen Wolf's Head Hill. Ruadhan was a fool. They would take the sheep that grazed at the bottom of the slope, the sheep he was minding. He would be punished.

Below him, like an adder woken from winter sleep, the river slunk through the valley. The sun glinting on its surface, the long day's work, hunger, and finally, the steady beat of a heron's wings on the still air had drawn him into sleep and he had not seen the sleek boats on the water. The sails had been lowered, the oars raised and the boats beached and half-emptied before Ruadhan became aware of the invaders. There was no time to warn the settlement. Crouched low, bent as tightly to the ground as he

1

could be, with his heart thumping like a rabbit running, Ruadhan burrowed deeper into the gorse.

The strangers quarrelled twenty metres below him where the slope levelled off at the edge of a small, treacherous bog that Ruadhan had been told to keep the sheep well away from. A tall, bent, fair-haired man with a reddish moustache was very angry and shouting. A shorter man with long, braided black hair and a vividly scarred forehead laughed at him. Ruadhan strained to pick up words that might make sense to him, but heard none. Red-Moustache's anger peaked. He raised his axe as if to strike but before he could, Long-Plait gave him a powerful push that toppled him into the bog. Some of the others laughed but some were furious. They jostled one another and brandished their weapons. Long-Plait turned, pushed through them and walked calmly up the slope closer to where Ruadhan was. Before he sat down, he stared intently at the bushes where the boy lay hidden. He saw the boy. Ruadhan stared back at him. Long-Plait raised a hand, palm outwards and made a short patting movement in the air and Ruadhan knew the stranger would not give him away to the others. It was then the surging began in Ruadhan's mind and his body twitched uncontrollably and the surges became thuds - one, two, three, four, five and then the first fire-burst erupted in his head. It was happening. As he slid into unconsciousness, Ruadhan prayed that he wouldn't cry out in his helplessness and made fists as tightly as he could as if that would hold the shaking and the whimpering fast within him and out of sight and hearing of the rest of the strangers. In shapes he had never seen, in motions he had never seen, terrifying creatures broke into his mind and rampaged over deep, dark, swirling landscapes: they milled and fought, all indeterminate until huge, scaled and winged beasts rose, then swooped and devoured half-cat, half-human beings.

In the swamp, Red-Moustache found his feet but struggled. A comrade in a yellow leather vest steadied himself at the edge of the bog and, holding his axe in both hands, reached with it as far as he could towards his friend. Two others held on to this man as he leaned so that he would not follow his friend into the bog, and two others held on to them. Red-Moustache grabbed the axe and inched out of the quagmire. At the point where he could climb out himself, he let go of the axe, angrily swatted at the hands then offered to help him, and plunged his arms under the surface of the slurry. He bent until the mud was once more up to his chest and strained to lift something heavy. It was a show of strength, an attempt to dismiss the humiliation he had suffered. He made a deep, guttural moan and his face became a fiery red but his efforts were rewarded when, with a loud sucking sound, the load came from its dark resting place. Red-Moustache rolled it from the bog and, smiling and shouting, clambered out after it.

Wolves? Foxes? Birds? Each animal was curled about another in a tall column that stretched to the sky and each sank fangs, claws, and beaks savagely into that other's flesh. Ruadhan waited for the column to tumble and for him, the watcher, to be caught up in the struggle but the picture froze. He came round with a shudder but with the awareness that he was safe and undiscovered. The band below him stood in silence around the corpse. It was a sign. They could go no further. With hardly another word being spoken and stopping only to round up six of Ruadhan's sheep, the Northmen returned to the rest of the raiding party at the river bank. Long-Plait did not leave as quickly as the rest. He knelt down by the body, rolled it back into the bog and watched until the disturbed surface settled once more.

Ruadhan's vocabulary had grown steadily with his body but only in his mind did he visit regularly all of its pages. The yelps and grunts that he had brought from the forest were all that most of the others, with the exception of Ite and Tulchán, heard. It was different now. He had to warn the village and in the telling, what he had seen by the bog and what he had seen in his during his fit became entangled in Ruadhan's mind. For a while, he stuttered and tumbled words out in a mesh of his vision and reality.

"They were as tall as trees?"

"No... no... that was when I was..."

"Scales like fish?"

"No, that was in the dream too."

"You lose sheep and then make up this ridiculous story. You will be punished for your lies." Fáelcar hit him sharply on the back of his head and the others pinned him to the floor. One forced Ruadhan's jaws apart and smelled his breath, "Foul! I've seen him sleep with his mouth wide open inviting devils in! Smell, smell! Sulphur!" Two more did and confirmed that Ruadhan's breath smelled of Hell and devils. "I don't know why I gave you a roof over your head," said Fáelcar, but pulled the other men off him.

3

Ruadhan brought trouble but he did not want him damaged since a man's strength was entering the boy's body and before long Fáelcar would be rewarded in work for taking him into his house. And besides, the boy had two powerful friends: Tulchán, the monk, and Ite, one of Fáelcar's blood children. Ite had a great liking for Ruadhan and would kick and spit fury even worse than her mother if she saw what was being done to him now. "Leave him be."

In spite of their doubts, Fáelcar with several others and Ruadhan went to the place. They could count sheep if nothing else. They all thought Ruadhan was a stupid boy and a liar. The village should have heeded the ones who had screamed for his death when, naked, filthy and little more than a babe but screaming like a beast, he had crawled out of the forest. And on Samhain Eve of all nights! And with that hair colour! Not the brightest; a deep, muddy crimson, but red all the same! Kill him or take him back deep into the forest's darkness, some had bayed. Let the wolves raise him! Fáelcar, weak, soft-headed some said, and prompted by the old monk, Tulchán, had taken the boy in. He and his family had suffered tribulations ever since and were mocked by many. The boy carries a curse; he brings ill luck; he would always be a hindrance and would never grow to be a full man; he belongs to the Evil One; he must never be allowed to plant corn; he is more animal than human. And when he was writhing and frothing at the mouth and nose, many believed there were serpents in his head that one day would break free and destroy the village.

It was late in the day. The animals were penned, the cooking fires burning. Darkness was slinking into the valley. Across on the southern bank of the river, the monks were gathering once more for prayer. It was a time for settling, for eating, telling stories, huddling against the night, gathering strength for the following day's work. Certainly, it was not a time to harvest corpses and, as they followed Ruadhan back to the place, the men's steps were slow and wary and their talk was full of tales of the dead who still walked in the land of the living and had been seen by this person or that one. They could kill a calf in its mother's womb with a glance; they could blacken ears of corn with a touch and they could dive into you like an otter into water and emerge with your heart bloody and beating.

Dusk shrouded the group thickly by the time they reached the bog. The evening was still and warm. Clouds of small flies hovered close to the swampy ground. Before they could stop him, the boy jumped in at the edge

4

of the bog and thrashed around with his arms. He found the body easily and managed to raise a foot above the surface. Midges haloed the swaying limb. Men waded in and roped the corpse. It was Feach who had disappeared two years previously. Perhaps the boy had spoken the truth.

ALEXANDRIA, Egypt
The Harbour

A dusty, brown foot, gnarled with a warty lump the size of a quail's egg just below the big toe, planted itself alongside Brecc's head. Ah yes, medicine made from a blue flower, delicate, four-petalled, would cure that ailment. What was its name? If you made a tincture from the whole plant... no, just the roots, or was it the flowerhead only? He would kill someone at Clonmacnoise one of these days with his potions. Anyway, whatever the infusion was, it would clear that nasty growth. Suddenly, Brecc remembered and felt for the gold. The pouches were there, sewn into his tunic at the small of his back. He felt again. They were intact. His satchel and prayer book? Brecc felt it by his right knee and, as he did, wondered if his waking mind had got its priorities right. The foot lifted and moved on and Brecc realised where he was. It was foolish to have lain down where they had, so close to the harbour and without any defences about them save the tall grasses, but Brecc had been exhausted and it seemed they had come to no harm. He was delighted to be on dry land once more. For the first time since they had left Marseilles, and in spite of the mosquitoes, he had slept well, missed his dawn prayers, and now felt refreshed and ready to meet the Patriarch. Even though it was a mere seven hours since he had completed this final leg of his journey, the hardships seemed to belong to a different age, and Brecc felt genuinely contrite for having told the vessel's captain that he could sail as well as he could fly.

Fiacc was still in a deep sleep face down in the tall, thick-stemmed grass they had trampled into a bed but even in his companion's repose, the old monk sensed tension, an aura of great matters unresolved. Which people was it in these parts, he thought, who buried face down men without heirs so that they might fertilise the earth of their grave? He couldn't remember. Brecc stretched his arms and hoped his own good mood would last but was not optimistic since his spirits wilted quickly in this climate. The message from the Patriarch had said that the matter was urgent and that only someone who could be trusted completely should be sent. Abbot Ronan had made it clear that Brecc was not his first choice for this mission, but that Diciul, who would have been ideal, was in the Kingdom of the Franks and could not be taken from *Liber de Mensura Orbis Terrae,* an important geographical text he was working on.

"Well," Brecc thought, "I suppose it is pleasing to be looked upon as trustworthy by your superiors, but, if I am honest with myself, I wish they thought of me less highly, because, much as this place fascinates, I would rather be home, swinging and pushing, pulling a hoe in my - tut tut – in *the* monastery garden."

Even though there was no pain that morning, Brecc rubbed his left shoulder slowly for a moment and gazed across the eastern harbour to the great lighthouse of Pharos that they had sighted when the boat was still a great distance from the coast. Rising one hundred and fifty metres, the massive granite structure dominated the Mediterranean entrance to the bustling city of Alexandria. The sun had barely risen but the streets of this great crossroads were already busy. Caravans from China, India and Ceylon brought silk, jade, tea and spices. From the south-west, across the great deserts, tireless camels carried ivory and gold. Timber, pottery, salt, and fish spilled on to Alexandria's quays, brought from a host of other Mediterranean ports. Brecc breathed deeply. After another glance at the still motionless Fiacc, he walked aimlessly among piles of grain, glassware and rich embroideries waiting to leave the port, and watched as great earthenware jars of olive oil were hoisted on to a ship. One swayed uncertainly above him, slipped from its ropes, fell and shattered on the ground close by him. The dark yellow liquid spilled in all directions but most found its way to a narrow gutter that led it in one thick stream over the sides of the quay. The sailor operating the hoist cursed the two on the dock for what had happened. One of them, thin, lithe and with deep black skin, pulled at the top of his tunic and bared his chest as if inviting death. In swift, liquid movements, he fell to his knees, placed both hands in the flow of oil, raised them heavenwards and then smeared the oil on his bared flesh. All the while, he screamed at the sailor on board the ship. Whether it was an apology or insult, Brecc had no idea.

He stopped and breathed in deeply again, too deeply, and for one uncomfortable moment felt the sway of the ship underneath him once more. He had to sit down heavily on a sack of grain until his breathing settled itself and the feeling went. "And the pilgrimage across the desert still to come," he thought. "Ah, well, must try not to complain too much when I get back to Ireland." He stood up very slowly and continued to enjoy the sights, sounds and smells, the energy of the busy quaysides. The sharp morning light drew his attention to details: a boy with much lighter skin, almost white, in the middle of a ragged group of children playing at the water's edge; the pulsing gills of the fresh fish scudding into baskets; the raised scar, like a rope with several knots tied in it on the back of a brown man naked to the waist; the straight, quietly confident step of women bearing pots on their heads; the dark, agitated eyebrows of a man in the middle of a furious argument with some Greek sailors. Everywhere he found the richness of creation. Give praise. He could have stayed there a long time, but recalled his meeting with the Patriarch and decided that he should go to him before the day lost its coolness completely. Brecc found the late morning Egyptian heat close to unbearable and had suffered severe sunstroke on his first visit. The memory of it made his skin prickle and so he turned his back on the sea, walked towards the first low buildings and along the front of them to a narrow street that led from the harbour. Before the corner, he had to jostle through a silent group of tall, lean and tough-limbed men whom he recognised as Abyssinian Highlanders from the long, greased braids their hair was fastened in. Brecc felt the edges of his calm begin to fray as he pushed through, but they remained impassive, ignoring his busy little presence and allowing their gazes to slowly take in all that was around them. He turned the corner, annoyed with himself for getting annoyed, and almost fell over a leopard held on a chain by a very large Egyptian. Brecc quickly pressed himself hard up against the corner building, the fingers of his right hand curling and gripping the upper edge of a large crack in the dried mud, but the animal moved closer, raised itself up – *was it Columbanus or Gallus who when confronted with a bear bade the creature put a log on the fire and then fed it bread? Gallus, it was Gallus* - and pinned him to the wall with its forelegs. The large Egyptian did nothing to stop the creature. Brecc closed his eyes, tried to recall recent sins, and said a prayer to himself. He heard the man shuffling closer and then smelt his sweet-scented breath as he bent down and said: "Be here at midday. The young monk, Makarius, will take you to the Patriarch. Please do not look for the Patriarch yourself. If you do, you will place him and yourself in great danger." Brecc could sense the man smiling at his discomfort but he did not want to confirm it and kept his eyes closed. He felt the pressure of the creature's paws lift but kept his eyes shut and prayed: *Yahweh my God, I take refuge in you, save me from all my pursuers and rescue me, or he will savage me like a lion, carry me off with no one to rescue me.* When he did open them, both man

8

and the leopard had gone. Brecc breathed deeply several times then strode back around the corner, pushing through the Abyssinians once more. He could not see the strange messengers anywhere. He thought of his earlier meditation: "Richness of creation, my *clocthech!*[1]" This was the last thing he wanted to meet on his journey; he was too old for intrigue. He wondered if the spring sowing and pruning was over at the monastery of Clonmacnoise.

---

[1]*Clocthech* is the belfry, the bell house. When Brecc was much younger, a fellow monk, bending very low in the garden, expelled with force and noise a great deal of wind whereupon Brecc stopped his labours and made his way to the church announcing that the *clocthech* had called them all to prayer. The term was coined on that day, among the more flippant of the brethren, to refer to a person's bottom. Brecc received six lashes of the cane for this.

CILLEBAIRRE
The Scar

There had been great argument over the boy and his *strangeness*. Two monks, certain the boy was a sack of skin packed full of devils, wanted him isolated on the monastery side of the river where he could do little harm and could be prayed over. Several felt sympathy with those villagers who were threatened by his fits and wanted him cast out of the settlement completely. Tulchán was wary since the world was a complex confrontation between the forces of good and evil, but he accepted none of this assessment and protected the boy. He reminded the community of the ancient Brehon laws of the land that granted respect and equality to those who had disabilities and of the heavy fines that could be levied on those who mocked or otherwise mistreated them. Ruadhan was different, his opponents argued. Ruadhan had come from the forest, was more animal than human, should not be recognised by the law. Tulchán had yet to witness the *crupán*, the seizures that afflicted the boy, but believed he knew Ruadhan well enough to discount any talk of devils. The boy spoke freely to him alone. The fits might be terrifying to behold but Tulchán was sure from what the boy himself had told him, that there was a stillness at the heart of all his struggling, ultimately a vision of things that were not of the Devil, a vision that might take him beyond the pain and perhaps beyond the limits of their earthly circumstances. The boy *saw* things, just as Tulchán himself had done from time to time, was shown pictures in his mind that glimpsed other places and perhaps, *the* other place, the happier place beyond. Tulchán was well-aware how the devil could, in the guise of enlightenment, snake into our thoughts and dreams and shape our actions to his ends and he always questioned, constantly kept guard, but did not believe that this was happening with the boy. There was something about Ruadhan, his quietness; his independence of spirit; his ability to endure hardship and his eagerness to learn, that convinced Tulchán otherwise and told the old monk that the boy was destined for a greater life than Cillebairre would offer him. That was Tulchán's conclusion and so firm was he in it that he had chosen Ruadhan for a special mission. True, the boy was simple, raw, unskilled, uneducated and there was a danger in favouring one so lowly, not least the danger of kindling fierce envy among young and old, but Ruadhan had been *given* by the forest, given for a special reason. Tulchán did not think he was open to fanciful interpretations of events but when this child had staggered, naked and starving from the forest to be beaten, scourged by fearful villagers and fastened arms outstretched to a tree like God himself, he knew this was someone who had a special destiny to fulfil.

Dawn entered the valley like a knife drawn slowly from its scabbard. Tulchán went for the boy as soon as there was enough light for him to use the stepping stones. A tall man, once he had been able to cross with a few confident strides but now had to be careful. Suppleness had left his joints several years before and he suffered painful falls frequently.

"Will they come back?"

"Finding Feach'sbody has deterred them, but for how long, I don't know. It could be days or much longer but they will return."Tulchán led Ruadhan back over the river and up the gently sloping bank through the stockade to the monastery. They wove their way through the small stone cells and wood and thatch huts. As they neared the school, Ruadhan heard a teacher asking questions and the students answering in a language he did not understand. "The Word of God?"Tulchán stopped and looked beyond the church to the dense forest that cloaked the shallow valley side and above it, moorland. He scanned the forest to the east. The cloak had been torn and pastures established in several places, lighter green spearheads into the darker forest green. He smiled to himself as, for a moment, he had a vision of the trees uprooting and rearranging themselves into letters and a sentence to give him an answer. The long hours in the scriptorium had taught Tulchán to value words, spoken and written, especially, of course, those that came from God. What he, Tulchán, said and wrote at any time could mean salvation or damnation for himself and the one who received the words. He shuddered and walked on. "Always, Ruadhan, always. That is the centre of their studies. They read his Word as in Holy Scripture, but... but..." Tulchán made a sweeping gesture with his right arm: "They also learn to see God's writing in the rocks and trees, the rivers that surround us; in... in the patterns of the stars..." The monk hesitated. He jabbed a finger at the air ahead of him: "And..." Jab. "And in..." Jab. For a moment, he looked as of he was in pain as he strained for further explanation. "In the mystery of numbers and geometry." He stopped walking and looked directly at Ruadhan, his face back to its usual intense expression, an odd swirl of happy belief and anxiety. "The histories of people in poetry and grammar; that's another source, as well. His Word.

11

The Word." Such talk belonged in a world that was much more than a river's width away from Ruadhan's. The handful of youths on this bank, the students, were the children of nobles sent to the monastery when they were very young. Ruadhan knew nothing of his birth. Perhaps animals *had* raised him. Tulchán kept looking directly at Ruadhan and spoke sharply. He wanted to know about recent history. "Tell me about the one with plaited hair, the one you say lingered by your hiding place."

You say: Ruadhan was used to having his word doubted but not by the monk. He kept his temper. "A strong one," he replied. "A leader."

"And you saw him make the sign of the cross?"

"He was half-turned from me but, yes, I think he did."

"You *think* he did?"

"He did it!" snapped Ruadhan and quickly, roughly touched his forehead, midriff and shoulders with his right hand.

Tulchán was deep in thought but not so deep that the boy's rudeness didn't register. "Don't speak like that. It's no wonder you are beaten. I am on your side. I want to believe you."

"You *want to*..." It was Ruadhan's turn to gaze at the dense forest and wish he were back inside its comforting darkness and away from questions, away from doubters, away from everyone, even the monk.

"Walk. Come on, keep up."

Ruadhan was *keeping up*, always *kept up* with adults, did what he was bid. That way he was more likely to avoid beatings. He smiled to himself. It was easy to *keep up* with the old monk whose legs looked as if devils were forcing one knee to go east and the other west.

Tulchán spoke quickly and became breathless. "These people from the sea do not worship the one true God. They claim there are many Gods. Odin is the name they give their chief God but we could be forgiven for thinking that the one they honour most is Thor, the God of war." He stopped suddenly and calmed his breathing. He did not turn to the boy. There were many of his own who, by their actions, worshiped the same God. He raised his head and looked to one of the cleared areas of valley side bitten into the forest beneath the moorland. Its semi-circle shape made him think of his tonsure. He stroked the front of his skull and realised he was in need of a shave. He smiled. There was life up there still. He walked on. "And the scar on this man's face; tell me about it." Ruadhan replied abruptly. "It was on his forehead; a bar about the length of my thumb and as thick. His complexion was ruddy but the scar was darker still." Tulchán nodded, "And he made the sign of the cross?"

"Yes, I have told you that!" Ruadhan almost snarled his answer.

"That's enough!" Tulchán retorted. He knew Ruadhan had told his story many times, had been questioned and called a liar many times, but this was no way to address an elder. "I do not doubt what you saw, Ruadhan, but if what I am thinking is true, the warrior with the scar is different from the other Northmen in a way you cannot imagine. Did you tell Fáelcar of the scar?"

"No."

"You should have. You must."

"Tell him and get another beating."

"I will speak to him as well. You will not be beaten."

Four monks worked at sloping desks in the cramped scriptorium. If people knew of Cillebairre, it was because of this place. The settlement had not advanced as its founders had hoped: poor harvests, the lack of strong royal patronage and Abbot Comgall's weak leadership coupled with his thin spirituality had stunted its growth. Neither zeal nor a deep love of God had brought Comgall to Cillebairre. He had been a lightweight in his clan's constant political struggles and someone whose sanity was questioned regularly. A lost dispute over inherited land had encouraged him to think half-heartedly of life at the small monastery and it had also come into his family's consideration as they debated what to do with a son who was displaying manifestations of advancing madness each day. They, the Máenmaige branch of the Ui Maine dynasty, acted swiftly when Comgall had returned after a disappearance lasting a month. He entered the dun in a seriously emaciated state and with his nakedness thinly concealed by freshly-picked and delicately intertwined flax flowers. After dressing him, they tied him to a horse and escorted him to Cillebairre. Comgall's relatives told themselves that the rigour of the monastic life and the power of prayer would drive the demons from him. And, to a noticeable degree, they had been proven right. Comgall settled comfortably if ineffectually into the role of abbot which his privileged background secured for him. He would never advance in sanctity like monastic predecessors such as Ciarán of Clonmacnoise or Ailbe of Emly but he said his prayers and did his best to sustain the Rule that ordered the community. He had no serious lapses into deranged behaviour and, at all times, he wore his tunic. Comgall's leadership did not bring Cillebairre to anyone's attention but the monk Tulchán's dedication to preserving knowledge through writing achieved that. He and those he trained had spread the name of Cillebairre throughout Ireland and beyond.

Light in the scriptorium came from two high, narrow windows set in each end of the stone building. Books in leather satchels hung from every wall. Tulchán nodded to the monks in turn and received serious, silent replies from all except one. This was the tall, thin, hollow-chested monk, Duach, half-brother to Abbot Comgall. Duach seemed delighted to see them. He smiled broadly and put his pen down.

"Always looking for excuses to rest from your labours, Duach," said Tulchán.

"My hand is cramped, Tulchán. Do not be so harsh. I love my work, but sometimes it does not love me."Tulchán walked to Duach's desk. Ruadhan had stayed at the entrance not sure if he was allowed inside. Tulchán gestured for him to enter. "Duach has been working for many days now on a missal for me."A small, ragged edged sheet of calfskin vellum was stretched and pinned to the desk. The lettering was in black except for the red capital. "The hour of my learning is early, Ruadhan. When you look on my work, you see only the murky, undistinguished twilight at the start of the day. Look on Tulchán's and you see the glorious midday sun."Tulchán laughed and patted Duach on his shoulder. "Ruadhan, this man is a scholar of law but with words like these aspires to become a famous poet." Then he led Ruadhan to an empty desk positioned so that it received most light from one of the windows. The worktop was cluttered with goose feathers, a squirrel's tail and a keen-edged knife. Tulchán sat at his desk, brushed the feathers to one side and gently lifted a large, blank, polished sheet of vellum to show the worked page beneath. The page seemed a blaze of many colours which would not die down, a blur in which Ruadhan, at first, could not see any pattern. As his eyes focused, he saw blues, golds and reds form the figure of an angel in the top left corner. The angel was half-seated with its back to a slender tree. The tree's delicate branches and leaves arched over the angel's head. Below the angel, the roots of the tree knotted into a complex design which was repeated and ran unbroken around the edge of the page. The pattern was even but seemed to change each time Ruadhan looked at it: one minute, fiery suns; the next, writhing serpents, the stuff of his visions; look again, chieftains'

14

shields or, and this is where his mind rested, the soft folds of a mother's cloak wrapped around her child. "This," said Tulchán, tapping the page gently, "is our lifeblood. Believe me, Ruadhan, if we spill and lose the Word, we lose the world, this one and the next." Tulchán paused. His eyes glazed over and for a moment he was a long way from the scriptorium. He shuddered slightly and tapped the page more firmly. "This, the Psalter, is almost finished. Another day or two, that's all. What next for Tulchán, Ruadhan? No, don't try to answer, since I think I know it all ready."

Ruadhan heard only part of what Tulchán said. His eyes were fixed on the page. The angel held a book and from it swirled the first letters of some sacred text. Ruadhan asked Tulchán what it was. The monk leant close to the writing, breathed deeply and with great deliberation translated the words:

"God is our shelter, our strength, ever ready in time of trouble. So we shall not be afraid when the earth gives way, when the mountains tumble into the depths of the sea, and its waters roar and seethe, the mountains tottering as it heaves."

The Two Brothers

Most of the community on the north of the river gathered at the meeting place, a large, uncultivated clearing that side of the stepping stones. A fire had been lit. The older generations knew the tale but all insisted that Fáelcar tell it. At first, he was reluctant. Words didn't cut wood or bring in a harvest. Stories! That's all some of them wanted. Tales to help them idle more time away. That boy had brought him more bother. Fáelcar did not want to accept what Ruadhan had told him about the one with the scar and, to make matters worse, did not like the way the boy had told him. He had looked Fáelcar directly in the eye! Fáelcar had smacked him hard across the side of his stupid head. The boy had been told off many, many times and punished many, many times for staring. Bran, Fáelcar's cousin, suffered eyes that wept pus for days without end after Ruadhan had impudently returned his gaze. Fáelcar lowered his thin body to the ground close by the fire. He was weary and ached all over. He thought he must be going down with something. His bones felt uneasy within his flesh. It was as if his skin was too tight for them and they were trying to burst through. With both hands, he scratched his scalp furiously through his matted, sandy hair. He looked about him. They were waiting for him to start his tale of the nobility. "If I had any say, I'd forget the lot of them, the rich, the highborn."

"Yes, yes, we know that but get on with it, Fáelcar! And embroider it; give it colour! A colourful story: that's what we want."

Colour! What *colour* was there in Fáelcar's life? He didn't acknowledge *colour* in his life whether in nature, clothing or temperament and was unlikely to weave it into any tale he told. Having to do what he was called on to do that evening meant little; did not excite Fáelcar. He regarded his life in all its aspects like this storytelling; an imposition. "Two brothers: their father, Mael..."

A shout came from the far side of the fire. "Stand up, Fáelcar! If you're going to tell the tale, get on your feet, man! That's the way to do it!"

Reluctantly, Fáelcar stood, taking time to ease and straighten stiff limbs and grumbling all the while. "Right! Right! I'm not preacher; I'm not a poet and I'm not a storyteller but I'll tell you what I know. No poet's great leaps of fancy. Just what I know. In plain words. Plain words from a plain man."

"Get on with it, then, *plain man*!"

16

"I'm trying to!"

"Quiet, everyone!"

From where he now stood, Fáelcar could see the cause of all this bother on the other side of the fire, sitting apart and well back. Ruadhan was scratching in the earth with a stone. The scoring, that simple back and forth motion of the boy's arm, irritated him. He wanted to stride to where Ruadhan was, stepping around the others, and slap him firmly once more about his empty head. A pest, a nuisance, a burden, and another imposition he, Fáelcar, could do without.

"We're waiting, Fáelcar!"

He would keep it brief. "Two brothers: their father, Mael... of royal birth, banished to the west from Mide. Indiscretion: silly man married a woman who was a, what'sit, er, a consecrated virgin. Frustrated; couldn't confine his lust to the slave women and angered the high-ups with his affairs. Lucky to get away with his life. I was his slave, just a boy, from one of their raids somewhere. Got banished with him and a few others. Fintan was one of them, weren't you, and younger than me?"

Heads turned. A short, swarthy man nodded an answer sullenly. The fire spat violently several times.

"That's what brought me and him here. Lucky us. This place wasn't much then. Not much now. Just a couple of monks here. No stone houses. Mael settled here. Could have redeemed himself probably and gone back to a small *tuath* somewhere in the old place but took up with a lowborn here and had two sons. Both were headstrong youths as most of you remember." Heads nodded. *You remember so why am I telling you this*, Fáelcar thought. He also reminded himself that he hadn't eaten since dawn and suddenly felt very hungry.

"The elder was Morann. When he was still a weak boy, foolishly he tried to join adults who were hunting in the forest. Got in the path of the boar they were chasing. Left him with a leg that still had power but that dangled from him like... well... I don't know... like an oak bough blasted in the storm."

"I can picture it, Fáelcar. Good image that. *Colourful.*"

"Let him tell the story!"

"He's doing well."

Fáelcar spoke without emotion. He was not a storyteller. He had been called upon to tell the tale especially for those who didn't know it and he would do just that. He knew he should feel closer to those whose history he was retelling, closer to Mael who had given him his freedom and towards Mael's sons who could be arrogant but who never harmed him and accepted his direction most of the time after their father died of the withering disease, but he didn't. Fáelcar had no strong allegiances even to his own family and Mael's two sons meant little to him now except for a few memories and mild grievances. If this scarred man was Conal, then so be it, but Fáelcar hoped nothing more than this story would be expected of him by way of responding to whatever else this man's appearance in the valley brought. If Fáelcar lived the rest of his life without a glimpse of either of Mael's sons, he would be content.

A tired Ruadhan stopped his scratching and dropped the stone. With some effort, he lifted his head and looked at Fáelcar, but not full in his face. Fáelcar's words came to him like the waves of a low sea. He forced himself to stay awake and listen. He was the reason they had gathered, the reason the story was being told.

"After the boar, he was too slow to join in chasing and hiding games. The others didn't want him to play and there were lots of fights. Him being a cripple, he should have been given many beatings but it wasn't like that. Once he had another boy at close quarters, Morann could fasten him close with that strange shattered leg. It was useless most of the time but in their fights, he learned to lock it into place like a great hook. Once he had someone there, it didn't matter how much they hurt him with whatever they could move, fists, feet, the fight was over for them."

Someone threw two boughs heavily in succession on to the fire and those nearest were showered each time with sparks.

"Conal: get on to Conal!"

"Now, Conal, the *special* child. *Special.... special...* that's what was said. *Conal is special and don't anyone forget it.* All others walked in his shadow. A *leader*, they said. Came from his mother's womb feet first and so, right from his first moments, after special prayers to ward off evil since that was no normal birth, they talked like this. *Special, special, special.* He came from the womb ready to walk, they said. Could walk, some claimed! Almost killed his mother. Long and difficult; the birth. I can remember her cries and the rushing in and out of the house of the old women as they busied themselves with the delivery. A frosty March night it was and the fire outside was a poor one. Some fool had put green wood on it and there was smoke and crackling but little heat. I could have done with going in and sleeping by my house fire but was not allowed. Would have been disrespectful. I sat shivering outside while special Conal was pulled into the world. What a fuss. Stars... stars... there was a lot of them... they... they crowded the sky."

"*Crowded* is a fine way to put it, Fáelcar, a fine way."

Fáelcar hesitated, bent and stared intently into the gloom where those words had come from. He could not tell who had said them but believed they were meant. He straightened. It was odd but Fáelcar was beginning to enjoy telling the story and beginning to think that, perhaps, he was good at such a presentation. Words did seem to be coming to him with ease coming like... like water from the hills in springtime. He coughed and spat on to the ground at his feet.

"In spite of the fierce cold that bit like an animal, I fell asleep where I sat. I can't have been asleep long when I heard Conal's thin cries like those of some... of a small wild animal caught in a trap, replacing his mother's low moans which were not unlike those of a... a larger wild animal caught in a trap."

"Keep it simple, Fáelcar. Too much embroidery."

"I sat up sharply and shook myself awake like a... like a dog fresh from the river. As I did this, I saw one star move quickly across the sky like a... a swallow darting under a roof..."

"Enough of the *likes*, Fáelcar! Tell the story!"

Fáelcar couldn't see who had shouted this. It was a different voice. He didn't recognise it. "The star left a bright trail behind it. The trail vanished as I shouted but others had seen it too. It was a sign, the old ones said. Another sign, they said." Fáelcar spat, this time into the fire. "The *special* one. Signs. Signs. Signs. Always *signs*. Learnt quickly and was eager to grow and do a man's work. As he grew, his *specialness* showed and one spring day, when, Morann had perhaps sixteen years at his back and Conal, perhaps ten, we had visitors. There was much fighting among the monasteries at that time and a war party of the Éoganacht Áine was just south of us. One of their women, a princess or something like that, what do I care, had been abducted, I think. Our lot came here recruiting. None of it had anything to do with us. I've never benefited from any of their battles and I've never seen inside their great halls or feasted till I'm bloated on the cattle won by their victories. All we see is broken bodies when the battle's lost and crops burnt and cattle stolen."

There were murmurs of agreement from round the fire but someone cautioned Fáelcar. "Strong words, Fáelcar, words that could get you into trouble. Mind them."

Fáelcar shrugged. "True words," he responded. "We have nothing before they come and even less when they've gone."

"The story! The story! Just tell us the story!"

Fáelcar cleared his throat loudly as if he was going to spit again but swallowed instead. "We'd had warning they were coming and many, including me, went to hide in the forest. Conal was too young and Morann was a cripple who would be no good to them. The soldiers threatened to burn the village. Conal stepped up and told the chieftain's son that no one of royal blood should threaten his own people. At least, this is the story that was told. The elders of the village expected to see him split from head to crotch for daring to speak in that way and some of the soldiers unsheathed their swords and closed in on him. The chieftain's son laughed and, leaning down from his horse told Conal that he was impressed. He stared at the boy for a moment and then announced to everyone that he would return when Conal was older for he would never win victories if Conal joined his enemies' ranks. Having said that, he ordered his soldiers to remount and they left the village. Saved by Conal, the special one.

After this, we got tired of hearing the praises of Conal sung on both sides of the river; tired, very tired, especially Morann. His hatred of Conal grew until he seemed more crippled by it than by his withered leg. A few days later it was Easter. We prayed with the priest at Holy Mass and here in the village, a great fire was lit, many cattle and sheep were roasted and much ale was brewed and drunk. Even the children drank till their stomachs ached and they were dizzy and fell down asleep by the fire. All except Morann. He did not drink and he stayed alert throughout the night. Early in the morning when everyone was deep in sleep, he took a glowing branch from the dying fire and went to where his brother Conal lay. Some say he was trying to put Conal's eyes out, others that he only wanted to threaten his brother. Some even claim it was an accident. As if from instinct, knowing danger was near, Conal woke, but before he could stop him, Morann thrust the branch in his face, branding him on the forehead."

Fáelcar looked about him. They were rapt. He *could* tell a story. "Morann was branded too from that day forward, branded as Cain who must be given no home, but who must wander the earth as a punishment for his crime. He was banished from Cillebairre and from that day, a good many years ago, I have never seen him."

Fáelcar stopped. Ruadhan shivered. He wasn't *rapt* and needed to move. The fire had died down again. He rose, stepped by the ones in front of him, stirred the embers and placed some branches on them. They flared quickly. Colman, a pale, sickly boy, not much older than Ruadhan, placed sods of turf carefully on top of the branches and nodded to Ruadhan as he did so. Ruadhan nodded back.

"Conal too has been many years away from his home. He was not sent running from here like a... like a... like a cur that has stolen meat; no, Conal was taken from us by force. As the older ones know, if the Northmen return, it will be their second visit. We suffered greatly by them that first time: we lost cattle and grain, and our homes were burnt. Conal should have been in the forest hiding but he was not. Even though he was so young, it is said that the *special* one fought like a chieftain..."

"Blood will out, so it will! He is descended from warriors."

"It is said that he took a sword from one of the dead raiders and the enemy began to fall around him like corn stalks to the scythe. That is what is said. I've no notion of what really happened. All exaggeration, no doubt. Much good it did us. Didn't stop them. More of their boats came up the river and they swarmed like... like... I don't know what over the few who had remained to fight. Some were taken as slaves. He was among them; Conal was among them. That's what happened. We heard nothing of him. He was dead to us. And now the boy... that boy...!" Fáelcar turned suddenly, looking for Ruadhan. This storytelling nonsense was draining from him quickly. "Come here! Come to me, boy!"

Ruadhan stood and did as he was bid. Fáelcar grabbed him roughly by the hair, pulled his head backwards and glared at him. "If this is some wild story come from your idiot imaginings, boy, you will suffer, mark my words; I'll... I'll flay you!" Ruadhan breathed hard and, even though he knew it would further anger Fáelcar, stared straight back at him. "You bring us this tale of Long-Plait, a Northman who blesses himself and who bears a scar like the one Morann gave Conal. You've made me believe you, boy. I didn't want to! I didn't want to! If you've taken me in and made a

21

fool of me... but..." He let go of Ruadhan. The boy continued to stare defiantly at him. "I am convinced, convinced..." Fáelcar remembered his audience. He should finish with a flourish, perhaps another simile or two. He couldn't summon the words. "I am convinced that the *special* one has returned like... like the birds do after winter days." Fáelcar spat once more into the fire.

ALEXANDRIA

The Patriarch

At midday, the streets were deserted. All sensible people were resting well out of the heat. The old monk was tetchy. Obedience was all very well, but if there was a next time, he would refuse to make the journey. He was too old for the travelling: long days in draughty, lurching boats; longer days on chariots that reordered all the bones in your body - the walking days were the easiest. And without any doubt, he was too old to play secret diplomacy with Copts in the boiling streets of Alexandria. He would refuse. "Abbot Ronan, I am not going," would be all he had to say and that would be the end of it. Let them thrash him till there was no skin left on his back. They could send a younger monk next time.

Brecc sat and tried to push himself further into the thin shade granted by the buildings at midday, but the fierce heat and light followed him into every recess. Out of the shade, a lizard scuttered along the front of a building opposite lifting its legs high as if the earth was too hot even for its accustomed feet. His mind grumbled continuously: wasn't the great Alexander himself killed by the heat in this place and he still a very young man? Or was it in Babylon? And was it the heat or his Macedonian drinking habits that finished him off? The drink, probably, or both, concluded Brecc, but the heat alone would be enough in his own case.

Brecc was surprised and irritated to see that Fiacc did not seem troubled at all by the climate. His companion declined to sit down and stayed alert all the time, scanning the entrances to the street and the doorways. Brecc wondered if he should have brought him but had concluded that it would do no harm and that it would be foolish to try to outdo the Copts in secrecy. He couldn't anyway. Intrigue was not in his nature. Some people are like icebergs: they show you only the tip of their personalities and have no difficulty in hiding their affairs from others. Brecc was the opposite: he was what he said and did and could be no other. Perhaps the scheming appealed to Fiacc. Brecc was not sure. Considering the time they had been together on this long journey, he had learnt very little about his fellow traveller. He had attributed his companion's silence to thoughtfulness and to a conscience which needed time to come to terms with murder, but this had not helped him feel at ease with the man.

Fiacc was of noble birth and belonged to a branch of the powerful Southern Ui Neill family. He had been sent to the monastery of

Clonmacnoise after killing a cousin. Drink had played its part but what the fight had been about, Brecc had no idea. The penitential discipline exacted by the abbot demanded that Fiacc spend five years in exile on a remote and barren isle off the west coast, living only on what that place provided. At the end of this period of penance, the abbot would examine him to test the quality of his repentance and, that being well, Fiacc would return to render service to the near relatives of the person he had killed. On examination, Fiacc had told the abbot that his conscience was calling him to be of service to others and the Church from that moment and he asked to accompany Brecc on his difficult journey to Egypt. On returning to Ireland, he said, he would willingly spend the five years in exile. This had impressed Abbot Ronan as had the way Fiacc had diligently joined the monks in all their prayers. He had granted the request.

Fiacc leant down and with a large muscular hand shook Brecc by the shoulder. "He's coming," he said quietly. "This must be Makarius."

Brecc did not stand. He shuffled, turned and looked but then quickly closed his eyes. He did not want whatever was going to unfold to happen. For a moment Brecc indulged himself in another memory of home and imagined he was sitting in tall, lush, cool spring grass. He sighed deeply, "What a poor, poor monk I am," he thought.

A tall, young Coptic monk in a black robe and carrying a prayer staff was walking along the quaysides. When Brecc saw him first, his eyes registered a mature man moving at a sensible, even pace. Fiacc helped Brecc to his feet and they watched Makarius approach. As he neared them, Brecc realised he had been painting the scene to satisfy his own demands and quell a rising uneasiness about what was happening. This Copt, in spite of favouring his right leg in a distinct limp, bustled towards them; there was nothing *even* about his gait. And he was little more than a boy. The features were deceptive. His face carried premature signs of elderliness. It was gaunt and the skin under his large eyes was darker than the rest of his pale olive complexion. Together, the colours brought to mind the streaky fresh droppings Brecc's few hens produced. After what had happened at that same corner in the morning, the Irishman expected this young man to be the quick, nervous type who conjured enemies out of every shadow, but was pleasantly surprised to find that, although cautious, Makarius was embarrassed by the way the meeting had been arranged. He addressed them in excellent Latin.

"I apologise for the manner and time of our meeting. This is not the best time to walk the streets of Alexandria but, as you see, there are few people about and it will be easy to know if we are being followed. We go to the Church of St. Sergius. Please come with me and I shall take you. You will find shade and a cool drink."

Makarius was impeded only slightly by his limp. At first, he led them at a surprisingly fast pace up the narrow sloping alley, away from the blazing sunlight of the quaysides but suddenly, anxious that the foreigners should not over-exert themselves in the heat, adjusted his walk and proceeded at a slow rhythm, taking them across the canal, and east along one of Alexandria's main thoroughfares to one of the oldest parts of the city, a crowded quarter where, in the middle of an undisciplined maze of quill-narrow lanes and small courtyards, the Coptic church of St. Sergius was hidden. Brecc, in his discomfort, turned his thoughts to what he knew of the Roman soldier, Sergius. He was reputed, at the height of his torture when one of his eyes had been poked out, to have thanked his two torturers for leaving him with an eye with which he could see only the goodness God had put into both of them. Brecc knew he could never find such forgiveness. He wasn't finding it for Makarius who had resumed his bustle and constantly, politely hurried them onwards. His discomfort led him to think of the Patriarch's palace. He had never visited that building, but his imagination conjured up white marble, cool colonnades, a fountain and greenery. He had never visited it but he knew that it was in the opposite direction to the one they were going. He sighed aloud, wondered about asking the Copt why anyone should bother to follow them but decided not to waste his breath in the stifling heat.

In spite of his handicap, nimbly, on dainty feet that seemed ill-fitted for his height, Makarius negotiated steps by the side of a wall and led them to a huge door studded with heavy bolts. Once through this door, they left the wide and marble-paved streets behind and made their way through lanes so narrow and dark that they could have been underground. Although the sun was at its highest, its rays were cut off by the cracked and crumbling, mud-walled houses that crowded together as if out of fear of the rest of the city. An unnerving silence controlled the streets: there were no shouts from children playing, no dogs barking, no simple reassuring sounds of cooking or of neighbours calling to one another. The padding of their feet on the beaten mud of the lane seemed loud enough to waken the

25

dead. Although he saw no one, Brecc felt sure that, from barely opened doors and dark apertures, watchful inhabitants monitored their progress through this Christian ghetto. He was glad they had Makarius with them and that they had not entered these threatening streets at night.

After walking steadily for what seemed a long time, checking regularly to see that no one was following, Makarius suddenly stopped halfway along one of the lanes. Brecc could see nothing to indicate that they might be close to a church, but followed Makarius through a low door made of tall Nile grasses into a courtyard where an ox lay on the hard mud in the shade of a stunted fig tree.

"I am disappointed," said Brecc, "I expected to meet the leopard again."

Makarius looked hard at the Irishman again, the thin, desperate smile of the accused on his face. "The leopard is very useful sometimes," replied Makarius. "It is quite tame but it frightens people and keeps undesirables away. However, I was told the creature upset you and I am sorry for that. I am also sorry that we have to be secretive, but the city is very uneasy at the moment. There is fresh persecution and the Patriarch has had to go into hiding. Even this place may not be safe for him soon, and he will have to go to one of the desert monasteries."

"Why is the persecution so intense now?"

"We are rebuilding the Cathedral of St. Mark which the Mohammedans burned down when they invaded. It is a sign of our great faith in Our Lord Jesus Christ that we are doing this after two hundred years of suffering under our Arab rulers. This is why the persecution is worse now. There is anger that such faith persists. But come, there is no need for us to keep the ox company. The Patriarch is waiting."

Makarius ushered Brecc and Fiacc into a small, simply furnished room divided by a curtain, and into the presence of the Most Holy Pope and Patriarch of the Great City of Alexandria and of all the Land of Egypt, of Jerusalem the Holy City, of Nubia, Abyssinia and Pentapolis, and of all the Preaching of St. Mark. Brecc expected to meet someone impressive both in character and physical stature. Instead, the seventy year old who greeted him was a squat, shabbily dressed man, with small eyes set deeply in a dark and serious face. His robe, black like Makarius', was frayed and stained. He looked insignificant, a peasant whom you would pass by on the streets without a glance. Brecc could not help feeling a sense of

26

disappointment that the Patriarch had not created a more favourable first impression: "This place is little better than a stable, and the Patriarch..." *Stable* made him halt and he began trying to regather his stupid and mischievous thoughts. "Our Saviour was born in humbler surroundings than these and yet I ... always quick to judge ... Will I ever change? The heat; perhaps it is the heat; it has curdled my little brain. What an idiot, I am. Penance, I must think of an appropriate penance to redress such stray and dismissive thoughts."

Makarius greeted his leader respectfully and waited for the foreigners to do likewise. Brecc realised this and quickly went down on his knees at the Patriarch's feet. He forgot to raise the hem of his tunic and heard it rip somewhere. Fiacc, unruffled, raised the hem of his garment and slowly knelt down. The Patriarch took a large, finely worked cross of Abyssinian silver from inside his robe and blessed each of them in turn. He then gestured for them to rise and to be seated on the rush mats that covered the floor. Makarius remained on his feet and announced that the Patriarch knew Latin but would speak in the language of their Church, the ancient tongue of the Pharaohs mixed with the Greek brought by Alexander and his successors. Makarius would translate.

"I greet you in the name of Christ Jesus the Lord and I welcome you as dear friends, the most recent of many Christian travellers from Ireland. Since well before the Mohammedan invasion, the Church in Egypt and the Church in Ireland have been linked. We have shared the vision of the Desert Fathers and brought the light of Christ to many. Although we in Alexandria have gone one way, the true way, in understanding the nature of Our Saviour, this friendship has remained."

The Patriarch, although his voice was weak, did not falter, and as he spoke, looked over Brecc's right shoulder as if half-expecting another visitor. Brecc winced at the mention of "the true way" and hoped he was not going to get a lecture from the Patriarch on the nature or natures, divine, human, of Jesus Christ. *Nature*: green shoots nudging their way through dark loam cooled his mind.

"I am a simple monk from the monastery of Der Anba Bishoi whom God has seen fit to raise to this position. I lead the Church at a troubled time. We are in some difficulties. Always the taxes, more and more taxes – they would milk the camel until it gives blood. And now the fighting on our streets and the increased immigration of Mohammedans. We are a persecuted people. Our Christian faith brought to us by St. Mark is in danger and we must do anything we can to preserve it."

He halted his flow abruptly and Brecc realised that the Patriarch was studying his face to learn if his words were receiving a sympathetic hearing. Brecc twitched uncomfortably, thought *green shoots* and nodded a response. The Patriarch's gaze shifted to the other Irishman. Fiacc lifted his head and stared straight back.

"When I was a boy, I met a saintly monk from Scetis who told me of a Chalice used by St. Mark, a glass Chalice made at Wadi Natroun. Since then, many others have repeated this story to me and have said that the Chalice was taken to Ireland many years ago, before the time of your blessed Patrick."

The Patriarch paused again and shook his head quite violently. Brecc was startled. Did the man's head ache? Sage and garlic would help with that and what else? There was more. Thyme? He was getting more and more forgetful. The Patriarch halted his speech abruptly, told himself off over how neglectful he had been of his guests and apologised. He called and another monk emerged from behind the curtain with bowls containing lemon drinks for the visitors. The newcomer waited while they drank. Fiacc sipped slowly, his eyes fixed on the Patriarch. Brecc emptied his bowl, desired another and then told himself off for being greedy. He must control his appetites. Leopards and glass chalices were creating confusion. He had heard of this chalice but had not given the stories much attention: a chieftain had carried it into battle and won the day against great odds. Something like that. A daughter of that same family had been cured of a leprous affliction. And there were more. The Abbot of his monastery, he was sure would know all about it. Ronan was a *learned* man. "He cares more for his books and for legends such as this than he does about the people around him," thought Brecc and then quickly asked forgiveness for letting such an uncharitable idea enter his head. Another drink would have been very satisfying. The newcomer was behind the curtain again and the Patriarch was back where he had broken off.

"Over thirty years ago, an Irish monk in priestly orders came to our land. He was a great scribe, one of two in your country who used the precious *lazhward* [2] in his work. He came to purchase a new supply and to

---

[2] Lapis lazuli

make a pilgrimage. For one year, he walked the Sinai desert and, alone or with the Greek monks, prayed and meditated. He spent the following year at the monastery of St. Anthony, passing six months in total seclusion in St. Anthony's cave itself. He was greatly respected as a very holy man. The story is told of how he left the monastery to wander and pray in the desert. The air had been heavy with the threat of storms but Tulchán simply smiled when he was warned and could not be dissuaded from his intentions. The storms came, the worst that had been seen for many years. Thunder galloped round the hills and lightning tore the sky. Tulchán returned physically healthy but his mind was in turmoil. He had lost the inner calm that marked him out from other men. At the height of the worst storm as he tried to find shelter by some rocks, he was given a terrifying vision concerning the Chalice of St. Mark. Before that time, he told the monks, he knew very little about the Chalice except that no one could say where it was. Tulchán was not able to stay dry in that storm. One rock jutted over his head but not far enough to stop the rain from running on to him. As he squatted and tried to pray, he noticed the rain was staining his tunic dark red. At first, he thought the water had picked up sediment from the rock but when he held out his hands to collect rain before it reached the earth, the cup his fingers made filled with blood. And then, he told the monks, the scene before him changed completely with each flash of lightning as he was granted a series of disturbing visions centred upon the holy Chalice. He would not reveal what was shown to him and insisted he had to pray about their meaning and the truth of them. Some concerned the past and some the future. Tulchán did not need to be reminded that what seems to many to be the emptiness of the desert is in fact a city crowded with devils wanting to confuse and lead us from truth. He had to be sure that the visions were not from an evil source. He left Egypt without speaking more of what had happened but the monks of St. Anthony's were sure that the visions had revealed where the Chalice was."

The Patriarch was short of breath and once more, he paused. Makarius moved nervously from one foot to the other. He was anxious and gestured that he would get his superior a drink. The Patriarch waved his arm in admonishment. Makarius looked quizzically at the Irishmen to see how they were responding to the story. Neither face told him anything.

"The Chalice is precious, treasured by all Christians, but most of all by we Egyptians. It belonged to the founder of our Church, a saint who, as a young boy, knew Our Lord and who, as an adult, recorded our Saviour's words and deeds. If it could be brought back to Egypt, it would be a powerful symbol to inspire our people to remain steadfast and resist, even to death, the persecution we suffer. They are talking about it already, not only the priests, but also the common people. These homes around us are alive with whispers about the return of the Chalice of St. Mark."

The Patriarch rushed the last sentences. This was tiring him. He was breathless. Makarius moved closer. The Patriarch waved him back. "The Chalice of St. Mark must be brought back as soon as possible." The Patriarch sat forward on his stool and spoke these last words with great feeling. The room was cool but a heavy coating of perspiration covered his brow and drops began to run down his face. Makarius moved to wipe them away with a cloth but, once again, the Patriarch brusquely gestured for him to stay where he was. "You must help us. You must find out where the Chalice is and it must be brought here. This is a sacred duty that I place upon you. If we can rebuild St. Mark's Cathedral *and* bring back the blessed saint's Chalice to enshrine it in that building along with his sacred bones, then once again the Nile will be the great artery of Christianity carrying the lifeblood of redemption to the whole world."

The Patriarch sat back and leaned heavily against the wall. He was exhausted and feverish. The running and the hiding and the never-fading anxiety over the future of his Church wearied him and made him sick. He beckoned to Makarius. The young man almost ran to his side and bent low. Makarius listened intently and then addressed the others. "The Patriarch would like us to pray with him, and then I am going to try to make him rest. He is not well." Makarius helped the Patriarch to his feet and they led the two Irishmen through a door in the far wall and into the well-hidden Church of St. Sergius. The space beyond the door was large and dark with the only light coming from two oil lamps on the walls. The nave was oblong in shape and several huge, grey, marble pillars supported its low roof. A semi-circular sanctuary extended from the eastern end and was cut off from the nave by a high wooden screen. A free-standing stone altar was just visible beyond the screen. After being helped to kneel, the Patriarch prostrated himself in prayer. Makarius leant on his T-shaped staff and murmured his prayers. Brecc stood silently reciting from memory psalms for the canonical hour of sext. Fiacc stared blankly at the altar.

CILLEBAIRRE
The Mission

The Northmen would be back. None of the adults doubted it. Abbot Comgall turned restlessly on his bed. In his mind, he went over the advice he had been given by Tulchán about measures he should take. His fellow monk seemed distracted as if he believed nothing could be done to deflect an attack and the great suffering that would ensue but had told Comgall to send a messenger to their chieftain, his cousin, asking for help and to get the people to make a dry store deep in the forest of any crops that were ready or almost ready. Comgall had overseen the harvesting of vegetables himself and any corn that might be edible after long cooking. On his own initiative, he ordered the strengthening of the stockade and the placing of lookouts. He also replaced *Tiert*, the late morning office of prayer, with weapons training. The messenger would take at least a day and a half without rest to get to the chieftain's dun – Comgall had thought of sending his wife out of danger as well, but that would not look good - and a day and a half to come back with help if the travelling was uninterrupted. Comgall wasn't optimistic. His cousin had an army, soldiers who did nothing else but fight and eat and drink, but it had been weakened by defeats in several recent clashes with neighbouring clans. A fast; perhaps a personal fast would help, a fast in reparation for the failings of the community and the failings in his leadership that could have brought this terrible threat to their home. Late in the afternoon, Tulchán found Ruadhan lashing posts together to strengthen the stockade. He remarked to himself that *boy* no longer suited him. He was strong, muscular and growing fast.

"Leave that."

"I'll get into trouble."

Tulchán was tetchy with him. He too had passed a restless night. A small bird that he did not recognise had flown into his cell and, in its panic to escape, and before Tulchán could usher it back into the open, had dashed itself to death against the walls. With this, Tulchán's burdensome premonition of his own death had returned and troubled him all night. "Do as you are told! Leave it *now*!"

It was a short walk south from the stockade. Neither spoke. Tulchán led them to where Brother Kevin was building a coracle by a quiet stretch of the river, a meander that had almost separated itself to form a small lake. Hazel poles, bent into an inverted, bowl-shaped frame were held in place by heavy stones and a pile of tanned ox hides lay in long grass nearby. Short, tubby Kevin was on his knees rubbing sheep tallow into one of them. Ruadhan and Tulchán sat on the bank and the youth dangled his bruised and dirty legs in the cooling water. The monk stepped into the river. "I will wash your feet."

Ruadhan pulled his feet onto the bank. "No."

"I *will* do it, not simply because your feet are dirty but for another, a *higher* reason."

Ruadhan ached inside. He knew it was one of those times when he had to listen hard. He wanted to understand; tried hard to understand but often the *higher* things and what they demanded of him seemed far removed from his life and impossible to undertake. He looked directly at the old monk's face: the dark beneath his eyes; his jowly, sad cheeks a lighter band; dark again at his chin. It made him think of the long-bodied wasps that mobbed the tall, yellow irises by the stepping stones.

"We find our true freedom through serving others, Ruadhan. That is hard, I know for you, someone so beaten by life, to understand, but what I tell you is the seed our God gave us through his Son. Only through planting that seed will we know fulfilment in this life and, most importantly, in the life that follows death. And it is of death I must speak. When the Northmen return, Ruadhan..."

"How do you know they will return?"

Tulchán did not answer him. "When the Northmen return, many of us are going to die, caught like fish in their strong nets. As a monk, I must be prepared at all times for death and the world to come. In the days I have left, I must fast and pray more and confess my sins."

It was strange to hear Tulchán speak so easily of death. Ruadhan did not want to hear such talk. Looking back along the river, he could just make out Fáelcar and others still working on the trench and the stockade. Fires had been lit among the houses. The women were preparing to cook. The steady, faint, reassuring sound of chopping reached his ears, then an indeterminate shout followed by what could be children's laughter. It was a peaceful scene. It could not change. The Northmen would not return, Tulchán would not die, the work would go on and the fires would stay alight.

"You wash my feet so that you can get into heaven."

Tulchán's face creased to the point where Ruadhan thought he was in pain. The old man sighed and his features relaxed. "I stand reproved by you. Indeed, you are wise beyond your years. It's true that sometimes we do good like we gather gold, a way of storing benefits for ourselves, but once we think that way, the good deed is worthless, the gold is dirt. Perhaps, I was guilty of that..." He hesitated for a moment, then stepped back on to the bank and sat alongside Ruadhan. "We'll talk of other things. I have a task for you, Ruadhan, a very important one. When the Northmen come..."

"How can you be certain they will? How do you know?

Tulchán looked away from the boy and west along the river. How could he tell the boy that he didn't need any visions to know that this would happen? It was inevitable. People lusted after power and land and wealth whether they were Northmen or Irishmen. The invaders were strong and not content, it seemed, with the land God had granted them – indeed Adam was not content with Paradise – and they were spreading over many lands like water from a toppled pail. "Don't question me, Ruadhan. Just listen. This is important. The Psalter you saw: I am going to hide it. It is finished. The Word must be preserved. It is the mind of God. I do not expect any of the monks to be alive after the Northmen have attacked and so I want you to know its hiding place. The forest will have kept you safe. A time will come when you must retrieve the book and take it to the great monastery of Clonmacnoise. You will be welcomed there and given an education."

"Why me?" Ruadhan almost spat the words out. Why not one of the clever, spoilt students, he thought.

"What will happen here will seem like the end of the world to you, but do not let it terrify you for long. Such happenings are sad and fill us full of fear; we moan for our loved ones dead and scattered; we tremble with thoughts of the future..."

Ruadhan felt confused emotions welling up. He looked across the river towards the hill where he had minded the sheep. A few metres from them, a fish made a muscular arc as it leapt high from the water, a flash of iridescence, before returning to the river with a gentle slap.

"Put your trust in God. What will happen is like that fish's jump, a small disturbance on a great river that is winding its way to His peace and his love."

33

Ruadhan kept his face from the monk and wondered how it was that Tulchán got so much from words written and spoken. He recalled a prostrate, drunken Fáelcar who didn't feel the blows he and Ite showered on him. Words worked on the old monk like ale worked on Fáelcar, making him smile at all the world, numbing him to the pain. If the Northmen returned, it meant death for many and hunger in the year ahead for those who survived. How was that like a fish jumping? Ruadhan was upset and confused by the monk's predictions but also angry that Tulchán had chosen him for a task he did not understand. Why give him such responsibility? When you do not belong and have had as many beatings as Ruadhan had, you keep well away from responsibility since failure always brought more beatings and an even greater sense of being the unwanted one.

"Ruadhan, I repeat, this is very important. At the foot of the tall stone cross which marks the boundary of the monastery's lands to the east is where the Psalter will be. I shall wrap it in a sheet of Brother Kevin's hides. It will not be buried too deeply and the place will be marked by a stone with the shape of a fish scratched on its underside. You must promise to do this. You have been chosen. Do you understand?"

A heron lifted from the water further along the river, perhaps the same bird that had helped lull him to sleep on that fateful day. He was tired, did not want this responsibility but could not refuse the one who had been so good to him. Ruadhan nodded his understanding to the old monk and made a promise. Promises, he told himself, could be broken.

The Return

Despite Tulchán's anxiety, the days came and went without any sign of the Northmen and, on both sides of the river, the people relaxed. No help would come from the chieftain - he had enough on his plate with a dispute over succession - but what did that matter now? Swords were put aside; the lookout posts were abandoned, the small militia band stopped drilling and the children played in the stockade trench. A steady, familiar working pattern settled itself on the days at Cillebairre.

Their return, two months after Ruadhan had encountered them, was not loud and obvious but near-silent and subtle and in the middle of a particularly hot, energy-sapping afternoon. Most of the villagers were busy in the fields on both sides of the river. The days were long and muscles ached by evening but people were content at the thought of fat grain stores in autumn. The advance party of Northmen crept along both riverbanks and through the high corn on the north side. They would have reached the heart of the settlement unnoticed and the slaughter would have been greater but for two warnings. Sun glancing off metal was one but the other, much more significant, was the clamour one of the invaders, well ahead of the others, set up. He broke from cover and ran openly towards the settlement, screaming, "Flee! Flee! Run!" in Irish.

When he heard the church bell rung wildly, Ruadhan was alone weeding onions and chives in Fáelcar's small plot near their hut. He looked hard towards the ford. A mass of people were racing across the clearing and into the river, ignoring the stepping stones and stumbling and splashing their way wildly to the monastery side. Several men and women who had sickles and hoes stood their ground. Ruadhan saw his two little foster-brothers being pulled by his foster-sister, Ite, the one who loved him. "I should join them," he thought, but the story of Conal, filled his mind. Conal had been young when the Northmen last attacked. He, Ruadhan, was on the edge of manhood. He would be expected to fight. Stay and face the Northmen? Don't be stupid! Look after yourself, like always, Ruadhan. You are a survivor. He remembered Tulchán's words. *I have a task for you... a very important one.* Ruadhan knew little of loyalty. He had not convinced himself that he would try to fulfil the task his old friend had given him, but now, confronted by the choice of fighting or fleeing, he knew he would. Was he being a coward? Was he using the responsibility Tulchán had charged him with to avoid the fight? *This is*

35

very important, Ruadhan. Only he and Tulchán knew where the precious Psalter was hidden and the monk was certain that *he* would not live beyond the Northmen's return. Ruadhan had to save himself and so save the Psalter.

His foster-brothers and foster-sister scrambled on to the far bank of the river. Ite urged them on but paused for a moment and looked back across the water, scanning the land. Ruadhan knew she was looking for him and he loved her for it. Her face was anxious. Her younger brother wailed. He sat down on the bank, gripped the grass tightly with both hands and refused to get up. Ite saw Ruadhan and screamed for him to follow and at the same time pulled the crying brother roughly to his feet. Two sods of sandy earth came away in his hands. She cuffed his ear and dragged him, his fists full of dirt and grass towards the forest.

Hesitation cost Ruadhan dearly. Screaming Northmen seemed to rise from behind every cornstalk, every bush, every unevenness in the landscape. He had to cross the river. The Northmen were close. He would never reach the forest. The stockade was still open and the narrow bridge over the ditch still in place. Ruadhan splashed through the water and up the south bank for its shelter. Just inside the gate, Cairech, his step-mother, was sharpening poles frantically into weapons with an axe. For a moment, he wanted her to stop what she was doing, pull him to her and wrap him in her brat that he knew would smell of smoke from the cooking fire, dust from the cornfield and her sweat. Twice she had comforted him in that way and he had felt he belonged. Cairech saw him but did not let her gaze linger and showed no emotion. It could be that the child from the forest had brought this terrible visitation upon the village.

Ruadhan ran into a half-built hut, curled himself under a pile of hides and prayed that the strangeness would not come over him. The attacker's advance stuttered at the stockade only momentarily. They used lengths of tree trunks to scale the stockade and it wasn't long before Ruadhan heard battle screams outside his hiding place. *Hiding*: he was always hiding from someone: from Fáelcar and the beatings; from other youths and their mockery of the wolf-boy; from twists and turns of the everyday that brought on his seizures, such as playing a ball game too hard or staying underwater too long. As a baby he had been hidden in the forest. When would he stop hiding? Ruadhan covered his ears with his hands but could not shut the sounds out completely. He pushed to the edge of the hides that covered him. Two struggling men reeled up against the side of the hut and before Ruadhan could move, crashed through the wall on top of him. A sharp pain shot through his right leg. In the blur as they came through the wall, Ruadhan saw that it was poor, weak Colman who had found unusual strength in battle and was bound in fierce combat with a Northman whose lank blond hair flailed about his face. Both had lost any weapons they had held and were trying to kill each other with their bare hands. Their sweating faces were twisted in hate and fear. Ruadhan felt ashamed that he was running and hiding. Perhaps it *was* cowardice that called him to fulfil the mission Tulchán had given him.

The two combatants rolled off Ruadhan. The Northman forced himself on top of Colman and beat the boy furiously about the head with large, hard fists. Colman weakened. His shoulders went limp. Behind them, Ruadhan tried to stand. His leg ached fiercely and he fell. He looked for a weapon. Fists alone would be useless. A branch that had been cut for the house but was too short lay just inside the wall. Lying full stretch, he reached and pulled it towards him. The effort exhausted him. He was breathing quickly, heavily, a bad sign. A fit was coming on, he was sure of it. Ruadhan told himself to be calm. He sat back against the wall, rocked himself backwards and forwards and gulped for air.

Colman, who had played his part, had fought alongside the adults, gave a screech and started to struggle once again, lashing out wildly with his arms and legs. The Northman stopped hitting, drew himself upwards off Colman and breathed deeply summoning the energy to finish the boy off. Ruadhan had to do something. He could save Colman; he had to save him. Using what remained of the wall, Ruadhan pulled himself to his feet. The fierce pain returned to his leg. He swayed and started to fall but managed to stay upright. The Northman's hands were around Colman's neck once more. Colman lifted his head and, under the Northman's arms, saw Ruadhan. As his eyes pleaded for his life, a sudden squall of fighting men tore through the walls. One Northman reeled from the mass clutching his head. Another, shorter, with dark, plaited hair, stepped after him crouching low, his short sword thrust forward and his body bunched tautly to conclude the fight. More blows weren't needed. His opponent fell lifeless to the ground and the victor spun swiftly to take in his surroundings. Before Ruadhan recognised him, the man lunged at Colman's assailant. Ruadhan turned away. He felt sick: sick with the killing and sick with relief. He heard several thuds and a scream and then felt a hand tapping his shoulder firmly. He turned, glanced quickly around. Colman had gone. The man's face was very close to his own. He saw the scar. "Conal?"

The man did not speak and was soon taken up once more by the milling crowd of men. Ruadhan crawled back under the hides and lay face downwards. The beating in his head started followed by the coldness. A fit was close. For what seemed a very long time, the fight ebbed and flowed about him. Ruadhan tried to calm himself but shook violently. Strong legs stepped backwards and forwards over him. Sometimes they kicked and stood on him; stumbled and cursed. He heard the clash of their weapons and his nose was invaded by a thick smell of leather and sweat. He pulled himself upwards and stuck his head from under the hides but the dizziness overcame him and he slumped back again. He did not know if what he saw was reality or the product of his delirium. Did he hear voices or the roaring of a river in spate? He thought his eyes were open but all he saw was a blur: figures like diving, swirling wraiths surrounded him; the abandoned walls of the house now rose unendingly into a black sky. Before he lost all consciousness, Ruadhan thought his hair was pulled from behind and his head wrenched backwards. He thought he heard his name spoken. Something hard struck the side of his head and he fell back to the ground. A great beast, a snarling dog but with antlers jutting from every part of its body raced towards him but just before the blackness completely overcame him, the page from Tulchán's Psalter flamed in his mind, the dog veered away from him and he was carried in the beautiful swirling pattern of the monk's work to the words at the centre.

Ruadhan had crawled or been carried over fifty metres and when he became conscious, saw that he was lying on his back by one of the stone cells inside the stockade. The sun was low in the sky. He sensed his chest rising and falling slowly, steadily. His head and leg ached but he felt strength coming back into his arms. He moved his head slowly. Trails of smoke rose from the remains of the house where he had hidden and from many more on both sides of the river.

It should have been hard to think clearly; hard not to panic, not to bring on another fainting fit, but Ruadhan was calm. His mind, although it was racing, was doing so with great purpose and devising an escape route. Back across the river and out of the village on the north bank would bring him to open ground, fields where the corn had already been harvested. He would be seen. He lifted his head slightly and looked to the edge of the forest on the south side. He wondered how many had found refuge there. That was where he should go but the direct route meant finding his way through the churches and houses and this was where the Northmen were concentrated. He saw one group sitting exhausted against the scriptorium wall. Irish resistance was over. Ruadhan lowered his head slowly and as he did, decided what to do. A length of the stockade had been smashed and flattened thirty metres from him. He rolled over once, twice, three times at then lay still again and waited to see if he had brought any attention to himself. From his new position, he could see the river through the gap in the stockade. The water would hide him. He had to get into the water, work his way upstream until he came to the place where the forest, like a friendly arm, reached around the settlement and touched the riverbank. There, he could clamber back out on the same side and find the survivors and, perhaps, safety. *Perhaps*: he might evade the Northmen only to suffer the wrath of the people he had never been allowed to call "his own". They would be suffering and in the midst of their grief, would be looking for reasons why this had happened. Ruadhan knew from harsh experience that some would point the finger at the boy from the forest. Could he survive on his own? He knew nothing of the world outside of the settlement of Cillebairre. Beyond the river, beyond the forest could be a life even more brutal than the one he knew. The quicker he moved, the better. Ruadhan didn't want to give himself time to think. He shivered and, for the first time, he noticed the ringing in his right ear. No! Not now! Not again! His heart beat faster. If he started convulsing now, in that open place, he was bound to be seen. He had to get to the river. The cold water might shock his body in a different direction. Smoke drifted over him from the nearest building. It would give him some cover.

Once outside the stockade, Ruadhan flattened himself on the ground once more. He needed a clearer picture of what or rather, who, was between him and the river. He raised his head and chest. A solitary Northman with his back to Ruadhan crossed the stepping stones, jumping to take two at a time. There was no one else, no one else alive between Ruadhan and the place above the stones where he would enter the river. He rolled slowly, stopping frequently, playing dead, down the gentle incline to the water. After his last stop, he became impatient and stood up. Crouching low and moving as fast as he could on his aching leg, he limped towards the river's edge. Almost there, he slipped and crashed into a patch of reeds. He lay there, waiting, panting, and listening to discover if his tumble had revealed his presence. Luck was still with him. Ruadhan scrambled to his feet and waded into the water. The tall reeds and a thick summer growth of pondweed would help him move down the river undetected. The reeds covered almost a quarter of the river's width and Ruadhan's only worry as he pushed through them was that he would make the tops of the grasses move unnaturally and that this would be seen. He went to the outer limit, took a deep breath, ducked, and walked as far as he could underwater. When he needed to take in air Ruadhan broke the surface of the water as gently as possible. The thick green pondweed helmeted his head. As he looked back towards the village, the last of the sun shone directly into his face. The fires were lower but a lot of smoke was still drifting slowly upwards on the windless air. Squinting in the bright sun, Ruadhan saw a Northman leading a line of six village women across the stepping stones. They were roped together and had their hands tied. Cairech was among them. Ruadhan breathed in deeply and ducked below the water again.

When he surfaced next, he edged steadily back towards the bank. Four metres from it, he was shielded from view behind the dense curtains made by the slender, bowing branches of a solitary willow. The dark sanctuary was comforting and the branches made him think of the tree that arched over the angel in Tulchán's Psalter and with that thought, the monk's body bumped against him.

Ruadhan did not want to believe it was his old friend but knew right away that it was. He parted the curtains momentarily to allow in light and to confirm it was Tulchán. The uncovered flesh was paler than any he had seen before and badged with large, dark bruises. Tulchán had said this would happen; had foreseen his death at the hands of the Northmen. Ruadhan remembered sitting by the river and how Tulchán had washed his feet and talked so easily of what was ahead. It seemed a long time ago. He bit his lip and prayed that his old friend was beyond harm in heaven. The noises in the ear became louder. The special task Tulchán had given him to perform had gone a long way from his thoughts but now came racing back. He would have to travel many miles through land and among people strange to him? Had he the strength of will? Had he the physical strength? And why was a book so important? How had it helped Ruadhan or the people of Cillebairre? A book hadn't stopped the Northmen's axes and swords. Could a book feed the village now that its livestock had been stolen, its crops razed? Emotion thickened in his mind and body. Ruadhan clenched his fists. Crying like a baby would not help. Ruadhan didn't cry. His feelings were a strange mix. He wanted to wish away what had happened, especially Tulchán's murder, but understood that the terrible events of the day meant a new beginning for him and with it, perhaps a new freedom. Perhaps. He had to move. The monk was face down in the water as if he was studying for a final time the complex patterns in nature that had inspired his work; here, the weeds underwater swayed gently in the current, intertwining, coiling, separating, shifting and returning to stroke the old monk's flesh. Ruadhan gripped and turned the monk's head so that he could see his friend's face one last time. He saw a change: those lips that in life had been almost permanently turned down at the corners, that seemed to express ruefulness and a doubt that he could rise to God's challenges; those lips now curled gently but surely upwards in a face that was at peace. Ruadhan let go and looked into the water beyond his friend's lifeless body. As he did so, the thumping started in his head and the weeds he saw began to thrash, became unidentifiable creatures attacking each other, twisting to eat themselves and then snapping their jaws to devour him. Ruadhan pushed Tulchán's lifeless body from under the willow branches back into the slow current. For a moment, Tulchán bobbed gently as if he did not want to leave the youth and then turned and drifted slowly from him. Before it was too late, and with a fierce fight raging in his head, Ruadhan pulled himself out of the water using the stub of a broken branch low down on the willow's trunk. He knew he was close to blacking out and lay down hidden now by branches that bent to the earth. He was safe as long as he did not shout in his delirium.

Not far from where Ruadhan lay, Conal, crouching low, ran swiftly along the edge of the forest. He could do no more on the battlefield. The band he had come with had overrun Cillebairre but before celebrating victory, would look for him, the traitor whose sword was dripping their blood. He had seen a member of the royal family unhurriedly dismembered for the treachery of contact with an enemy clan. He knew that if he was caught, his death would be even slower and more painful. He would not let himself be captured. There was work to be done. The idea had crossed his mind more than once and seeing the young man hiding in

41

the gorse had convinced him that he should return to Cillebairre, his home. The settlement had been ill-prepared; it was a child pushed over easily. Conal had foolishly thought that with a warning and with his blade fighting on its side, Cillebairre could have repulsed one boatload of attackers. He was wrong. There had been individual bravery but no weaponry or fighting skills to match those of the Northmen. Conal vowed to himself that this would not happen again; if another attack came, Cillebairre would be prepared. There was a lot to do.

Ruadhan stayed safe and when he came round, made his way carefully into the forest. He knew the refugees would be at *Na Lámha*, a widespread, complex pattern of rocky outcrops that looked like a furious giant had hurled them to earth in a failed attempt to stop the forest advancing along the valley side. The tallest grouping of these rocks pointed skywards like stubby fingers and gave the place its name. It was a place still revered by some, avoided by others, since bloody sacrifices had been offered there to the old gods. Many believed that evil spirits inhabited the stones, but at this troubled time, such misgivings were put aside since they offered refuge. A good half a day's walk east of Cillebairre, it was a gloomy place but the two streams that forced their way through the rocks, the clearing between them and the trees and the stones themselves, piled and overhanging, offered benefits for encampment and defence. The open space was in permanent shade and damp the whole year round but the place helped satisfy the refugees' need to feel closeted and hidden. The distance to *Na Lámha* was too great for Ruadhan to accomplish after the day's exertions and so he limped until hunger and exhaustion pulled his aching body to the ground. On all fours, he burrowed into a thicket, lay down, and a healing sleep with no warring beasts or churning landscapes overwhelmed him.

Ite met him before he reached the encampment the following morning. It was fortunate since the huge rocks of *Na Lámha* had once more echoed talk of sacrifice. Ite was picking small, tart, early blackberries on a slope above the forest. She dropped her basket and smiled broadly when she saw Ruadhan but pulled him quickly back into the darkness of the trees he had come from. "They are smarting, Ruadhan, and some of them blame you for what has happened. You know how they go on. And Tulchán is no longer here to defend you. You must not enter the camp.

They say that Cillebairre has had nothing but bad luck since you came. I think they may kill you."

Could he be to blame? Had he carried some curse with him when he crawled from the forest? Had he brought this suffering to Cillebairre? Ruadhan was not one to look for causes. He never thought about why things happened. He was too busy surviving, avoiding beatings, making sure he was warm and had enough food each day. One thing followed another. It didn't need thinking about. And yet, others did that; they stopped and wondered and came up with reasons. Tulchán believed that God was shaping our lives and that his Word had to be preserved to give us a clearer understanding of His ways, of that *shaping*. The villagers of Cillebairre believed that Ruadhan had brought evil and suffering into their lives. Some of them did. They rewrote the past. They convinced themselves that their lives were free of suffering until they had given Ruadhan a home; they could plot each step downwards from a happy, prosperous Cillebairre to what they were reduced to now, a diminished, cowering community living like animals in the forest. Certain individuals, such as Ruadhan, broadcast evil like seeds.

Ruadhan did not want to sit on the ground and feel sorry for himself, as he had done often in the past. At that moment, he was almost glad to hear that the people had turned against him once more. He was on his own and maybe that was to be the life ahead of him. He was on his own, almost. "Do *you* think I am to blame?"

Ite smiled again. "You know my answer to that. And there are others who don't blame you. Maybe they just need time. We are frightened and when we are frightened we find strange patterns in our lives." These were adult words. She reached for his hand. Ruadhan looked directly at her and realised for the first time how *adult* Ite was. Her dark, sharp-featured face was all thoughtfulness and calm, far removed from the teasing, mischievous face of his childhood friend. "Water: let me show you a stream not far from here and bushes close by that will hide you. I will bring you food."

"For how long?"

"What do you mean?"

"I can't hide for the rest of my life."

Ite smiled again but this time only with her lips. "They will come round. Things will settle. Give them time. We'll go back and the stupid

43

things they are saying now will be forgotten. Only one thing is constant among these, my people, and that is *fickleness*."

"*Your* people. I should go away."

"Where would you go?" Her eyes betrayed her anxiety.

"Tulchán entrusted me with a mission. I have to go to the great settlement of Clonmacnoise."

ALEXANDRIA
Spies

"You may stay here for as long as you wish, but I must stress the urgency of the mission the Patriarch has entrusted to us. We must find the Chalice soon." Makarius tried to express the urgency in his voice and by clasping his hands together in front of him, but found it difficult, as always to tell others what must be done. He was nervous and almost stammering. He had great strength of character, but it showed itself in serving others and not in trying to give them orders. "Other monks are nearby and they will bring you bread."

The room was to the right of the small courtyard with its own exit to the alley. It was small and contained two pallets, an urn full of water and a large washing bowl. A high window let in a narrow ray of weary sunlight. Brecc acknowledged the kindness with a shallow bow. The prayers with the Patriarch had not calmed his mind. There was no doubting how important retrieving the Chalice was to him and his people, but why had he, Brecc, been chosen to play a part in it, given this "sacred duty"? And what did this trickle of water of a boy mean by saying that *we* must find the Chalice soon? He would eventually accept what was happening as God's will - his life as a monk was meant to shape him into an unquestioning instrument of that will - but at that moment an uncomfortable itch of resentment disturbed his spirit. He answered Makarius abruptly.

"With my companion, I shall make a pilgrimage to the desert monasteries, Baramus in particular."

"I would like to accompany you. I could be of help to you."

Brecc believed that Makarius' real intention was to make sure that their return to Ireland was not delayed too long, but decided not to protest. He would be pleased to get back to his home and away from the Egyptian heat, and, besides, he looked forward to having another companion alongside the sombre Fiacc. Nevertheless, he could not stop himself from retorting. "And you could prod us from behind all the way, couldn't you, like cattle you are eager to pen for the night. Pilgrimages are not meant to be hurried, Makarius. Meditation will not be easy when you are reminding us constantly that we should have left the monastery two days before."

Makarius was not sure how to respond to this. From the time they had met, this Irishman's face had been a checkerboard of moods in sharp contrast to the other one whose serious expression seldom altered. The young Copt did not know from Brecc's present tone of voice whether he was angry or not. Of course, he hoped they would not linger too long in his country now that they had been given this important mission, but no one should ever think that he would interfere in their pilgrimage. Their prayers while in his land might be *the* means by which the Chalice was found. He, Makarius, believed in prayer; knew that prayer was a personal and communal need and was a force for change. He, Makarius, would do nothing to make them stumble on any step of the pilgrimage they planned. No, he would never do that. How could the Irish monk think that? He, Makarius, must have been indiscreet, must have suggested somehow in his clumsy manner or tone of speech that they must hurry their pilgrimage. He was a fool and had alienated the Irishman.

Brecc saw the Copt's pained and apologetic expression and withdrew his words immediately. "I am sorry for saying that. My tongue, as you are no doubt learning, has a life of its own which it uses in the service of the Devil. Perhaps, like your predecessor, Agathon, I should place a stone in my mouth to enforce silence. Forgive me, I have a lot of thinking to do concerning the task your Patriarch has set us. I shall do all I can, as quickly as I can, to return the Chalice if that is possible. And so shall Fiacc who is tied by a temporary vow of obedience to me. Don't worry, for we shall not linger here. But tell me, other than pushing us back to Ireland, what part will you play in this mission?"

Makarius smiled hesitantly, relieved by Brecc's frankness and eager to answer the question. "The Patriarch wanted to tell you everything but as you see, he is weakened by the least exertion. I am to follow you to Ireland and join in the search. It is best that we do not travel together. I cannot tell you my feelings when the Patriarch chose me for this task. The recovery of the Chalice is so important to our Church." The Egyptian's excitement was innocent and childlike, but it did not carry to the Irish monk. "Leeks," thought Brecc, "I would have planted a lot more leeks this year."

That night, Brecc was sure his body had only just lowered itself on to the bed when Makarius burst into the room. A picture of his - tut tut – of *the* monastery orchard, a storm of blossom, had filled his mind, when he was pulled roughly into a sitting position and given a cup of water.

"We must leave the city at once. Mohammedans are invading this quarter. They say they are looking for Christian spies, foreigners who have come to lead the Copts in rebellion against them."

Brecc drank and then splashed some of the water on his face to try to clear the blossom from his mind. The crackle of fire and cries of pain seemed very close. Fiacc was already alert and standing guard by the open door. Brecc gripped Makarius' arm and protested: "I really am too old for this and if it weren't for your Chalice, I would lie back down and finish dreaming of my sweet smelling orchard and the abundance of fruit it will bring come autumn."

Fiacc closed the door and gestured for him to be quiet. Moonlight penetrated the gloom of the alley. A group of men, women and children were trying to outrun some of the invaders who were only twenty metres behind them. Before leaving their houses, they had made the mistake of grabbing possessions, and these slowed them down. A large woman carrying a cooking pot fell heavily outside the entrance to the monks' house. The pot shattered and shards of the red earthenware spat under the door into the room. Her husband turned and came back to help her. He grabbed one of her arms and tried to pull her to her feet. She managed to bend one leg into position for rising but the other would not obey her. She fell back to the ground. The man tried again with his hands under her arms but she moaned loudly and pointed to her left leg. They could not escape and so he let her fall and threw himself on top of her. The leading pursuer, in his wild chase, stumbled, screaming, over them but quickly regained his feet. All, seven in number, stood over their silent victims and brought their swords down swiftly. One urged the others to take up the pursuit again but they faltered. Eagerness drained from them. They stood panting by the bodies and quizzed each other with their looks. All they heard was the sound of their heavy breathing. Their lust for blood cooled, not because the killings had fully satisfied them but because now their fear peopled the empty lane ahead and behind them with vengeful enemies. In those alien streets, every shadow held a flashing knife, every corner an ambush. Cautiously, they moved back the way they had come. One, a small, wiry man with a full beard, stood on one of the pieces of broken pot, winced with the pain and drew his foot back quickly. He hopped a couple of paces onwards and then stopped to pull the shard from his foot. The others rushed ahead of him.

Thinking the invaders had gone, Brecc stood up from his bed. The sound of the straw easing itself spilled into the lane. The Arab bristled with fright on hearing this but moved towards the door. He pushed it inwards.

47

His curved sword came through the entrance before him. He swung it rapidly from side to side and took another step. Fiacc, flattened against the wall just to the side of the door, grabbed the wrist of the man's sword arm with one hand and his throat with the other. With great strength he pulled the man into the room and, using the hand at the throat, lifted him off the floor and slammed him against the wall. The Arab dropped the sword and his arms fell and flapped limply by his side. Fiacc continued to hold him pinned to the wall and squeezed steadily until life guttered from his face. It happened quickly; a blur of figures in the insipid moonlight thrown through the doorway. Fiacc did not acknowledge Brecc's fists on his back at all and seemed unmoved by what had happened when he finally let the man fall to the floor.

Fiacc turned to the monk. "He was going to kill us."

"That is true and he had killed already," added a very shaken young Coptic monk.

Brecc looked from Makarius to Fiacc and shook his head: "You may have an argument to justify the killing, but you can never, never excuse the pleasure you took in doing it."

Brecc was not sure if Fiacc smiled at this point or whether the shadows the younger man was standing in deceived him. He blamed the shadows. "We had better go, and go quickly. They will miss their friend and may return." Makarius nodded his agreement.

As they left the house, Brecc remembered Makarius' words when he had woken them up: *they are looking for Christian spies, foreigners...* Did the Mohammedans think Fiacc and he were the spies? Were they, simply by being in Alexandria, to blame for the killing that was taking place? The thought terrified Brecc. He looked down, first at the Arab's body and then outside at the corpse of the Coptic man. They were dressed almost identically, the Moslem in the white woollen tunic of the Sufi sect and the Christian in a plain white cotton tunic.

The Venetian and the Precious Powder

Rusticco da Torcello locked the *fondaco*.[3] As he turned from the door, he belched and almost blew out the candle he carried. Sluggishly Rusticco made his way to his sleeping quarters. It was late but he knew that a troubled conscience and a turbulent stomach would pull him away from sleep. He blamed Egyptian wine and Egyptian religion. Venice was bad enough for plotting and intrigue; for religious and political scheming, violence and treachery, but at least there he had some understanding of who was with one party and who was with another, and what those parties stood for, and why they fought each other. In Alexandria, the quarrels baffled him. He wanted to trade and did not care whether the people he traded with were Christian, Jew, pagan or Moslem or whether they were supporters of Al Amum or Al Amin, or whether they belonged to the Lakhm or Mudlidj tribe, or even if they were Andalusian corsairs! *I give; you give.* He would do business with them! He should leave the place.

"Dried leaves;" he thought, "comfortable enough, but a mattress stuffed with feathers would be better, and more befitting a man of my standing." He belched loudly again and looked anxiously towards the door of his bedroom half-expecting his servant to come running in response to the noise. Flat on his back, Rusticco gazed for a moment at the great bulk of his stomach, started to shift on to his left side, but changed his mind. A physician had told him that the weight a heavy man places on his heart when he lies in such a position causes that organ to become misshapen and this weakens it greatly. Rusticco had been plagued by thoughts of his death in recent days or, more precisely, of damnation. Even in the heat of buying and selling, the most insignificant event or object would make his thoughts lurch into contemplation of hellfire. Two days previously, while negotiating a price for some fine Byzantine silk, his eye had fixed on a simple sewing mend just below the left shoulder of the tunic the Moslem dealer was wearing. A repair in the shape of an inverted *V* became a single flame and that single flame became a raging fire and that raging fire roared in Rusticco de Torcello's conscience. Such terrors made him assess his life and its excesses: fornication; over-eating; fraudulent dealings with other traders; neglect of his religious duties. Rusticco knew he had to make amends.

---

[3] warehouse

The business about the bones made his stomach churn anew but it could be his salvation; the sacred bones of St. Mark. Several days before, he had been visited by two Copts, one a merchant with whom he dealt regularly and the other a priest. Their business had been most unusual and disturbing. The priest leant on his staff and kept quiet; the merchant was the one who assailed Rusticco's conscience. He, Rusticco de Torcello had been chosen to write a page in history, the merchant announced. "Accounts, ledgers: that's the only writing I want to do," retorted Rusticco in his mind. His could be the pivotal act around which a new, Christian circle could be drawn about the Mediterranean. "Euclid, now," he thought, "but haven't they burnt all the books?"

"First of all, the bones and all that they represent - the works of the early Church in our land; the physical connection with Our Saviour; the graces brought through intercession - all that and more, since I have but drawn a cupful from that well, will be preserved. And you, Rusticco de Torcello will be the preserver."

"Preservationist," interjected the priest.

"Possibly," snapped the merchant.

Rusticco was terrified. They wanted him to smuggle the sacred bones of St. Mark from Alexandria on board one of his ships!

"For safekeeping. It's a great privilege that you have been chosen to carry them from here; temporarily, you understand. A great privilege."

"That's your opinion. I differ."

"The present troubles will blow over," continued the merchant.

"They usually don't last long. Why worry?" suggested Rusticco.

"I never know who's fighting whom. They run around like children finding grievances in a word, a touch."

"Possibly. It could be like a desert sandstorm and calm, smooth dunes are just ahead of us. Give it a little time."

"*Preservator* could be the correct form," said the priest.

The merchant ignored him. "However, there is a serious risk, if the rioting gets worse, that the bones will be desecrated."

"A terrible risk," added the priest.

"But forget about that. Even if they were not under threat that way, I would say take them to Venice."

"You would?"

"Definitely. Most of the time, life is reasonable for us Copts. We pay the poll tax to keep our faith and to keep our heads, but otherwise we don't do too badly. You agree, don't you?"

What the merchant said was true. It was patchy, but for most of the time, there was an accommodation, a working relationship in which the discrimination by the Arabs against the majority Copts was burdensome, but tolerable. The Copts had considerable freedom to worship, their language was still the most prominent and they held many high positions in the land, even in the government. The rioting, the stupid attacks: these were the work of fanatics, men who did not understand how the world and especially its trade worked. Rusticco had agreed with his visitor.

"But we cannot be complacent, my friend. Change is coming. Slowly, we are being pushed from those positions of power, economic and political, that we hold. Slowly, our ancient language is being buried under Arabic. Slowly, the fierce hatred of their most radical sects is being raised higher up the mast. When the Mohammedans settle their own quarrels, they will turn on us with great force. When that will be, I don't know. It could be a hundred years from now, but what I do know is that the prudent farmer always fills his store with droughts in mind."

Rusticco wished they would just go. He did not want this but, as if prompted by that thought, an insect that had penetrated his undergarment, bit him fiercely on his right testicle, an unmistakeable reminder of his sexual indiscretions, his mortality and his need to make things right with God. He suppressed an expletive but stood, reached under his clothes and scratched furiously.

"Displayed in Venice, the bones of St. Mark would draw attention to us, to the Copts and our situation."

Rusticco reordered his clothes. Avoiding damnation was a priority but never rushing into deals was his way in business and would be with this delicate matter. Take a step back. Give yourself time to think. "You're not liked particularly by the Catholics, you know, in Venice and elsewhere."

"We are your fellow-Christians. In troubled times, that is what matters."

Rusticco wasn't so sure of that. He felt a duty to help his fellow-Christians, but he also had great allegiance to his business. True, trade in some commodities was moving elsewhere but for him, after a difficult passage, business was brisk enough to bring a good profit. Rusticco was visiting Alexandria more frequently and was doing very well trading in spices, silks and fine linen. He had no way of knowing if it would last but while it did, the fabrics especially were making him a rich man: the Pope himself wanted Alexandrian silks as gifts for churches and the linen was of such an excellent quality that the flax sold for its weight in silver. The city was shaking itself into life once more. The canals were being dredged. The present rioting was nothing compared to the turmoil in the past especially that which erupted when the Arab adventurers were thrown out of Spain. Rusticco had worked hard to become known and trusted by the Alexandrian merchants, Mohammedans, Christians and Jews, and was doing much better than his Venetian and Genoan rivals. He could not leave the place.

Try to turn a profit in life and try to turn a profit in the afterlife. It had appeal. Rusticco had told his visitors that he would consider what they had said but could not do anything with the ship he now had in the harbour because it was loaded and would sail on the next tide.

A sharp, insistent, burning pain pressed high in his stomach. He tried to remember if sleeping on his left side had been his usual practice before the physician had warned him. His heart could be misshapen already. "Perhaps if I sit up or walk about the room, it will be eased," he suggested to himself, "or perhaps it won't. Perhaps I am being punished for not agreeing right away to help those two. Perhaps this is a foretaste of Hell."

When the insistent knocking started, Rusticco got out of bed. His troubled conscience told him that the merchant and his priest friend were back and that he was being given a chance to make amends. He imagined them standing outside with a box containing the blessed saint's bones. He would aid them in their cause. It would go a long way to saving his soul, he was sure. "Pork," he thought, "a basket of salted pork for the crew: if I hide the bones among that, the Moslems will never inspect." He had been delighted with his idea but was both surprised and relieved when he found that his servant had opened the door to Makarius and two Irishmen, and that the idea would not be put to the test right then.

Makarius knew it would be foolish to try to leave the city that night. There was too much confusion on the streets and it was probable that the guard on the gates had been doubled. He took Brecc and Fiacc the length of the pillared Canopus Road to Eastern Alexandria, through the large but quiet Jewish quarter, to a sector by the harbour where Venetian merchants lived. A priest friend had told him that de Torcello was going to smuggle the blessed bones of St. Mark for safekeeping to Venice; that the merchant had agreed to be the *preservator* of the relics. If he was willing to undertake such a task, then surely the Venetian would shelter the foreigners for a night.

Rusticco agreed to take the refugees as a step down the way to assuaging his guilt and was not surprised when, with one final belch, the burning pains left him, his stomach settled and thoughts of hellfire receded. They could sleep in the small courtyard and his servant would stay awake to make sure they had not been followed.

Brecc hardly closed his eyes. He gazed at the stars and wondered if one could predict the future from the patterns they made. Where was The Plough? There was a pattern he understood, the earth unfolding its richness to that tireless blade. He had a sudden longing to quit Egypt, to forget about pilgrimages, Chalices and oh, of course, lapis lazuli. Let them use verdigris or woad; woad would do. He yearned to journey north to greenness and coolness. Makarius dozed fitfully, twitching and whimpering, and Fiacc slept soundly. In his room, on his leaf mattress, Rusticco de Torcello slept for a short while but was woken abruptly by a hideous dream in which a pig's head on a table set for a feast told him that death and God's judgement were close. His body was running with sweat and the pains high in his stomach had returned. He would transport the relic to Venice.

Makarius and the two Irishmen waited until the streets were busy before leaving their refuge. The Copt wanted to lead them from the city quickly and head for the desert monasteries. As the markets were filling, they could slip through the city gates unnoticed among the crowds. The guards would be busy accepting bribes and helping themselves to whatever the traders were carrying. Brecc gripped Makarius' arm. "I have a weight to shed, Makarius, as you well know, and I must be unburdened of it before we leave Alexandria."

Makarius stared at Brecc as if he hadn't heard. He did not want to hear. What did the Irishman mean? Was he speaking of a *spiritual* burden? Were there sins he needed to confess? He, Makarius, was being tested again. They had to leave the city as soon as possible but how could he deny anyone such blessed relief and sustenance? They could be in great physical danger from those searching for the foreigners but death could threaten the Irishman's soul if he was not allowed the sacrament of repentance. Makarius remained silent and continued to stare as if that alone would resolve the situation, perhaps change the Irish monk's mind.

Brecc studied the look, not furtive, but one of unnecessary guilt that creased the Egyptian's face. "Lapis lazuli, Makarius, or those in Clonmacnoise who sow The Word on paper, will pierce me to death with their quills. Take me to a supplier. Lead on."

"It had slipped my mind."

"You'll forget the Chalice next."

Once more, Makarius did not know how to respond. How could Brecc make such a suggestion? He, Makarius, would never forget such a sacred task. Isaiah had prophesied that an altar of the Lord would be established in Egypt and so it had come to pass and he, Makarius, would do all that he could in his lifetime to make sure that the Holy Sacrifice would continue to be offered from that altar down through all the turbulent years that might visit the land. He could not answer the older man directly.

"Then the sun will be high before we leave the city."

"I am the oldest and the weakest and I will suffer the most but I must complete this business."

Makarius snapped out of his stare. "I know where to go."

Rusticco de Torcello was another keen that the guests move quickly from his quarters. After profuse thanks to their host from Makarius, the three of them left the *fondaco* and headed for the market. Makarius led them further along the stretch of shore within the arms of Alexandria's great eastern harbour. After the terror of his night, Brecc expected people to be licking their wounds and the streets to be tense in expectation of more trouble. He was surprised by the normal way in which life was going on and people were mixing. The city had quickly absorbed what, alongside other disturbances, had been a minor affair, nothing that would stop the market traders from littering the ground with their goods: fresh dates, olives and figs, dried fruits, wine, goats, salt; fabrics, from simple wool weaves to rolls of the finest brilliant silks; perfumes; pottery; wood and metal tools; delicately wrought gold and silverware and precious stones.

Makarius stepped carefully among piles of peppercorns, cloves, nutmegs, cinnamon sticks and ginger roots and lead Brecc and Fiacc into the portico of one of the market street buildings. There, by one of its huge green marble pillars, he introduced them to a Moslem dealer it would be safe to do business with. From somewhere within the building proper, a small boy brought samples of levigated lapis lazuli. Brecc inspected them. He knew he had to concentrate, had to do this well and not allow his impatience to let him and the monks in the scriptorium down. The colour could vary considerably from sky blue to a pigment with a greenish tint. Brecc was under instructions to buy the variety known as *nili* because that was what produced the serene and royal indigo colour with which the Clonmacnoise monks illuminated the gospels.

Although he did not let Makarius know, Brecc too wanted to be out of Alexandria but not through any urgency prompted by a search for the Chalice or by any fear of discovery. Tranquility; peace; prayer: it would be a long time before his mind and body could find rest in the soft greenery of his home but the wilderness of the Egyptian desert might bring some repose. With a clear sigh of relief, Brecc had no trouble choosing. It was good quality. That sprinkling of gold specks among the blue was a good sign. Those who had bought and loaded the stone in Badakhstan knew their trade. The haggling was simple, a calculated, *I start high, you low and we meet exactly at the middle.* Makarius smiled. It was a good price. He was surprised at the Irish monk's quick and efficient bargaining. Through Makarius, Brecc told the trader what the powder was for. The Moslem nodded and told Brecc that it pleased him to know that through his simple trade he was helping spread knowledge and praise of God. The transaction was over quickly much to Brecc's satisfaction. He was pleased that the boy had not brought the drinks which were customary during such dealing and told Makarius sharply to refuse when the trader apologised and ordered some. Makarius, he could see, was being pulled apart by two straining horses once more. Tradition and tact demanded that they sit with the trader but, now that the purchase was done, contingency pressed them to make their way to the emptiness and what Makarius hoped would be the safety of the desert. Brecc told him to tell the man; tell him now. He did, apologising profusely. Brecc tucked the bag containing the precious powder into a pocket inside his tunic. He would sew that pocket shut as soon as he had an opportunity to do so. One task completed and the desert ahead of him, the vast expanse where many believed the fierce pull of temptation to sin slackened. Brecc hoped for peace of mind; prayed for peace of mind but knew the silence, the heat, the stillness, the barrenness could provoke one's senses and imagination ferociously and in the turmoil, it was as easy to find the Devil as it was to find God and peace of mind.

CILLEBAIRRE
Conal's Return

That first night in the forest Ruadhan was more troubled by what was going on in his mind, a strange, complex mix of thoughts and feelings than by his painful leg. Anger roiled within him, anger against those who were dead or had been taken by the Northmen. With the exception of Tulchán and one or two others, he had felt little love towards them, but now that they had gone from his life, he ached for their presence and became anxious about his new "freedom". He had been tied, beaten, ignored, laughed at and had spent a great deal of time on his own. He had raised himself but, nevertheless, Fáelcar, Cairech and their children had become his family. They should have done more to be with him still. The rhythm of the days, the hard work, the scraps of food, even the beatings had provided a routine which, now that it had gone, memory made reassuring, almost comforting. For the same reason, he was angry with the old monk as well. In the forest, no new family had extended its arms to him. The morning after his arrival, in spite of Ite's warnings and much to her annoyance, he had entered the encampment and stirred great anger. Tempers cooled and clearer reasoning prevailed among the majority, but the exiled community had decided it was better if Ruadhan stayed in his hermitage by the stream and outside its protection until the return to Cillebairre was agreed upon. From dusk to dawn, he would be roped to a tree unable to defend himself from enemies or wild animals. If he had done no wrong, he would come to no harm. Ruadhan wanted to run when Ite told him what they were going to do. The man he was becoming would not tolerate it. His strongest impulse was to refuse to submit and leave, fend for himself. Would a life wandering, begging, offering work wherever it was needed be that different from his life in Cillebairre? Ite fought him over this. With her ardent eyes fixed firmly on him, she used all her powers of persuasion and the memory of the mission Tulchán had entrusted to him to make him stay and accept further indignity.

"I will be with you," she promised, "I will be close to you."

A guard was set during the day. Just before nightfall, before he left his post, the guard tied one of Ruadhan's wrists, passed the rope around a tree and fastened the end to Ruadhan's other wrist in such a way that he could not bring his hands together. With her daily duties done and the guard removed, Ite sneaked away from the main camp and, as she had promised, lay close to Ruadhan. Each night she passed on stories her mother had told her of paradisal lands where barns overflowed with grain; where every tree was laden with fruit and where no blood was ever shed. Tulchán had told similar stories: lions living with lambs; leopards lying down with goats; children putting their hands into a snake's hole and not being bitten. Why should Ruadhan put faith in any of their stories, Ite's or Tulchán's? Nothing in his life mirrored the stories except... except for Tulchán's belief in him and the devotion that Ite showed. Ite. He longed for the time she left her daily tasks to bring him soup, hard pieces of bread and once, a lump of cheese and he longed even more intently for the evenings. As her low, wavering voice told the stories, he felt comforted and even content in the intense dark of the forest but when, on the fifth night, she lay closer and hugged him for warmth, Ruadhan thought the *strangeness* was coming as his whole body tensed and part of him - the part that had to be hidden; the part that drew special attention but wasn't spoken of; the part that confused and worried him - stiffened and expressed itself in a way it had not done before and when it did there was something like a burst of light in his mind and he relaxed and felt intense pleasure. It was not the *strangeness*. Ite knew it wasn't. She smiled. The pleasure wasn't Ruadhan's alone. He knew little about such things but enough to realise it was a sign that he and Ite were children no longer.

Ite slept soundly as Conal cut Ruadhan free before dawn on the twenty-fourth day after the raid. The boy had been sleeping lightly, had heard the warrior's soft approach and easily distinguished it from the faint rustlings of small creatures in the grass and the stirrings of the birds in the branches above him. There was nothing he could do to defend himself. Ruadhan had turned as much as the fastenings would allow and, even in the dark, recognised Conal immediately the trees disclosed his powerful figure. He felt a slight tremor of apprehension. It was not fear. He had no close knowledge of this man but a bond between them had been sealed at the strange encounter by the bog. What made Ruadhan shake slightly, as Conal bent and freed him, was his own foresight, a clear, thrilling understanding that with this man's arrival, life in the valley would never be the same again. Conal gripped his shoulder.

"Be still, my friend from the gorse. I did not betray you then. You must not betray me now. Not a sound must spill from your mouth. Come, show me where the guards are placed about the encampment and bring the rope that bound you so strangely. There are hard lessons that need to be learnt before Cillebairre can live again."

The first hint of light infiltrated the gloom. Ite woke, saw the kneeling, bent form of Conal gripping Ruadhan and panicked. She rose and flung herself at the intruder. "Leave him! Let him go!" Conal grabbed her by an arm and pulled her back to the earth. She resisted and, with her free arm battered furiously at his shoulder, arm and head. "Ite, it's Conal," Ruadhan said quietly, "a friend." Conal smiled and with his free hand pointed to his scar. Ite nodded but pushed the other hand roughly off her.

Ruadhan looked hard at Conal and wondered how he would teach the *lessons*. The adult's long, dark, oily hair was pulled back tightly to free that high, square, and cruelly marked forehead and he was dressed, sword, dagger and buckler at his back, for battle. For a moment, Ruadhan wondered whether he should pass over the information. The truth was that the encampment was guarded casually. The people of Cillebairre believed the forest provided protection as well as shelter. "Forests hold many fears for the invaders," someone declaimed. "They are a very superstitious people. The holly trees close by this place will stop them for they worship the everlasting leaves." Others had echoed this. In the early days of their exile, many experts claiming close knowledge of the ways of the Northmen sprang up like green shoots under rain and intense sun:

They never attack at night.

If they know the sticky-leaved plant, the fly-trap, flourishes here, they will leave us alone.

At Inishbofin, it is said that their attack was impeded by red-haired women lying on the ground in front of them.

If we pin moss that has been used to staunch a woman's menses to trees about the camp, they will never pass.

And so on and so on. Some even went so far as to argue that since Na Lámha had been a place of sacrifice to the old gods, protection was assured. "We are safe here." In spite of such talk, few went far from the damp enclosure. Those who did venture into the forest went only as far as they needed to gather or cut wood or pick berries to add to dwindling food reserves. No one hunted, convinced by one of their number that a defeated people, a hunted people, must wait for the full transformation of the moon until they hunt again. Many old notions as were revived. They were a beaten, cowed and hungry people without leadership.

Blue eyes stared straight back at the boy. Ruadhan nodded reassurance to Ite. He knew for certain that this man had fought for his people and not for the invaders. She could trust him. Ite knew the positions of only two guards. One sat below the furthest spill of the great rocks and to the east of Na Lámha. From this vantage point, the guard could scan a great stretch of the forest's edge. Sometimes, Ite told Conal, the guard climbed above the rocks to the bare ridge and a place that commanded a view into the next valley.

Conal pulled Ruadhan to his feet. "Take me there."

"I'm coming too," said Ite.

Conal shook his head. "No, you wait here."

Ite moved quickly. She got on her feet, reached behind her, pulled a knife from her cinture and pressed it to the side of Conal's neck. Conal smiled again. "In one land I have visited, there are large, spotted cats. They are faster than any other creature I have seen and as fierce. Now, I see they have come to Ireland. Girl, you are welcome to accompany us."

The first guard was at his lower post beneath the rocks. The weaponry did not encumber Conal. He crouched low and became a stealthy darting creature springing on the lesser stones until he was close enough to grab and overpower the guard with ease, gagging his mouth and trussing him firmly with the fastenings that had bound Ruadhan. A second sat slumped forward by the communal fire at the centre of the clearing. His spear, stuck in the earth, was to his right. It was the squat figure of Fintan, an unsmiling man who never missed an opportunity to twist his pock-cheeked face into sneers and to abuse others, especially Ruadhan. His fists, had Ruadhan not great alacrity, would by now have beaten out a pattern on his skull. Conal smiled as he recognised the hunched figure who, like his father and Fáelcar, had been exiled from the Kingdom of Mide to Cillebairre.

"A feckless man; he always was; a fool," whispered Conal to Ruadhan and Ite. "Let the flames die down no matter how cold you are. And don't sit in the fire's light so that your enemy can count your hairs." Still in a crouch, Conal dropped down the slope, entered the forest and closed on Fintan. With the guard's back to him, Conal left the trees, bounded the two streams and crossed the clearing to where he sat by the fire. Ruadhan and Ite followed him at a distance. As Conal suspected, Fintan was asleep. Conal pulled the spear easily from the spongy earth, took it in both hands and pricked Fintan's neck sharply with the point. Fintan shuddered awake, realised he was threatened and staggered to his feet shouting and flailing right and left for his spear. The camp came quickly to life. Axes, spears and swords were grabbed and brandished as the refugees of Cillebairre surrounded the intruder and his young accomplices.

Fintan knew who was confronting him. He stroked his neck and held the hand out towards Conal. "You drew blood!"

"You won't forget then, will you," replied Conal. "Next time, remembering that prick, you might stay awake and do what is expected of you." He threw Fintan's spear to him. Fintan reached for the shaft as it came towards him, connected, but could not grip it and the spear fell to the ground. Already humiliated, Fintan did not look for more. He left the spear where it fell and glowered fiercely at Conal.

Conal's name was being passed from mouth to mouth by some but there was confusion and scepticism. All knew the story but, apart from the telling scar, only a few could see the boy they had known in the features of this mature, well-travelled and battle-hardened stranger. He was dressed differently in a kilt of skins they did not recognise and cloth with patterns unlike any the Cillebairre women wove. The hilt of the sword by his side was studded with bright, semi-precious stones they had never seen. The cry of "Northman" went up.

Ruadhan watched closely the one who had freed him. Conal did not flinch. He was not the tallest of men but he seemed rise above all others in the assembly as he spoke with ease to the crowd.

"Give me a few warriors and I could have overrun this camp of yours without having to take a deep breath!"

As if to prove him wrong, three men, two with blackthorn clubs and a tall man with a short sword, rushed him. Ruadhan shouted a warning but Conal was ready for them, clenching his buckler closer to him and swiftly drawing his sword. The first to close on him lifted his club high to strike but, before he could, Conal took a quick step forward and rammed his shield into the man's chest. The attacker was caught flat-footed and unbalanced by the thrust. He fell, winded, to the ground, and in his fall, took the other club-bearer with him. The tall swordsman attacked from

Conal's left side, crouching and lunging. Conal spun, dipped and deflected the sword with his shield. He could have driven *his* sword up under the man's ribs but stood upright, tilted the blade towards himself and brought the pommel down sharply once, twice on the man's forehead. The attacker crumbled, stunned, to his knees, clasped his head and howled. The other two rose to their feet to renew their attack and were joined by several others. They ringed Conal.

Conal shouted at them. "I do not wish to kill my own and that is who you are, but I will if it means keeping my life!" He held his sword on high. "This close friend has struck and killed more than most of you could count, men of more colours of skin than you could count in more lands than you could count. It needs to rest. Let it return and sleep within its scabbard!"

Ruadhan and Ite pushed through the attackers and joined Conal. Ite drew her knife again. Conal shook his head but smiled. The ring closed on them. One man pulled a long branch from the fire and joined the circle. "We'll brand him anew!"

A loud cry from somewhere among the huge rocks made all of them falter. The survivor monk, Duach, had been evacuating his bowels in frightening gushes at a shallow latrine behind the longest finger of stone in Na Lámha when he heard the commotion and realised a newcomer was in the camp. *Buinnech* had plagued him on and off since they had come to this place and as he tried, falteringly, to rush across the two streams, a sharp pain in his gut told him it was not over. Duach was as thin as a wraith but his voice was strong: "Stop! This is not the way! There has been enough killing!"

Duach had no knowledge of the newcomer's secretive and threatening entry into the camp but, squatting regularly at the miserable toilet, he had had plenty of time to consider what was happening to the displaced community of Cillebairre. Old feuds going back generations had resurfaced; each day, hunger bred fights over the little food they had; quarrels exploded over accusations of stealing; frustrations over how they had been defeated and driven from their home to this dank, gloomy sanctuary pitted brother against brother. No longer did the people share all things in common as the first Apostles had. It was fortunate that there had been no serious injuries or even killings but both could not be far off if the disorderliness continued. Duach could have done more, should have done more, to staunch the disorder in the camp and would have done more, he told himself, had he not had to spend so much time trying in vain to staunch the chaotic flux from his bowels. This exile in the forest was doing no one any good. The people had lost purpose, direction. They were not enslaved as the Israelites had been by foreigners, but - and here Duach surprised himself with his cleverness of thought - by days passed in idleness and ill-thoughts towards their neighbours. They were reverting to older, primitive ways of living and with that they were drifting away from the true faith. Superstitions were ruling lives! That business, such nonsense, with the menses should have prompted him, *buinnech* or no *buinnech*, into action and he had had an idea of telling the people to think of the great rocks they camped below as hands that were blessing them and that God would point the way from this dismal place. He should have done so. He had to shape his thoughts with more clarity and lead with determination. Their backsliding had to be stopped. Twisting right and left while trying to adjust a poorly bound undergarment, Duach shouted at them. "This man, even were he an utter stranger, should be welcomed to our home, miserable as it is! And those young ones: what is going on? Food and shelter, not weapons should greet the stranger! Refuse him these and we refuse Christ! Let me through!"

"Does that include the well-armed stranger who creeps upon us Duach?" shouted Fintan.

The crowd parted for the monk. He saw the stranger close up for the first time and, despite the fierce pains in his gut, smiled. "It's true, he should not enter bristling with weapons. Those should have been left at the edge of the encampment but, as you can see, this is Conal, one of us, without doubt." He pointed to his own forehead to draw attention to Conal's scar. "The one the boy saw, the one with royal blood from somewhere, I understand." Here, he nodded to Ruadhan and, in a gesture of reconciliation and apology, put a hand on his shoulder. "This is the one Ruadhan brought us news of and the one Fáelcar, father of this girl, God rest his soul, spoke of."

Duach's intervention, his mention of Fáelcar, who had been killed in the raid and the certain knowledge that several more of their community would join Fáelcar should they rush Conal, brought a stutter to the crowd's resolution. The ones closest to him lowered their weapons.

"We will feed him and then hear what he has to say. There…"

Conal interrupted Duach and, from that moment, like a smith breathing forge embers into new life, he began to exert control over the people of Cillebairre. The *special one* believed it was his destiny. He spoke and, as if to confirm that understanding, the sun made its dawn presence felt forcefully and streaks of light raced through the trees to the assembly. Several were sure they had never seen such brilliance so early in that sombre place. It was another sign to add to those that had accompanied Conal's birth. The *special one* had returned. At close quarters, Ruadhan continued to watch the one who had set him free. Even he, in his youthful ignorance, recognised a force of character that would be hard to resist, a new leader for the broken community.

"My story can wait; my stomach can wait; wait until we are back where we belong," announced Conal. "Return to Cillebairre today! Do not stay in this damp, stygian place a day longer less you grow gills and think you belong here. There is nothing to fear back in your home. I have come to tell you this. The boat that came here and the Northmen who manned it have rejoined their fleet and the fleet has gone far from here. I know this for certain. The commander of the fleet has his eyes on richer pickings than those found in Cillebairre. You must return." Conal's gaze slowly swept the crowd before him. A few for whom the raid had confirmed that life was full of sorrow, hardship and uncertainty wouldn't be healed by shallow optimism and walked away. It was only a few. Most stayed and were urged to do so by Duach the monk. They were not far from awe as they listened.

Brother Duach knew that his half-brother, the dead Abbot Comgall, had been a weak leader. His family's influence had kept him in place but it was Tulchán who had provided what discipline and spiritual focus the community had. Duach also acknowledged that *he* had not the willpower or skills to direct this community. He wanted nothing more than to go back to the simple, strict rhythm of the days at Cillebairre, days filled with writing and prayer. Duach wanted to copy the Gospels and pray and fast his soul into Paradise *and* get rid of this terrible affliction that *not fasting* had brought him. There was a vacuum in the small community where there should have been leadership. Duach listened as someone started to fill that void. There was the matter of Duach's family. He wondered whether the lordship of Máenmaige, his and Comgall's family, the lukewarm patrons of Cillebairre, would be content to allow Conal to rule the settlement but dismissed the thought as quickly as it came. That stream would be crossed when it was reached. Conal was here with them now, someone who could unite, who could heal. God had sent him. God had pointed the way. Na Lámha, The Hands *had* blessed them.

"The Cillebairre raid was the mistake of headstrong warriors on one ship, one ship only. They will suffer for their foolhardiness, believe me. I know the ways of these people. The path is clear for you to return, to return before winter extends its grasping fingers."

Looking around, Ruadhan saw that there was a general assent. The time spent at Na Lámha had not been easy and conditions were deteriorating. Food stocks were low; illness was rife; quarrels were many: the people of Cillebairre needed to be shown what to do and Conal had arrived to do that.

"There is a lot to do but nothing insurmountable. We will make your home bigger, stronger, more easily defended. All it takes is your brawn and your determination. Others are there before you, and have started the task of rebuilding. Some are strangers on a pilgrimage who came to Cillebairre in the hope of learning from Tulchán. Perhaps they will not stay but others have come to make Cillebairre strong, to create a settlement that will match any in the west. Come back even if it is only to give your dead deeper graves than we have. They deserve better." Conal stopped and scanned the crowd. Even the dissidents had turned and were heeding him and most, without doubt, were with him. "Gather what you want to take back with you! Don't linger any longer in this dreadful place!"

Restoration

When he tentatively stepped from the sanctuary of the forest, Ruadhan half-thought his old friend, Tulchán, would greet him. The wreckage of the settlement assaulted his eyes and drove such a childlike attempt to deny reality from his mind. For a moment he thought of turning back to lose himself in the dark burrows and niches of the forest. The days ahead of him were going to be more uncertain than they had been in the past. He had stood alongside Conal at Na Lámha. Would the newcomer take him as a slave? If so, he would be protected and some might begrudgingly give him respect. Could he hope for more? Perhaps Conal would become his guardian. That was too much to wish for and who could tell what the warrior's *guardianship* would bring? Conal was not Tulchán. Tulchán's presence had brought calm, a calm that came from the monk's deep belief in a God who loved all, even those who crawled mewling from the forest's depths. Conal was strong, resolute, and, thought Ruadhan, wise, but he would not bring calm. He looked like a man who grew restless with calm. Ruadhan was stepping from the forest depths once more to be reborn in the new Cillebairre. He took a deep breath and, hardly thinking about it at all, recited from Psalm 46: *"God is our shelter, our strength, ever ready in time of trouble. So we shall not be afraid when the earth gives way..."*

Ite came from behind him, gripped his arm and urged him onwards. The few beehive cells looked as if they had been untouched. The stone walls of the church and scriptorium remained. Their roofs had been burned but some on the former was intact. For the rest, on both sides of the river, only a few charred poles marked the dwellings that had been. Two monks, Nuadu, a physician and Mochan a carpenter, the pilgrims Conal had referred to, met the returning exiles as they came out of the forest. A rugged pair, these men had lived and prayed first on Sceilig Mhichíl and then in craggy recesses in the mountains to the south of Cillebairre. It was their intention to walk to the great Slighe Mor Road and Durrow on the first part of a pilgrimage that would see them following the steps of Colmcille to Ioua Insula. Their path had led them to the ruins of Cillebairre where, clearly, they were needed. God had brought them there at this crucial time. It could be a sign that their pilgrimage had ended. From a pile of cut wood that Mochan the carpenter would work, they were restoring roof of the church

Close to the stepping stones, three more newcomers lounged on the riverbank. These men were not in Cillebairre to do any rebuilding. They were soldiers, dissatisfied ones who resented the deception used to recruit them. Conal had lied prodigiously to them and that was the main cause of their resentment. A great feast is being prepared, he had told them. That's what would welcome them in Cillebairre! In the great hall of Cillebairre that matched anything the High Kings had built, the long table would be piled high with the crackling roast carcasses of specially fattened pigs; with a shoal of salmon stuffed with herbs; with succulent poultry and even a porpoise or two. Servants there would be; three at least for each of them. They wouldn't even have to lift the food to their mouths. That would be done for them. Drink? Rich wine from the Kingdom of the Franks, mead and ale would flow like streams from high mountains, and as for women, well, the most beautiful on the whole island of Ireland were there; warm, soft, palpitating flesh waiting for the strokes and probes of Ruarcc, Beccan and Eoin's strong, rough hands. With these promises rearing themselves in their minds and conversations, they had ridden their horses hard through mountain passes and along valley bottoms, barely sleeping, barely eating. And what had greeted them? No great hall; no feast; no servants; no compliant, beautiful women. Ruins: miserable, burnt out hovels, a few sheep, wasted fields; the remains of the small monastic settlement of Cillebairre. One, the large, lumbering man called Ruarcc nursed a wound to his shoulder. When he saw what he had been brought to, he had turned on Conal, drawn his sword and tried to kill him but his opponent's superior fighting ability overpowered him easily.

"Stirring only in your old home for cattle raids against weak neighbours has made you flabby and effete," Conal mocked as he stood over him. "I don't see why anyone would run from you. You need some real fights to shape you into a decent opponent for battle-hardened Northmen."

Ruarcc believed he was about to die and tensed himself for the finishing thrust of Conal's sword. He felt one deft, humiliating slash to his right shoulder, a wound that, as it was inflicted, he vowed to revenge.

"And foolish too, Ruarcc. No soldier worth his salt and with hair as long as yours fights without hair tied back. You have a good many years at your back but still have much to learn. Remember your first lesson by that cut, Ruarcc, and think of this as well. Your lord did me no favours when he gave you three to me. You are the least among his fighting men as this…" -

he pricked Ruarcc's other shoulder with the tip of his sword drawing blood once more - "...weak attempt to attack me confirms. He is more battle-ready now than he was with you three at his side."

Conal stepped back, sheaved his sword and offered Ruarcc a hand to help him stand. Ruarcc was sick with hurt pride. He knew little of this man who boasted of fighting with and against the Northmen. He stood without help.

"But I can change that. I will teach you to fight." Conal laughed. "But to fight and win, Ruarcc. That's what brings you feasts and servants and women. You will have earned them then."

Conal could have been resentful as well. He had wanted more than three soldiers to help him shape the new settlement of Cillebairre and had wanted men of a better temper. Knowing Cillebairre fell under the loose patronage of Fearghal of Máenmaige, a sept in the Ui Maine kingdom, Conal had conducted his first diplomatic mission there requesting help in the rebuilding of the community. He had convinced all of his royal background in the Kingdom of Mide and reminded all who received him how his father, before he fell from grace, had hidden one of their family for several years from enemies intent on killing him. Some thought any debt accruing from this act had been paid in full by a daughter offered in marriage but others, especially the elderly Fearghal, were so impressed by Conal's gall, by his superb, finely-honed sword, by his pledge of fealty and by his wondrous stories of voyages[4] with the Northmen that they were happy to receive him and furnish him with a few fighting men and horses. There was even talk and preliminary negotiations of a wife for Conal. A river of ale was drunk and all agreed that there were sound reasons to encourage the rebirth of Cillebairre. For one thing, tributes... yes... tributes that had dried up... that clown, Comgall... they could flow once more and... and... a stronger Cillebairre, a settlement at the edge of the Kingdom, could act as a useful shield against enemy clans and the Northmen. Yes, Conal could have his warriors and there would be more discussions, certainly, in the future over the matter of a wife. Warriors! Conal knew full well what he was being given and knew too that Máenmaige was a weakened and ill-

---

4   Some had tried to match Conal with their tales but the truth was that the household had no appointed storyteller. The last one had been skewered by Feargal who, in a drunken rage, believed the man was mocking his stutter when in fact, he had been struggling to recall a particularly obscure Pictish name.

governed sept under Fearghal's rule. But as raw, ill-disciplined and inexperienced as Ruarcc, Beccan and Eoin were, Conal believed in his own power to create a small but purposeful military unit that, like a small Roman square, would protect the people and land of Cillebairre.

On the day of the return from the forest, movements at first were sluggish and reluctant as if people were still infected by the melancholy their gloomy forest sanctuary had given rise to, but soon, encouraged by their forceful new leader, one who did not tolerate idleness or complaining, bustle and a sense of purpose returned. Like ants scattered by a child's stick raking the dirt, a confused people eventually found the familiar paths and started the hard task of reclaiming their home. The monk-pilgrims, Nuadu and Mochan, hung cloths in front of the sanctuary and told the returning villagers that the rest of the church could be a temporary home for some. The women lit fires, fetched water and quickly set about making flat bread and vegetable and herb broth. Groups of men and women worked together to make simple, temporary rough shelters from sods and branches. Others scattered to the fields to see if any crops still stood, to consider planting anew before summer was lost completely, to collect honey and beeswax from hives that were intact and to milk any sheep, goats and cows that they could find.

Conal was determined to restore the community of Cillebairre. He was a driven man. Throughout his exile with the Northmen, no matter what foreign lands he visited, what adventures he participated in, what company he kept, Conal had yearned to return. This small piece of Ireland had come to mean everything to him. He did not understand why. The landscape had not the grandeur of the fiords he had navigated or the mystery of desert lands he had almost died of thirst in. The growing collection of hovels and the few half-stone structures were ants to the elephants of cities to which he had travelled. The people of Cillebairre were cowed, small in ambition when compared to the Northmen. With the exception of the few monks, they were thin in learning when compared to such as the people of the Abbassid Caliphate but they were the ones he wanted be among and, more than that, wanted to lead, wanted it so much that, when the opportunity arose, he felt no compunction over turning on those he had voyaged with. He had become convinced that he would return on one particularly long night following a riverbank skirmish with Khazars who had used faulty scales to weigh their silver payment for pelts and weapons. A wound to his shoulder had been washed with goat urine and then cauterised with a heated knife. He had lost consciousness briefly but for the rest of that night, the pain kept his mind awake and surging furiously like a high sea. The sword that had inflicted the wound was one they, Conal and his band of Northmen, had traded to the Khazans. Once again, he had been attacked by his own and had another scar. This had turned his mind to thinking hard of the place he had never stopped calling *home*. Blood? Destiny? Returning to Cillebairre and shaping its future alongside his own was, perhaps, what God wanted him to do and here, Conal hesitated since his mind was unclear on how exactly the deity or deities intervened in human affairs. When he raised his sword and brought it down on an enemy, was he an agent of God's will or was the action simply something that *his* needs compelled and nothing more? Conal was not a great thinker on such matters and being among the Northmen had confused what little theological understanding he had. He had never denied his Christian God publicly and had never been asked to do so, but to avoid questions and because the feasting that followed was hard to resist, he had honoured the pagan Gods of the Northmen with sacrifices. Trying to understand the ways God played a part in human affairs was not for Conal. He acknowledged the existence of such a being but happily left such analysis to the monks.

In the revived Cillebairre, the survivor monk, Duach, provided the blood-link with the Máenmaige sept and took Comgall's place as abbot-leader of the whole monastic settlement. He held sway among those whose concerns were for the rebuilding of a spiritual community but his reticence happily let Conal lead in the regeneration of the wider society of Cillebairre: its politics, its economy, its social and military organisation. Duach told himself always to be cautious and steadfast in his decisions since certain teachings were inviolable but was content to place Conal's initiatives on theological foundations whenever it was required.

On the second evening after their return from the forest everyone lay down their tools, put aside all thoughts of work and gathered in and around the church. All came to eat and listen to the *special one* tell stories from his voyages with the Northmen. It was the first of many such gatherings and proved to be a way in which Conal could impose his authority, impress with his experience, convince all of his loyalty and insist on theirs. That evening, ignoring protests that the sheep be kept for milk and cheese, Conal ordered that three of the small flock found grazing close to Wolf's Head Hill be slaughtered. To this he added two deer his militia had hunted.

In assertion of *his* new authority and mirroring the rule applied in many monasteries, Duach imposed a strict dietary regime which forbade meat for himself and the two other monks, the intention being to strengthen spiritual awareness (and, he believed, keep at bay the dreaded *buinnech*). He told Conal they would absent themselves from the feasting but that he was not to interpret this as a slight. Conal hoped Duach understood that after the deprivations of Na Lámha, he wanted his people to eat meat. He wanted them to enjoy ale as well but there had not been time to brew any. Duach's mind winced at Conal's reference to *his people* - it seemed premature and arrogant - but accepted that the weakened community had no alternative but to accept this appropriation.

Butchers went swiftly about their work skinning the creatures and then deftly stripping the meat from the bones in huge slabs as blood streamed over them and the grass. They were impatient. The meat spluttered but was only partially blackened by the flames before portions were carved, still bloody, from the spits. All bar the monks ate meat that evening, Conal's warriors first, then the rest of the men hunched as close as possible to the roasting fires, fat guttering through their beards, and finally, the women and children. As appetites were sated and as dark came, talk and laughter wrapped a comforting blanket around them and a feeling of contentment almost as perceptible as the smoke above the fires rose to the few stars that had appeared. There was nothing to fear. Conal insisted that the much-prized viscera were given to him and his warriors. He speared the heart of the larger deer on a pointed stick, turned it in the flames for a short time and offered it to Ruadhan.

"Put the heart of this fine beast inside you and draw upon its strength."

Ruadhan hesitated but knew he could not refuse his guardian in public. Ruarcc watched this gesture closely and spat his disgust on to the earth close by. Ruadhan nibbled at first but then began to gnaw the mix of soft portions and chewy membranous meat with relish cramming the heart into his mouth. There was enough for two. He had never fed like that before and felt bloated. Conal nodded his satisfaction. Dogs circled the gathering picking up what few scraps were left.

When the eating was over, Conal stood on Mochan's woodpile inside the church and brandished his sword. He had never felt more certain that he was fulfilling his destiny than at that time. He could almost feel the sting of Khazar goat piss on his wounded shoulder once more and the thrill of the revelation that had followed. The mercenaries, Ruarcc, Breccan and Eoin, clutching spears, ringed the woodpile and faced the crowd. Ruadhan, still uncertain of his place in the community and well-aware that the granting of the deer heart would have been resented by more than Ruarcc in this reordering of Cillebairre, looked about for Ite and when he didn't see her, sat outside the church, his back to one of the walls. Conal demanded and was given silence.

"I lived with the Northmen, learned their language and their ways but, I swear, I never forgot my people and my home. The only way I had of ever returning was to impress the Northmen with a keenness to stand alongside them in battle. I became more of a Northman than the Northmen themselves. So keen did I prove myself in fighting skills, I was given my freedom and this magnificent sword and I was allowed to join them when they sailed on their raiding missions; *fara i viking*. And, let me tell you, I was eager and proud to fight. I will not pick a quarrel like some for whom it is like throwing a stone in the river, but I tell you, fighting is in my blood. My people were rulers in the Kingdom of Mide. Were it not for my father's banishment I would have been raised in the ways of a true Irish warrior. Cillebairre would not have granted the young Conal such an education as that I got from the Northmen. It took foreigners to recognise the royalty in me and confer a higher status. The Northmen trained me to be a warrior and I would match my fighting skills against anyone on this island." Conal stopped talking and swept the crowd slowly with his gaze; an invitation to anyone there to contradict and challenge him. No one did but one stern face carved from the hardest wood softened to a smile.

"Stories! Let's have some stories!"

Conal's head was crammed with stories from his time with the Northmen and many times he had rehearsed the telling of them. That evening they tumbled out of him. He told of people who lived in holes in the ground far away in the lands where the sun rose; of precious treasures looted from the courts of great kings and thrown like old pots into the Northmen's boats; of men blacker than the darkest night who fought like demons; of those with sharpened teeth who fed in a frenzy on the flesh of those they had killed in battle; of mountains of floating ice that crushed boats as easily as hands snapped a dry twig; of rivers ten times as long as Ireland, of fields of sand wider than Ireland. Conal told his listeners he thought he would never see his native land again until that last voyage with the Northmen and the shock, after being separated from most of the fleet, of his boat coming up the river to Cillebairre. He was interrupted only once. A gaunt young man whose head was bleeding from several cuts received in a recent shave asked a bold question and then became hesitant, nervous over how it would be received.

"You were with them for a good few years. Did... did you take a woman, a Northwoman?"

Conal stared directly, sternly at the man for a moment. The man backed into the people immediately behind him as if making a way for his escape. They protested and pushed him forward. Conal smiled. "There were women. There was one Northwoman. We hunger and thirst for more than food and water as you well know."

The young man relaxed a little, smiled back and nodded.

"I have never been summoned by God to suppress such appetites for the Kingdom. I took a woman. She died giving birth to my son. He died too. There was fever and vomiting in the place; a plague that killed many."

The young man wanted to ask if their women were beautiful but, after Conal's answer, kept that question to himself. There was a general murmur of sympathy. Cillebairre's people knew of babies dying and of plagues that sprang like sudden mists bringing death to all ages. This brought Conal closer; this put flesh on his bones; brought sympathy to their hearts.

Conal finished his first evening of storytelling by recounting the second time his boat came to Cillebairre and the attack. "I could not warn you and I could not stop them when they returned. There are those here who can testify which side I fought on." He searched the crowd, found young Colman and pointed. "He is one of them!"

Colman enjoyed being singled out in this way. "He is speaking the truth. I would not be standing here were it not for Conal."

"Six Northmen lost their lives at my hands before I fled to the forest. Had I not, I would have been slaughtered for my treachery."

"He's telling the truth!" Ruadhan shouted over the wall. "He saved my life as well!"

73

Someone retorted that Conal should be damned for doing that and a few nods and the looks on some faces echoed that statement. Fintan, who had kept himself at a distance and who was the adult nearest Ruadhan, strode to where he was, pulled Ruadhan to his feet and told him to get back in the forest where he belonged. He smacked the side of Ruadhan's head and pushed him away from the assembly towards the trees. Enough; he had had enough. Ruadhan rounded on Fintan ready to fight but Conal moved quickly. He leapt from the woodpile, pushed people out of his way, vaulted the wall and claimed the youth. He led a reluctant Ruadhan back past a snarling Fintan to his platform and held him by his side in silence for a moment, making a bold statement. The three guards formed a tighter knot about their leader. Conal said nothing to Fintan. What he was doing said enough. Conal had placed himself at the centre of the resurrected community and now he was placing Ruadhan there too. Ruadhan did not want this. He knew it would breed resentment. Conal's guardianship would mean a better life than previously but Ruadhan vainly wished it would not bring with it more attention than he had already. As if remembering his first meeting with Ruadhan, Conal gave an order to the assembled.

"On all of the approaches to Cillebairre, I want beacons to be built at the highest points. We will share the watches. I want to know if someone comes to visit us, be they friend or foe, single or many, well before they penetrate our length of the valley. This will be done tomorrow."

There was a general murmur of assent.

"We must defend ourselves. We will grow to be a strong, united community. Believe me! Learned men, men of God; more of them will come. We need their wisdom. We need physicians, lawyers, smiths. We *will* grow. I will lead you. And we will be strong enough to repulse any who try to invade our valley. If it is the Northmen, we will cast them all the way back to the sea. There will be no more running and hiding. Cillebairre will prosper!"

Once again there was an approving murmur in response to his words but this time, the murmur swelled to a great yell of agreement.

On that, the second night back at Cillebairre, after Conal had addressed the assembly from Mochan's woodpile and before settling for the night on the rough beds they had made, he told Ruadhan that he was to be a warrior. Ruadhan did not know how to react. He had hardly a notion of what Conal was talking about but enough to know that this was not what he wanted. The monk, Tulchán, and now Conal told him that he was destined for a life grander than that he was used to. First, he who knew no letters was to be a scholar and now, he who had hidden himself from the marauding Northmen, was to be a bold soldier. Ruadhan laughed scornfully; no one *grew* to be a scholar; no one *grew* to be a warrior. You were born into such status. He told Conal what he thought and the man who, telling his stories, had controlled the people of Cillebairre like a horseman using reins became angered by the youth who was not responding to his words, who contradicted him. And this was the one he had given the deer heart to, the one he had chosen in front of all the others as his favourite! Conal was drunk on the sense of power that had rushed to his head that evening and on the conviction that what he was doing in Cillebairre had been ordained. He came close to beating Ruadhan out of pure rage. He gripped the young man's shoulder roughly, looked him full in the face and spoke each word like the fall of a hammer on an anvil. In the gloom, as his brow creased, the paler scarred skin seemed to glow.

"I... have... said... I... will... make... you... a... warrior."

"Tulchán..."

"A true man of God by all accounts but by all accounts he is dead."

"I have not the breeding."

It was Conal's turn to sneer. "Breeding? My training will *breed* the warrior in you. We need warriors. You will be one."

"I don't want to fight."

"You will do as you are told!"

"I have a mission..."

"So have I."

"I promised to deliver the Psalter."

"You are not a man of books. Scholarship is not for you, Ruadhan. Scholarship will not rebuild Cillebairre. Scholarship will not repulse the Northmen. I have other ideas for you. I need you. You will obey me. Put the monk and that book out of your mind."

Many who returned to Cillebairre were happy to be away from Na Lámha and cared little who led them. As long as your life, daily food and the roof over your head was not threatened, what did it matter? They rejoiced in having decisive leadership that brooked little opposition but,

75

among some, deep suspicions remained. They could not stop hating Conal for his *foreignness* and his arrogance. To them, he was a *Gall-Goídil*, half-Irish, half-foreigner and therefore not to be trusted. They mocked the old stories of his childhood, of his specialness and the new stories of his time among the Northmen. They had heard the story of the two lost brothers, accepted that this man was Conal but he was tainted; he had been with the Northmen, had gained their trust and had, to all intents and purposes, become one of them. He had been taken from the village and corrupted, they said. And so, in the early days after Conal's return to Cillebairre, his presence was pecked at consistently in conversations outside his hearing: he had changed in many ways: his clothes were not like theirs; his speech had a very different rhythm to it; his vocabulary included Norse words; simple, traditional, everyday Irish courtesies had disappeared from his behaviour and speech to the extent that it was not possible to regard him as Irish any more. He had changed radically and it seemed he wanted to change them. *We should be like the Northmen.* Conal urged this often. The Northmen were powerful because of they did *this*; the Northmen's influence was spreading because they did *that;* their boatbuilding, their military tactics, their weaponry were far superior. To prove the last point, Conal was seldom without the double-edged sword with the bejewelled hilt and an edge so sharp that the momentum created by its own weight sliced through leaves. Swords were a rarity, especially ones of such quality. Few, Northmen or Irish, possessed them. This one, Conal told anyone who would listen, was made of a harder, purer steel than anything to be found in Ireland. To the sceptical, the foreign ways and ideas Conal brought to Cillebairre would not take in Irish soil. And to make matters worse and condemn himself further, he had the wild boy, the possessed one always by his side. The two of them together now were *the curse*. The village would be better off rid of them.

Ruadhan did not believe that Conal could make a warrior out of him but, from respect and fear, was obedient and did what he was told as well as he could. He watched Conal closely. He had learned from the monk, Tulchán. Could he learn from this man especially from his decisiveness? To Conal, issues were clear cut. There was no need for sophisticated thinking, writing or debate. The Northmen had sailed huge tracts of water, trampled over great swathes of land, made their farms in far-flung places and defeated many in battle because they did not ponder things for too long. They made decisions and they acted and that is how Conal would rule Cillebairre. He would be fair. He believed he could be and he also believed that if he was an unjust ruler, not only the people, but the land itself would groan. Nature's spirits would respond accordingly to good and bad rulers. Like most of the people of his home, a mist of the old religion still coiled about Conal's awareness.

THE DESERT
Journey to Scetis

They succeeded in leaving Alexandria by the southern Bab al Sidra gate without being questioned. Makarius kept well away from accepted routes and once he had arranged for them to be guided through the dense reed beds surrounding Lake Mareotis and then ferried across its water, he hired camels and told them of the journey they would undertake. They would rest till nightfall and then head south to Wadi Natroun. At a steady pace, being careful, the whole journey to Baramus would take them three days and nights. They would find shade and rest during the hottest hours of the day and travel as much as they could in darkness. Brecc knew the change of pattern would grant him little sleep, but reminded himself that Abba Arsenius who lived as a hermit for forty years in the desert had stated that one hour in slumber is enough for a monk. Makarius knew that it was Brecc's intention to visit several of the monasteries, especially those at Nitria and Cellia but – and here the young monk displayed a steeliness which surprised the Irishman - he could not allow that on this journey since well-worn trails led from Alexandria to those monasteries.

"If they are looking for us, they will go to those places, and so we will skirt them and head for the wilderness of Scetis. There are no tracks in that wilderness. Only the sun and the stars will be our guides."

Brecc's mind took some time to come to terms with not being *allowed* by this... this... *boy* to complete his pilgrimage but that concern was overtaken, once Makarius decided it was time to leave, by the struggle to ride a camel. Progress was very slow at first as the Irishmen adapted. Fiacc's ride was a mettlesome animal and Makarius volunteered to ride it himself, but the taciturn Irishman would not let him. Fiacc was used to tough, shaggy little horses, and training them out of their wild state into animals that obeyed every dig at their flanks and every pull at their manes, but the wondrous creature he now had to control was nothing like them. It responded quietly and obediently most of the time and stored its stubbornness and viciousness for odd, unpredictable moments. As Fiacc mounted, he showed, for once, a hint of uncertainty and vulnerability, but, from his manipulation of the reins, there was no mistaking his determination to become the animal's master.

Brecc's camel was older, quieter and more predictable, Makarius said.

"Very like myself ," replied Brecc and looked directly at the Copt.

Makarius lowered his eyes. There was nothing he could confidently predict about the older monk. "Perhaps," was all he said.

"You will have time on our pilgrimage to get to know me better, Makarius, but do not plague me with talk of glass chalices." Makarius bowed as if agreeing and Brecc realised he was being testy and that the tall Egyptian, for all his *not allowing,* did not deserve this attitude. Arsenius came to mind once more: *Many times I spoke and, as a result, had to repent but I never regretted my silence.* He should try harder. It was the thought of the long ride that was troubling him. He had ridden in the desert on his earlier visit and had taken two heavy falls. An older Brecc would take much longer to recover from similar tumbles.

Brecc found that he still had the riding skills those punishing falls had helped him gain. However, realising this did not let him enjoy the ride and throughout its long miles he yearned for the journey to be over. Even though he ached and felt exhausted, Brecc resented the long daytime halts when Makarius would find them shade beneath one of the many huge rock outcrops. To add to his discomfort, a bitter wind from the Sahara's interior blew stirring the surface of the sand with a constant rasping sound each night they travelled. Makarius made them bind their faces tightly to protect them from the stinging particles but their progress had been slow. Few landmarks had distinguished the way to and past Nitria, and the second half of their journey from Nitria to Scetis was even more of a featureless wasteland. At what Makarius thought was the mid-point of the third night's travel, they ate dried fruit and took an hour's rest, the last before reaching the monasteries. Brecc dozed fitfully and from time to time prayed. After lying for only a short while, he noticed that the wind had dropped. Across the valley he made out high dunes like the heavy folds of a highborn woman's cloak. *God's cloak*, he thought. *I am wrapped in the deep, dark folds of God's cloak.* He uncurled himself from his camel's side and turned on to his back to gaze upwards at the huge desert night sky swarming with stars. As he lay there, an unnerving awareness that this experience was alien gradually came over him. It was so unfamiliar. There was nothing to interrupt his gaze; no branches or eaves overhead; no yardarm and furled sail; no valley slopes raising their arms upwards in praise of God. He suddenly became dizzy and felt that he was falling into the depths of this sky. He grasped for a handhold to anchor himself to earth, but there were no roots, not even grass stalks, only stones and the sand which ran quickly through his fingers. It was a long, half-awake minute before Brecc realised that he was not falling but was still firmly bound to the earth. He breathed heavily and looked about him for reassurance. The camels, their heads erect, looked as immovable as the ancient desert monuments; Makarius shifted and pulled his blanket closer about him; Fiacc slept soundly.

A cloud drifted before the moon and a pool of shadow spread down a dune and over Fiacc. Brecc shuddered and stared at the young man's still figure. At least twice to Brecc's knowledge, he had killed. Perhaps that was not the only blood on his hands. In Alexandria, he had been defending them from the Arab, that was true, but the strength and ease with which he had killed the man and walked calmly away frightened Brecc. He had shown no compunction at all. And what about the death of his cousin; why had they fought and was Fiacc truly repentant? Abbot Ronan thought so; he believed that Fiacc was a monk in the making and that the pilgrimage to Egypt would confirm this. Brecc was not sure. He found his fellow traveller an unsettling companion. The intense cocoon of silence he had wound about himself at Clonmacnoise and on the journey from there made Brecc's questions multiply. It did not seem to be the silence of a soul coming to terms with great sin. On the contrary, to Brecc it seemed the threatening, brooding quiet of a man who has been told he has done wrong but who does not acknowledge it himself and waits until he can reverse the judgement upon the judges; it was the calm of the windless treetops before rooks scatter cawing from their high perches.

That third night in the desert, as he watched Fiacc sleeping, the pains that rushed from his shoulder to his hand came back. He rubbed the shoulder vigorously. Perhaps it was the cold. The pains were not important. By praying the Psalms he could forget about them and consider his own sins instead of judging Fiacc.

Makarius pushed on relentlessly with only the stars to guide him and they traversed the gently sloping sides of the Wadi Natroun and skirted its natron lakes before dawn. As if to reprove Brecc for his doubting, Fiacc questioned Makarius at length about the monastic vocation. The young Copt was animated.

"We must not let our body rule us. We have to overcome all except its most basic needs in order that the soul might grow nearer to God."

"And the desert is a place where there is so little in the way of luxury that you can avoid temptations of the flesh?"

"No, that is not the way we see it. We come to the desert because that is where temptation is greatest. Satan was at his most persistent and strongest when Our Lord went into the desert. The body is more demanding when faced with the severities of life in the desert and it is more difficult for us to resist those demands. For example, you have carried those heavy goatskin bags from Alexandria and you have drunk water from them whenever we have stopped. Your body demanded that you drink; this is what the desert does even when you travel at night. I have taken only a little water. Forgive me if this seems to be boastful. I do not intend it that way. All I want to do is show you how the demands of the body grow in the desert; they are not left behind in the cities or the green valleys; they multiply and have to be resisted by prayer and discipline. It does not seem to do us much harm. Our blessed Anthony reached one hundred and five years leaving only his sheepskin tunic and a worn blanket that had served as his coat and his bed."

Makarius stopped abruptly, looked even more solemn than usual, and then let a broad smile crease his face. He would show that even his flesh had needs.

"We cannot deny the body completely. I think we should stop and rest a moment and I would be grateful if you would grant me a mouthful of water from one of your flasks."

They halted and the camels knelt for them to dismount. Fiacc gave one of his rare smiles in return and unhooked a flask from his camel's side. Makarius took half a mouthful only, swilled it slowly around inside his mouth and then swallowed it. He handed the flask back to Fiacc. Brecc let them know that he was unhappy about the rest by not dismounting and by refusing water. According to his calculations, they had only a few miles to go to the monasteries and so should press on. He was eager to end the journey and get off the camel's back. The long ride had brought many forgotten aches back to life. Brecc's camel stirred gently under him. The monk breathed in deeply. The air was sharp, dry and cold, for all the world like an early March morning in Ireland. He closed his eyes and allowed himself to dream momentarily: he was walking briskly to the great church of Clonmacnoise and the divine office of *prime*; the grass was firm but springy beneath his feet and his breath rose like incense.

When he opened his eyes, the sky over Sinai, the vast and terrible wilderness where God made his covenant with Moses, began to change colour subtly and swiftly, with first, a mauve light insinuating itself into the blackness like a cat stalking its prey. The mauve eased into indigo; the indigo paled towards a green and then, streakily at first, the gold of the sunrise began to dominate. One of the camels snorted. Brecc wondered if they were as close to the monastery as he thought and recalled words from Exodus: "By your grace you led the people you redeemed, by your strength you guided them to your holy house." When he looked back to his companions, he saw that at last they had remounted. As the sun began its quick ascent, Makarius confirmed that they were close to their destination. Brecc urged his camel on and the others followed. From the top of the next low sand hill, they saw in the distance three faint brushstrokes of grey among the pale browns of the desert; they had sighted the monasteries. Only a few miles of flat, empty sand separated them from their destination.

No tracks led to the first monastery of Baramus. As they approached, the three travellers saw that a high wall surrounded it. Just nudging into view over the wall were several domed buildings and tall palm trees. A large square tower dominated the entrance gate.

"At one time," said Makarius, "our brothers would have swarmed from their cells to greet us, bring water, wash our feet. Now..."

Brecc did not listen. He was allowing dangerous thoughts of comfort to enter his head once again when Fiacc slapped his camel's rump hard. The animal jerked forward almost throwing Brecc, and then broke into its loping gallop. Brecc slowed the animal down and was overtaken by Makarius and Fiacc. The Irishman was shouting and pointing back the way they had come.

Judging by the clouds of sand they were raising, the riders in pursuit were numerous and were travelling fast. They clearly wanted to intercept Brecc and his companions before they reached the monastery. Brecc spurred his camel on but it objected to the erratic orders it was getting and kept to a sluggish pace. Every glance backwards confirmed that the pursuers were gaining.

Fiacc was the first to reach the gate of Baramus monastery. He leapt down from his camel and called for entry. Several monks watched him from the tower above. He shouted at them, pushed at the huge gate and pulled frantically at a long bell-rope. The monks continued to gaze impassively down, now and again exchanging a few words with each other. Fiacc was furious but as soon as Makarius joined him, and pulled away the cloth from his face so that he could be recognised, the monks above became very active and lowered a large basket down the outside of the wall. Makarius shouted at Fiacc: "Forgive them! They have to be sure it is their friends!"

"Tell them to open the gate!"

"It will be barricaded. There is no time."

Brecc reined his camel to a halt beside the others. The animal knelt and the monk clambered awkwardly off. This was not the desert experience he wanted on his pilgrimage. He wanted the solitude, the emptiness of the desert, and the peace that the sunrise had brought to him momentarily.

The basket hit the sand with a thud and the ropes fastened into a net around it slackened. Makarius grasped Brecc by the shoulders and ushered him to the side of the basket. "Please, brother, you go first. There is only room for one."

Brecc turned and smiled at the Egyptian as if he was going to accept the invitation and then pushed Makarius into the basket. Any other time he would have been delighted by the young man's politeness, but not now. If anyone was going to be killed, it ought to be him, the eldest. As the monks started to haul the basket upwards, Makarius tried to climb out, but fell back heavily. His ascent was painstakingly slow. The basket stopped every three metres or so as the ones pulling took a new grip on the rope. As soon as Makarius scrambled clumsily out at the top of the wall, the monks threw the basket back down. This time it dangled two metres from the ground.

The first pursuer closed on Fiacc and Brecc. He crouched low and out to one side of the camel with his sword raised above him. Brecc staggered up against the wall - its hard caked mud was just beginning to warm in the sun's rays - closed his eyes and knelt with his arms fully extended from his sides. He felt his tunic rip once more as he knelt. Through his eyelids, he sensed the rider and his mount coming between him and the sun. He tried to examine his conscience. The last time he had confessed to a priest was in the Kingdom of the Franks. That was too long ago: his undisciplined mind and body, and in particular, his bad temper, frequently led him into sin. Even now his mind was drifting from its

83

important task and taking him to the garden at Clonmacnoise. The apple trees were laden with fruit. He picked one, two plump green apples flecked with red. The sharp, decisive snap of their stalks was so satisfying; another year's harvest secure; the tables full once again.

The Arab was puzzled by the strange behaviour of the smaller man and checked his camel's approach slightly. This hesitation was enough for Fiacc who grabbed the basket and swung it fiercely against the rider's sword arm. The basket's hard wooden rim rapped the soft inside of his wrist with great force, the weapon fell harmlessly into the sand, and the shock of the blow made the rider rein the camel almost to a halt. In his panic, he tried to turn but gave the camel confused signals. Fiacc was upon them swiftly and grabbed the Arab's bare foot. The rider pulled a dagger from his belt and slashed at Fiacc's face. Fiacc twisted the man's ankle until he screamed and then used his great strength to pull him from the camel. The Arab fell heavily on the sand but rose quickly and tried to get away. He had moved only a few paces when his damaged ankle gave way and he sat down on the sand. Fiacc grabbed him from behind and locked his forearm around the man's throat.

After Brecc had snapped that second apple free from its branch, he expected to be killed by the Arab; to be killed and to be born to a new life in his real home with God. "In a way," he thought, "I should be grateful to my executioner." When he heard the scuttering of hooves and feet close to him and felt sand stinging his face, but was not assaulted, he opened his eyes and saw the two men in an unequal contest nearby. Fiacc was going to kill the Arab. Brecc struggled to his feet in the soft sand and pulled at Fiacc's arms. His companion's face was fixed in controlled fury; the lines of his features were like the planes of a crystal. He was going to wring the life completely out of his victim. The Arab lost consciousness and his body sagged in Fiacc's fierce grip.

Fiacc ignored Brecc's pleading, but paid attention to the other riders who were only forty metres away. He let the Arab fall and pushed Brecc back towards the basket which was swinging wildly along the side of the wall. "Get in, and be quick!"

Brecc started to protest but the younger man lifted and dropped him in the basket. "No red martyrdom for you, Brecc! Go!"

The monks above pulled furiously at the rope and the basket started to move. When Brecc looked above he saw the anxious face of

Makarius peering down. Brecc had an uncharitable thought: was the Egyptian worrying about Brecc or about the Chalice of St. Mark?

Fiacc found the Arab's sword half-buried in the sand and, brandishing it, turned to face his attackers. His heart was beating fast but he was calm and alert. All his senses were as sharp as chipped flint. He backed to the wall and scanned the riders' formation. Five were ahead of the others and had fanned out to attack him from the sides as well as from the front. They would crowd him with their camels and crush or cut him to death. Fiacc realised that he had no hope of defeating this vanguard and since he had no intention of dying so young and so far from home, he jumped and grasped the net of ropes which cradled the basket. The monks were surprised by the sudden extra weight and the basket dipped back towards the sand, but once they had compensated for the extra load with increased effort, it began its steady ascent once more.

The Arabs raced in under the basket shouting and slashing at Fiacc's legs. Fiacc curled his body upwards as far as he could and just managed to avoid their blades. One of them tried to stand on his camel's back to gain more height, but the animal lurched and toppled him on to the sand. When the basket was halfway up, another threw his sword at Brecc and Fiacc, but it missed and clinked impotently against the wall.

Soon they reached safety. Brecc was helped out of the basket and Fiacc swung his legs over the parapet and on to the top of the wall. Several of the monks who had been helping, dropped the rope and started hurling stones from huge piles on to the attackers below. The Arabs backed out of range, taking three captured camels, and then slowly retreated over the crest of the nearest sand hill.

After two hours of sleep, Brecc rose, and crossed the central square and the garden crowded with palms, fig and citrus trees, to the refectory. The trees were completely still: "At peace," thought the monk, "like I shall never be." Above the walled monastery, only a few faint hairs of cirrus straggled across an intense and otherwise cloudless sky. Makarius was already seated at the long and wide stone table which ran the length of the light and airy refectory. The table was littered with small and very hard loaves of bread and lumps of rock salt. Makarius was softening a loaf in a bowl of water and when Brecc joined him, he lifted it out and tore it in half. He crumbled salt over both pieces and handed one to Brecc. The Irishman nodded his thanks. "Those Bedouin knew we were coming, didn't they?"

"The desert tribes are constantly attacking travellers, Copts and Arabs, and raiding the monasteries. It is always dangerous to travel in these parts. They saw that there were only three of us and thought we were easy prey."

"When I was in the basket, they did a lot of shouting. I know enough to realise that they kept shouting about a *cup*. That can only have been the Chalice."

"I did not hear them saying that," replied Makarius, and Brecc, looking straight into his eyes, gave him the benefit of the doubt. He did not think he would lie about this or any other matter. This young man's mind and motives were as clear as a mountain stream.

"Even the monks here know that we are the ones expected to return the Chalice."

"That is easy to explain. As our Patriarch told you, the people are all talking about this; it is helping them to be strong in the face of terrible suffering. They have been expecting someone from Ireland. They do not know you are the ones but they hope you are."

Once again, Brecc began to feel bent under a very heavy burden and questioned whether his old back was strong enough. Anger rose within him and he felt powerless to stop himself. "Faith in God should not depend upon a drinking cup, no matter whose hands have held it! We should be content with the great revelation of the Gospels, the appearance of the Son on earth, and not be looking for trinkets and daily miracles to keep our faith alive!"

Makarius was shaken by Brecc's words. He and his people were not looking for *trinkets* or *daily miracles*. "Many stories are told about the Chalice. Do you doubt them?"

Brecc realised that he had said more than enough but went on speaking loudly. "God can choose to work his wonders through anything and anyone he has created; that, of course, I believe. I also believe that God is more likely to choose the saints and the objects in their lives as channels of his grace but I worry that you are making an idol of this Chalice, that your people will worship it and not God who may choose to work through it."

"God *has* worked wonders through the Chalice: miracle cures; irreverent hands crippled; rains brought to drought-stricken lands. They are stories which I do not doubt for one minute, but you do me and my people wrong if you think this is the only reason why we want the Chalice returned. We look for miracles, yes, but first we look for a symbol that will keep us united in the face of persecution, that will remind us that our Church has existed since the time of Our Saviour." Makarius was becoming excited and talking much faster than normal. Brecc wanted to interrupt him and withdraw his angry words, but the Egyptian would not let him.

"You are fortunate, brother; in your country, you do not suffer because you speak out loud the name of Christ. Here we are forced to whisper it and to hide our priests and churches. The Chalice can change that. My people need the Chalice, brother."

Brecc realised he had offended the gentle Makarius deeply with his foolish outburst. He looked down to the compacted earth beneath him. A lizard raced across one of his feet and up the wall behind him. *My stupid, stupid mouth.* He felt ill. "So, the Copts have been looking for Irishmen, but that does not explain why the Mohammedans are chasing us as foreign spies."

"Try holding water in your hands, brother. There is so much excitement among my people that the return of the Chalice could never have remained a secret. And in addition to this, there are those who count themselves Copts but who have sold themselves to our invaders. They will report anything they hear. People, both Copt and Arab, will be looking for you. You are in danger. I cannot hide that fact from you."

Brecc clenched and unclenched his left fist in an effort to ease the aching. The whole left side of his body was numb and almost useless. "I can do little to direct what happens in this business of the Chalice while I am here," he thought. "I must put it out of my mind and give myself to prayer or the pilgrimage will be pointless." *Prayer*: his repetition of the psalms was bringing no fulfilment, no slaking of *that* thirst. A desert in a desert. He was so easily distracted. Brecc wondered if the roof of the main granary at Clonmacnoise had been repaired. Which brother had he entrusted to see that it was done?

PART TWO

CILLEBAIRRE
Ruadhan's dream

It was grey. It was all grey and he could *see* that it was all grey. The thought of colour had never entered his dreams before, but now he was aware that this dream was grey, different shades of grey: the green-grey of ash bark; the black-grey of nut-hatch feathers and more. Tulchán's tunic was dark blue-grey but his face was much lighter. His arms reached out to Ruadhan. Grey must be the colour of death. Ruadhan put his hand out to touch the monk but it would not enter his dream. The dream would not let him touch his friend. He felt anger at this in his dream, anger that he thought would wake him up, but it did not and the dream continued.

Tulchán's mouth moved but he was not speaking as people did normally. His mouth opened much too far and twisted itself into the strangest shapes. And no sound came out. Nevertheless the words entered Ruadhan's head and his mind held the words the monk communicated, held them until he woke into a cold misty morning.

Imprisoned by rocks; see the darkness fall.
The Word stays unchained where seabirds call.

This had to be a sign that he must take the precious Psalter to Clonmacnoise. For a year it had lain untouched among the reeds of the roof, well-protected by the greased hides the monk had wrapped it in. Ruadhan had retrieved it from where Tulchán had hidden it and put it securely above where he lay to sleep. He shifted on to his side and looked across to where Conal, his woman Carnait, and their recently delivered baby lay well wrapped in blankets and skins. It had been an eventful year in the new Cillebairre. Conal now had a son, Cearbhall, one whose veins ran with his blood, one whose destiny seemed to have been as clearly drawn as the brightest of the monk's pictures by a father who had named him *fierce in battle* and by the fact that he had been born with a tooth. Conal doted on his son and Ruadhan, the surrogate, prompted by clear signs from Carnait, felt an interloper. He was the cuckoo in the nest but this chick, Cearbhall, would reverse Nature's pattern and the cuckoo would be evicted. It was clear to Ruadhan that Tulchán had chosen the time of his return carefully. After a difficult first few months in that first year, the settlement had grown fast. Encouraged by Duach, Conal had walked the bounds, determining the full extent of the monastery's land and influence

88

and confirming the allegiances of isolated farms on both sides of the valley. Fearghal of Máenmaige had mentioned unpaid tributes and these were discussed, debts excused and new commitments made. At the settlement, under Conal's direction, the forge raged from dawn to dusk. He wanted more axes, more adzes, more saws, more mallets, more chisels. Trees were felled to prepare more land for planting and erecting buildings on. At Conal's insistence, more stone than ever before was quarried, all for new dwellings more substantial than the ones erected in haste on their return from Na Lámha. In the fields, careful husbandry was practised and the numbers of livestock increased. Neglected land that weeds, scrubby bushes and reeds had invaded was cleared and planted anew with cereals and vegetables. The weather favoured them with a soft first winter and early spring. They were granted rain and steady sunlight when needed. Livestock grew fat and granaries were filled. With Conal's support, Duach universally reinstated tithes and the practice of firstlings and first-fruits to the church which had become inconsistent under Comgall. News of the resurgent community spread and drew immigrants from the surrounding hills and neighbouring valleys swelling the number of *manaigh*[5] and their huts on the north bank of the river. With this growth in numbers, Duach became anxious. None of the monks was ordained. Conal acknowledged the monk's growing concern at the absence of the Eucharist and tested his inchoate influence with the lordship of Máenmaige by requesting a priest. In the new year, a cousin of Duach's, a priest-monk called Bréanainn, arrived from the monastery of Clonfert and Holy Mass was celebrated once again in the church.

Conal knew of the mission Tulchán had entrusted to Ruadhan's care but refused to give it attention. Yes, the man was emerging but Ruadhan was young and knew little of what dangers lay beyond the valley. Besides, there was important work for him to do and important things for him to learn in Cillebairre; the ways of a warrior. And the ways of loyalty. He had to concentrate on those. *Put the monk and that book out of your mind.* Conal did not beat him savagely on any pretext or through excess of drink as Fáelcar had done but his discipline was quick and harsh if Ruadhan did not fulfil his orders. In this way, Ruadhan was pulled in

---

[5] Here the word refers to monks who were tenant farmers on the monastery lands. Their status in the monastic community differed from settlement to settlement. In some they had more influence than others. They were married and often lived according to strict rules.

different directions by two masters, the dead monk and his guardian, Conal. He did as he was told with one exception, a small, secret act of defiance. Instead of forgetting him, Ruadhan thought *more* of Tulchán, dwelt on the time they had spent together and tried inadequately, he believed, to decipher the serious matter in those discussions: *we find our true freedom through serving others.* How could he who had crawled from the forest serve others? Did warriors *serve others*? Was fighting, killing the way that the King of Kings had taught?

Once his new status was conferred on him and much to the anger of the haters in the community, Ruadhan was excused certain duties that had been his normal workload. He did not dig latrines; he did not work in the fields and neither did he mind the sheep on the hills as he used to. He did not cut or fetch wood or feed the fires. He was part of Conal's elite warrior-band. *Ridiculous*, the haters thought and sometimes whispered but this was Conal's command and not to be opposed openly. Good food, including goat or deer once a month, daily exercises of running, throwing, wrestling and climbing fattened and hardened Ruadhan's muscles until *boy* was no longer a fitting appellation.

Build a strong, disciplined fighting force to defend the community and maintain order: Conal gave this task primacy above all others. For Ruadhan, the training alongside the brutish Ruarcc, Ruarcc's close friend, Beccan, and the slightly built but agile and intelligent Eoin was intense and demanding. Conal drove them hard and did not favour Ruadhan. Soon after the return from the forest, he chose two others to join them: Colman, the thin young man he had rescued in the heat of battle but who had fought so courageously and Corraidhín, a new arrival, an older man, an adventurer who claimed to have fought and defeated the Northmen with the tribes of Ulaid. Conal took one look at him, had doubts but liked his open face and his boldness and, a rare thing, had made a joke. It concerned the new man's name: "Naked, you may only have a small spear, Corraidhín, but I hope you can carry and use a big one in battle."

"I favour the axe, Conal, but if you want me to carry a spear I will not let you down."

As part of his discipline, Conal insisted that contact with others in the community of Cillebairre was strictly controlled. The warriors comprised a select group which would, given time, expand in numbers and which, when the eventuality arose, would be augmented by a militia raised from all the able men in Cillebairre. To impress upon all that they were an elite, the warriors, their weapons and horses, were separate from the rest of the settlement. All except Ruadhan lived in a small, single building compound on the north side of the river. It stood close by Conal's house but well removed from the cluster of homes occupied by the *manaigh* and others. Conal did not demand celibacy of his warriors but strict self-control over their bodily needs and their emotions. Living together would, he believed, bring benefits but he worried that there was the possibility it could bring an undesirable outcome. Comradeship, an essential quality among men who would fight for each other in battle, would be fostered but confinement in the one building could also encourage the close relationships such as those he had witnessed among some of the Northmen. It was a fact that he had never witnessed anything to confirm that those affairs weakened the men's performance on the battlefield but he was adamant that he would not tolerate it among Cillebairre's warriors. He himself had never indulged in such practice and never would. For one of the males to be submissive was, to Conal, like the coupling itself, an act against nature.

Duach was one with him in this and echoed his concern. The Penitentials laid down punishment for such lapses among monks and lay people. He confided in Conal that he himself when he was younger had struggled with regular involuntary nocturnal emissions and had frequently risen in the night to recite psalms and, when morning came, since he had polluted his body, had not taken communion.

"*Involuntary*? Your mind never deliberately conjured lust-filled dreams?"

Duach nodded rapidly several times. Conal was not his confessor and they had gone far enough down this path of personal revelation, "Yes, yes, there were those times too, Conal, when I have burned with physical desire and ached for relief, terrible passions for which my penance was greater. The devil sends such visions and dreams to test us, to defile our purity. Cassian, em, yes, John Cassian, I am sure, writes of this. Replace lustful desire with spiritual desire he tells us. These acts, as you know, are sins against God's natural order, physically and spiritually damaging. Aretaeus the Cappadocian counselled that frequent ejaculation brings on premature ageing; that men become timid, stupid, enfeebled and effeminate; that it is semen that makes us to be men, with body-hair, well-braced in limbs, strong to think and act. We must not lose it casually. And sodomy in particular can spread like a contagion. Be aware of this, Conal, and instruct your men in these matters. Prayer and physical labour will discourage these actions. Tire them out. Gregory recommends this."

Urges: they came. Conal *would* work his men hard but that might not be enough. If his soldiers were discreet in such matters, Conal would not make a quarrel of it or deny them such relief but if it all became obvious, it would offend him personally and would cause scandal. Then Conal would not hesitate to act swiftly and sternly.

Ruarcc had never tolerated discretion. He beat Colman badly. In the middle of the morning, Conal found the young man by the river dabbing his face with a cloth soaked in water. "Who did this?"

The young man struggled with a storm of emotions: humiliation, anger and hatred in no way balanced by loyalty towards his fellow warrior. He did not reply.

"Tell me!" demanded Conal.

"Ruarcc: the foul beast, Ruarcc!"

"Why?"

"I resisted him."

"Where? When? In what way?"

"He regularly puts his penis between my thighs when we lie down to sleep."

"And you do not want this? You have not encouraged it?

"No, never! I do not want this attention, Conal! It fouls me and goes against God. Let him spill himself on Beccan. Beccan does not care but that is not enough for Ruarcc's appetite."

Ruarcc sat at the side of the warriors' house, pulling at his beard to find stray lengths and then roughly trimming them with a knife. The day was warm. As Conal crossed towards him, a soft breeze brought the smell of earth drying after overnight rain. It brought calmness to him and even greater control over what he was to do along with conviction that it could not be avoided. Conal strode up to Ruarcc and before the big man could rise, kicked him sideways to the ground.

"You have a simple choice. Leave Colman alone and you remain whole. Let Beccan be enough to satisfy you." He bent low, his face very

92

close to Ruarcc's. "Thrust at the young one again in that manner and I shall remove that which you thrust at him."

He turned and left immediately. Ruarcc lay on the ground for a moment and seethed. He would have replied to this affront with a weapon but since he had only the knife, did nothing except rage within and add to his already bulging store of discontentment. "We might as well live on the other side of the river and pray and scribble!"

As the settlement grew, so did the individuals who inhabited it and none more so than Ite. She was still slight of build but womanhood and undeniable beauty were emergent. Her loose-fitting *léine* could not hide plumping breasts and thick, unruly brown hair hacked short only sharpened the focus on her face: the penetrating green eyes, sculpted cheekbones and a golden-brown complexion that drank the sun and wind.

Ruadhan saw Ite almost every day but was seldom allowed to approach and speak to her. His feelings towards the young woman were confused. Part of him wanted to preserve the childhood friendship, the natural loyalty and the simple games they had played while another strong current within him strained to explore what had happened that night they had lain so close at Na Lámha. She frequently minded sheep at the grazing fields along the river and this provided Ruadhan with the opportunity to see her. Whenever he could slip away from the others, he joined her there. These meetings did not go unnoticed.

The embittered Ruarcc was one to bear grudges beyond the grave. He smarted from his fight with Conal and now, from the additional humiliation brought on by tales Colman had told. Boys, not men, were ruling Cillebairre! Like the sceptics, Ruarcc did not like his leader's choice of the stray from the forest, did not like the fact that he was the favourite, separated from the rest of the soldiers and sharing the same house as their leader. Whenever the opportunity arose, he encouraged the community's doubters and haters in their superstitions: without doubt Ruadhan *had* brought a curse with him from the forest; in the past it was he who brought disease to livestock and blight to the crops; he belonged to the Evil One and there would be more ill luck because of him, just wait and see. Ruadhan was Conal's weakness. Ruarcc watched him closely and became aware of the young man's fascination with Ite. He followed him and discovered their meetings. "You want to lie with her, don't you?"

Ruadhan did not look up and did not interrupt his rhythmical rubbing of the stone on the axe blade. "She is my friend. I was brought up with her."

"Her body is ready."

"I don't want to talk to you about Ite."

"I wouldn't turn her away from my bed, young one. Virgins are always the best."

Ruadhan's anger rose quickly. His breathing quickened. Why was this man who disliked him and hardly spoke to him talking about Ite in this way?

"You need to snatch the honey from that bee cluster between her legs before someone else starts lapping it."

Ruadhan stopped sharpening the axe, lifted it and rammed the blade hard into a tree trunk.

Ruarcc leant close and grinned: "I hope you're not thinking of doing that to me, Conal's favourite. Try anything like that and I'll send you crawling back to the forest and your animal friends."

Ruadhan pulled at the axe but it did not come loose. Before he could try again, Ruarcc pushed him out of the way and released the tool from the tree with one simple jerk. Ruadhan was furious, wanted to react but did not know what to do without humiliating himself further. Ruarcc laughed out loud and planted the axe deep in the tree once more. "There, try that. You're nowhere near ready for a woman, Ruadhan. They would laugh at you as I am doing now."

Each day there was training. Weaponry: the ambidextrous use of a spear, axe, sword, club, dagger and shield with the emphasis always on attack. "Only take a step back if you are seriously outnumbered and are forced to. Never let your enemy even get a hint of any thought you might have of losing. Intimidate: don't think of your height, or the fact, Colman, Ruadhan, that you are just stepping into manhood. Make up for any physical smallness with ferocity. Ask the people to describe the Northmen and they will tell you that they are as tall and solid as mature oaks but it is not so. Many are slight but fight with a ferocity that leaves the enemy believing he has been attacked by ten. They believe they are destined to be conquerors and that's how they become conquerors. Some are wild, crazy. Some eat mushrooms to make them crazy. I don't want this for you. I want you to be fierce but always in control of what you are doing."

Riding: a wild mount was roped and broken for Corraidhín and Conal showed the older ones subtle ways of making the beasts respond to squeezes, pulls and taps, weaning them off brutal thumps and whips. He taught them to fight at close quarters with a sword while on horseback and how to spear a target riding at speed, all skills he had been taught by the Arabs he had lived among while on his longest voyage with the Northmen. One regret Conal had was that he had not learned the skills of the Northmen's bow makers and bowmen to be able to pass them on.

Once, only once, in that first year did a fit come over Ruadhan and it was the one time he wrestled Ruarcc. The wrestling bouts were strictly regulated. The idea was for one to gain total control over the other until resistance was useless. Each pretended to carry a knife. At first and as usual, Ruadhan and Ruarcc circled each other, feinting moves forward and sideways to try to put the other off balance and find a way to get to close quarters. Ruarcc, the much bigger man, was expected to win quickly and easily but that did not happen. His body had grown in all directions and he was strong but clumsy. Ruadhan was quick and lithe. From an early age he had learned to dodge and ride blows and wriggle out of holds. He knew that if Ruarcc succeeded in grabbing and holding on to him, the fight would be over. He had to keep moving, dodging, striking quickly and he had to control his anger. He disliked Ruarcc, intensely so since the lewd comments about Ite and the humiliation with the axe, but knew that with anger he would defeat himself. What was it Conal had taught them about the Northmen? *They believe they are destined to be conquerors and that's how they become conquerors.* Ruadhan told himself he could defeat the bully, Ruarcc. They circled each other. Each time Ruarcc closed on him, Ruadhan slipped easily out of the half-hold and gestured to show that he could have inflicted a serious wound on his opponent were he carrying a knife. Ruarcc became angry. *He* was being humiliated. With his anger came clumsier, more ineffectual moves. He was sluggish turning. At one point, Ruadhan trotted his "knife" over Ruarcc's back making contact four times before the big man managed to turn and swipe it away with a swinging arm. The others started to laugh. Ruadhan realised that Ruarcc would not accept what was happening and knew there would be repercussions but was thrilled by the skills he had exhibited. His heart was racing, he was still in sharp control over his body and ready for whatever Ruarcc should try, but, as he once more ducked under Ruarcc's slashing arm and drove a fist into his attacker's side, he sensed a change. The sounds about him, the encouragement from Colman, the laughter of the others, the mutter of the river, the low breeze in the leaves of the trees close by, all became one, a loud hissing in his ears. However, he did hear Eoin call time on the bout and turned smiling and panting away from Ruarcc to walk to the river and bathe. The cold water would hold the *strangeness* in he was sure. To an enraged Ruarcc, the fight was not over. He charged after Ruadhan. Eoin stepped forward to intercept him but Beccan fastened his arms from behind and held him back. Before Ruadhan could turn, Ruarcc had one of his powerful arms around his neck, hoisted him off his feet and started to choke him. Ruadhan remained aware enough to realise that all rules had been abandoned. He swung a fist backwards into Ruarcc's testicles and then grabbed them fiercely. The older man let out a loud howl as Ruadhan squeezed and twisted with all his might. Ruarcc released his grip and Ruadhan wriggled free. He turned quickly, balled his right fist and hit his assailant as hard as he could in the middle of his face. A shocked Ruarcc staggered backwards and tripped over a stone. Ruadhan fell upon him immediately and beat at his head with both hands. As he did so, he realised that it was going to happen. The hissing became thunder in his ears; light, like blown dandelion seeds, exploded in his mind; he started to shake and his surroundings no longer made sense. He may have been pummelling Ruarcc but it had little effect. The bigger man reached and pressed violently at Ruadhan's eyeballs with his thumbs and then threw him off with one eruption of his torso. Ruadhan fell to the ground writhing and thrashing furiously with his arms and legs as if a hundred devils were attacking him. In his head, trees became serpents and the serpents slid into every opening they could find in the huge naked body of a grossly fat woman who lay at the foot of mountains that took fire and crumbled down on the woman who became a wolf that became a lake whose brown water was churned into white foam by the wings of an enormous black bird that suddenly took flight. He heard angry shouts that he was sure weren't in his mind. He knew his right hand was touching stone. The water calmed and Ruadhan calmed. His body flapped like a fish just pulled out of water. He tried to rise and collapsed.

Wiping a bloody nose, Ruarcc walked to the side of a still, unconscious Ruadhan and was about to kick him viciously in the stomach when Conal arrived. He had been watching from among the trees keen to see how the young one acquitted himself against the brute but keen not to influence the fight in any way. He pulled Ruarcc away and clubbed him behind his ear with a fist like a hammer. Ruarcc went down on one knee but reached to his belt for his knife. Conal stood over him and smiled.

"That would be even more foolish than what you have already done, Ruarcc."

Full of defiance, Ruarcc got up stiffly and for a moment, the others believed he would challenge Conal. Then, as if to calm himself and also to remind himself of his deep grievance, one that could wait to be truly satisfied, Ruarcc rubbed slowly, steadily through his vest making contact with the scar Conal had raised on his shoulder. He pointed to Ruadhan. "Look! He is cursed! There are devils in him. He should not be with us."

"Keep this up, Ruarcc and you will pay dearly. I have warned you. The man who does what you have done here has more quarrels with himself than with... with barely a man who got the better of him. I am not sure I want you beside me in battle. You have a lot to prove, Ruarcc."

Ruarcc spat blood. The boy had burst his lip as well! He turned from Conal and the others and slunk towards the forest. His humiliation was complete. He wanted to be alone and get drunk. Conal shouted after him. "And before you fight again, Ruarcc, tie your hair back!" Apart from this last order, Ruarcc did not understand Conal's admonition and neither did he understand Conal's relationship with Ruadhan. His anger did not abate. It intensified towards the *boy* and towards Conal.

Conal had dealt quickly and decisively with what he had come across but knew that such disturbances were like the sea's tide and would, without doubt, return. It was the first time he had witnessed Ruadhan's *strangeness* and it left him with conflicting feelings. He was fond of the boy and, until one of his own blood was given to him, happy to treat him like a son, guiding him, shaping him away from the softness the old monk had bred in him. But this manifestation was perturbing. The Northmen and many an Irish clan would have got rid of him, some by putting him to death. Conal would not allow that but what if he proved a liability on the battlefield as he would if such storms wracked his mind and body? Why was the boy like this? Could it be devils like many said?

A Marriage

It was Bréanainn the priest who, soon after his arrival in the new year, suggested that Conal should marry and confirmed that Fearghal would provide the bride. Correspondence passed between the two settlements negotiating the terms of the union. And so it was that the first formal duty for Conal's small band of warriors had been to provide an escort as he returned to the household of the Máenmaige sept to claim a wife. Fearghal of the Máenmaige had regretted the excesses of Conal's first visit, especially his call to the house of Carnait, later that same night. Carnait was the orphaned daughter of a second cousin and one who had consecrated her life to virginity. He had forced himself upon her violently. With her apple-plumpness, rich black hair, green eyes and complexion as white as the sand on the shores of the far west, she had to take a great share of the blame, but nevertheless, Fearghal told himself he had done wrong and would do penance for this serious lapse. Sometime in the future, he would make a pilgrimage, pray for a whole day, fast, do something like that but for now, it gave him an opportunity to strengthen this curious new relationship with the impressive *Gall-Goídil*. Conal expected to be offered a woman who was of Fearghal's family and he, Fearghal, needed to satisfy that wish but not offer someone who was too close in blood to himself. That would exaggerate Conal's importance and the importance of Cillebairre. Carnait would do. She was of his family, but well detached from the policy-making centre. Let her be the one. Conal would also, since he claimed he had the blood of chiefs in his veins, expect to be given a virgin. Well, let him *expect* and let him believe. Fearghal considered slitting Carnait's tongue to secure her silence but this would diminish her value and might discourage Conal. Besides, she had great reason to say nothing since her younger siblings would remain at the dun with Fearghal and since she would not want the shame that would follow the broadcasting of what had happened. He nicked her tongue just behind the tip on the right and left sides. To Fearghal, the slight speech defect this gave her was quite charming, not unlike his own mild stammer, and would act as a permanent reminder for her to take care over what she told her husband.

Under a watery sun on a cold, late January day, Conal entered the land of the Mainmaige as he had Na Lámha with a display of stealth and strength. Ruarcc, Breccan, Eoin, Corraidhín and himself had pressed their

98

stocky horses and one packhorse hard on lesser routes while Ruadhan and Colman, no longer a sickly boy but a tough, wiry soldier, ran behind them. On the third day, closing on the dun, they stayed high, avoiding Fearghal's sentries in order that their arrival would be unannounced. As they approached the dun itself, they came down from the high track and followed a stream through dense woodland and bowed bracken until they could see cleared land. Still they hadn't been sighted. Hidden by the trees, they rested and prepared their entry.

Conal rode to the gates of the dun with Ruadhan and Colman walking behind carrying staffs. Fearghal, unready and furious, was told of their approach and buckled on his sword quickly. His fury became disappointment when, on horseback with ten spearmen about him, he rode from the dun to receive the visitors. Doubts entered his mind. He had not ordered a great feast. This was a simple, political marriage. No one thought otherwise. Carnait had no great status but some of the same blood flowed in her as in Fearghal and therefore Conal should have arrived with a more impressive retinue than these two youths and with some sign of gifts, perhaps that fine sword he had coveted since their first meeting. And where were the soldiers he had given him? Had they deserted? Why should they do that? Surely they would have returned to him. What was happening at Cillebairre? Fearghal maintained his position in the Ui Maine kingdom by trusting only those closest to him in blood and few of those. Was this man to be trusted? Was Fearghal being punished for letting his guard down? The marriage should be *lánamnas comthinchuir* with the two parties contributing equally but, impressed by the stranger's boldness, effrontery and downright courage and with his thought and speech blurred by ale, Fearghal had accepted Conal's argument that since he had no property he could not contribute any property and so had agreed to *lánamnas for bantinchur*, marriage on the woman's contribution. The lawyer-clerics had advised against this but Fearghal was tired of their constant whispering in his ears. Perhaps this was why the Máenmaige was considered a lesser sept in the Ui Maine Kingdom. Perhaps he had too many advisers and lawyers. He had told them to go and fast and pray or be slaughtered. Besides, Fearghal reassured himself, Carnait was not of great significance and the woman's contribution did not amount to much: a small plot of pasture, a hectare of woodland, four head of cattle, six sheep, two goats plus a stock of cheese, honey, cured meats and other miscellaneous chattels. The land would remain hers anyway. The man would have no real claim in Máenmaige.

Conal urged his mount onwards gently with his thighs. Ruadhan and Colman quick-stepped alongside. In spite of his disappointment, Fearghal acknowledged that Conal was a fine-looking man. He had the demeanour of a natural leader who, with his confidence and effortless manner, could have been at the head of hundreds. Fearghal held his tongue, greeted Conal civilly and ushered all three into the dun. At this sign, Ruarcc, Breccan and Eoin raced their horses at breakneck speed from the wood towards the gates. Corraidhín followed at a more sedate pace pulling the pack horse behind his steed. All four were in full battle attire. Ruarcc, Breccan and Eoin whirled their weapons high and shrieked as they charged. As they closed on the dun, Ruarcc lowered himself to the side of his mount as if to cut down a terrified wood-gatherer. The man dropped his load and raised his arms but, at the last moment, Ruarcc lifted his weapon in an arc over the man's head, bringing it low once more to slash and slice cleanly through one, two, three sturdy trunks of ash saplings.

Fearghal turned his horse and watched this exhibition. Eoin was next, racing his horse towards a wooden frame to Fearghal's right, hurling his spear and splitting a waterskin, one of several hanging there. Breccan followed. As he approached the gates, he raised and placed both his feet on his horse's back and, for a moment, still waving his axe, squatted there. Legs safely astride the animal's back once more and in time with Ruarcc and Eoin he reined the horse to a halt in front of the reception party, some of whom had angled their spears in combat readiness. Fearghal sat stiffly feigning indifference as soldiers he had considered of little account, displayed some of their newly learned military skills. He was impressed by what he saw but smarted from the failure of his security and the effrontery of this secretive entry into his land. Conal should have arrived in a straightforward, subdued manner as part of his obeisance to Fearghal as a chieftain, albeit a petty one. This cleverness and stealth did not bode well. Before Fearghal's misgivings could fester, Corraidhín led the packhorse in front of his comrades and dismounted. Conal nodded to Ruadhan who rushed to the horse's side and with a deft slash from a dagger, released its load of three hidebound packages. Ruarcc, Breccan and Eoin also dismounted, lifted the parcels and, kneeling before him, unfolded the gifts to Fearghal. The first revealed washed fleeces, several of them dyed.

Fearghal was unmoved. This was nothing out of the ordinary. He had sheep; he had fleeces by the dozen. The second, smaller package was unwrapped and Fearghal found he was in possession of precious items Conal had looted from his previous masters: several copper bracelets studded with tears of amber and onyx and a finely made short battle axe with one horn of the head a sharp blade and the other forged into a spike. Fearghal's eyes widened. He nodded: this was a more fitting tribute. He pointed and one of his soldiers picked up and handed him the axe. Immediately, Fearghal experienced and was stirred by its lightness and balance and imagined himself wielding it to great effect in battle. Finally, Eoin slowly, formally, opened the last, the smallest parcel and Fearghal gazed with clear lust at two simple, pure Irish gold torcs stolen in Ulaid before the Northmen's expedition reached Cillebairre. He nodded again and this time also grunted his satisfaction. This gift and the ale that followed the greetings at the gate was enough to balance any reservations Fearghal had of forging an alliance with this *Gall-Goídil*.

Simple politics brought Conal and Carnait together. Conal did not know the woman but, when he saw her, liked the look of her well enough. Some would have been repulsed by her strange speech defect but Conal though curious, did not give it room as he assessed the woman's attributes. What attracted him in addition to her beauty was the bold way she returned his gaze, letting him know that he was not the only one who had a right to evaluate the other. They spent that first night in guests' quarters that had been set aside for them by Fearghal. It was a testing night for Conal as he learned that behind that bold gaze was a strong will. Carnait had sat sedately at the high table with her uncle and new husband but left the meal early. Conal, sensing he had offended Fearghal by his unorthodox arrival and not keen to provoke him further, remained in the great hall. He ached with desire for his new wife – it had been a long time, far too long a time, since he had lain with a woman – but counselled himself with patience. He wanted a clear head for what was to follow and did not try to keep pace with the older man's drinking. Besides, such indulgence had never been his way. A score of feasts among the Northmen where drunkenness had blinded men to friendships and caused them to maim and kill each other and, at times, opened doors to treachery, had taught him to be circumspect. Conal felt contempt for those who blurred their mind and senses to the point where they could do little to defend themselves. He remained watchful and sober. He did not expect to meet bad faith in any guise that night but he wanted to be sharply alert for the delights Carnait's body could give him.

Conal was bitterly disappointed when he entered the guesthouse. With the aid of a servant, Carnait had improvised a partition of their sleeping place using wall hangings and blankets. She was nervous but resolute and told him that she would sleep one side and he the other. She did not expect Conal to respect this separation and prayed that his forcing of her would not be as crude and distressing as Fearghal's violation. She spoke from her side of the divide with the strange slurring that her wounded tongue created. "Before this day, before this union, I had given myself to God, and undertaken to commit myself to virginity and a life of prayer and humble obedience."

"A nun? You want to be a nun? Why take such a vow?" Conal snapped the questions out. He was angry and to him his anger was righteous. Why should he tolerate this rejection? She was his wife. If others heard of this, he would be diminished in their eyes, seen to be vulnerable.

"Many women do. It..."

"Ones that marry?"

"It can bring one closer to God."

"And lying with me will carry you away from God?" Conal was shouting now.

Carnait did not reply. She had no answer to that question. There could be no doubt that the union between a man and a woman and the begetting of children was ordained and blessed by God but her only experience of such physical union, Fearghal's brutal attack, seemed as far removed from God and His grace as it was possible to be. There was anger in Conal's voice but without looking on his face, she could not read his intentions. Her mouth went dry and her throat tightened as she anticipated him tearing the partition down. Fearghal had schooled her in men's lustfulness and brutality.

Conal did lift his arms to rip the curtains away and gaze upon the woman whom he had married that day, gaze upon her and then drown himself in her nakedness. He stopped and lowered his arms. As on the battlefield, so in love-making: there was passion and there was rashness and stupidity. "Why then did you give yourself to me in this marriage?"

"I had no choice. Fearghal forced it. He made the arrangements. I pleaded with him but he would not listen to me. He wants your friendship and your support. He trades me for those."

Conal turned and gazed at the glowing turf sods. It had been a long, tiring day, the full length of which he had anticipated having sex with Carnait and now it was ending with great disappointment. A low, throbbing ache established itself behind the scar on his forehead. "You give me the fire to lie beside. I suppose I should be grateful but I would prefer the warmth of your body."

"Give me time, I beg you. Perhaps God will send me a sign, a vision that will confirm me on the path I must follow."

"Perhaps I am that sign." *Sent by God*: Conal smiled at his arrogance. "Your old master, without doubt, would force you. I will not though my craving is like torture. And it would be justified, you realise that, don't you?"

Once more, Carnait did not reply.

"Sleep. Be assured, to force you is not my way."

"I am pleased to hear that from you."

Conal moved hides and blankets even closer to the fire and sat. "Tell me, your speech. Have you always been afflicted that way?"

There was a long silence and then Carnait tried to answer but stuttered badly and incoherently. That answered his question.

"Who did it to you? Who maimed you in that way?"

"It... it... is a burden I have to accept."

"It was a man, of course. Perhaps this is why you punish me in this way, me who has done you no wrong. Will it always be like this? If so, I will not cast you aside but I *will* take another. It will be my right. And perhaps not just one, several."

"Give me time."

In the early days of the marriage, Carnait had maintained her refusal to sleep with her husband. She was adamant that she would enter the Church as a religious and that this would free Conal to divorce her. She even consulted Duach over the matter which the monk found very disturbing. He knew there were precedents for such separation but was unclear how Conal would react if he gave it his sanction. "Pray, Carnait, pray hard," was his only advice.

Conal was patient. Rather than repulsing him, her rejection made her more attractive. He sublimated his frustration with work: the relentless drilling of his soldiers; personal intervention in disputes over grazing, planting, ownership of livestock and the enforcement of any judgements in law that Duach might pronounce. He directed the building of a fine house for his wife and the children he hoped she would give him. Four courses of stone were topped by great lengths of split timber and a deep thatch. Carnait remained impassive but Conal's forbearance and tenderness towards her began to wreak a change. With her, he was a different man. Only she, she told herself, knew the Conal who gave way to another; who, since their return from Fearghal's *tuath*, had never raised his voice to her; the Conal who had beautiful jewellery crafted for her, a penannular brooch set with millefiori glass and enamel which, he said, represented their marriage, an incomplete circle; the Conal who courted her with poetry learned in a faraway place he called the Round City:

She who caused me to taste their love now makes me weep;
She awoke my heart to passion,
But then her heart yielded to slumber;
She roused me, but when I stood up with the burden which she placed upon me,
She sank into repose.

Carnait delighted in the attention he gave her and was stirred by genuine affection towards all that he was. *She* began to want him and, one evening, made plans. Conal had ridden into the next valley to investigate a report of cattle raids and returned after dark. Carnait ordered Ruadhan out of the house and told a servant to bring hot water. When Conal entered, she undressed and washed and dried him and asked him to do the same to her. He ran his rough hands slowly, tenderly, over all her body and sighed deeply.

"The circle is almost complete," he said.

"I was told by Duach that the circle is a symbol for God," Carnait replied and led him to her bed.

On the morning after Tulchán had made his presence known in a dream, one year after the return from the forest, Ruadhan heard the baby wake and cry softly. He watched as Carnait stirred immediately and led Cearbhall's mouth deftly to her breast. The baby fed greedily. Carnait caught and returned Ruadhan's gaze, her face unemotional, betraying nothing except a lack of feeling towards one who shared the living space but who remained a stranger and an interloper to her. She had allowed one male to come close. That was enough. Ruadhan held Carnait's gaze for a moment and then rolled on to his back to gaze at the roof and the place where the Psalter was hidden. The dream returned to his mind and with it the terrible events of a year before. Tulchán had spoken from beyond the grave. The dream, as clear to him as the people he had been looking at, could not be ignored. The book had to be taken to the great monastery of Clonmacnoise on the Shannon. Conal would have to accept that this must happen.

CLONMACNOISE
The Abbot

"Ah yes, the famous Chalice. Didn't what-do-you-call-him... em..." The Abbot sat forward and gestured as if trying to grasp the memory out of the air, "... of Durrow carry it before him into battle and win a famous victory against the people of Birr? Yes, I'm sure that's what happened. Marvellous... marvellous." The front of his tunic had bunched as he sat down and he fussed to straighten it as he talked.

Brecc flexed his shoulder blades back and inwards. The stiffness of almost a year's travelling had not started to work itself out and a long session standing listening to the Abbot as he displayed his learning would not help at all. He moved his weight from one foot to the other and wriggled his feet to keep them warm. Something was wrong with the left one. He wriggled it again and found that the sandal was holed, holed badly for if he arched his foot and brought his big toe back, he could stick it through the sole.

Abbot Ronan put a hand to his forehead and brought the fingers and thumb together in a squeezing motion as if he was drawing knowledge from his head. "Our links with the Church in Egypt go back a long way, even to before the time of our beloved Patrick. We always attribute the bringing of the Gospel to that saint, but it is certain that descendants of those who heard the evangelist Mark were here before him, and so was Palladius, of course, but the impression he made was insignificant." Abbot Ronan moved his hand from his head and placed it before him, palm outwards as if he was telling someone to stop. "Don't ask me for details of those Egyptians. Any reading I did on this was a long time ago, but it is certain that the way we live now, the life of a monk, was learned by us from the Coptic Church and from the first monk of all, Anthony. Or was Paul the first monk? There is considerable debate about that, you know. Yes, yes, Egyptians are buried at Dysert Ulidh and Patrick himself found an altar and four of their glass Chalices. The Chalice we speak of is one of those four: in fact, according to Abbot Colman of Tir da Glas, whose learning on these matters I have no cause to question, it is the only one remaining, the others having been destroyed.

And now we hear that Tulchán of Cillebairre knows where the Chalice of St. Mark is. Well, I would have sent you immediately to seek his assistance, but your journey would be in vain for Tulchán, that giant of learning and Christian fortitude has joined the triumphant band of those who have been martyred for Christ's sake in Ireland. Cillebairre has suffered terribly at the hands of the pagan invaders who plague our shores. Tulchán is dead."

The Abbot bowed his head in silent prayer for a moment. Brecc did likewise. He had known Tulchán and admired his gentle, loving personality and his beautiful work as a scribe. Fiacc stared straight ahead.

"You say Makarius, an Egyptian monk is coming to us. Well, he is welcome but it is sad that we will not be able to give him news of the Chalice. It is sad that we will not be able to return the Chalice. It is precious to all the Church, not because of what it is made of - glass should never be used to hold the Precious Blood - but because of what it has been used for and by whom it has been used. If I remember rightly it was this particular Chalice that was referred to in our annals by one of my predecessors, also Ronan by name. His was a troubled incumbency - I give thanks to God every day that the period of my rule has been a peaceful one - and there was much fighting with the Durrow people. Two hundred of the enemy fell in one battle, and the Clonmacnoise commander was ... em ... I shall not let my memory fail me on this. His name was ... He was one of our finest soldiers; the son of Murchad. Em... Bresal, that was his name: Bresal!

The Abbot was delighted and looked from Brecc to Fiacc and back again as if he expected them to congratulate him for recalling the soldier's name. Both remained motionless and silent. "Somewhere else it is recorded that he had the largest feet ever seen in these parts and that they equalled the length of the then Abbot Ronan's forearm, from the tip of his fingers to his elbow. Now, I find that hard to believe unless Ronan was particularly small of stature and nowhere is it recorded that he was; at least, to my knowledge it is not recorded anywhere. Such facts as these are not written in our annals, you understand."

The Abbot paused and gazed hard at Brecc without seeing him. Brecc heard a blackbird singing early in the garden. "I have no idea where I got that fact about Bresal's feet. It eludes me completely. It will be in our library somewhere. Now, feet: why did you bring up the subject of feet?"

Brecc imagined a whole cow's hide being used to provide shoes for Bresal and then remembered his own footwear. His big toe curled back to the hole in his sandal and he tried to work out how large it was. Fiacc remained silent. Brecc had to answer Ronan. "The Chalice, Abbot Ronan, you were talking about the Chalice of St. Mark."

The Abbot frowned and looked from Fiacc to Brecc: "Then please do not distract me with talk of feet, Brother Brecc. Now, the Chalice of St. Mark ... and, yes, our Coptic brothers." He paused once more as if his mind was turning pages until he found the right one. "St. Patrick himself may have said Mass with that Chalice and before him many Desert Fathers whose example in spiritual greatness we try so feebly to follow. Strange that seeds from that distant dry land should sprout such a harvest in our greenery. It is sad that Makarius will return empty-handed. You say the Mohammedans are once more persecuting the Copts. They are not a soldier-race, you know, the Copts. The Greeks were there before the Arabs, and the Copts were quite happy to see the last of the Greeks driven out and new rulers installed, ones who were closer to them in many ways, and who seemed, at first, content to let Christians practise their religion in peace. However, that did not last and they have suffered severe persecution for their faith. I have all this from Diciul who knows a great deal about that land and its people. Probably more than yourself, Brecc. Have you seen him since your return? He will be off again soon to the Emperor's court. You should go to him soon for you may have some knowledge that will be of interest to him in his studies. His work is excellent and his influence is spreading through many countries. Of course, he owes a lot to his master, Suibhneus, who, it ought to be said, learned a great deal from myself, but he is now ploughing his own furrow. Have you read, *Liber De Mensura Orbis Terrae*? No. Well, you ought. Diciul has built upon the cosmography of Caesar, Pliny and Solinus, and is bursting with quotes from all kinds of learned sources: Pomponius Mela; Orosius; Isidore of Seville; Priscian the Grammarian. It is a wonderful book to which you should refer. It is in our library. And go to see him. He will impart much knowledge to you."

Brecc took a deep breath. He did not think he would ever have need of Dicuil's maps no matter how excellent they were because he had no intention of ever again leaving Clonmacnoise and his garden. He did not dislike Diciul, but, if he was honest, had to say that he did not enjoy the man's company. He was far too learned. The Abbot had not finished.

"Now, I called the Copts "brethren" a moment ago, but, please understand me: I say that out of charity for the truth of the matter is that they are cloaked in heresy by their denial that Christ's nature was both divine and human. If I am right, and I think I am, it was ...em ... Chalcedon, yes, the Council of Chalcedon in 451 which confirmed their heresy. You will find some reference to this in our library, I am sure. However, ...em... we must help the Copts for, as you say, many are being forced by persecution to deny Christ all together. The Chalice would be a call to remain firm in their faith, and who, knows, with the grace of God, it could lead them to a renunciation of their heretical ways and to the true understanding of Our Saviour's nature."

The Abbot struck the arms of his chair several times as he spoke the last sentence; seemed pleased with the sentence and with its delivery and pleased to have reached what he believed was a fitting conclusion. Fiacc spoke for the first time. "We can still search for the Chalice."

Abbot Ronan smiled and looked directly at his protégé. "Yes, yes, you are right, Fiacc, we could. Thank you. We have no Chalice. It is possible that the Chalice is lost forever, buried with Tulchán and his knowledge. I do not know where you can turn, Brecc, in the search, unless it is to our library where, somewhere among all those learned volumes you are bound to find a reference or two which may direct you towards that precious relic of St. Mark. Yes, the library: that's where the search should continue, and Diciul, Brecc: speak to Diciul about it."

Brecc frowned. The learned had a dryness which people who had never watched plants grow often have. Brecc would in obedience speak to him but hoped that nothing would come of their conversation. And he had no intention of sitting long hours in the library in order to solve the mystery of the Chalice of St. Mark.

The Abbot gazed hard at Brecc but his fellow-monk could have been a stone. A long pause. His mind turned pages again without finding the right one. "Em... em... terrible... em..."

Once more, Brecc heard a blackbird singing in the garden and yearned to be outside. "The Chalice, Abba Ronan, you were talking about the Chalice of St. Mark. Diciul. Library. Copts. Heresy."

The Abbot frowned and looked from Fiacc to Brecc: "Now, the Chalice of St. Mark ... and, yes, our Coptic brothers. Diciul will know something. Yes, he knows a great deal about Egypt. Go and see him for he may be able to help you find this Chalice if that is possible. There must be references to it in our library."

Fiacc spoke: "I wish to ask the Abbot's permission to begin my exile upon one of the barren islands to the west."

The frown was converted to a satisfied smile on Ronan's face and he nodded his agreement. He looked directly at Fiacc and was impressed by the spiritual strength which he saw expressed in his quiet, solemn manner. There was great power in the man which could be harnessed for the greater glory of God. "You have my permission, Fiacc. There is one of a shower of islands upon which an oratory was built by... em... I think it was Ciarán, Ciarán of... em... I forget where; not our own founder, of course, but another one of the saintly Ciaráns. You will go there. Five years was it not? Yes, well... we shall see how you fare. I have the power to cut the length of your exile. Em... once every two months, I will send someone with a supply of bread and perhaps some cheese and milk. Yes, I am pleased with your acceptance of this, Fiacc, and convinced that the isolation will bring you closer to God. And we shall all benefit from your prayers and denial of physical comforts. Yes, you have my permission."

Fiacc lowered his head in acknowledgement but spoke once more: "Do not send any bread, Abbot."

Ronan smiled once more upon the determined man in front of him. Clearly, he had learned from his desert pilgrimage. The abbot nodded and agreed. Fiacc would be an example to them all. Ronan stood and looked as if he was going to dismiss them both. Brecc had been tensing his shoulders all the time. Now he allowed them to sag. But the Abbot had not finished. His mind had gone back to the Chalice of St. Mark and he looked very upset. "It disturbs me deeply to think of such a vessel being used in the sacrifice of the Mass. Oh, I do not mean this as any criticism of those who employed such a receptacle, since they must have been driven to do so by their circumstances. No priest, if he has the choice would allow the Precious Blood to rest in anything but a Chalice made of the most precious metals. A clay cup cannot be considered at all, no, but I am inclined to think that certain precious stones such as onyx are acceptable. I have read somewhere in our library that the cup Our Lord used at the Last Supper was agate. It is in Spain, you know, but where exactly has slipped my memory for the moment... Em... Where was I? Ah yes, base metals or wood are unthinkable. And yet, I am told, such materials have been used. Poverty, I suppose, may force you, but... em... wood... no... never... It..."

Brecc interrupted crudely: "I quote Boniface to you, Abbot Ronan, begging your pardon for interrupting but earnestly asking for your leave to go since there are urgent matters in the garden I must attend to. This too is to be found in our library: *In ancient times golden priests said Mass in wooden chalices, but now wooden priests say Mass in golden chalices.*"

The Abbot studied Brecc long and hard. He wondered what it was in the garden that could be making urgent demands upon his fellow-monk. Then, in his head, he repeated the words Brecc had quoted. Who was it? Boniface? Was this a personal comment upon his own attitudes and personality? Surely not. No, Brother Brecc was headstrong and sometimes loose-tongued but he would not be so bold and offensive, and that quotation was very fitting. What was it again? *Golden priests and wooden chalices and wooden...*

CILLEBAIRRE
Conal's Tower

Why a tower and why a *round* tower? At first, Conal protested weakly that the people of Cillebairre must be getting fed up with his tales and someone else should stand at the centre but several voices contested one with the other to plead that this was not the case.

"We have little to speak of. The boundary of our lives is a short stretch of this this valley."

"We don't want to hear of how Gobnait lost a sheep beyond the Yellow Stream."

"Or how Aednat dropped a needle yesterday."

Most of the men and a few women and children had gathered and sat around Conal at the meeting place. There was still light but many brought blankets to ward off the mid-October evening chill. Duach, the priest, Bréanainn and a few other monks crossed the water to hear what Conal had to say. Ruarcc attended out of duty and the rest of the militia came with him but Conal had insisted there be no guard about him.

"I will tell you then of The Round City and its round towers."

Brother Duach found pleasure, perhaps to excess, in the scriptorium but Conal had spoken of a new building and he believed it was his duty to address the gathering. He did not like preaching or teaching, was born for neither but as Abbot, had responsibilities. He set off with confidence at a quick pace. "Ah, yes, a round tower; very fitting since the circle has a meaning that stretches way beyond our understanding. It is a great sign of our God. Augustine it was, I think, who wrote of God as a ... perhaps it wasn't, but someone among the learned and holy wrote of God and his love. Like the circle, it has no beginning and no end and *that* divine love was demonstrated by the sacrifice of His son at The Place of the Skull. The centre of the circle is... nothing. That, well, that is the mystery of God. There will always be mystery. Intertwined, three circles give us the Trinity, Father, Son and Holy Spirit... we can see such intertwining in some of the illustrations we draw..." Duach's mind and mouth started to stutter. He was losing his train of thought. "The circle..., well, the circle... think of God's love like a stockade, surrounding us, keeping... em... keeping us..."

"The story! Let's hear Conal's story!"

Duach nodded in agreement at this rude interruption. He had just about drained his knowledge of circle symbolism anyway and had found himself grasping for more ideas: *bracelets, amulets, God's love keeps us safe; God's love is like a warrior's round shield (how?); the burnt circle fires leave in the grass; God's love is like the fire that creates those circles...* "The story: a round city, you say, Conal, and a round tower. That could be very pleasing to God."

"And it must be built completely in stone, Duach." Conal gestured to the lengths of wood that topped the half-stone walls in the completed church. "Well-built, I know, but we can do better. Buildings that are mostly of stone are easier to defend; harder for an enemy to destroy and they keep the wind and rain at bay better than other materials. We must build in stone as much as we can. And everyone must work together. And..." Here he broke off and stretched his arms as far as he could upwards. He held them there for a moment and a smile spread slowly over his face as he came to a resolution that gave him great satisfaction. "We will build it high, high and round!"

Ruadhan was not close to Conal. He stood to one side with Colman, a sign of the discreteness that had come to the household in the days following Cearbhall's recent arrival. There had even been talk of his going to live in the soldiers' compound. Ruadhan gazed over the river at the great black, brooding mass of forest. He would return to its uncertainties before sharing living space with Ruarcc. Ruadhan knew why Conal had called the meeting; he knew of the plans. For weeks before Carnait gave birth, Conal had puzzled him with long and private talks of such a building.

"With the Northmen, I travelled sea roads that only they know. No two days were the same. One day, the boat would lurch in seas with waves higher than many a hill in our land; the next, it would rest in water as still as my hand." Here, Conal stretched out his right arm, his sword arm full length and held it there as all focused on it and acknowledged the steadiness. Those closest to him noticed another scar, pink and puckered that ran across the back of that hand.

"Usually, we sailed and rowed to the north and west but one great voyage took me in the opposite direction. I have told you little of this. It was my longest voyage and it was to places even my dreams could not conjure. My masters formed an alliance with others from distantly related tribes. They came from a place called Birka and were as fearless and intrepid as my own. These people favoured different trading routes. They knew of great lands far to the south and east and we were persuaded to join them by tales of rich trade. The world I travelled to with them is full of so many wonders; the strangest places and the strangest people. We sailed through fields of ice and along rivers wider than lakes. We were merchant-warriors. We would fight if needs be but, first and foremost, our intention was to trade. We packed our boats with furs - beavers, black foxes - seal fat; the gold-red amber which many want for adornment and which Fearghal of the Mainmaeige now carries on his arm. We took slaves along the way and these too we traded. What did we get in exchange?" Conal stopped talking momentarily and looked around at his listeners. Ruadhan looked too and once again saw the power this man asserted in so many different ways over the people of Cillebairre. Here, it was through his ability translate his experiences into stories that held them spellbound and convinced them even more of his "specialness" and his right to lead them.

Conal reached under his vest and drew out a, carefully bundled and tied piece of cloth. The petty-chieftain Fearghal had not been given all that Conal had looted from his old masters. From the untied cloth two dozen silver coins tumbled on to the earth in front of him. Some were whole, others halved or quartered. "This is what we received from the Khazars and, further south, the Arabs." Those closest were wary of picking the dirhams up as if they were sacred objects that they had no right to touch and which, if they did, would bring some supernatural punishment into their lives. Conal encouraged them. "Go on. Touch them. Look at them. The finest of silver and much prized by your unwelcome visitors; in fact, prized more than gold. This coveted precious metal is what they choose to be buried with in order to buy themselves a pleasant resting place in the afterlife. Duach, did the raiders find any of this among Cillebairre's treasures? They would certainly be looking for it."

"All – and I don't mean much since ours is not a large monastery – was well-buried before they got to it, except for one Chalice of Irish silver given by Cathal mac Murchadh. I don't know why it was not hidden. That, they took, of course."

Ruadhan strode forward through the crowd and picked up one of the whole coins. His understanding of trade was basic. He knew what was needed to live – to feed, clothe, shelter and protect yourself and those closest to you. Those needs gave value to certain goods but beyond that level of understanding, Ruadhan was lost. He had learned enough to know that the litter of silver on the ground was of great value but he did not know why. He recalled Fearghal's childish glee when he saw the copper bracelets and gold torcs Conal had brought. As marks of their rank, wealth and power, noblemen and women decorated themselves with jewellery made from such metals. Acquiring and wearing ornaments seemed to be a great reason for existing. Ruadhan did not know why it should be so. And those same people ate and drank more than their fill. Tulchán had done the opposite. He had few clothes, no jewellery and ate and drank little. Ruadhan tossed the coin back to the earth.

Conal had the attention of all present and did not need to command more. Nevertheless, he raised his voice. The fire glinted strangely on his forehead scar giving Ruadhan the impression that his guardian had a third eye. "After many months travelling south along rivers we reached a great sea far east of the Roman one and we crossed it to the port of Jurjan. There we left our boats and transported our wares over a hot, dry, stony land to the Round City I want to tell you about. We carried them on the backs of strange humped creatures twice as high, I'd say, as our horses, to the Round City. What a place! The Arabs, their architects, their builders and their engineers have made it like no other settlement on earth and certainly, there is nothing to compare with it on our island. It is a place that makes strangers gasp at when first they see it. They stay for a lifetime and are still gasping."

As ever at such times, many of the people who had gathered had little idea of some of the things Conal was talking about. *Cities*? Cillebairre and a few clusters of hovels further up the valley along the river's edge were the only measures they had of human settlements. *Island*? It had to be explained to some that water surrounded the land upon which they lived. Conal's storytelling was constantly interrupted by individuals wanting certain references explained. What was *amber*? Who were *Arabs*?

"To walk across this great city takes the best part of a day. Its heart is protected by, not one, but two high, mud-brick walls. The main wall is higher than the tallest tree our forest boasts and as wide as our river on the top. Around this wall, a barrier of wide water flows. It is more than twenty long strides wide and is led there by a canal from a great river. The Round City is the centre of a huge empire. Four gates break the walls and four roads lead from them to the four quarters of that empire. It teems with people from many lands and its markets are choked with goods from those lands. It is a green place. Although we trekked through dry, desert land to reach it, great rivers flow there and provide many cool and fertile spaces within and without the city walls. There are parks where the noblemen and women walk; gardens full of vegetables and orchards bursting with fruit that you have never seen. It is like Paradise itself."

Conal stopped momentarily. It was as if the recollection of that place had made him breathless. "They build in stone as well as mud. Marble, there is much marble: palaces with steps down to the water's edge. I tell you this place has riches beyond imaginings, slaves beyond number. And it is also a place of great learning. Many books, Duach, Duach the Scribe... where are you?"

"I am here, Conal. I have not moved. I am at your feet and listening intently to every word you say."

"Books: buildings full of them and the words are not written on skins. Plants, Duach, they make sheets from plants to write on."

"I have heard of this, Conal, and have, in fact, written on such."

"I was offered all that I could ever wish for to stay there. Like everywhere in this fallen world, there is jealousy and treachery, sometimes from those who almost stand in your clothes. Because of this universal fact, the Arab nobles buy mercenaries from outside their land. Such purchased loyalty is less suspect. That is their thinking. Those mercenaries are far from home and dependent upon their masters in a strange land. And the people they admire most for their military prowess and weaponry are the people they call *Rus*, the Northmen. To the Arabs, I was a *Rus*. Yes, I could have stayed. I was given great freedom there. Let me tell you of one time, and I swear this is true, one time in a lush green park, when an Arab lord asked his daughter to pick some of the fruit for me, huge oranges..."

"What's an *orange*?"

"He's told you. It's a fruit."

"Now, many hid their women from us and would never allow a meeting between them and foreigners under any circumstances but this man was different. And his daughter was very beautiful. It is hard for me to describe well the beauty of this young woman: rich black hair like my own Carnait, face half-hidden but eyes dark and alive like fast-flowing water reflecting bright sunlight. She left where we were sitting in the orchard and crossed to a far corner and a tree that was larger than the others. Her father saw me watching her.

'She is beautiful, isn't she?' he remarked.

I was wary. I was learning quickly but did not know much about their ways. Was it acceptable for me to let him know that I did think his daughter was beautiful and perhaps, in so doing reveal that I had been admiring her beauty – no, let's not play with polite words – that I had been lusting after her? I was not sure but nodded and muttered that she was, indeed, a beautiful woman.

'You will stay,' he said. 'I need someone strong and fearless, someone who will guard my back from those who would plant knives in it; someone who will be loyal to death.'

I watched his daughter stretching to pick fruits, with one hand and then, the other. I will be honest and tell you that, as I watched her strain to pluck the fruit from the branches, and I apologise to no one for my thoughts, I imagined *my* hands stroking, plucking fruit from every part of her beautiful body." Several men nodded their understanding of what had been in Conal's mind.

" 'She and what she brings you now can be yours if you agree to stay,' her father told me.

With her hands clutching the fruit held out straight in front of her, stepping confidently and heading directly to me, his daughter returned slowly. I say 'stepping' but 'flowing' is a better description. She moved towards me like a stream sliding around stones. How I wanted to bathe in that stream! It wasn't until she was almost by me that I realised one of those *fruits* was very different. One was the juicy orange I had been expecting; the other, as large and of the same shape, was made of metal, the same metal scattered on the earth here." Conal gestured to the dirhams.

"She handed me the orange. The other *fruits;* that is herself and the silver wrought into the shape of an orange, would be mine and more, much more, if I stayed in the Round City and protected that Arab nobleman. She picked the two from the same tree, I swear. I watched her do it. Silver; solid silver."

"And you came back here!" It was too dark. Ruadhan could not see who spoke.

"You see me! You hear me!"

"I'm telling you, Conal, I wouldn't have quit that place! I'd be with her!" There was a general murmur of agreement among the men.

"I had made a decision to return to Cillebairre long before we reached that city and the temptation her beauty placed before me is not the reason I tell you this story. I talk of this city because of the towers: there are hundreds of towers in the walls of this great city; towers that command the land in every direction. These towers are round. The greatest city in the world has round towers and now, I tell you, Cillebairre, will have its very own, a tower that will reach towards God and that will defend us from the most resolute of attacks by the Northmen!"

A general shout of agreement went up. There were still dissenters but they kept quiet since most of those present loved being transported by Conal's memories and glimpsing people and places so different from themselves and their own land. They rallied to his call. Yes, they would build a tower for him and it would reach higher than any other building in Ireland. And yes, it would resist the Northmen and any other marauding enemy of Cillebairre. Duach had not liked the references to the Arab woman and Conal's lust for her and neither had he been happy with this tower "reaching towards God", which he recalled, had a biblical precedent. However, these were minor objections Duach quickly put aside. Cillebairre was changing for the better and Conal was the main reason for that. His own family's interest in Cillebairre was still, at best, lukewarm and could not be relied upon for patronage. Duach was not going to undermine Conal's leadership in any way. He spoke a blessing over the assembly and told them how a tower would enhance the monastery's status as a place of refuge and security. In the secrecy of his own mind, Duach hoped his faith in Conal was not misguided. The light had faded and the air was cold but most went to their homes and sleep warmed by Conal's vision for their community.

There were grumbles. *We haven't the skills. It is much harder work. We will need more tools and better ones. A bigger forge is needed. The quarry is a great distance.* Some damned Conal's tower from the start. It was a foolish project, a waste of time, and would never stand. Also, it would bring ill luck to the community. It was, like the one who planned it and those who had built Babel, arrogant and divisive. It was too high a building and like Babel would topple. Everyone would be punished for the hubris of one man. In spite of the muttered opposition and the fact that winter was closing on the valley, Conal got his way, appointed Conchad the monk as architect and ordered every adult to give time to work on this building. That included the warrior elite. Duach gave his approval.

In the early weeks, the work progressed steadily. There was enthusiasm for it and the task was favoured by a gentle autumn. With the exception of a few who would never waver in their suspicion and hatred of the one who had returned and of the forest boy, the people of Cillebairre, the whole new community, monks and lay people, wanted to contribute. They were determined and united by Conal's vision of a future dominated not by fear but by hope. Stone was cut and hauled. The initial courses were laid. Scaffolding was erected. Pulleys and ropes lifted more stone for higher courses. New skills were learned by all: men became quick-eyed at spotting which stones should go on top of others already laid, and dextrous at plugging gaps with spalls. Teams of women laboured long and hard at packing rubble firmly behind the stone outer wall to give the tower strength and solidity. Carpenters cut wood for several floors to be installed. Mochan's adze rarely rested as smooth lengths were fastened strongly and snugly together on joists firmly sealed into the thick walls. For purposes of defence, the first floor and entry to the tower could only be reached by means of a ladder. Many shared Conal's vision and echoed his words when he had spoken of the tower as a sign of their faith which reached upwards to God.

The *grey* dream stayed with Ruadhan. He tried to speak to Conal about his need to fulfil his mission but the man was so rapt in the building of the tower that he all but ignored him. "Some dreams are important and some are not. Don't trust them. There is work to do here and I need you. Besides soon it will be the wrong time of the year for you to travel."

But not the wrong time to build. Through a particularly harsh winter, the people did more than Conal thought possible. They hauled and built even when snow fell but by spring it was clear that enthusiasm was waning. He had told them to be careful about the work right at the start: always make sure no one is working beneath you when you are cutting stones in the quarry or placing them in the tower; never overload yourself or the oxen; always use lengths of the strongest wood for the scaffolding and lash them firmly together. At first, eager to do the work, they had listened to him and there had been few accidents - a stone dropped on a foot, a slip on a ladder - cuts and bruises, nothing more. With two deaths, one from a rock fall at the quarry, the other from a tumble off the scaffolding and a subsequent fever, the flurry of work and the enthusiasm for building waned. More began to question the wisdom of building the round tower. The tower brought bad luck. *That boy* climbing up and down ladders fetching tools and water brought bad luck. Complaints other than *bad luck* multiplied: the fields were being neglected and the crops would be poor; warriors should not be engaged in such a task; the tower wouldn't store that much corn; not many could shelter in it and only the elite would be chosen; the Northmen would not return; what was the point? Every little job became a huge task. The work slowed; quarrelling increased; everyone was getting careless, and accidents were commonplace. Work on the tower became sporadic.

It came to a head with Fintan's death. Conal was above with Ruadhan and shouted as he saw the stones begin to move - a huge window lintel and the others about it - but his warning was too late for Fintan to get out of the way. He had time only to glance upwards as the shower of heavy stones and rubble crashed through the scaffolding and felled him. Conal clambered quickly down from where he was inspecting the highest course of stones and ran to where Fintan lay.

Before he reached him, Conal knew that Fintan was dead. His body moved, flinched as if the stones were still falling on him, but Conal knew life had gone. With the Northmen on their battlefields, he had seen death come in many different costumes, so many that it could no longer disguise itself from him. Too much deep red, almost black, blood had already spilled from the terrible gash in the side of Fintan's head and was fingering its way through stone dust and grass blades. Futile as he knew it was, Conal knelt at the man's side and placed his hands over the wound to staunch the flow. As he did he saw that the lintel stone had also struck Fintan's chest. Conal ripped Fintan's tunic apart from the neck and saw splintered ribs like barley stubble piercing the flesh. Ruadhan arrived and copied his master by pressing his hands over the second horrific injury.

"Leave it be. He is beyond us now. Send for Bréanainn."

As he lifted Fintan, Conal was dismayed to hear bickering voices around him. *We are going too high; the mortar is weak; Conchad does not know his business; the joists for the last floor are not properly embedded in the wall's thickness.* They angered Conal. He wanted to shout; punish in order to remind them of one reason why they were building the tower and bring back to their minds pictures of the Northmen rampaging over the settlement, of loved ones slaughtered or taken into slavery, livestock stolen. That would happen again unless they worked together. Peace, the weight of a hoe in their hands, fat food stocks and their backward attitudes made them forgetful. The Northmen were strong and determined and could only be matched by a people who were equally strong and determined.

As he walked from the half-built structure, cradling Fintan's lifeless body in his arms, Conal himself felt disillusioned. For once, his confidence thinned. The strong-willed man, purposeful to the extreme of never accepting correction, had doubts. He questioned himself. Perhaps Destiny was a fickle and deceitful friend. Perhaps he had misunderstood the experience amid the Khazars that had steered his return to Cillebairre. Signs. You could find them everywhere and they could mean everything and they could mean nothing. He felt a stranger, Long-Plait who had spent so long with the Northmen that perhaps he *was* more foreigner than Irish. Did others truly share his vision of a Cillebairre that would make a mark in the history of the island of Ireland or had they simply come back from Na Lámha ready to follow anyone who would lead them? He knew he could not build a Round City in the western world but he had been confident that he could create a settlement that was admired and feared. The early signs had been propitious. The community had continued to expand as its status and the tower rose, and as winter's cold drove migrants to it from neighbouring valleys. The monks on the south side trebled in number. New arrivals brought new skills as well as young men with an eagerness to learn. Their simple cells had sprung up like molehills and once more the scriptorium of Cillebairre was talked of throughout the land. Similarly, Conal's warrior band had swollen with the arrival of hardened soldiers fleeing conflicts among feuding Eoganachta monasteries to the south. Cillebairre was, without doubt, stronger.

Two swords clashed in Conal's mind: the first directed he stay a leader close to his people, listening to them, working alongside them and sharing the wisdom gained from his experiences. The second which was sharpening itself in his mind had him distancing himself from his people, ruling autocratically and forcing change upon them. Conal wanted to drop Fintan, Fintan the whiner, Fintan the sleepy guard; he wanted to drop him, abuse his body in death and declare to the world that the dead man had been the prime example of the ignorant thinkers in Cillebairre; the

121

naysayers who, with their small minds, opposed any change and had no ideas of their own. Never a day had gone by without Fintan complaining about the building of the tower and the work he was given. Conal wanted to stifle the mourning for Fintan before it began. There was no time to grieve. There was work to be done. That second sword swung high. He had the power. His militia was much stronger. Conal could lash out and punish anybody who stood against him. He could not afford to lapse and show weakness. In his experience, the most successful leaders were the cruellest. To secure the future, he should tighten his control. He had been too soft, too gentle, too conciliatory.

We are never ourselves

A few made half-hearted attempts to restrain Flann as she crossed to Conal's house on the evening of that day. She burst in and made for him. Ruadhan had already lain down to sleep, as had Carnait and the baby, but Conal was sitting close to the remnants of their fire gazing into its fading embers. He rose quickly and, in a reflex action, grabbed the battle-axe which he always kept close. Carnait gripped the handle of the knife which was hidden in the rushes of her bed and then lay as still as she could with her body covering all but the baby's head. Flann faltered and stopped. Several women followed her inside. Two went to her and gripped her arms gently. Ruadhan sat up and wrapped his blanket around him. Conal released the haft and let the axe drop.

"At the least, Flann, this violation of my home is disrespectful."

Flann screamed at Conal. "That tower is yours, Conal! I never wanted it! Neither did Fintan! Now, *your* tower has killed him; *you* have killed him. He goes to his grave following others *you* and this foolish venture have broken. Their blood is on your hands but *you*... you feel nothing for them. To you, our dead are like those stones cast to one side at the foot of your tower; the misshapen ones that are no use."

"The blood that runs in his veins is in mine, Flann. I grieve like you for a lost kinsman."

"Were you not there, Conal? Did you not carry Fintan home? Did you not see that it no longer runs in my husband's body? His lifeblood spilled from him as quickly as if a raider had split him with that axe. Be honest. You are happy to see him dead. You wanted him dead because my Fintan did not like you or your schemes."

Conal lowered his eyes to the fire. It was easier to deal with men. He wanted to dismiss her as he might brush a fly from his arm but those two swords were still clashing in his mind. Restraint was called for. He had to acknowledge the grief she bore.

"You do me wrong, by speaking like this. If... if... I ..." Conal stuttered, clasping and unclasping his hands by his side. He would mourn with Flann but familiarity with killing had dulled his ability to respond at such times as this. He could seldom find the words and now they were well hidden from him. "If I could change places with him ..."

"Change places you cannot, but join him you can," screeched the distraught woman and shook herself free from the grip of her companions.

She rushed towards Conal and as she did, Ruadhan saw a small dagger in her hand. He fell to the floor from his sitting position, stretched and grabbed one of her ankles. Flann screamed louder than ever as she felt Ruadhan's grip and tumbled headlong. She kicked and writhed and spun almost a full circle on the floor scattering hot embers. Conal reached down, firmly held her wrist with one hand and wrenched the dagger from her with the other. "We are never ourselves when one so close dies," he said but angrily and without expression of sympathy.

From the floor, Flann spat out her reply: "Don't betray yourself by believing such words, Conal the Builder. From this day on, guard your back from me, Flann, wife of dead Fintan; Fintan who was an oak in a forest of willows."

Breccan, armed with a spear, rushed through the entrance. Conal gestured for him to stay back. The danger was over. Two of the women helped Flann from the floor. Her anger, for the moment, was spent, but she brushed her tangled hair roughly to one side and faced Conal again. "You don't belong," was all she said quietly and then rubbed at her face furiously with both hands, streaking it with dirt and tears.

"Come, Flann, come now," said one of the women in a soothing voice, "you can do no good here."

Flann wept bitterly as they pulled her back through the door and tried to drag her away from Conal's house. She pulled free once more and threw herself on to the ground outside. "Here I stay!" she screamed. "I will fast until I have satisfaction or I die, *Gall-Goídil*! You have my husband's death on your hands! Soon you will have mine!"

One woman went to lift Flann but another stopped her. "It is her right to try to force him to make amends this way. Leave her."

Conal watched them go and then kicked some glowing embers back from the bed rushes they were dangerously near. For the first time since Conal had returned to the settlement, Ruadhan saw signs of vulnerability in his guardian. He looked tired and smaller. The energy that usually flowed in spate from his compact, muscular body seemed to have been drained by the events of the day. He was shaking from this confrontation with Flann. "Do you see this knife, Ruadhan, the knife which, thanks to you, did not find my heart? Fintan made it for me when I was a boy. He served at the forge of one of our most skilful metalworkers and was a craftsman of sorts in his own right. Not that this is an example of his skill.

It's a simple weapon. Look: a blade, a wooden handle and strips of leather to bind them. Simple. I skinned a few rabbits with it; nothing more. It stayed here when the Northmen took me."

"It was her grief talking, Conal. You are not to blame for what has happened and she will realise that when daylight comes."

"It's true, Flann's mind is turned by the death of her husband but in the midst of her ranting, there is a refrain that others would play as well. I am not liked; I do not belong, they say. And now she corrupts me, my family and my household with this ridiculous fast!"

Carnait released the child from her secure grip and extended her arms to Conal. "Come to bed. This is where you are loved and belong."

"My wife, most nights your caress would draw all poison from my mind and body, but I have an aching at heart that I cannot describe. It will not let me rest." The baby stirred and began to whimper. Carnait lay down and drew its lips to a breast. She spoke as she did so. "You are a fool if you let this pass. You have shown weakness by allowing her to go."

"I know that. Be quiet," was Conal's only reply and he turned his back to her and addressed Ruadhan.

"They are ready to abandon the tower. Fintan's death will convince more that it is a foolish venture." Conal paused and began to pick up bits of kindling. "I don't expect to sleep much tonight. This business is not over. And don't misunderstand any of this. My restlessness comes more from anger than from sorrow; anger with myself. I should not have tolerated any of this show by Flann. Carnait is right. Flann has to be punished for this boldness. I have that to consider. I shall need the comfort of the fire. Get some wood."

"Should Breccan alert the others?"

"No, if she enters and even if she brings more vengeful ones, I can cope. But no others will come. They are cowards."

"I will stay," said Breccan and stepped outside to stand guard.

Conal placed a hand on Ruadhan's shoulder. "And anyway, I have you, Ruadhan, as well as Breccan. Sit with me. Let the others sleep." He threw straw and twigs on to the embers. They smouldered for a moment, then crackled and burst into flame. Ruadhan brought lengths of ash from just inside the doorway and placed them on the flames. He would stay awake. The aftermath of Fintan's death had brought a change. Conal had shown vulnerability and because of it, Ruadhan felt as close to his guardian as he had ever done. Conal sat down wearily, cleared his throat noisily and spat into the fire.

The sound of Flann's keening broke into their thoughts. It was no longer hysterical screaming and sobbing but a steady, surging wail. The river beyond nudged its way through the stepping stones and sustained a steady murmur to accompany her sorrowing and declare the universality of what had happened. Conal sighed deeply, shuffled closer to the fire, and, with a foot, pushed several scorched brands back into its heart.

"We could sit and crowd our heads with sad thoughts, Ruadhan, but that is not the way of those who lead. I must not be seen to be weak. I will only go so far in sympathising with Flann in her loss." Conal laughed, "*An oak among willows*: Fintan wasn't much when he was alive and now he is no more. He will be given the relevant ceremonies for someone of his status but I cannot allow his death to interfere with what I am trying to do. If I allow it, these people will slide into a slough of grieving and the grieving will go on and the grieving will be an excuse for indolence and indolence will see this place overrun by any armed band no matter how small. That's what will happen. Mark what I say. That's what will happen if I allow it. Cillebairre cannot fail! Cillebairre must grow strong! I don't want them feeling sorry for themselves! It was happening before Fintan's accident; it will be worse now. I won't allow it. There is work to be done and they will do it!"

Conal looked across the fire to where Ruadhan was sitting with his blanket wrapped round him once more. The youth – no, the man - was listening intently, straining forward to catch every word. The light from the fire lit up his features and showed how much they had changed in the year since Conal had returned. His face had lost a lot of its fleshiness and was now long and angular with the high cheekbones and strong chin prominent. His hair looked a deep cherry red in the firelight. Conal had meant to crop it regularly but had forgotten and now, roughly parted in the middle, it hung almost to his shoulders.

Ruadhan was not sure of Conal's mood and whether he really meant what he was saying. There was still that hint of frailty he had never witnessed before; there were arguments going on inside his guardian's head where before there had been unquestioning belief in his mission.

"And what of Ruadhan? Will you stay by my side? Will you watch my back?"

"You have a son now; your own blood."

Conal smiled, "It will be a few years before Cearbhall will carry a sword."

"He will be your warrior."

Conal nodded. "His coming does not mean your going."

"The wind has changed. Carnait looks at me as if I am a stranger."

"She does not rule here."

"You too look at me differently. You know we are not as close."

"As you said, Cearbhall is my blood. You... you came from the forest as many keep reminding me."

"It is better if I go."

"And if I say no?"

"I made a promise to Tulchán."

"Tulchán singled you out and *he* made a promise. He promised you an education. You will learn to write. I was taken roughly from my education when we had to flee Mide and since then most of my learning has been on the battlefield and in the planted fields, woods, mountains and rivers. I read weakness in an enemy's face; I read the freshness of deer spoor; the direction of the wind; the yellowing of the corn; the rightness of wood for the handle of a tool; the temper of a blade in the forge's heat. I know little of the monks' learning but I have respect, Ruadhan. I can hold a story in my head and I can tell that story. Others might remember it but it is likely that when I die, the story dies too. The monks do more, much more. They capture the stories in the letters they write and the books they make, capture them so that they cannot die. The strange marks mean little to you or me but, if you know those letters, you know the stories especially those of the God who came to earth. The books are important. Even I know that. They have to be saved. Tulchán was a wise man, a prophet. He would not have entrusted anybody with the Psalter."

The words were meant to calm Ruadhan, but they did the opposite. He began to feel and resent a great burden of expectations resting on him and prompting him from beyond the grave. He pulled the blanket closer around him. He knew from the dream that he had to fulfil the task Tulchán had entrusted to him. He would take the Psalter to Clonmacnoise. Then he hoped that would put an end to his *specialness*. He was not like Conal. To grow quietly and not be singled out was what he wanted. He shivered in spite of the fire.

"You're tired. You should sleep."

To himself, he had vowed that he would sit awake with Conal through the night. So many thoughts were running through his head that Ruadhan thought sleep impossible. Nevertheless, he lay down in his blanket. Conal crossed, squatted and placed a hide on top of him. Ruadhan wanted to stay silent but the words came without any bidding: "I must go soon to Clonmacnoise. I must take the Psalter. I must go as soon as possible." Ruadhan related the dream once more in detail was startled by Conal's reaction.

"That was a strange dream, Ruadhan, a compelling dream." The words came sluggishly from his mouth but he agreed wearily that the journey should be made soon. The sun was leaving them. Winter would be upon them before long and travelling would be difficult.

"We shall talk more of this, but you must sleep now. I shall stay awake, mourn Fintan and decide what to do with Flann." As an afterthought, he added, "I will lose a warrior, a good one, one who taught Ruarcc a lesson." Conal laughed, "Not one that fool will learn from. There are no such lessons." He stood, "You will need a good weapon. You cannot travel without a weapon. If you go, I shall make you a good blade, a sword, not heavy and long, but light, and well-balanced with a carefully crafted pommel. Easy to travel with and easy to use in battle. You are lithe and quick. I know the sword for you."

Ruadhan's words rushed out of him, did not seem to be his own but were the right ones. "No! A knife, that's all. A knife to cut my food with. Nothing else." Tulchán had never carried a weapon. The monk was speaking through him and he expected a sharp retort from the one who had trained him to use spear, sword and axe; the one who believed he had shaped the warrior Ruadhan.

"That would be foolish," was all Conal muttered.

Ruadhan turned on to his left side, the position he favoured when trying to sleep. Conal had not fully sanctioned his going but neither had he opposed it. He began to feel sleep's soft hand stroking him. Hunched over the fire, Conal spoke in a low voice.

"Fighting comes easily to me, Ruadhan. Be a man of peace if you want, but be warned; it is the harder path to travel." He paused and then laughed quietly, "I would have enjoyed working the forge."

Poison

The following day, Ruadhan found Ite minding sheep on the lower slopes of Wolf's Head Hill. She had cut herself a pole of hazel wood and sharpened it to make a simple spear which she was throwing at a target on the ground made from a circle of stones. Ruadhan smiled. *She* was the warrior. Her aim was better than his. She did not see him approach through the stubby thicket of goat willow that edged the riverbank. He stopped and watched her. Each time she flexed her body to throw, her breasts were thrust forward and Ruadhan's gaze was drawn to them. He felt a need touch those breasts that was as strong as the baby, Cearbhall's was to suck on his mother's. Each time she ran to retrieve her spear, Ruadhan urged her to go faster, turn and get back to her throwing place, a spot that she had marked by scuffing the grass. When she took her stance, Ruadhan felt her thigh muscles stiffen. When she eased her body backwards; Ruadhan imagined he was pressing against her. When her breasts pushed out, Ruadhan held them firmly. Then it started. It came from nowhere. Turmoil. He began to shake. His vision blurred. His mind clouded, pushing out the images of Ite and his chest heaved as he tried to calm himself. A loud hissing sound grew in volume in his right ear. He could not control his breathing. The *strangeness* was coming over him again. He squatted down out of sight and gulped air into his lungs. Ite must not see him like that. Never. He tried to slow his breathing; clear his mind. How? He looked hard at the nearest magenta bloom on the raceme of a tall plant he had partly crushed as he knelt, looked until it came into focus. A bee looped from flower to flower, probing each one. Ruadhan swallowed hard. He was breathing more slowly! His head was clearing. The bee left the flower. The *strangeness* was not going to happen. As he made to stand up, he heard a soft *whoosh* as Ite's spear arced through the willow he was hiding behind, scraped his calf and embedded itself in the soil close to his left foot.

"Come out! Show yourself! I have a knife!"

Ruadhan stood and pulled Ite's makeshift spear out of the ground as he did so. "You have no knife."

"Why were you hiding?"

"I wasn't. I... I needed to piss."

"You were watching me."

Ruadhan nodded. "You make me different."

"What do you mean?"

"Looking at you. My body changes... and my head."

"You're not looking at me now."

Ruadhan turned away from her. He was confused. Being in the depths of one of his fits would be better. He stared at the ground. A large beetle scuttled over his toes.

Any anxiety that her face had shown disappeared and Ite smiled as if she ruled a great city of secrets and held the keys to unlock every door in that city and Ruadhan's confusion along with them. "We will lie together soon, Ruadhan."

"We lay together at Na Lámha."

"Then we were children playing."

Ite led the way up the slope away from the river to a rocky ledge where they could sit and see all the sheep. Ruadhan was quiet. He had resolved to tell her that soon he would leave. Ite knew of the Psalter and of Clonmacnoise but could not conceive of a world larger than the short stretch of the valley that she had grown up in. Neither, until that moment, had she thought of any reason for leaving the place. Ite had convinced herself that Ruadhan would stay in the valley and now he was telling her of a dream, one that, he said, compelled him to go to the great monastery. "I'll come with you."

This idea had never come to Ruadhan. The mission had been given to him alone. Would it be right for him to take Ite? What would Tulchán have thought? Part of him argued that this should not be a matter of choice but the rest of him believed that taking the Psalter to Clonmacnoise had to be a solitary task; that all his concentration should be on the Psalter. *The Word must be preserved. It is the mind of God.* Ite noticed his uncertainty.

"You don't want me to come with you, do you?"

"I... I didn't think such a thing could happen. Tulchán..."

"Well it can," said Ite.

Carnait had carried the baby slung in front of her and left the house empty when she went to the river late in the day but her arms ached and so she had placed him hastily on the bed when she went back for water a second time. There was nothing to be concerned about. The baby had taken milk and was sleepy. And Ruadhan was there. He had returned from the warriors' compound and was pressing new reeds into the thatch.

Flann, in the third day of her fast, sat silent, weak and unmoving outside the entrance, a vigil broken only by Fintan's burial.

Cearbhall was not quiet for long. He woke and cried. He kept crying. Ruadhan left his work and lifted him from Conal and Carnait's bed but could not comfort him. The baby's face looked ready to burst with crying. Several women nearby heard and came to see to the child. One of them offered her breast but Cearbhall screamed louder and beat at it with his little hands. Ruadhan ran for Carnait.

Not even she could quieten him. "I will lie with him. That usually soothes him."

Carnait placed her baby on the bed but immediately lifted him back again as her hands were pricked and scratched through the blanket. She freed a hand and pulled the cover back. Several blackthorn branches had been stuffed among the rushes.

Still holding him close to her Carnait swiftly undressed her baby. Red spots covered his small body and Ruadhan could see where some of the long thorns had snapped and were embedded in the flesh. Carnait's screams were so fierce that word soon reached Conal and brought him back across the river from the tower.

Nuadu the *liaige* [6] was sent for. He was puzzled but nodded confidently when he was told of the blackthorn branches. He left and returned quickly with herbal poultices to apply. Cearbhall continued to scream and writhe in Carnait's arms. His skin became cold and clammy. Conal felt useless. He wanted to hold the babe but thought his rough hands would bring more discomfort and pain. The roof and walls of the house seemed to be closing in and squeezing the air out. Conal found it hard to breathe. His great physical strength and determination meant nothing at that moment. "Do something, Nuadu! You are the healer!"

Nuadu asked for the branches to be brought back from where they had been thrown. Ruadhan fetched them, then went back outside, and walked aimlessly along the riverbank hoping that when he returned health would have been restored to Cearbhall and peace to the home. He too felt inadequate in the face of the child's suffering. In the house, Nuadu examined the branches closely, rubbing a finger and thumb along the thorns. They came away coated with a thin residue. He smelt it once, twice

---

[6] *physician*

and looked puzzled. "Try to cool and calm the child," was all he said and left.

In spite of their attention death came quickly to the baby. Not long after nightfall, under the poultice, the places where the thorns had penetrated Cearbhall's flesh turned a vivid black. The poison travelled leaving red trails and creating strange red blooms over the rest of his small body. Carnait tried with cold wet cloths to lower the baby's high fever but failed. He screamed continuously and his small heart beat like the writhings of an insect trying frantically to escape a spider's web. At the door to the house a crowd of women stood silent and almost motionless waiting for the end. Flann joined them for a moment. "My fasting is over," she said quietly, then left.

"He is the one! He is cursed!" screeched Carnait. She should never have left the child. She knew that and blamed herself but that alone was not the cause of his death.

Conal jeered, "He is cursed! You are cursed! We are all cursed! What do the monks call it? Original Sin."

"He carries ill luck with him. Many will testify to that."

"If you believe that why did you leave him alone with our child?"

"I had to return to the river and I... I was away for such a short time. I never thought..."

"You have others to do that for you! You left. With Flann outside our door! Did you leave our son alone at other times?"

A distraught Carnait did not want to be questioned by Conal. Her mind swirled. Flann? Ruadhan? Whether or not he had placed the *draighean*, the cursed boy had brought ill luck to their house. Why was he so favoured? What was he to Conal? Nothing. "He should have gone from this place the moment our child was born. He is not of our blood and there are many stories of his powers."

Conal sneered, "What powers? We all have power enough to stuff blackthorn in a bed. He has been alone with Cearbhall many times and nothing ill came the child's way."

"Perhaps one of those fits you have witnessed came upon him; times when he is possessed."

"I have had devils inside *my* head that have urged me join you and others with idle tongues who would blame Ruadhan for every misfortune that comes Cillebairre's way and right now I have devils telling me to make you suffer for your neglect of my son but I refuse to listen to them. For that you should be eternally grateful. This evil came from Flann and will be answered."

"Kill them both! If you are a true man; if you are a true father, kill them both!"

Nuadu visited Conal's house one more time that night to tell him that he was certain now that the thorns on the blackthorn branches had been smeared with aconite, a deadly poison.

Earlier on that same day, Ruarcc watched Ite walk along the riverbank. She and a few children were driving a dozen sheep to graze on Wolf's Head Hill south of the settlement. The children would go to the hill and return while Ite would mind the sheep on her own for several hours. Ruarcc slipped into the forest. Eagerly anticipating the encounter, he ran swiftly for a heavy man up the slopes and through the trees. This girl was a temptress and he would now crop the harvest her wiles had sown.

When she saw him coming, Ite stood and firmly gripped the club she carried. She knew what he wanted. "It happens," the old women said. "It is the way things are. They will do it and you will give way and accept it." For a moment he stood smiling a few metres from her. Ite did not show the fear that rippled through her being. This angered Ruarcc and a snarl replaced the smile. He stepped towards her. She swung at him with the club. He stepped back and circled her. He moved towards her again; she swung at him again but this time too forcefully and almost toppled. He dodged the blow and rushed in before Ite could regain her balance and bring her arm and the club back to a fighting position. Ruarcc's violation of Ite was brutal. He quickly disarmed her and pinned her to the ground, a forearm across her neck. With his other arm he reached for Ite's most private part and spread her crudely with his large, rough fingers. Ite did not accept the wisdom of the old women. She resisted fiercely but, although spirited and tough, she had no answer to that man's strength. He pounded her cruelly. Ite beat at him and screamed her throat raw until he clamped a hand over her mouth and dug his nails deeply into her cheek. She felt blood trickling to her neck. Still she punched and tried to kick but her strength waned and he thrust and thrust inside her and her body went limp and she imagined her red-haired Ruadhan and how she had wanted it to be with him and not like this, not this... this fury... this hatred... this stabbing. Ite remembered something else the old women had said and her last thought before losing consciousness was that, since it had been such a foul act from which she had taken no pleasure, it was not possible that a baby would shape itself inside her.

Ruarcc raped Ite, strangled her to unconsciousness, broke her neck and threw her body into the same bog that Feach's body had been pulled from on that fateful day Conal and that band of Northmen first visited the valley.

Brother Duach, though not a *brehon*[7], had received training in law and was told by Conal to lead the questioning. He did not want the job but there was a lot of agitation in the settlement over Cearbhall's death and Ite's disappearance and so he had accepted the position and started gathering evidence. Flann never moved from the place she had chosen for her fast. That was the testimony of two women, friends of hers, who said they had been with her while Carnait was absent from the house. Ruadhan had gone to Wolf's Head Hill the day Ite disappeared claimed a fellow-warrior. There was a consensus in the community. Ruadhan was responsible for both deaths (most had concluded that Ite had been murdered). For some, this was vindication of how they had regarded this person, no, this creature, since the day he had crawled whining from the dense forest. Duach felt the weight of great responsibility upon his shoulders. He was the dispenser of the greatly respected laws which had accrued through thousands of judgements down several centuries. In his training he had read many legal texts but not enough to equip him to assess the present cases. Besides, that reading was many years ago and he was not certain he could recall much of it. He would pray for guidance, for the wisdom of Solomon, and call upon his common sense and what he believed to be his sharp assessment of character. In dwelling upon these matters, Duach recalled a visit to the scriptorium made by Tulchán and Ruadhan. The boy had been quiet, polite and serious, *intense* was perhaps a better description. Tulchán had believed in him; that said a lot. Ascertain the facts and judge accordingly, Duach told himself. Do not be influenced by rumour, by superstition and by depositions that are tainted through close relationships such as those women had with Flann and by pleasant

---

[7] *Judge*

memories of a fellow-monk who was an inspiration to many. The boy divided the community, more so since Tulchán's death. Duach had never sided with the "Of the Devil" faction but Ruadhan's unfortunate birth and upbringing could not grant him immunity from the sanctions of the law. Duach shivered involuntarily as he thought of what he had to do. He feared that the young man might be dealt with summarily if he did not intervene and show clear leadership. It was not to be contemplated. He called Ruadhan to the empty church.

"You admit that you used to meet her in that place?"

"Why would I want to deny it?" Ruadhan snapped.

"Please do not become aggressive towards me," said Duach softly. "It will not serve your cause."

Ruadhan didn't know he had a "cause". All he knew was that Ite was seen last by the children who had accompanied her to the pasture below Wolf's Head Hill, the place he used to meet her. That day, before attending to the thatch, he had been sent to the forge with Eoin and Corraidhín to see a sword being shaped for the first-named. Conal believed that the closer you were to a weapon from its origins in stone to the times you wielded it in the heat of a fight, the more likely you were to use it effectively. If you knew its struggle to emerge from the earth; if you took some part in that struggle, the mining, the smithing, the more likely you were to overcome *your* own feeble origins in the dirt.

"As a soldier, you are subject to certain rules. You broke those rules."

"I did not meet her that day."

"You were seen following her."

"I did not meet her that day."

"You are calling someone a liar?"

"Who said I went there?"

"They claim not to be alone in seeing you go there."

"Whoever said I went there is, without doubt, a liar."

"Perhaps you were unable to control yourself. Perhaps you were corrupted by lust. Women can exert..."

"I did not go there!"

"I can admit to being tormented by desire of a woman, aching to such a degree that I had to inflict the harshest of physical discipline on my body in order to control myself."

"I did not go there!"

"Did you suffer a convulsion? Perhaps one of those strange episodes overwhelmed you so that you did not know what you were doing?"

"I did not go there! I did not meet Ite!"

"I have a judgement to make, Ruadhan. We will return to this. For now, we will pray."

Conal sat inside the church with his back against a wall. With the death of his son and now this accusation pointed at the one whom he had held as close as a son, Conal was drained of energy. He closed his eyes and clenched his teeth firmly in an attempt to contain the grief and anger that had overcome him. Neither would serve him or Cillebairre well. He could not surrender to this personal tragedy. He had to act. Usually his decisions were like his sword thrusts, forceful and direct. The thought quickly became the act. Answers were found in action. Now, nothing was clear in his mind. Now, his body felt limp and vulnerable, incapable of decisive effort. The *law*... the *law*. If harm had been done to Ite it was not by Ruadhan, of that he was sure. Conal should have acted swiftly to deny the *law* this pointless questioning of him. He should have acted to suppress all suspicions, and all the foul *he is cursed* accusations that once again coursed through Cillebairre like the poison that had flooded Cearbhall's body. And Flann who he should have punished had disappeared, escaped, Cearbhall's death on her hands. Even if she did not smear the aconite or place the blackthorn she knew of it and had, more than likely, directed the act. Conal would be mocked for his leniency, his weak leadership. Now, Carnait's keening had replaced Flann's. Day and night she raved over the death of her child.

Conal quit the church and forced himself to act. He banished Carnait from his bed and sent her to sleep in another house. Ruadhan, he sent from the settlement. "You must go away. There are some who would get rid of you, who have always wanted rid of you and, in my present state, I may not be able to curb them. They are cowards and have skulked in the background until now. Today they crawl from there into the shadow cast by Ruarcc. He has a faction to lead and not just against you. I am no fool. He seeks my downfall."

"I did not kill her, Conal."

"Some men in the tempest of lust are capable of terrible evil but not you. Tell me, who was with you at the forge?"

"Eoin and Corraidhín."

"Ruarcc was not there?"

Ruadhan nodded.

"A day of reckoning will come but not just yet. I never thought anything would shake me as Cearbhall's death has done. From a height, in a far eastern land, I once watched a sudden flood after a storm. It raged along a dry valley destroying all in its way. Those who survived walked in circles, contemplating the destruction, wondering why they suffered so, dazed in what had become an alien land. That is how I feel. It will pass but while it is on me, I am defenceless and so are you. I will become the Conal you know once more but I don't know when. Until that time, I may not be able to protect you. Make yourself a shelter in the forest but hide it well. I will come for you as soon as I have laid my son in the ground. You will go to Clonmacnoise and we must make preparations. You have my permission and my blessing."

Ruadhan did as he was told and entered the sanctuary of the forest once more. As he was always being reminded, he was a child of that place. It held no fears for him and neither did solitude. Before sleep on the first night in a hollow formed by the muscular roots of an oak tree, he recalled the time spent close by Na Lámha with Ite. Was she alive? If so, where was she? Would he ever see her again? Would he ever hold her close and once more know those strange, wonderful eruptions of his mind and body?

A grave was dug for Cearbhall and lined, on Conal's insistence, with stone slabs. When the child was placed therein, Eoin offered his new sword and Conal placed it diagonally on top of his son, the warrior's shrouded body.

It is Time

"I could have clubbed you into unconsciousness before you knew I was here."

Conal found what he thought was Ruadhan's hiding place and, to startle him with another lesson in survival, crept close. Ruadhan had shaped grass and branches under a spare blanket to make it seem like someone was sleeping there. He startled Conal from behind. The older man smiled broadly when he turned and, as he looked at Ruadhan, he saw a warrior of sorts, a young man becoming hardened and alert to the dangers that were everywhere; a warrior regardless of the fact that he would not carry a weapon.

"Look, Ruadhan, I have brought you something."

Conal pulled the Psalter from a satchel he was carrying. Ruadhan smiled and nodded, "So, it is time?"

"Come, we have work to do."

It was just before noon when they reached the quiet stretch of the river where Brother Kevin had built his boats.

"It will make a change from lifting stones and from twisting my mind all ways to find sense in recent events," Conal said. "This is work we shall do on our own, Ruadhan. I have forbidden everyone except Duach to come here. He knows I am with you and he knows what is planned. He muttered some words about the law but will not interfere. There are others, one in particular, who will be curious, others who know a day of reckoning is not far off."

"Ruarcc?"

"Yes, the one who testified falsely against you and who is corrupting Cillebairre against me. If he has any sense or someone close to him has sense and tells him, he will flee this valley. That would slow the reckoning but not cancel it. A stupid, baneful man."

The frame of bent, tied and weighted hazel rods was still where Brother Kevin had left it, upturned and unfinished, when the Northmen raided. Signs of interrupted work were all around: a bowl half-full of wool grease; a bronze cooking pot; a pile of ox hides tanned and trimmed of leg and shoulder skin; a truss of long leather thongs; a heavily rusted knife with a blade thin from great use; two awls, a bone needle, strong flax thread and even, so anxious had the monk been to flee the Northmen, his sandals. Tall grasses and nettles had speared their way upwards through

138

the framework of the craft but the wood was undamaged. Conal pulled at the hides and turned them over, revealing a large patch of flattened pale yellow grass.

"Tulchán had some gift of prophecy, that's for sure. You say he knew he was going to die, don't you? And you say he brought you here? Perhaps he also knew you would travel in this coracle."

Ruadhan was not pleased to be reminded of his friend's death. "He knew his death was close," was all he replied.

"You cannot travel by land. There is fighting not far from us. A succession dispute, and every minor chieftain who can hold a sword is out roaming the country with his soldiers to see what he can plunder in the chaos. Monasteries have been attacked; they are no sanctuaries for anyone, it is said. Brother Colm passed through the region south of us a few days ago and saw smoke rising from two razed settlements. Anyone he saw on the road either hid from him or questioned him suspiciously and threateningly. You will travel by rivers and sea."

Conal separated the hides and held each one up to inspect. Huge slugs adhered to the underside of the bottom one. "Kevin knew his work. Look: well tanned with oak bark. Check them for holes. Do it slowly and carefully. I'll see to the frame. Remember, your life will depend on this leather and those poles. Brendan had three wrappings of leather. You have only one but it will serve you well enough for your voyage."

They set to work with a will and as if by an unspoken agreement, never mentioned Cearbhall or Ite although their minds were filled with thoughts of them. Ruadhan examined the hides on the ground for rips and holes and then crawled underneath each one to see if any light penetrated. If she was alive, he couldn't leave without seeing her, perhaps taking her with him as she had said. A few small holes had been eaten at the edges of the hide that lay on the grass but, otherwise, they were flawless. Following more instructions from Conal, Ruadhan placed stones, set and lit a fire in the middle of them, put the bronze pot on the flames and then, after pouring a year's rainfall from the top of the bowl, ladled handfuls of the foul smelling wool grease into the pot. Ite could not be dead. There was so much energy in her.

"Not too much flame," Conal advised, while he continued inspecting the poles to see that they were bound tightly together where they crossed. "Heat it gently to make it easier to apply. When it's right, rub

139

it well into the hides." He had to avenge Cearbhall's death. He knew that spending this time with Ruadhan was neglect of duty, a running away. If a thong was frayed, no matter how slightly, he untied it and chose a new one from the truss. His warrior son had been taken from him. He tested each length by wrapping the ends around his hands and pulling them apart with his great strength. If it was sound, he soaked it in the river water for a few moments and then fastened it tightly around the join. To honour his son's memory, Conal he knelt down to help Ruadhan.

The afternoon soon went by. Conal stopped rubbing the grease into the hides and stood up. "Leave them, Ruadhan. We have done enough. Let's get this mess off us." He pulled at the long grass until he had a handful to wipe the grease from his hands. "Eat. We must eat. And trample a bed in the bracken on the slope down to the little stream that feeds the river beyond those alder trees. We have no need of shelter. The night will be dry. From there we can keep an eye on the work here but be hidden from anyone seeking to do us harm. Tomorrow, we'll put the hides on the frame and do the sewing. It's hard work. Your fingers will be like a boar's tusk before this work is over. I'll clean and sharpen the awls. Finish tomorrow and then you're ready to row from here."

The work had been hard but Ruadhan was more than satisfied with the slow tempo of the day and the simple, mostly silent strengthening of his relationship with Conal. In the night that followed his mind would not let the work go: overlap the hides; stab with the awl; bring it back slowly and follow it from the other side with the threaded needle before the leather closes over the hole; pull the thread as taut as you can on each stitch. *A boar's tusk*: his hands were calloused from the needle and awl and hatched with cuts from the tough thread.

Early on the third morning, Ruadhan prepared to leave Cillebairre. The vessel looked frail and vulnerable - little more than a piece of eggshell - even on the calm water of the river. Through wishful thinking and after the hard work, Ruadhan had expected something more substantial. Conal climbed into and stood in the coracle on the water, balanced carefully. He bent over checking once more that the thongs binding the frame were tied securely. The little boat bobbled dangerously as he shifted his weight. "It's a good, strong boat, Ruadhan, and there's enough grease on the hides to keep out all the sea around Ireland."

Ruadhan nodded a reply. He did not want to leave. The days and nights spent with Conal had brought him closer to his guardian than he had ever been and that man's strength and conviction had started to run in his veins. And there was Ite.

As if he knew Ruadhan's thoughts, Conal spoke of her. "She has not returned, Ruadhan. Believe me, Ite is dead. I know who killed her. But I *have* returned. I will bring Cillebairre to its senses. Try to empty your mind of Ite. Justice will be done. Leave that to me and God, and..." Conal smiled broadly. "And, of course, Duach, the *brehon*."

Ruadhan felt afraid but did not admit it. A warrior shouldn't, should he? There was anxiety about travelling on the water and venturing into new places but there was the greater worry that he might not be able to fulfil his mission. He felt resentful of Tulchán for placing such a responsibility on his shoulders and confessed this.

At first, Conal did not know how to respond. Vacillation: the one who was spending so much time brooding over the death of Cearbhall and neglecting to do what needed to be done answered Ruadhan by telling him, "Just *do*, and don't waste time brooding." He paused, remembered something fitting and found more words. "I have watched Northmen initiating youngsters into adulthood, Ruadhan. They made a rope hammock between two trees and fastened the young man into it with his arms and legs tied. They then lit a huge fire beneath him. It quickly snarled upwards, scorching him and snapping at the ropes until it severed them and the young man tumbled into its jaws. He rolled away. He had burns and bruises but he was smiling because he knew others would now see him as an adult. Things had changed. This journey is your fire; your initiation. It will change you. It will confirm you as a man."

The coracle bucked violently and water splashed inside as Conal stepped clumsily out of it and into the river. He had found words for Ruadhan but whether they were the right ones, he did not know. As he stood in the river, he sensed loss once again. Another son was being taken from him. *See how Jesus suffered on the Cross*, Duach had told him, *and Mary, who also lost her son*. Even though he felt it, Conal would not express his sadness. It would not help this youth to grow. Among the Northmen, there were always boats leaving the villages and partings had been many. Men fought for the privilege of going in the longships and were not going to shed foolish tears as they left. And yet - perhaps the company of too many children and women in this place had softened him - Conal was going to miss Ruadhan. He looked at the bottom of the coracle and found a distraction. "Of course, you will get some water coming over the sides and spilling from your oar into the boat, but don't worry. Row to the river bank if too much gets in, and tip the coracle upside down."

"And the sea, Conal?"

"The sea?"

"Has the sea banks like the river?"

Conal smiled broadly. Ruadhan had never encountered the sea. "The sea you are going to has only one bank that I know of, Ruadhan, and you will stay close to it for your journey. I have always found the sea a friendly rogue; an acquaintance you like but are never sure you should trust, one who might take advantage of you if you let him. On every voyage I took, except for the last, it made promises to return me to my people, promises it never kept. Try not to fear the sea; if you do, it will notice your anxiety and take advantage of you." Conal snatched the side of the coracle and in one motion pulled it out of the water, turned it upside down and held it over his head revelling in the display of his strength. Water fell to his cheek and trickled slowly down his chin to his shoulder. Ruadhan froze then almost shouted out loud in terror as what he was looking at became a vision of Ite with a bloodied face and what seemed like a boulder being brought down over and over again on her body. He shuddered. Conal lowered the boat to the water and did not see Ruadhan's distress.

"She *is* dead," Ruadhan shouted.

Conal looked hard at his young companion. Why this now? He felt a slight surge of anger with Ruadhan but also with himself for the mawkishness of recent days. "Yes, I think she is but whether she is or not, she has gone from you and you have a task ahead of you. Listen to me. If there is too much water inside, make for the shore and empty the boat. You do not know the sea, but at times, if you are not far enough out, you will find that it pushes you back to the shore, telling you that that is where you really belong."

Conal reached to the bank for two leather bags and slung them into the coracle. "Even men on holy missions need to eat, Ruadhan. There's oatcake, barley bread, cheese, eggs and salt pork. Fill the empty one with water, fill it well before the sea starts mixing with the river." He had said all this before and now, by repeating it, showed his reluctance to lose the company of his young friend. "Go, Ruadhan. Go now. By the third day you should sight the place where the greatest river in Ireland meets the sea. You will leave the sea for this river. Its mouth is huge and its water flows long into the ocean. You will know it. Go now! The sun has barely risen and you have plenty of daylight ahead of you. You will know the sea well before nightfall."

With the satchel containing the Psalter hanging from his shoulder, Ruadhan stepped from the bank and joined Conal at the edge of the water. They searched each other's faces for emotion, Conal's big and hard with a strong growth of beard, Ruadhan's thin and still forming with its sproutings of bristle. They embraced briefly. "God speed your boat," the older man said.

As Ruadhan stepped gingerly into the coracle, Conal, for the first time wondered if this venture was wise. He steadied and held the craft as Ruadhan, still trying too hard to be careful and clutching the heavy Psalter closely, sat down clumsily and made it lurch away from the bank. Conal's hand felt the thick smearing of grease he had put over the leather and the poles, and doubt, that rare and unwelcome visitor, needled its way into his mind once more. He wondered if the coracle was adequate. After all, he had never made a boat before, and even though he understood the theory, he might have made a mistake, a mistake which could cost Ruadhan his life. Had he been over-confident, rashly believing that whatever he turned his hand to, he could do? The round tower was a failure: could the coracle be another? Conal shivered inwardly at the thought, but did not communicate his anxiety to Ruadhan. One boy had died from burns received when he tumbled from his initiation hammock. "I know you are eager to go, Ruadhan, but have you not forgotten something?"

Ruadhan looked about the small craft and then at the riverbank. He had the Psalter and food. Conal was wrong. "I don't think I have," he replied.

"And you the great sailor who would be twice round Ireland before the rest of us are off our beds tomorrow morning!" Conal pushed the coracle away from the bank, laughing as he did so. The boat shook violently and then settled in the gentle flow of the water at the meander. Ruadhan was puzzled at this parting and nervous now that he was on his own on the river. He placed the Psalter in the bottom of the coracle and looked for an oar to steer with. Conal walked along the bank. An oar! The boat could not find its own way to Clonmacnoise! What a fool Conal must think him. In all the preparations, he had not once thought of an oar. He looked to Conal on the bank and could not help smiling back when he saw a grinning face and the oar brandished above it.

Conal shouted: "Now you've remembered, have you?" He jumped down from the bank once more and waded out, holding the oar high. The water was up to his chest when he reached the coracle. For a moment, Conal the man of strength, of action, looked as excited as a child and full of emotion: "Oak, they said, make it of the oak's heartwood so that the ocean's strongest currents cannot break it. I did not listen to them, Ruadhan. I listened instead to my memories of an old boat builder among the Northmen and made your oar from a solitary mountain ash. This came from the right tree; a tall and proud tree that stood alone amid barren scree; one that, from the bursting of the seed, struggled to survive in meagre soil and vicious winds. Your oar comes from that royal tree, as strong as oak but lighter. Think of that tree, Ruadhan, think of its struggle and its triumph."

The river carried Ruadhan slowly towards the southwest, the sea and his future. He had never considered that future closely. He had a task to perform and once that was done, other tasks would be put before him. Tulchán had spoken of doing God's will but Ruadhan could never really understand what was meant by this. "Love God and love others," Tulchán taught him. Was he doing that by taking the Psalter to Clonmacnoise? Perhaps it would become clearer at that great monastery. Perhaps there he would be given more signs that he was doing God's will. Tulchán had said he would receive an education there but Ruadhan knew that it would be very unusual for someone of his obscure origins to be granted such a privilege. He released one of his hands from the oar and reached out to touch the tightly bound package in the bottom of the boat. Immediately, the beauty of the Psalter's pages burst into his imagination like those pictures that came with the *strangeness* but with this vision he felt calmed and reassured. Doing God's will. Ruadhan returned the free hand to the oar and began stroking steadily, on one side and then the other, in the quiet water. The rhythm of the simple action satisfied something within and the loneliness he had anticipated on the riverbank left him.

He passed no other settlements on his way and the only sign of human life he saw was smoke rising from a distant encampment by a forest. The river hardly altered its sedate pace, but gradually broadened as it neared the sea until, to Ruadhan, it seemed wider than the whole valley of Cillebairre. He steered away from midstream and nervously kept the coracle close to the south bank. The land on both sides was flat and stony. Soon the only trees in sight were stunted and wind-blown ones standing on their own. They all leaned spectacularly away from the sea as if telling Ruadhan to return to his home.

The river took one final long curve before it met the sea. Waves broke beyond a thin, curling finger of coastland that forced the river south. He thought of rowing for the bank in order to eat, but admitted to himself that he was not hungry and that stopping would be an excuse for delaying his first encounter with the sea. He kept rowing down the estuary.

On that first day of his journey to the monastery of Clonmacnoise, Ruadhan met and became acquainted with a friendly sea. At first the breakers frightened him, and he was sure the coracle was going to capsize as it headed into them, but beyond the surf, his confidence grew. The bobbing of the craft on the sea was more marked than it had been on the river, but he quickly became used to it and, at one point when he rested from rowing, he was almost lulled to sleep by the regular dipping and rising. The sea was a friend helping him on his way and the muffled slaps of its waves on the coracle were words of encouragement. Ruadhan headed south. Initially, his progress was slow and the rowing, which he was unused to, was hard but his body responded well, the action became familiar and the boat moved at a steady pace. The low land of the estuary was replaced gradually by a rugged grey-black coastline fretted into rocky bays and headlands. When the ache in his arms became too much and when the sun was low in the sky and the air cooling rapidly, Ruadhan decided to go ashore for the night. Until that moment, fearful of the sea's vastness, he had avoided looking westward. Now he glanced furtively to where the sun seemed to be drowning in the sea and was certain he heard a sharp hissing just like at Cillebairre forge when red hot iron is pulled from the fire and thrust into the cold water vat. He looked away, breathed deeply and heard only the constant soughing of the calm seawater as it lapped the boat's sides.

Calm and Storm

Before the sun had fully set Ruadhan found a broad, calm bay with few rocks to snag his fragile boat. He was among the breakers before he spotted a small fishing settlement, some huts and upturned boats, just above the shoreline at the northern end of the bay. Three men came out of the huts to see who their visitor was and, for a moment, Ruadhan wondered if he should have taken Conal's advice and carried a weapon. "Be on guard; always on guard," Conal had told him. "Do not trust until you are sure of your company." It was too late to change his mind. He jumped clumsily into the surf and dragged the boat up the beach. The Psalter. Quickly, he knelt and digging furiously, scooped a hole in the sand to bury it. That done, he turned the boat upside down over the hiding place.

A giant of a man and his two grown sons, all carrying long-handled clubs, reached Ruadhan just as he finished doing this. All three were dressed roughly in vests and trousers of sackcloth and the father also wore a sheepskin jacket. One son, like his father, had long, dark, unkempt hair but the other, who limped badly, had red hair and a fair complexion. The father said something about Northmen and they all laughed. Ruadhan was no threat. They were friendly but very curious and as they took him past the long, sleek *currachs* they questioned him. Why was he on the sea alone? Where had he come from and where was he going? Ruadhan did not speak of the Psalter but told them he had been sent to Clonmacnoise to be of service to the monks there.

The rough thatch of one hut seeped smoke and the stench of drying fish. Freshly scraped sealskins were draped over large rocks nearby. The mother cooked large lumps of the seal meat on sticks over a fire and the other member of the family, a young woman, sewed seasoned sealskins together. The girl turned away shyly when Ruadhan passed but her red-haired brother caught her attention and pointed to the cause of his limp, a serious gash on his thigh. "I need the needle more than they do," he said.

She left the skins and attended to him. With the others watching in silence, he stood stiffly and clenched his teeth in readiness as she, without a word, splashed seawater over his leg and then knelt to sew adroitly the edges of the wound together. When she was done, she turned back to the skins and the red-haired brother flexed and unflexed the leg several times. She had done well.

The men took Ruadhan into the largest of the huts, which had reeds covering the earth floor and a small fire burning at the centre. They were not going to go back to their work. They had a guest and in return for shelter and food, the stranger was going to entertain them that evening by telling them about his home and the people there. As fisherfolk they knew little of any other place except their bay and the coast half a day's rowing to the north and half a day's rowing to the south. Occasionally they carried fish inland to exchange for corn and meat with farmers, and sometimes people came to the bay to trade, but for most of the year, they lived in isolation fishing only to feed themselves. An unexpected visitor like this was very special. In return for their hospitality they wanted his stories.

Ruadhan told them about Cillebairre. His sharpest memory was of the Northmen's raid and he was about to speak of it when the red-haired son clambered awkwardly to his feet.

"You know very little of the sea, visitor. The tide tonight will take your boat if we leave it where it is."

Ruadhan's thoughts immediately went to the Psalter. He scrambled out of the hut and followed the limping red-haired son along the beach in the dull-metal grey of the evening. The sea was still lapping languidly several metres from the coracle when they reached it. The fisherman lifted the boat with the same ease Conal had done, placed it on his head and carried it from the sand on to pebbles and above a distinct shelf the sea had shaped in them. He was puzzled by Ruadhan's digging in the sand and curious to know what was wrapped in the hides the visitor had disinterred.

Back in the hut, his hosts were stern faced and silent. Ruadhan explained as best he could what the Psalter was and why he had buried it. He spluttered an apology for what he had done; he was a stranger; he did not know who was crossing the beach to meet him; he had not meant to insult them in any way. The women brought the cooked meat but no one started eating. Ruadhan told them that the Psalter was a precious treasure, not because it could be exchanged, like gold, for a lot of corn, but because... because it was the Word of God... the One who had come to save us... the son of God. Such words had come easily from Tulchán's lips. For Ruadhan, it was as if strange birds had nested in his mouth. They scrabbled about and eventually flapped their way out but did not seem at ease in the open. "That is why I hid it," he explained. "I was not sure what kind of people would greet me on this shore."

The sons heard only one word, *treasure*, and became excited and angry with Ruadhan. The dark-haired one stood and looked as if he was going to beat their visitor but the father told him harshly to sit down and told them both to be quiet. When they had settled, he spoke to Ruadhan very seriously. He *was* offended that Ruadhan should have been so suspicious of them. However, he knew how precious this thing was. As a boy, water had been poured on him and prayers said by a wandering priest. The priest had had such a book and from it he had told stories of Jesus the Son. Ruadhan was right to protect it. Could Ruadhan baptise his sons? Ruadhan could not but he would open the Psalter and show them wondrous pictures and writing.

"Eat first," the father said, "and then show us."

They ate in silence and when he had taken his fill, Ruadhan asked for water and sand to clean his greasy hands. That done, he unwrapped the Psalter carefully. They made him show every page and gazed, wrapt, at the Psalter's beautiful illustrations. The whorls of colour about one initial letter of script, made the red-haired son think of eels coiled about one another below the quivering surface of the sea. Ruadhan told them what Tulchán had taught him about the Psalms: they were songs written by the people of Israel. In some, they thank God for all they have been given. In others they sing of their sorrows and ask for God's help. These were people who had suffered but no matter what happened to them, they believed, trusted and praised God. From memory, Ruadhan recited number 46, the psalm he had watched Tulchán copy and which the monk had translated into Irish for him: "*God is our shelter, our strength, ever ready in time of trouble...*"

The fisherfolk listened intently and the father nodded his agreement with the lines,

"*So we shall not be afraid when the earth gives way, when the mountains tumble into the depths of the sea, and its waters roar and seethe, the mountains tottering as it heaves.*"

He knew all about roaring and seething sea waters and about trusting in a power greater than himself. More birds fluttered in Ruadhan's mouth. He told them all he knew about Jesus and brought great smiles to their strong, weather-etched features when he said that the first people Jesus asked to follow him fished the sea just as they did.

148

The two women, faces still grimy from the smoke of the cooking fire, overcame their shyness and emerged from their corner to look at Tulchán's work. The girl, Samthann, was not much older than Ruadhan. She was timid and, most of the time, cowered animal-like away from the others. Like most of the family, her hair was a rich black, but, unlike the others, hers was tidily braided. Prominent upper teeth gave a smile to her face even when her lips were turned down. She studied Ruadhan with quick, intelligent, part-frightened eyes, but never let him see her doing so. She was pretty and Ruadhan found *he* wanted to look at her. Was it wrong to look at another as he had looked at Ite? Ite. Was she dead? Had that beast, Ruarcc murdered her? If Ruadhan had stayed at Cillebairre, perhaps in a year or so, there would have been talk of arranging a marriage for him. Even the boy from the forest would be expected to take a wife. If she still lived, would it have been Ite? For a moment, the sight of the shy fishergirl's face through the flickering firelight cleared Ruadhan's mind of anything else and the girl's father had to shake his shoulder roughly to bring his attention back to the Psalter.

It was well past midnight before they let him stop. The father insisted that Ruadhan leave the Psalter open at Psalm 46. As soon as he woke, he wanted to see its beauty in the morning light. It would be safe, he assured Ruadhan. "Treasure. Yes, treasure."

Before they slept, the father told his family that God had sent Ruadhan and that they were all followers of the God of the Cross now because they had heard the Word and seen the pictures. He thanked Ruadhan several times. Ruadhan was exhausted. Tulchán had said that when *he* travelled it was in order to bring the Word of God to people who had not heard it. That evening, he, Ruadhan, the forest-foundling had brought the Word to these fisherfolk. As he lay down on the reeds he heard the girl murmuring something to her mother and the woman laughing quietly in reply. The fire died down quickly and the picture on the page of the open Psalter seemed to glow with its own light.

Ruadhan slept deeply. This was company he could trust. When he woke, he found he was the only one left in the hut and the Psalter had been moved. Had his trust been misplaced? Had he fallen at the first obstacle placed in his path? Ruadhan rushed from the hut. Just outside the entrance, the father sat with the Psalter in his lap. It was still open at the same page and he was gazing at Psalm 46. He had carried the book there in its hide wrappings but had not touched the pages with his large, gnarled hands. He turned to Ruadhan, nodded to show that he was satisfied, and then put the book on the ground for Ruadhan to close and wrap. After watching the visitor carefully folding the sheets of hide around the precious book, the father fetched a length of sealskin. "Put this tightly over all and the sea water will never harm it."

A bleary sun hardly penetrated the thick, cold sea mist that blanketed the whole of the bay. Everyone had rough woollen cloaks over their shoulders. The two sons had already been to check lines they had placed and were pulling bronze hooks from several fish. The women lit a fire and as soon as the men had finished, they scraped the scales off the fish, speared them on thin sticks and cooked them in the flames. Samthann stopped what she was doing and brought Ruadhan a cloak. She handed it over without looking him in the eye and went quickly back to her mother's side.

As they ate, the father rolled his shoulders stiffly a couple of times and then addressed Ruadhan. "The sea is difficult to the south. It is fickle, hard to judge, never the same from one day to the next. It can change its face in an afternoon..." He paused and looked directly at Ruadhan. "It is like a polite, shy stranger invited into a family home who becomes disrespectful and ogles the family's daughter."

Ruadhan was pulling a very hot, charred piece of fish from a stick Samthann had handed him when he heard these words. He could not judge the tone in which they were said. He dropped the gobbet of fish. *Did the father think Ruadhan had been so rude?* He brought his head up slowly and met the man's gaze. The fisherman's face remained impassive for a moment leaving Ruadhan unsure but then it brought him relief as it broke into a great smile. Ruadhan looked around the others. All except the girl were smiling as well. Ruadhan blushed and the girl turned her head away.

"It can become very angry. There are many islands, and channels, with strange, unpredictable, fast-running currents among them. Stay too close to the shore and your boat will be ripped by rocks that are scattered there. Stay too far away from the shore and you will have to fight these restless currents. Take care, young sea-farer."

A short time later, Ruadhan said farewell to the fisherfolk, to all except Samthann who was nowhere to be seen. Once again, conflicting emotions confused him. If they accepted him, it could be a simple matter to stay with these people, be part of a family, test his feelings for the girl and forget about the demands of his *mission*. Who was he to have a *mission*? The father broke into his thoughts by handing him dried fish for the journey. He apologised for having no bread or cheese. "We must visit the farmers once more," he said. Ruadhan breathed deeply and thanked him. He had to go on.

The mist was beginning to break up. Only small patches drifted about the bay. Ruadhan handled the coracle with more confidence than he had done the day before. He pushed it into the water, clambered in and soon had it free of the breakers. The surface was slightly more agitated than on the previous day but Ruadhan quickly settled once again to a steady rhythm with the oar. Back on the shore, what looked like a huge beetle headed for the water as the fishermen hoisted a currach and carried it upside down on their heads. He wondered where the girl was and as he rounded the southern tip of the bay, he saw her. She was on the headland sitting in a small cleft in the rock face where her family could not see her. She watched Ruadhan as he rowed steadily past.

Midday came and Ruadhan's journey had been uneventful. He calculated he had travelled a good distance. The mist had cleared completely and, ahead of him, Ruadhan saw the cluster of islands the father had spoken of. He let the coracle bob in the water while he ate some of the bread Conal had given him. The boat drifted slightly, or so Ruadhan thought, but when he looked towards the islands, he saw that they were much closer. The coracle was caught in one of the strange, fierce currents the father had spoken of and was travelling faster than when he had been rowing. It was as if his boat was trying to outrun the storm that, out of nowhere, was about to break.

At first, the sea was just bothersome and frisky; a petulant child anxious for someone to play with, grabbing at the boat with its small hands. Ruadhan took the oar and tried to row for the shore but realised his strength was no match for this sea's. He was no longer in control of the coracle and another greyness surrounded him as in his dream of Tulchán, a living, writhing greyness that, time and time again, lifted its misshapen hands high above him and then brought them swiftly down to batter the little boat. The sea that had guided Ruadhan, that had been his friendly companion, that had almost lulled him gently to sleep the day before, had been transformed. It was as if a tumour deep within its heart had burst and

151

poison was racing through its bloodstream. It was now a sick and angry friend driven to hate by its pain, pain it could not understand, pain which clouded its mind and drove it to maim and kill.

Ruadhan lay flat and clung to the frame of the boat. He tried to tie one of his wrists to it using the loose ends of the leather thongs that bound the cross-poles together but he and Conal had cut them neatly short. He did succeed in fastening to his ankle one long end of a leather strip that criss-crossed the wrappings round the Psalter. As he did, the boat lurched and reared on the side of a huge wave. His grip broken, he was forced upright and then toppled backwards as the coracle rode the crest. He fell heavily and one of the cross-poles dug into his ribs. He rolled off it and gripped the side of the boat with an arm and his head over the rim.

His world was in chaos. There were no fixed points, but a constantly moving greyness of sea and sky. His world soared and swooped; it spun one way and then the other. It created levels and angles that he could not comprehend: sea mountains, valleys, crags and crevices. A denser grey in the midst of it all? An island? He closed his eyes but his fear grew. He wanted to know when the end was coming; to see the grey hand that finally snatched him from the boat and pulled him under. If only it would end! Ruadhan wanted to find again the peace of a summer's day in his childhood when he wove grass boats with his friends and raced them on the river. He wanted the colour of spring, the splashes of blossom at the forest's edge, the fleshy green shoots in the fields. He wanted the calm at the end of the day, and Cairech's murmur as she built the fire to last through the night and as he rolled himself more tightly in his blanket. He wanted the deep sleep he had experienced in the fishermen's' hut.

Ruadhan did not see the bough until one wave formed a fist around it and hurled it at the coracle. Torn from the trunk of a mighty oak by a bolt of lightning, one end had splintered into five thick wooden spear points. Like well-honed swords, the wooden prongs cut through the tough ox hides and broke the frame in several places. Ruadhan tried to stand, but was only half-erect when the smashed boat lurched and threw him heavily towards the damaged place. There was a split second when he knew what was going to happen but also knew that he could do nothing about it. The back of his right thigh was impaled cleanly upon one of the oak spear points. Ruadhan stopped himself from looking down. He felt for his leg. The point had penetrated his flesh deeply. It ached but the viciously cold seawater pouring into the boat dulled the sensation. Ruadhan felt all resolve to act draining from him. The pain of the wood in his leg was preferable to the greater pain and loss of blood if he moved. A wound must be staunched immediately; he knew that. You must keep the blood in. If the blood goes, the life goes. Ite placing moss on his gashed forehead; a friend's stone thrown carelessly. *You must stop the bleeding, Ruadhan. Let me.* Forget everything except keeping the blood in. Forget the Psalter? Keep the blood in. Don't move.

The water gushing through the holes quickly filled the coracle. A wave hit Ruadhan fiercely in the middle of his back, flung him violently forward and freed his leg. Terror of blood flowing unrestrictedly fastened round his heart. Under the water; going down; swallowing water; batted from side to side by the maelstrom; deep in the water; never this deep in the river; swirling water inside his head? Gasping; must stop the blood. Can't. Deeper still. Arms flailing. Choking. Let go. No more.

First Ite's face and a fleeting recollection of lying with her at Na Lámha and then Samthann's eyes flashing in the firelight. Live. Live. Ruadhan struggled to find the surface, kicking and thrashing the water. His lungs were a fierce fire inside of him. He would die... die... if he, if he, if he didn't reach the surface, the surface and air, and drink that air, that blessed air, drink it deeply, deeply.

Complete blackness first and then the memory of making acorn people. With Ite, he sat outside their hut with a bowl of the fruits. He was six and Ite four. Cairech was heavily pregnant and sat just inside the door, teasing wool. Ruadhan and Ite pulled the biggest acorns from their cupules and used them as the bodies of their play-people. He whittled short sticks for their game. They pushed these into the bodies as arms and legs and necks. Sometimes the wood broke and Ite became angry. Ruadhan laughed and helped her. They searched in their bowl for smaller acorns with their cupules still on and stuck these on the necks. They must have made thirty that day and they placed them all around the walls of their hut and in the thatch.

"They will guard us all through winter," Ruadhan told Ite.

When he regained consciousness, Ruadhan was clinging to the bough that had speared his thigh. The thought of the blood he must be losing made him feel faint once more. There *was* an island. He had seen it through the convulsions and gloom of the storm. It was near. He could reach it. He would reach it. Ruadhan clung fast to the bough and tried to propel it forward by kicking his legs. For, several minutes he kicked furiously but made little headway. He stopped when a voice inside his head - Ite? - told him to be still, be patient.

THE ISLAND
A Remote, Hidden Little Spot

Ruadhan was at the water's edge, lying face down on rocks uncovered by a retreating sea. The bough that had wounded him and then, as if atoning for its violence, had brought him safely to the shore, was nowhere near. Painfully, Ruadhan stretched an arm and groped about his ankles for the precious package. The Psalter had gone. He twisted upwards and round into a sitting position and for a moment, shook with a sense of defeat and irresolution. He had failed Tulchán and Conal and was probably going to die in this storm on this desolate island. A curious thought entered his mind and Ruadhan started to laugh/cry as he realised that throughout his ordeal, the *strangeness* had not visited him. He had been spared that.

The sea had released him but the furious wind and rain continued to attack. To slake a terrible thirst, Ruadhan tilted his face, mouth wipe open, to catch the rain.

"Move fool, or the tide will return and cover you!"

He had come very close unnoticed by Ruadhan, a strange figure shrouded by the ferocious downpour. Ruadhan could not focus on him. He was a blur, a changing, serous shape; he was the stuff of Ruadhan's ravings, perhaps a chimera. He spoke again and took a step closer.

"Move, fool!"

Leather shoes with long thongs that were wrapped around his legs and tied together above his knees; green leggings the colour of the seaweed that clung to the rocks where Ruadhan sat and a short tunic that was the grey-green of the rocks themselves. He was an adult but was very small in stature, and had a head that seemed much larger than it should have been. It was no fantasy. Light brown hair fell, tied like a horse's tail, almost to his waist. His eyes bulged making Ruadhan wonder if this was this some creature, half-human, half-fish, that looked after suffering sailors on this island. When he raised the staff he had been leaning on and spoke again, the creature's words knocked that idea from Ruadhan's head. He shouted through the tumult of the storm. "I am Ungorn. Remember my name. Before long you will wish the sea had taken you to its ugly depths because it knows only one way to make you suffer and die while I know so many ways that were each an ear of corn, I could fill all of Ireland's barns with my evil harvest. Do not expect me to provide you with shelter, to feed you and pour ointment on your wounds. You were not invited to this island. You trespass and foul the air with your stench!"

Perhaps it was a joke. Even the whirling wind and lashing rain could not disperse the foetid smell that came from this creature.

"Get up now and follow me! I would finish you off here but someone wants to have a look at you." He swung the staff swiftly and rapped Ruadhan's side before turning and heading inland. Although used to scrambling nimbly over these rocks, Ungorn stumbled and almost fell to the ground. As he righted himself quickly, he pulled a short sword from his belt and turned on Ruadhan brandishing this new weapon and his staff. "I won't think twice before using it!" he screeched. "I've killed much bigger men than you with this sword but it's a long time now since it tasted blood and it has a thirst on it like a Cork monk. So beware, my friend from the sea. Now, come, follow me or die where you lie."

Slowly and painfully, Ruadhan pulled himself up. His legs were half-immersed in a rock pool and several fronds of wrack fluttered their fingers about the wound, a gentle touching in the midst of a world that seemed intent on hurting and perhaps destroying him. The storm continued to scream and only a few metres away, huge trees of seawater reared upwards where the waves broke against the rocks. Ruadhan ached all over and when he removed the seaweed, he saw that his wounded leg was seeping blood steadily. *Must keep it in.*

Once he was upright, Ruadhan found moving was not as painful as he had expected and gingerly began to step forward in the direction the dwarf had gone. He fell frequently, slipping on the slick seaweed, and grazing his ankles and calves on the barnacle-covered rocks. Ungorn kept screeching for him to follow but Ruadhan couldn't see him through the curtains of water. He kept moving in what he thought was the direction of the voice until he staggered from the rocks on to a great slab of stone. Its black smoothness led to the foot of a sheer cliff that rose out of sight into the mist. Ungorn was already ten metres up the face of the cliff, but Ruadhan could not understand how he had reached that point. Favouring his wounded leg, he shuffled forward over the glassy surface of the slab. It was not until he reached the cliff face that he saw narrow steps cut crudely into the rock. They zigzagged upwards changing direction by ninety degrees every twenty metres. Ungorn was out of sight again. Ruadhan was considering how painful and slow his ascent was going to be when the first stone clattered on to the ground close to his feet. Ungorn shouted for him to move and threw a second stone that hit Ruadhan's shoulder. He put his uninjured leg on to the first step and searched with his hands for a grip on the cliff face.

Slowly, carefully, Ruadhan edged his way up the steps, his body shrammed by the water and wind, but the climb seemed never-ending and his strength began to fail. He stopped frequently and breathed deeply. It was no use. Give in. The storm centred its violence on him, hurling itself against the cliff face in an effort to dislodge him. Still he kept going, a step more, a step more, until he couldn't see the rocks below and knew he was at a great height above them. When would this end? His stops became more frequent. After every two or three steps, he had to rest. No more. He no longer clung to any fingerhold he could find on the rock, but slumped on the steps with his head and an arm hanging over the edge. The grey emptiness below called him, enticed him to ease himself a little further from the cliff face and fall into its forgetfulness. *So pain ceases, ceases,* the wind, rain and sea-spray spoke. It would be so, so easy to slip over the side, thought Ruadhan, and so pleasant to be rid of his pain and the ugliness of this bleak place. Perhaps below he would find Ite. Hands of wind that had pushed him into the rock, now plucked at his tunic, urging him over the edge. So easy. No more pain. *So pain ceases.* He clenched and unclenched his fingers as if trying to feel safety in the void beneath him. He pushed a leg over. A little more and then nothing, no feeling, no pain. Ite. *So the pain ceases, ceases, ceases,* the storm hissed.

At the point where one more gentle push would have sent him hurtling from the steps, Ruadhan's grasping hand touched a plant growing from a small crack in the rock below him. He had not expected to find such evidence of life and beauty growing in this barrenness. His fingers closed on the plant and pulled at it. The roots must go deep, he thought, to find sustenance there and he was surprised at how easily the flower came away in his hand as if offering itself to him. Still half over the edge, Ruadhan lifted the flower to his face. Its papery petals were of the palest pink, but were still bright flags of colour to Ruadhan. There was a faint rustling as he closed his fingers around the flowerhead, pressing its life into his flesh and then releasing it.

The flower fell and was quickly out of sight. Ruadhan pulled back from the edge angry with himself for having come so close to giving in, at having been seduced by that whisper in the wind into believing that there was nothing left for him in life. These steps had to be climbed and whatever was waiting for him at the top had to be faced. This fierce wind, the drenching rain, the wasteland of rock did not tell the whole story. They howled of a never-ending hopelessness, a short, brutal life, but the flower spoke to Ruadhan of a different world, one of beauty and hope, a world Tulchán and the Psalter wanted him to believe in. He was going to reach the top.

The grassy shelf of rock was two hundred metres above the shore, and another twenty from the clifftop. It was strewn with loose stones. Ruadhan dropped to his knees exhausted but thankful to see and feel a soft cushion of springy grass beneath him.

Ungorn squawked from above, on the steps that continued up the cliff at the back of the ledge but Ruadhan could not make out what he was shouting. With difficulty, Ruadhan stood and started towards them. He did not see the building until he had mounted the first steps. The driving rain eased and the small stone structure showed itself. It stood at the furthest extremity of the shelf on his right, sideways on to the sea. It was no bigger than a large rock, perhaps three metres by two and a half, and had been constructed painstakingly from hundreds of flat stones placed one on top of the other. These stones were its walls and they were its roof: each one had been placed overlapping on the inside the stone underneath so that the side walls rose with gentle curves to meet each other and form a compact beehive shape.

Who could bear to live in such a place as this? Who would choose to live here? How could a person survive in this harsh land unless the angels of God fed them? The large, heavy slate that served as the door was moving, being dragged to one side. A monk! Relief surged through Ruadhan's whole being. Ungorn must be some twisted malignant person who has been banished to the island in the hope that he would learn from the holy man and change his ways. This must be an anchorite, one of many who chose to live apart from others and from the snares of the world. Tulchán had talked of such men and women, holy people scattered about the western islands, existing on the simplest of diets and spending their time in prayer and contemplation. The monk crawled from the cell and uncurled himself outside the door obliterating the cross cut into the lintel. He was over six foot and heavily built and his face was not thin and drawn as Ruadhan expected, but strong-boned, well-fleshed and ruddy; a handsome face that you might find in the court of a wealthy chieftain; the face of a man used to eating meat every other day. The monk's thin-lipped mouth smiled at Ruadhan, but the green eyes, under thick, curling brows did not. His coarse woollen *casula* was of deepest grey flecked with black and, in spite of his height, it trailed on the wet ground. He pulled his hood up over thick jet-black hair.

"A remote, hidden little spot: for forgiveness of my sins, a conscience spotless before holy Heaven, I dwell in this remote high place. I am Fiacc." His eyes fixed themselves on Ruadhan's.

Ungorn came swiftly back down the steps. "I didn't think you would be here. I was bringing him to you."

Fiacc turned his head slowly and looked contemptuously at the little man, "Where else would I be except my simple dwelling place?"

"I thought perhaps the..."

Fiacc dismissed him curtly, "Go, attend to your work! There is someone in need here and I must assist him. Go!"

Ungorn scuttled up the steps and out of sight in the storm. Fiacc turned once more to Ruadhan. "That will be your dwelling place. A simple hut but it breaks the winds and keeps the rain out." He pointed over Ruadhan's shoulder and when the young man turned he saw that there was another beehive cell on the ledge. "But for now, come in here. I must pray soon, but it would be un-Christian of me not to feed you, tend to your wounds and give you shelter."

Ruadhan's relief was so great that he felt tears welling up inside of him. He started towards the monk, but his legs gave way and he fell heavily to the ground. Fiacc moved quickly to his side, lifted him and took him into his cell. Ruadhan felt himself being lowered roughly on to a bed of straw. Fiacc replaced the door and subdued the sound of the storm. The interior was dark with the only light, until Fiacc lit a candle, coming through chinks at the side of the door. Ruadhan's eyes took a while to adjust. Several hides lay at the foot of the bed and near them more candles. Close by Ruadhan's head, the monk dipped a wooden spatula in and out of several pots and prepared a salve for the wounded leg. "The wound is deep but if my flesh were pierced like this, I would choose for it to happen at sea. The salt water has started the healing and my ministrations will finish it. Turn on to your side. Do it now."

The abruptness with which Fiacc addressed him did not worry Ruadhan. This man was his rescuer; the one who was saving him from the storm, from bleeding to death, and - he had begun to forget him already - from the malignant Ungorn. Relief and gratitude controlled Ruadhan's responses to what was happening, and also the fond memory of another monk, the gentle Tulchán. Fiacc rubbed black ointment with a pungent smell into the wound. Ruadhan winced and his body stiffened with the pain. "I shall bind it. Then you will go to the other cell." Fiacc packed the wound with sphagnum moss and bound it with a strip of linen. Ruadhan felt fearful of getting on his feet again and facing the storm. A huge tiredness was pulling at his body but he knew from Fiacc's tone that he would not be allowed to rest where he was. Without speaking another word - was this some special time for prayer when his thoughts had to be on God alone and when communication with others was forbidden? - the monk pushed the doorstone to one side. The storm eagerly entered. Fiacc pointed to the other cell and Ruadhan crawled reluctantly from the straw, through the door and across the patch of grass that separated the two buildings. Finding him once more, the wind and rain pushed and pulled at his tired, aching body and made the few metres seem like a continent of space. He collapsed through the doorway, pulled himself along the floor and then up on to a stone sleeping platform that jutted from one side of the cell. This cell had no door and the straw on his bed was damp, but in his exhaustion, Ruadhan did not care. It was a shelter. The monk - ah, dear, gentle Tulchán - would care for him and help him with his mission. His wound would heal. He would find the Psalter. All would be well. But now, forget all and sleep.

CILLEBAIRRE
Harsh Penance

The boatbuilding had stayed the grief and anger for a little while but Conal was still in a rudderless vessel. Known for his iron will, he was now was weak and riven by indecisiveness. The loss of Ruadhan he could understand. The young man had a mission, a task to complete. It was the loss of Cearbhall, his first-born, that baffled him. He would never know if his boy would have grown to fulfil the potential his name expressed and be *fierce in battle*. His first-born would undertake no missions. His first-born had known little beyond his mother's breast and his parents' bed. Death had stripped Conal of companions in many ways. There had been horrifically violent departures contrasting with gentle, unremarkable retreats and, in most instances, his mourning had been instinctive, ritualistic. He had known grief but it had quickly scampered to the edges of his days and not climbed on his back and burdened him beyond understanding as it was now doing. There was much within the settlement calling for Conal's strong leadership: work on the tower had been abandoned, heavy rains had damaged crops, Ruarcc's muttered incitement was becoming a roar - but he could not respond to any of it. It was a time of deep grieving for the loss of Cearbhall. Carnait returned to their home but after only one night, Conal left it to occupy one of the small stone cells close to the church on the south side of the river. There he spent ten days accompanying the monks in their daily office and seeking consolation and understanding from Duach. Was God punishing him? How had he offended God? Would he see Cearbhall again? While with the Northmen, Conal had seen so much death at close quarters that he had begun to question whether resurrection took place.

"Our Saviour guaranteed that, Conal."

"Bodies, brimful of vigour hacked apart, severed arms, legs; faces alert, shining with life torn beyond recognition and stilled."

"All healed, Conal, purified. The righteous, that is."

"Will I see my son?"

"Attain heaven, Conal, and you shall."

"Will I see him as a man in all his might?"

"Attain heaven, Conal. Start with prayer and fasting."

"The marks, those hideous imperfections on his flesh that haunt my sleep: what of them?"

161

"Wiped away. Our Lord died and rose that we may know this."

Duach was flattered by the attention from Conal but, in truth, did not want it. First, more legal matters to consider and now to be the soul-friend of such a complex, dominant man as Conal. It was all very demanding. What could he say? Duach found it hard to shape words that would guide others even simple, superstitious farmers. The Word and pictures illuminating the Word: that is how he could direct people to God. The monk had never advanced himself as one clever in theological argument or spiritual direction and believed the priest, Bréanainn, would give better counsel, but God had directed Conal to Duach and he would respond as best he could. In the scriptorium, reluctantly, he passed the gospel text he was working on, Christ's arrest in the Garden of Gethsemane, to two others.

"Do not interfere in any way with the opening page depiction of the evangelist Mark's winged lion." They were young in learning and not skilled enough to attempt that. "I will complete that at a more settled time which I hope will be soon. It can wait."

Duach's immediate and urgent concern was Conal. The man had a strong moral centre. Duach knew that and it was confirmed by the piety and deep questioning that were now exhibited each day. The man had to be healed of his melancholy and quickly since the community was threatened with lawlessness but the theological discussions did not provide the balm. Conal himself came up with the answer.

"A penance, Duach, a harsh penance to purify my spirit as agrimony does the blood."

Duach was averse to prescribing penance to others; there were graduations of severity in response to sins confessed but he had little knowledge of such. Besides, he could not take rule and callipers to any moral lapses Conal had confessed in their discussions. The killings? He was a soldier. He fought. He maimed. He killed. Duach could punish himself for his failings willingly and impose the harshest of penances but he found it difficult to minister to another in that way. Conal begged him and so the monk sent Conal to climb *Sliabh Naofa*, the holy mountain several days walking to the south of Cillebairre. Hardship and tough physical effort might bring the man out of his torpor; a physical challenge to rid him of the doubts and restore his confidence.

"Take the most difficult route to the top on the slope that faces the sea. There is no path only a mountainside of scree that you must climb on your knees. Pray as you go. At the top, find shelter and pray and fast, find stillness until God... yes, until God gives you a sign and makes the way clear for you to return."

Duach should have foreseen the freedom Conal's absence would grant someone. Ruarcc could not stop himself. Ruarcc did not want to stop himself. His needs were basic. For too long, he had suppressed his appetites; for too long he had walked away from confrontations with Conal; for too long he had followed and not led. The rape and murder of Ite had unshackled the evil that was in Ruarcc, that *stupid and baneful man*. With pleasure, he noted the mental and physical fatigue that had overtaken Conal and saw the opportunity to assert and prove himself to all. The anger and bitterness that he had been holding close could now be released. He would claim what was his by right, take some of what Conal had promised on his first visit to Fearghal's dun: the feasts, servants and beautiful, amenable women to satiate his sexual needs. Ruarcc would grab what he could while he could and experience something of that Paradise Conal had said would be theirs. Ruarcc could not plan other than consider how next to satisfy his cravings but, in a vague way, he convinced himself that as well as satiating himself on food, drink and women he would make himself the quasi-chief of the community of Cillebairre, usurping Conal's position while that man was crawling like a slave up holy mountains. He had enough awareness to know he was stepping on to a dangerous path, one most likely leading to his death but alcohol helped him to dismiss all caution. He would have pleasure beyond his dreams before any reckoning. To start, there would be feasting. Meat! He would eat as much as he could and in so doing ingest the qualities of the animals he feasted on! Wild boar. Hunt. He would hunt that aggressive creature, stuff himself with as much of its carcass as his body could take, and then he would be ready for Conal. On the first afternoon of Conal's absence, after drinking heavily, he and Beccan rode east along the valley to "hunt". At an outlying farm, they abused shamefully the men and women living there and stole two head of cattle. They butchered the animals crudely, hid the meat they did not roast and, although well soaked in ale, denied all knowledge of the crime, when, a day later, they were confronted by Duach in their quarters. "This will bring no good! You are shaming yourself and the community! Unfettered appetites..."

Ruarcc raised himself slowly from a lying position and farted noisily adding to the foetid smell of urine and vomit that already filled the place. "That's my prayer for you, Duach! Now, go! Stay on your side of the river and keep your head down over your desk, monk."

"I am displeased and so will Conal be."

Ruarcc stood, turned a full circle on the spot staggering and almost toppling. "Who? I don't see a Conal in this place, monk."

More complaints were brought to Duach. He did not know to deal with the renegade Ruarcc and, in truth, feared the man. The community was already taxed to provide foodstuffs for the warriors' compound but Ruarcc decided the portions were not enough for his constant feasting and took more without recompense. And as well as insisting that their table needs be more than satisfied, he forced Cillebairre to sate his bedroom appetite by abducting two women from their homes.

Duach tried to turn a blind eye to what Ruarcc was doing and sought sanctuary back at his desk in the scriptorium. It would not last, he told himself. The man would fill himself like the glutton he is and then see the foolishness of his ways. Conal should have appointed someone to lead in his absence, someone who could restrain Ruarcc. Duach should have pressed for this and approved the one appointed. He told himself all would calm down; go back to normal. No one had been killed and eventually, when Duach thought the time was right, he would call on the law and pursue the matter of compensation for those the farmers who had lost livestock and the families of the women who had been abducted. He consoled himself when a day passed and all *seemed* normal in homes, storehouses, in fields, barns, the forge and the central buildings of the monastery. There on the south side of the river, the monks said their daily office, ran the school, library and scriptorium and often crossed to the north side to join in the seasonal farm work with everyone else. Duach knew those days did not mark the end of Ruarcc's misrule but they brought the time of Conal's return closer. He thought of sending a messenger and speeding Conal's homecoming but there was still unrest in the country to the south and besides, a Conal who had not found peace of mind could bring problems worse than Ruarcc's reign had. He turned to prayer. In the main church, Duach prayed hard and long, his knees

164

lowered to a flat stone he had placed for this purpose at one side of the altar. He prayed that Conal was finding a calming closeness to God on the holy mountain and would be back with them soon.

Ruarcc squatted and relieved himself noisily just a few metres from the door of their hut. A heavy morning mist had coated the grass with droplets and was cold on his bottom. He tore at it angrily and wiped himself roughly. Ruarcc was angry. His gut ached but that was not the true cause of his anger. That was brought on by the simple fact that the debauchery had not brought satisfaction. It was all beginning to pall, the ale and the routine coupling with unresponsive women. He stayed in a squatting position, moved slightly from side to side and found odd gratification in the touches of the spiky grass on his buttocks. Great feasts in a great hall, Conal had said! Tables piled high! Livestock pens, rivers and seas emptied of all manner of creatures to satisfy Ruarcc's appetite. Ale, mead and wine would flow like streams, Conal had said! Servants, Conal said! Ruarcc would not even have to lift the food to his mouth. That would be done for him so that his hands were free to fondle the most beautiful women that Ireland had reared, plump, fresh, untouched by other men; women yearning for his attention, compliant. He recalled last night's dull, drunken kneading of a captive's sagging breasts. The most beautiful, Conal had said! That's what would welcome them in Cillebairre, a never-ending feast. That's what the lying Conal had said!

Ruarcc stood quickly, too quickly and his head spun. He staggered and held himself upright by extending an arm to the wall. When his head cleared, he righted his clothes, breathed deeply and smiled. It wasn't over yet. Appetite was returning. He knew where to find a beautiful woman. She was only a few strides away from him. This was a woman who would give him great satisfaction.

"You have no right to enter here and you know it!" Carnait's deformed tongue corrupted her speech and *right* came out as a strange guttural utterance that Ruarcc mimicked. "*R...r...right*, Carnait? I have a *r...r...right*, Carnait. I have *the right*, Carnait. Look..." Ruarcc drew a dagger from his belt. "Here is my *right*."

Carnait backed off but felt with her foot for the blade she kept in the rushes of her bed.

"Ah, but wait precious Carnait, let me present my greater *right*. Look at this, my lovely!" Ruarcc lifted his tunic, unfastened, and dropped his trews to reveal his erect penis. "Look how this *right* asserts itself above all others! Look upon *my* tower! Didn't take long to build, did it? Where is your *right*, Carnait? Your *right* is kneeling on stones on some holy mountain. I don't see your *right* here."

Carnait dropped to her knees, frantically scrabbled for the knife and found it. Ruarcc watched her, teetered and laughed. Still on her knees, Carnait thrust the knife upwards. "Leave me, leave me now!"

"Does Conal know you welcomed Fearghal more graciously than this, Carnait?" Ruarcc gripped his penis. "And look, look, Carnait, this playfulness of yours helps me grow!"

"It is my time. I flow freely. You will be damaged. Go, go now!" As she shouted, Carnait noticed that the light from the entrance had dimmed. Eoin and Colman stood there. "Stop him!"

Eoin spoke quietly, "You have done enough, Ruarcc."

Ruarcc spun while pulling up his trews and stumbled to the floor.

"Kill him!" Carnait screamed. "Conal would want him killed!"

Writhing on the floor to adjust his clothes, Ruarcc announced that he was answering a call of charity. "This woman has been without her man for too long. She was in need of comfort. None can give comfort like Ruarcc." He made more adjustments shoving his member into the trews. "Look I have my comforter here."

Eoin bowed to Carnait and, without saying a word, helped Ruarcc to his feet. Once up, the big man pushed Eoin away. At the entrance, he paused and repeated himself. "No, no one can give comfort like Ruarcc." He slapped Colman lightly on the cheek. "You know that, don't you, my pretty one." Colman shoved Ruarcc's hand away and pulled back from any contact with him. Ruarcc stumbled outside roaring, "There's nothing for me here! Nothing!" and made his mazy way to the warriors' hut where others, dazed from a surfeit of drinking, stood and watched.

Eoin, like Duach, thought Ruarcc would rein himself in. He despised the man and his actions but knew what he was capable of and, like most of the others, lived in fear of him. He refused to join in the excesses but did not challenge Ruarcc. He knew this was steadily drawing the big man's wrath his way and surprising him with Carnait had hastened its arrival. Later that day, after a long sleep, Ruarcc found and confronted

Eoin as he stood on guard outside Carnait's house. He pushed himself up against the slighter man and inflated his chest. A sword could not have gone between them. Eoin concentrated hard on what he should do if Ruarcc did more than this and provoked a fight. Conal had taught them to go without hesitation for the very vulnerable parts: neck, balls, eyes, and to use hands, feet and head *like* a crazed man but one who is in command of what he is doing.

"What was it you said? Done enough, have I? Disapprove, Eoin, do you? You were a prissy little thing as a child and you still are a prissy little thing."

Colman came running from behind the house carrying a spear. He lowered it and held it within striking distance of Ruarcc's ribs.

"Ah, the midget completes your army, Eoin. You will conquer many lands." Ruarcc took a step back and poked Eoin hard on the chest.

"You will feast with me, Eoin, or you will fight me."

"I have no appetite for either, Ruarcc."

Ruarcc drew a line in the dirt with his toe. "You are the absent Conal's man or you are mine. Step this side if you are with me."

Two factions formed and clashed later that day. It was nothing but a melee without a killing or serious injury apart from young Colman who had to be treated in the infirmary for serious blow to the head but it hardened a clear division in the camp. Eoin, Corraidhín, Colman with nine others left the warriors' compound and crossed to the south side of the river to speak to Duach. They took Carnait with them. They would do whatever the abbot commanded them. Carnait occupied the guesthouse and the soldiers made their sleeping places in a simple wattle and mud hut roofed by branches and sods that stood at the back of it. Eoin did not think that Ruarcc would instigate serious conflict but mounted a guard at the stepping stones, the guesthouse and Duach's cell. Duach agreed that a militia of at least twenty more be raised from among the monks and the *manaigh* and that, if Ruarcc did not mend his ways, an assault should be made on the warriors' compound.

THE ISLAND
Prisoner

It was six days before the fever began to abate. Ruadhan remembered very little of what happened during that time. Other than snatches of strange dreams, all he retained were hazy recollections of being fed soup by Fiacc and of waking once to see, through the fog of his delirium, Ungorn at his side. He pushed himself up into a sitting position and felt aches all over his body. His leg was stiff and sore with a blue and yellow bruise extending up and down his thigh well beyond the wound. His tunic had been changed but the new one already stank of stale sweat. Ruadhan drew his knees up to his chest and clasped his hands around them. His mind, like his body, did not want to do anything, did not want to go over what had happened or consider what might happen now. Fiacc would help him. Fiacc would tell him what to do.

Six days on but from the sounds on the walls, the rain and wind had not eased. However, the cell was darker and not as open to the cold as when he had crawled there from the storm. Someone had placed a simple rush windbreak over the entrance. Fiacc pushed the new door to one side and bent low to enter the cell. He sat down facing Ruadhan. "You have returned to us, young one."

"I am grateful to you for sheltering me and nursing me through my illness."

Fiacc carried a bowl of oats soaked in water. "I have never seen a fever that raged as furiously as yours. Until the fourth day, I was sure you were lost and that only Fiacc on this lonely spot would see your soul pass into eternity."

"I should express my gratitude to the other one, but I still fear him from the way he treated me when I was carried to this island."

Fiacc looked at him quizzically. "The *other one?* There is no one else on the island, young man." Fiacc's answer was sharp but he quickly softened his tone and added, "Tell me, now, who but a foolish servant of God would choose to come and spend their life here when there are barns full of grain, larders full of cheese, and fields full of fat sheep and cattle on the mainland? This *other* you speak of is a creation of your mind, your fierce fever, a devil sent to deceive and tempt you." He let out a great sigh. This island is full of devils and I battle with them day and night. They come in shapes most hideous and tempt me with visions most lurid."

168

"Ungorn is his..." Ruadhan started to reply, but even in his weakness, was able to see that this was a subject on which he should not contradict the monk. Could he have been wrong? Could Ungorn be a creature of his imagination, a devil? Had he suffered some new form of the *strangeness*? Was his mind to be trusted? For a second, Ruadhan had doubts but then pressed a hand to where Ungorn's staff had rattled his ribs. The place was still tender.

Fiacc handed him the bowl of oats. "You must begin to eat again. This will give you strength." With his fingers, Ruadhan scooped the oats slowly, steadily from the bowl to his mouth. Even this little effort exhausted him. His appetite for food still had not returned and all he wanted to do was drink water. However, he knew the monk was right and tried to force the food down. Fiacc looked at him intently. "You spoke of many things and many people in your fever. Several times, you mentioned a monk called Tulchán. I know the name and have heard others speak of him as a very holy man, Tulchán of Cillebairre."

Ruadhan imagined an intense ray of sun penetrating the clouds that shrouded the island and entering the cramped cell by any opening no matter how small. *Tulchán*. That was his response to hearing someone speak that name. It was better than medicine, and once Ruadhan started to talk, in response, about Tulchán, the great weakness the fever had brought seemed to retreat from him. His memory began to burst with simple recollections of his gentle friend and his tongue could not give words to them fast enough. He told Fiacc of the talks he had had with Tulchán; of the prayers the monk had taught him; of the scriptorium and the beautiful manuscripts, of the belief that man had in him, belief that no other adult mirrored. He spoke, his imagination reliving those happy times, as if he was talking to a child who could never have experienced such things. Then his mind ran with a jolt into the unhappy memory of Tulchán's death, the Psalter, and the mission which he, Ruadhan, had been given. He told Fiacc about them but struggled for words and felt weak once more.

A vain hope stirred him. "Perhaps you have found the Psalter. It was with me in the boat. I had it tied to..."

"I know nothing of that." Fiacc interrupted abruptly, shaking his head. His features remained still and inexpressive. "The loss is unfortunate but there are other scribes in Cillebairre and other monasteries who will replace it." He did not want to speak of books. There was a lull in their

169

conversation. Fiacc reached for the bowl in Ruadhan's hand and tilted it slightly to see inside. "Finish this if you want to get well."

"I intend to get well, leave and no longer be a burden to you."

Fiacc made an indistinct reply, gathered himself as if to rise and leave but suddenly stopped: "Perhaps your friend, Tulchán of Cillebairre spoke of a Chalice, a special Chalice made of glass. It is of interest to me."

Fiacc had sat in stony silence while Ruadhan spoke of Tulchán's murder and had offered no words of consolation. Ruadhan took time over replying. He wanted desperately to please the man sitting before him and regard him as a friend, but felt uneasy in his presence. "No. Why should he speak to me about such a thing?"

As quickly as the storm had risen in Ruadhan's path on the sea, so anger came to Fiacc's features. He rose quickly, and, bent low over Ruadhan in the small cell, pushed his face forward and shouted his answer: "Because, so you tell me, he spoke to you of many wonderful things! Therefore, he must have spoken of the Chalice! It is an object of great sacred significance, high value and an object of great beauty!"

Ruadhan breathed slowly and deeply. He would stay calm. "I am sorry. I owe you a great deal, perhaps my life and so would tell you if I had heard of this Chalice from Tulchán but I know nothing of it."

The storm subsided as quickly as it had arisen. Fiacc sat back down, lowered his head for a moment and then reached across to put his hands on the boy's shoulders. Ruadhan flinched away from him. "I have been watching and praying over you for many nights and my body is weak. Often, when the body is weak, the mind juggles with all kinds of ideas that mean nothing. Forget my words."

Ruadhan's eyes searched the monk's face for answers. It told him nothing. Features drawn in uncompromising angles and planes were as hard and unyielding as the great slabs of rock at the base of the cliff face.

"I must go." Fiacc crossed the ledge angry with himself for the outburst of temper and especially for the apology it had pushed out of him. Was the unwelcome guest lying? Had Tulchán taken him into his confidence, told him of the wondrous glass Chalice and its great value and then sworn him to secrecy? Fiacc thought it unlikely but the mention of that dead monk's name had thrown a bundle of dried, seasoned branches on to a fire that burned within him.

Each evening for a week, Fiacc brought food, the simplest fare of wind-dried fish, oats, and sometimes bread and cheese, but did not eat himself. "I fast so that my spirit may grow strong." When the boy had eaten and before they both slept, Fiacc told Ruadhan more stories of the devils that swarmed about the island. They had the power to take any form. All were hideous. Some had a human head and the body of a lizard; some had frog's heads and human bodies, and others took the shape of the huge boulders that were scattered about the island. Perhaps Ungorn was one of them, thought Ruadhan. The sure sign that you were in the presence of a devil, Fiacc said, was the smell of scorching flesh that they carried with them from the depths of Hell. The ledge was sacred and they would not come to it, but beyond that consecrated ground, they roamed freely. Fiacc told stories of the devils and then unfailingly would ask again if Tulchán had ever mentioned the Chalice. Ruadhan's reply was always the same; that Tulchán had never spoken of the Chalice, and, Ruadhan reminded himself, neither had he spoken of these devils that crowded Fiacc's world.

Those visits stopped and the days went by even more slowly in Ruadhan's eyrie high above the churning sea. Fiacc had let Ruadhan know very clearly that he must not leave the ledge and must not enter the other cell or disturb him in any way. "Food, water will be left for you. Simple fare. It is impossible for us not to meet but you must do everything you can to avoid contact with me. My mind and body must have one focus only; that is God. I must pray. I must contemplate all that is holy. I must overcome this army of demons. I have tended to your wounds but I have other healing to do and you must not come in the way of that."

"Then I will leave the island."

Fiacc's usually inscrutable features twisted into a grimace and there was a long pause before he pronounced. "You will stay... you will stay here until I am certain that you have fully recovered and that I know it is safe for you to cross to the mainland. As you have found out, these are dangerous waters. No matter what time of year it can be difficult to launch and direct a boat. And confronting the sea is not the only danger. All manner of cut-throats and thieves scuttle among these islands." Once more, there seemed a hint of genuine concern in the tone of Fiacc's voice but it vanished when he told Ruadhan. "You will depart from here when I tell you and until then, leave me alone to pray and confront the many devils that crawl about this place."

CILLEBAIRRE

A Sign

It was a desolate place. The sky was leaden. Dark clouds smothered the mountaintop. As he climbed, Conal saw them as smoke belching from deep within the earth, rising from the depths of Hell. He tried to fight off such fancifulness but it stayed with him throughout his ascent and during the three cold, damp days he spent enshrouded on the mountaintop. In simple shelter he found under a rock balanced atop others and overhanging a patch of heath grass on the eastern side of the summit, Conal fasted and prayed for a deeper understanding of Cearbhall's death and of what lay ahead of him. The praying was difficult. Duach had told him there were four types of prayer: supplication, asking pardon for sins; prayer promising to serve God in the way we live our lives; intercession, petitioning God to aid others or ourselves in some way and thanksgiving, by which the mind, conscious of past or present favours or in anticipation of future blessings, gives thanks. Duach had added that, with discipline, the mind reaches a way of praying that goes beyond contemplating an image or reciting words or listening to the voices of others. The mind and heart, he said, are transported, lifted beyond speech, beyond the visible, beyond all senses. He himself had never experienced such mystical prayer and ecstasy but he knew others who, after years of practice and devotion, had. Conal wanted more than anything else to be taken beyond recent experiences. They had crippled him in a way he had not thought possible. He understood discipline; had practised it as a soldier and imposed it strictly on others, but could not bring it to bear on what Duach had called *spiritual growth*. At first, it all felt very strange to Conal, talking to rocks and to the sky as if they were living things. A simple prayer of thanksgiving Duach had taught him to say every three hours seemed foreign when he uttered it out loud on the mountain. He could not make it his own. His only company was a fox that regularly came from and went to its den in the earth beneath the rocks. They stared at each other on the first encounter and the fox had rightly assessed the man on his knees as no threat. Conal persisted. Wait for a sign from God, Duach had told him. Would he know a sign from God? On his third and last night, Conal found sleep evasive. When a large moon broke through the clouds, he opened the small leather wallet Duach had given him.

"Through Bréanainn, our priest, I am bestowing a great privilege on you," the monk had said. "You will carry God in this special form. Say the *Our Father* and reverently consume what this contains, saying as you do: *This is the Body of Christ.*" Conal followed Duach's instructions.

Conal did not believe he was given clear answers on the mountain top and still not sure, after what had happened that he could give unreserved thanks to God, but he woke, stiff and weary, on the third morning to a changed world. The bright, rising sun seemed to single him out for its attention and he basked in its pure, healing light. Looking westward, he was stirred deeply as never before by the sight of the fertile land beneath the holy mountain, land intensely green in forest and field. Was this the sign? He gazed upon it, breathed deeply, and steadily and, without shaping any words, knew he was giving thanks. Did he experience the stillness that Duach had said he must find? Perhaps this was it. His body and spirit felt recharged with energy and purpose. It was time to return to Cillebairre, leave the *scailp* that had sheltered him so well. Conal raced and skidded with great leaps down the scree. He felt renewed. The isolation, the debates with God, the kneeling, all very strange at first, had found a temporary home within him, but work, action, the satisfaction of exerting physical strength: this is what brought purpose to Conal's daily life. The darkness in his spirit had vanished like those clouds on his third morning at the summit of *Sliabh Naofa*.

Duach clasped and unclasped both his hands repeatedly. Each day stiffness and aching increased in the joints of his fingers and sometimes his arms. He wondered how much longer would he be able to express his skills in the scriptorium.

"I have much to tell you, Conal, but first I must counsel you not act rashly when I have done. You must promise me you will not act hastily. Please try to find the stillness again before you do anything."

Carnait, Eoin, Corraidhín and Colman confirmed what Duach had told Conal. They also told him that Ruarcc's band had dispersed by either fleeing the settlement or abjectly crossing the river to express regrets and make amends.

Word was brought to Ruarcc that their leader had returned and for a moment, some small stirring of his awareness told him he had been foolish beyond all measure. There was no going back. He would face Conal.

Before that happened, there was still ale to drink and the enslaved women to grope, still time to find his *Paradise* in Cillebairre. In his drunken ravings, Ruarcc soared to great heights of strength and martial prowess. No one on earth could stand in his way! He would out-monster Cú Chulainn himself! In battle, dozens charged him and he lunged, slashed, parried, thrust, repelling or killing all. Conal would meet his match! Conal would fall! In those same ravings, he also scoured great depths of despair and saw Death searching for him in many guises about the settlement. Death was a piglet racing through children's legs then suddenly stopping to grub with its snout in the earth and uncover Ruarcc's face rotting in the mud; Death was a monk with long, strangely articulated limbs crossing the river by the stepping stones to bend awkwardly and peer into homes looking for his victim; Death stood by a pit of fire as a beautiful woman beckoning to him. Ruarcc had sinned grievously but these visions of Death and what would most likely follow did not bring remorse. Even in his drunken state, assailed by such visions, Ruarcc rejected remorse, regret and confession as expressions of weakness and cowardice.

He was hideously drunk and unconscious when Conal found him in his quarters. One of the hobbled captive women was pinned to the ground beneath him and could not shift his great bulk. Conal pulled him off the woman, dragged him outside and tied him, sitting up, to a tree. He ordered Eoin to throw cold water over him regularly until he was sober. Then he was to be freed and allowed to sleep under close guard. When he had slept, he was to be fed again, fed well. When Ruarcc's revival was complete, he had to prepare to fight Conal to the death. If Ruarcc had a preference, he could choose the weapon or weapons to be used.

"Why honour him in such a way, Conal?" asked Eoin.

"It is my way. Don't question it."

When Eoin returned for the third time with water to the tree where the prisoner was bound, he found the two women who had been enslaved stabbing him repeatedly. There was to be no honour in the manner of Ruarcc's death.

THE ISLAND
The Shore

Ruadhan tried to keep watch through the gaps at the side of his door but could never completely follow Fiacc's movements to and from the place. The monk was quick and furtive. From inside his cell Ruadhan tried to interpret noises but with little success except for the soft rustling he heard when food and water were placed outside his door early every third morning. He thought Fiacc rose early and spent most of the day away from the ledge but could never be sure. There were times he slept in his cell but Ruadhan was certain he was not there every night. Ruadhan began to feel like a prisoner on the island. He told himself that this was foolish and that he had every reason to be grateful to Fiacc but on the rare occasions he saw him and spoke of continuing his journey, the monk changed the subject or found some reason for stopping him. Even when he felt strong and asked if he could take a walk, Fiacc opposed him:

"You have not fully recovered, are still weak and must take more rest. Remain here in this spot freed of the loathsome devils. Do not leave this ledge. And there are other dangers. The paths up and down are treacherous and in your feeble state you could easily fall."

The words alone suggested that Fiacc was deeply concerned for Ruadhan's health but from the tone, the boy knew that this was not so and that, for reasons he did not understand, he was being given an order not to leave the recess in the cliff face that the two beehive cells clung to.

Ruadhan lost track of the days but calculated by two full moons, that he had been on the island over a month. The bruising on his leg faded and the encrusted blood of the wound was like a long, dark leech. Winter had raced towards the island and any journey to Clonmacnoise would be much more difficult. Ruadhan's days were humdrum, wearisome. No doubt, Tulchán would have lectured him on the preciousness of such days and the opportunity they provided for coming closer to God through stillness, prayer and contemplation. No doubt. Ruadhan did not feel privileged in any way. More and more each day he knew a growing resentment of Fiacc his gaoler, of the island his gaol and, he realised, of Tulchán who had started him on his ill-starred journey. He had very little to occupy his days. Each day and no matter what the weather, he limped the length of the ledge – fifty strides – backwards and forwards. He had studied the remaining seabirds before the cold drove them south, watched as they flew with ease to and from the cliff face and dipped to the sea. He envied their freedom. On clear days, he gazed hard into the distance trying to see the mainland and searching the sea for signs of human life. All that entered his gaze was a great expanse of water and he concluded that the storm had driven him to the far side of the island. It became his greatest desire to climb to the ridge above and cross the island. He imagined what he would see. Once there on the other side of the island, he told himself, he would glimpse Clonmacnoise across a narrow channel of water. In his mind, it appeared like Conal's great Round City in that far-off place, a vast walled and moated settlement sprouting a forest of towers and teeming with people. One glimpse of it would kindle thoughts of escape, and those thoughts would lead to action. Ruadhan had to get away.

Why not climb up from the ledge and explore the island? Ruadhan asked himself this question every day and the answer was simple. Ruadhan cowered below the ridge and never set foot on the steps above the ledge out of fear; fear of Fiacc, this strange, gloomy monk, and fear of the devils Fiacc had inhabited the island with. It was a fear that had intensified after an evening of Fiacc's tales and brought on an attack. The ringing in his ears had started, grown louder, changed pitch, become a wasps' nest and brought on a dizziness until he fell to the floor of his cell. His body and his mind writhed and he saw visions of huge, towering sea waves that had the faces of unnameable animals. Jaws and teeth pointed and sharp like knives filled his mind until the waves crashed on the shore and became slithering, inter-twined serpents that spat and bit each other repeatedly until they transformed into a stream of dark liquid that entered the mouth of a sleeping woman who convulsed as if poisoned until a cliff face tumbled on top of her and brought calm. Fear kept Ruadhan rooted in that small, vulnerable place.

A bitterly cold winter attacked. Dense cloud frequently blanketed the island. Hardly a day passed without powerful fists of wind and rain trying to knock the cells from their narrow cliff ledge. Monstrous seas attempted to scale the cliff and join them in their efforts. When the storms abated, Ruadhan walked as near as he dared, stretched out on the ground and pulled himself forward so that he could look over the edge. Even at that height, sea spray doused his face and a sense of the fall grabbed his breath and the clashing of the waves made him want to scuttle back to his cell. Once, for a moment, despairing of ever leaving that place by any other way, Ruadhan inched further forward until he felt his head and shoulders begin to pull downwards. He contemplated the state when he no longer had earth beneath him and was hurtling to the rocks below and to brokenness and... ? Was there another world that Tulchán had spoken of, a heaven where pain was no more? *God is our strength.* Ruadhan could not understand those words as Tulchán had but they drew him back from the edge and from the thought of suicide.

Frequently, after storms, Ruadhan had to replace stones dislodged from the roofs, and to do his best to mend the battered rush door to his cell. He longed to do more, to break the monotony and to fight off the cold. One evening, his world was enlarged when Fiacc pulled aside his door and announced that he, Ruadhan must fetch his own water.

"Where do I go?"

"Below us, three *fertach*[8]. On the right you will find the supply."

"Devils?"

Fiacc did not answer. He crossed quickly to his cell leaving Ruadhan's entry open.

Throughout a harsh day when the ledge was stunned by frequent attacks of hail, Ruadhan huddled under his blanket and wondered when, if ever, he would get away from the island prison. That night, looking out through the doorway he saw that scowling, turbulent clouds had been replaced by a calm night sky crowded with stars. He resisted the urge to go immediately to fetch water. He would save that adventure for the morning and prayed that the quiet night would lead into a quiet day.

There was warmth in the winter sun that greeted Ruadhan the following morning. Even though he was about to perform the simple task of filling a jug with water, he was excited. After his extended confinement, this was an adventure; it was a glimpse of new life. On all fours, he moved slowly down the stone steps until he saw the source of water. Someone had cut a cistern into a jutting rock just short of an arm's length from the path and, to help fill it with rainwater, had roughly chiselled two wide grooves that entered at a slant from the top of the cliff. Ruadhan drank and then cupped his hands and scooped water all over his head. It felt good. The sun maintained its warmth. He sat and lifted his face to it in reply. For the first time in a long while, Ruadhan believed he would leave the island.

---

[8] one *fertach* is approximately three metres

Going for water became a blessed time in Ruadhan's dreary existence. He became so used to the steps that even when the gales screamed at him, he descended upright and confident to the cistern and drew water. He began to speculate on going further. There had been no sign of devils. Ruadhan waited for clement weather and was granted four still days very late in the year. The sea ebbed only a short distance at the base of the cliff and it was then, at low tide on the last of those days as the weather held that he took a deep breath and worked his way carefully down the steps to explore the rocks below. In his optimism, he thought a way of escaping would present itself once he reached the bottom. Perhaps he would discover a passage to the rest of the island and there find someone to help him or a boat that he could row to the mainland and the Clonmacnoise of his imagination. He had lost the psalter but was still intent on reaching the monastery. Tulchán's name would assure him of a welcome. The descent was easy but Ruadhan's heart pounded harder with every step he took. There *was* a world beyond the ledge. What a fool he had been to delay his return to the shore. The great tables of rock at the foot of the cliff were wet and slippery from the tide and spray. Ruadhan stepped gingerly over them towards the water's edge but stopped when the huge waves crashing against the rocks created spouts of water that arced over his head. He scanned the bay and was dismayed to see that even at low tide the cliffs held the bay in a tight embrace. The only way of leaving was by swimming through dangerous, choppy channels among rocks that had edges as sharp as Conal's sword. Any attempt in winter would end in failure and most likely in his death. He would have to wait for spring.

CILLEBAIRRE

The Egyptians

The chariot was not out of control but it was going too fast. In the driving rain, Makarius had not been able to judge the condition of the track. He should have travelled at a different time of the year. Why had no one told him of the weather in this country? The slope was much steeper and muddier than he had thought it was going to be. Georgis' mouth was tensed open with terror and he gripped the side of the chariot tightly. He relaxed his grip slightly as the slope eased off, but the horse and chariot continued to hurtle along the road. When he saw a huge stone in the middle of the track, Makarius pulled furiously at the reins to slow the horse down. There was a deep ditch to the right and a tree on the left. He had to keep the chariot straight. They both braced themselves just before the axle hit the rock but were thrown from the back of the chariot and fell heavily to the ground on top of one another. The horse and chariot careered along the road until they were out of sight.

Georgis lay in the middle of the track moaning continuously. His leg was hurt badly. There was a large lump at the front of his right thigh which was where Makarius thought it had broken. He would have to carry his fellow monk to Cillebairre. The rain was relentless. There was little shelter. Trees had been felled and laid in the making of the road. The few that were left dipped their branches, heavy with moisture, almost to the ground. There can be no deserts in Ireland thought Makarius. He looked around and saw no sign of human activity but as he was trying to lift his brother monk from the ground, a very ragged man and two small, equally ragged children, stepped out from behind a blackberry and hawthorn thicket. All had long, greasy hair and mud-caked feet.

Makarius spoke some Irish, but not enough to understand this man or make himself understood. However, Georgis' pain was all the language needed and soon they were both out of the rain and lying on straw in the man's smoky hovel. A thin herb soup was being heated over a fire of heather roots in the centre of the hut and, as soon as Makarius had cleaned some of the mud from himself and his injured friend, their host handed them wooden bowls filled from the pot. He took some himself, drank it quickly and then left.

All that night, Georgis was in deep pain. Nobody slept. The ragged man's wife and the children huddled together in a corner and watched the strangely coloured people who had come into their home.

The man returned early in the morning with help from Cillebairre. Others found the broken chariot but the horse had disappeared. A sled was made to transport Georgis to the monastery and the two strangers were taken there. At first, the children of Cillebairre ran away from them. When the adults assured them that these men meant no harm, they examined the strangers more closely, pulling at their tunics and, if they got the chance, touching their pale black skin.

The word quickly spread that Makarius and Georgis were monks who were looking for Tulchán. They were Egyptian, the Irish monks said. Duach welcomed them as representatives of the Desert Fathers who had prompted and inspired so much of Ireland's own monastic practices. Conal had never been to Egypt with the Northmen and so knew it must be a very distant country. The Northmen had spoken of it frequently; a dry land with no timber and one huge river.

THE ISLAND
The Devils

Time passed slowly for Ruadhan, an intensely lonely winter. He saw little of Fiacc and when he did, the older man ignored any pleas Ruadhan made to leave the island. When the days lengthened and the weather softened slightly and the raucous mob of seabirds returned to ledges abandoned through the dark days of winter, Ruadhan planned his escape. First, he would see if the bay below now offered opportunities. He looked forward to descending the steps again and intended to do so one morning after he had gone for water but his resolution faltered and fear took its grip again. The cries of the gulls became the screeches of devils. He turned his thoughts to the opposite direction. He could ascend the final twenty metres from the ledge. Perhaps his freedom lay that way. Ruadhan considered it but every rustle, every movement in the grass above was a sign of impatient demons waiting above the ridge. For three days, he did nothing but sit and brood over what might be waiting for him beyond the cistern and above the clifftop. Over and over, he recited the prayers that Tulchán had taught him, especially Psalm 46, and tried to bring into his mind the beautiful pictures the monk had painted, but the words and the pictures were as cold as the grey stone surrounding him in his cell. On the third night before sleeping, Ruadhan tried to pray again: "God is..." Immediately the words were lost in a flood of memories: those rare occasions when Cairech his step-mother had hugged him close; Tulchán patiently explaining the wonders of his painting: Ite helping the others escape from the Northmen; Ite holding him close in the forest by Na Lámha; Conal anxiously testing every knot binding the coracle, his muscles taut with the effort; the fisherfolk eager to share their meal with a stranger; Tulchán looking intently at him, looking *into* him, believing in him. The memories brought sadness but in the midst of them and without fully understanding, Ruadhan began to rediscover hope and the determination to escape.

Tulchán had told him that monks followed a strict timetable of work and prayer. Ruadhan would do similar but the prime reason he disciplined his days: his rising, his sleeping and his watching, was in order to plot Fiacc's movements closely and he succeeded. Fiacc was a creature of habit. Once he believed he had sure knowledge of Fiacc's comings and goings, Ruadhan made a decision and each day, as soon as he was certain Fiacc was clear of the ledge, he made his way confidently, steadily, zigzagging down the steep stairs to explore the bay. Once at the beach, each step he took, each glissade down the expanses of smooth slanted rock and each scramble over the smaller stones filled him with excitement and belief but he was quick to assess that the changing seasons had not granted him the possibility of walking or swimming to freedom. The tide never receded far enough and the water was never calm enough. Even the great Cú Chulainn would struggle. One large, deep cave at the northern end of the bay brought him hope. At first, the sound of the seawater flowing and ebbing in that stone chamber was like a repeated sigh of suffering and regret, a confirmation of his plight, but when he took in all that was about him, the curl of the waves and their rush forward became a call of encouragement: *leave this place... now; leave this place... now*. It was a treasure trove. The cave was a vertex to the many currents that drove around the headlands. Boughs and branches from storm-damaged trees had been driven into its huge mouth and nestling like a cracked egg in the midst of this clutter was Ruadhan's coracle. He did not think he had the means to mend it but convinced himself at first glance that he could make a raft from the great pile of driftwood, a simple vessel that would carry him from the island. Ruadhan waded into the water, selected six solid boughs of similar thickness and length and dragged them well back into the cave where they would remain dry and where he could work on them. In the water once more, he retrieved the coracle and untied as many leather thongs as were salvable. He had made a start, nothing more on that first day but the change in Ruadhan was palpable. It was as if he breathed fresher air. Building the raft gave purpose to the days that followed and he took great care not to alert Fiacc to what he was doing. Each day he erred on the side of caution by making sure he was back in his high retreat long before the saturnine monk returned. Always as he was scrambling down the steps, Ruadhan felt a pull to explore in the opposite direction, to go to the top of the cliff. He was curious about what lay there and believed he might find materials to help him in his efforts on the shore.

A dense mist packed the early morning. If Fiacc's devils were roaming the island, they could surround him before he knew what was happening. Through gaps in the rush door, he saw Fiacc's large figure move from the cell to the back of the ledge. He heard a slate being dislodged as the monk climbed the remaining steps to the top of the cliff. Ruadhan waited until mid-morning before leaving his cell. The mist had thinned but only slightly. The steps were not as steep as those below the ledge and yet he went up them slowly on all fours. In spite of the cold and damp of the morning and in spite of telling himself there was nothing to fear, he was sweating.

He pushed his head cautiously over the top, hoping that the view would give him some idea of the size and shape of the island and perhaps even a glimpse of the mainland. He was disappointed again. He could not see more than twenty metres in front of him. Cautiously, he stood and walked inland, all of his senses sharply alert. The slight spring of the short heath grass felt good under his feet. He was alert to the gentlest depressions and disruptions of the dew that could be footprints and responded guardedly to the softest of scufflings in the grass. Soon huge isolated rocks loomed on all sides and Ruadhan's mind seethed once more with Fiacc's stories. He stopped, closed his eyes for a moment and bit his bottom lip. The noise in his ears was still at the same pitch. He must not let fears paralyse him. He knew what he had to do, and as soon as he opened his eyes again, he ran, stumbling, towards the nearest rock. When he reached it, he slapped both his hands on its surface and ran them all over it. It was a rock, nothing more than that; a rock, grey and partially coated with pale green lichen. It was no devil. There were no devils! To calm his racing heart and thudding head, he took several deep breaths, before stepping more confidently onwards.

The land sloped gently downwards to a bog studded with higher areas of rough heathers. Here, Ruadhan made slow, careful progress but found plenty of black bog-rush and occasionally, dense tussocks of tough purple moor grass both of which might serve as extra bindings on the raft. He sawed at them with a rough edged stone sure that each small swathe he harvested brought him closer to making his dream of escape a reality. Using more grass, he tied his collection in several bundles. He had to keep aware of time passing. Through the mist, he glimpsed a watery sun and estimated that the day was close to noon. If he hurried, he still had time to go to the shore.

Ruadhan made his way back along what he thought was the track he had taken, but soon realised he was heading in a different direction. He stopped, turned, looked hard at the ground about him, thought he saw the right way, and set off again. The rocks had reordered themselves. He closed his eyes hoping that when he reopened them, the way forward would be clear. It was not. He was lost in the mist. He could not shout because that would let Fiacc know he had disobeyed and left the ledge and he could not walk blindly on since that might take him into danger at the cliff face or in the bog.

Ruadhan had to move. He trembled with cold and fright. The murk was not going to clear. He turned a full circle on the spot. Nothing seemed remotely familiar. He turned a half-circle and started walking. The ground rose again and underfoot became much drier. Ruadhan thought he was heading away from the ledge but kept going in the hope that the terrain would soon explain itself to him. After he had walked steadily for half a kilometre, a sudden rustling in the heather made him crouch down. Ahead of him, something moved. He strained to see what it was. Although the shapes were indistinct, Ruadhan had no fear of demons because he knew right away what they were. The sheep were the first sign that Fiacc, Ungorn and he might not be the only inhabitants of the island.

He continued to make his way up the slope where the sheep cropped the grass steadily, hardly disturbed by his presence. Their wool glistened with droplets of moisture which hung delicately on every strand. Well before he reached the top, Ruadhan was stopped in his tracks once more, this time by the sight of a light penetrating the mist and by the faint sounds of voices.

Ruadhan's spirits should have lifted and nothing should have stopped him from running towards the light. However, experience since birth, including the months spent on the island, had taught him caution and suspicion. Not for one moment did Ruadhan think that these were friendly signs and that not far away, there were people who would help him leave the island. That light, he felt certain, threatened him and yet he had to go closer. Fear of the devils came back but it fought and lost to an intense curiosity. He had to find out more. What kind of creatures shared the island with him, Fiacc and the sheep?

The main light came from a bonfire at the tip of a steep headland and, set back from the cliff edge and protected from inland by a long, low, curving stone wall, was a well-established encampment. Ruadhan walked forward slowly towards the wall of the dun and now felt grateful for the mist which helped screen his presence. The grass bundles slung over his back rustled continuously but as he neared the camp, his sounds were lost in the crackling of the flames and the shouts from the people around.

The dun was not guarded and no one saw Ruadhan scramble over the wall. He scraped his ankle harshly on the stones and crouched low until the pain, but not the steady bleeding, eased. The camp was on clear ground cupped right and left by more huge grey rocks. Two fires burnt at the centre, one a brazier from which flames leapt and crackled furiously sending brilliant sparks high into the greyness, the other, a carefully tended cooking fire. Ruadhan crawled forward, put his bundles down and climbed up the shelved sides of the tallest rock to overlook the scene.

Thirty men occupied the camp. A few stood by the brazier but most sat talking loudly near the cooking fire with their woollen cloaks pulled tightly around them. A spit stood just to the side of the flames and a young man not much older than Ruadhan was slowly turning two legs of mutton. He was fed up with his work and drowsy from the heat. Every now and then, his head lolled forward and he had to shake himself to stay awake. His hair was short and his beard scant, but the rest of the men were the roughest and fiercest Ruadhan had ever seen. All were shaggy-haired and dirty and, from their scarred faces, looked as if they had spent most of their lives fighting. Their weapons were strapped to their bodies or lay close by and one black-bearded giant was running a stone firmly, forward and back, along the edges of his sword blade. Whoever they were, they were well settled on this part of the island and had made crude lean-to shelters using the natural walls of the rocks. A woman was filling waterskins from a wooden bucket outside one of the huts. Another woman entered the camp from the far side carrying two more buckets and joined her. Somewhere, Ruadhan was sure, bread was being baked for its smell mingled with the roasting mutton to make him feel very hungry. Any bread he had tasted on the island was elderly and as hard as stone and mutton was a faint memory from Cillebairre. He was startled out of his dream of a good meal by the sound of two voices that, in the midst of the hubbub, insisted on his attention. He had heard them both before and could not be mistaken. Almost directly below the rock he was lying on, in shadows well away from the fire, Fiacc and Ungorn were having a heated discussion. Ruadhan strained hard to hear but only sparse fragments of their conversation reached his ears.

"Do not let it burn low. It has to blaze through the night *and* on days such as this, and, when the day is clear, make smoke, plenty of it. I have told you this a thousand times."

186

Ruadhan pushed himself forward carefully to the very edge of the rock. He had to check with his eyes what his ears had told him. Five metres below, he saw the tall figure of Fiacc with his unchanging, expressionless face, standing beside the cruel little man. So, Fiacc had lied about Ungorn, thought Ruadhan, but not about the devils. There were plenty of devils on the island, all of them two-legged, and he, Fiacc, the greatest of them. Ruadhan pulled back from the edge, lay flat on the cold rock and thought of his raft and of fleeing the island.

Fiacc bent low to address Ungorn and spoke slowly, deliberately. "You are failing me. They could be here any day. There must be a beacon to guide them."

"It is not so easy."

"Get these scoundrels to help you."

"They will not lift a finger. They sit all day and eat and fight amongst themselves. Give them an enemy, Fiacc, before they create one for themselves. The Grey Wolves are fighters and servants of no man. I warn you, if your great allies do not come soon, guard your throat. This lot feed on killing and you have brought them to a famine."

Fiacc's anger rose: "Don't warn me about anything, misshapen thing. See to that beacon fire and concern yourself with nothing else."

"I have to pass the days and nights with this murderous pack and the only protection I have is the amusement my misshapen body gives them." Ungorn clambered awkwardly onto a smaller rock which stood beneath the one where Ruadhan lay hidden. He pointed upwards to the great rock. "When they are really bored, two drag me up there, swing me by the hands and feet and throw me to their friends below. It is great entertainment for them." He jumped back down and pointed several metres from them towards the centre of the clearing. "See the stake in the ground? That is the furthest they have succeeded in throwing me. When they drop me, Fiacc, who will keep your beacon fire alight?"

Fiacc mumbled a reply. He was becoming anxious. The Grey Wolves were a ragged band of near-savages brought together by strange fortune and outlawry. From all the four provinces of Ireland, they had united to pester the west coast with their small-scale banditry and piracy. Fiacc had worked hard to win their respect and to exert authority over them, but that respect rested on the many promises he had made, promises that he could not fulfil unless the foreigners came soon.

187

On top of the rock, Ruadhan shivered uncontrollably and felt very tired and dejected. He had to return to his cell on the cliff ledge and make good his escape. He shuffled backwards down the rock when Ungorn's raised voice stopped him. These words came clearly to his ears. "*He* has to be killed. I found him so let me do it."

His name was not used, but Ruadhan knew he had to be talking about him. The voices, lowered and indistinct once more, told him nothing else.

"And what of this. What use is this to us?" Ungorn rummaged among straw piled in a cleft between two rocks and lifted out what looked like a bundle of small hides. "Will the Northmen give us money for this?"

Ruadhan rolled on to his stomach. He was going to leave the camp but, as if another look below might reveal a completely different world to him, one that welcomed and comforted him, he inched forward once more to the edge of the rock. He saw Fiacc take a package from Ungorn and realised what it was. Another of the monk's lies was uncovered. They *had* found the Psalter when the storm drove Ruadhan to the island. The *creature* must have cut it from his ankle. Ruadhan let his head fall to the rock once more.

Fiacc unwrapped the book, placed it on the top of a rock and began to turn the pages. He stopped at one where blue dominated the illuminated margin. "Do you see this colour? It is made from a special powder. Monks pay in gold the size of my fist for a small bag of that powder. Tulchán was one of only two who used it, and he also knew where the Chalice is."

Ungorn was not interested, "You have told me this before. How does it help us now?"

Fiacc stared at the page as if waiting for it to reveal a great secret to him. "It doesn't." He closed the book and ran his fingers over its rough leather binding. "Monks and their scratchings! What profit's in it for anyone! I am no closer to finding the Chalice than when I was in the middle of the Egyptian wilderness. Soon our visitors will be here and I have only this pack of mercenaries to offer them. No, they will not give you money for this, Ungorn. Even if it was encased in gold and studded with precious stones, they would not *pay* you for it. These people are *takers*, Ungorn. Remember that and tread warily when you meet them."

Fiacc wrapped and returned the Psalter to its cleft in the rocks, then walked briskly away towards the cooking fire hugging himself powerfully to ward off the cold. He stopped suddenly. He seemed uncertain about what to do. After a moment, he turned to face Ungorn again. "They have been promised the Chalice and so must not know that I cannot lead them to it." He returned to the rocks and lifted the Psalter in both hands. He had made a decision: "I shall return to Clonmacnoise tomorrow. This bundle may yet serve us. It gives me a reason for leaving my poor little hermitage and visiting the monastery again. I shall present it to the Abbot and it will convince the fool further that his humble servant Fiacc is repentant and advancing in holiness. I shall also see my travelling companion, Brecc. Perhaps he has some news of the Glass Chalice. Who knows, perhaps they have found it and it is there waiting for me. This will be my last visit before leading our seafaring friends and the Grey Wolves to that place. Then we shall see if monks' prayers can stop sharp steel from biting them."

Ungorn sneered at the idea that going to Clonmacnoise would help them. He doubted everything to do with this glass chalice. He had never heard such nonsense and believed his master must be losing his mind to want to chase all over Ireland in search of such a thing. Well, let him go back to the monks for a while. Perhaps he, Ungorn, could have some enjoyment at the prisoner's expense.

Ruadhan began to ease back down the rock when he heard movement below. It was the huge, black-bearded man who had been sharpening his sword by the fire and he had come behind Ruadhan's rock to piss. Ruadhan stayed as still as he could. Blackbeard finished but then started, out of curiosity, to kick at the bundles of grass. Why were they there? And there was blood on them, and blood above them; fresh blood in a patchy trail up the side of the rock. A great commotion broke out by the fire just as Blackbeard looked upwards. If there was any fighting, he did not want to left out of it. He abandoned his investigation and ran back to his friends.

The whole company was on their feet brandishing weapons except for one man who was lying full stretch clutching his arm. His cloak had fallen from him and his long brown hair had fanned out on the ground under his head. His chest heaved rapidly and he stared transfixed at the dark blood seeping steadily from a vicious wound to his arm just below his shoulder. The scene was tense with the threat of more spilled blood until Fiacc's voice boomed above the others. He moved into the milling group, pushing them apart. "You fools! I did not bring you here to fight among yourselves! Sheathe your swords and save your energy for some real battles! I..."

Another figure came shambling from the shadows his right leg strangely articulated. Fiacc stopped talking and turned to him immediately. There was a hint of uncertainty in Fiacc's voice when he spoke again. "This, I tell you, will spoil everything."

"You tell us many things, Fiacc," Morann replied in a low monotone and then raised his hands to make a patting motion in the air. Reluctantly, his men separated and put down their weapons.

Blackbeard burst into the middle of them. "That son of a cur, Mochua, deserves what he was given. There is nothing he hasn't seen or done and he's never finished bragging about it. He had seen the whole world and fought every man in it before his mother gave him his first suck of her milk. Maybe this will quieten him for a while."

"Bring him closer to the fire," ordered Fiacc. Blackbeard looked to Morann who nodded consent. Blackbeard grabbed the wounded man's legs and dragged him roughly into the light. Mochua wanted to scream with the pain that this brought but the only sound he allowed to come from his mouth was a low moan. Fiacc knelt and, with a gentleness that those who knew him thought he would be incapable of, tore and eased the sleeve of Mochua's tunic away from the wound. The gentleness veiled the violence of what was to follow.

Fiacc inspected the wound. The arm was all but severed. Mochua's eyes had moved from his arm to Fiacc's face where he looked for signs to give him hope. He saw none. He saw pools of dark, rank water. Prompted only by gestures from Fiacc, Blackbeard knelt on Mochua's chest and good arm and, as he did so, passed his newly sharpened sword to Fiacc. Nobody spoke. Mochua turned his gaze from Fiacc and his wounded arm and tensed his body for what was to happen. Silence filled the clearing. The blood that had been racing through the fighting men's veins was stilled by this cold violence.

With two swift, sharp hacks, Fiacc removed the arm. Then he dropped the sword, took a brand from the fire, and, in order to seal the terrible wound, ran it several times across the stump that was left. He did this all in an efficient, matter-of-fact way, as if it was a daily operation for him. Mochua could not confine himself to moans; he screamed throughout until he lost consciousness and two men carried him to a shelter.

The sure sign that you are in the presence of a devil is the smell of scorching flesh. Ruadhan remembered Fiacc's words as he slid down the back of the rock. As quietly as he could, he gathered the bundles of grass and left the place. The mist shielded him until he was well away from the headland and then lifted momentarily to allow him a clear view of his surroundings. Large stones strewn around the foot of a young, wind-battered ash tree told him where he was. If he skirted the bog on his right until the land dipped sharply and then rose again, he would be close to the cells. He ran as fast as the ground allowed him. He had never thought he would ever be as pleased as he was to scramble down the few steps to the ledge and stumble, tired, aching and with his mind full of questions, into his bleak home.

Ruadhan had heard little of what passed between Fiacc and Ungorn, and his knowledge of why these people had gathered on the island had advanced only slightly: he knew that Fiacc was connected in some way with Clonmacnoise and was going there the following day; he knew that that same man was a liar; he knew that Ungorn was not a creation of his imagination; he knew that his life was in danger, that the Psalter had not been lost, and that *they* were coming.

On Board the *Sea Bear*

A couple of huts; that's all; not even a village. A pile of dried fish, some of it rotting; no pigs; not one sack of corn; poor pickings indeed. Rorik looked back to the shore and the burning huts. He was happy to be leaving it but full of uncertainties about what was ahead. The past weighed heavily. He had returned from his last voyage with only half his men, empty holds and broken ships. He was cursed, some said. It had been hard to get people to invest money and labour in new ships and a new voyage under his command. His own brother had laughed when he said he wanted two of the big warships, the *drekkars*, and several of the smaller *snekkjas*. He had had to settle for three of the latter and, with them perhaps his last chance to make a name for himself and grasp political power. The raid had been a waste of time and energy. Perhaps he *was* cursed. Ill fortune had dogged him and very little had gone right since they had left their homes. When only a day at sea, one man had been lost mysteriously overboard and much later, with Ireland close, a violent storm had capsized one of the longboats and broken the *Sea Bear's* mast. Rorik had been forced to winter on the west coast of Caledonia. It had taken a week's rowing among bleak islands to find good pine wood for the mast and oak for the damaged gunwale. By the time the new mast had been shaped and stepped into its bracket in the keel, the weather was so threatening that Rorik had no alternative but to camp and wait for spring and a change in fortune. The land and the impoverished native settlements offered meagre sustenance. Only the chance meeting with Gudrod in that dismal place had brought any encouragement and convinced him to continue.

Now, it seemed, failure once more pushed its face into Rorik's. Cursed? Could Oddrun be behind it? The men were tired, fractious and provisions were low. Even the corn wine which dulled their appetites for meat had all gone. A quick, surprise raid on a fat village had seemed the answer. The evening before, they had scanned the coastline intently for signs of life until, just before nightfall, they had seen smoke. Their tired bodies quickened with the expectation of a brief fight and a long feast. Old Harald swore he could smell roasting pig and was cutting great slices of it in his imagination. He could feel his teeth sinking into the fibrous meat and the fat running down his chin. What a let down it had been.

The father had put up a good fight but staffs and knives are no match for the well-forged blades of axes and swords. His two boys faced up to us as if it was the first time they had ever been in a fight, thought Rorik. They had killed and gutted plenty of fish but never a man. Poor pickings and Gunnar caught by the old man's flashing knife. He had died during the night and would be buried unceremoniously at sea. One man for a pile of dried fish; a very high price to pay. There would be a reckoning. Old Harald did not get his pork and refused to touch the fish. He needed to piss more than ever that night and sat up for most of it with ten others muttering discontentedly against Rorik. They had not left their homes in Trøndelag, suffered hardship and put their lives at risk to raid peasant huts for dried fish. Their leader was weak. And, Old Harold argued, voyaging with a lone woman on board, even though she was a priestess and the captain's wife, brought ill luck. When was there going to be some real fighting and some plunder worth fighting for? This was an ill-fated voyage. The gods were playing with them and would soon turn their faces away from them. Something had to be done. Their eyes had searched each other's faces. Without saying it, they all knew what that meant. It frightened them, but a drastic sickness called for a drastic cure.

He spoke little to add fuel to the unease but prominent among the malcontents was Bjorn, Rorik's nephew. Another, Adils, sat alone, well apart from any group but not far from Rorik. He stayed alert most of the night like a dog guarding its master. Being alone did not trouble him. Adils was Rorik's son by a slave woman. He had been born before Rorik's politically motivated marriage to Oddrun and when he reached his majority, his father had insisted upon making him his legitimate heir in preference to the three children his wife had given him. Oddrun and her birth family had reacted with fury, but Rorik was unmoved. Oddrun had never forgiven Rorik and ever since that time, had honed her resentment of Adils to sickle-sharpness. It did not trouble Adils. His early upbringing and the hatred of his step-brothers and step-sister had given him a steely, resourceful and independent personality. At seventeen, he was a strong, big-boned, healthy young man. He cared for no one else except his father whom he was willing to die for.

When Rorik saw Bjorn muttering with Old Harald and his friends, it confirmed that this family hatred had followed him all the way from home. He had been foolish and not followed his usual self-discipline. On earlier voyages and unlike many other captains, Rorik had not allowed women on his ships, but back in Trøndelag, craving the satisfaction of regular copulation he had been weak and selfish and had made her accompany him. She in turn had insisted that cousin Bjorn be a member of the crew. The young man was a favourite of hers and an ally against a husband who had disinherited her children in favour of a slave girl's whelp. As a priestess and *volva*,[9] Oddrun claimed to have divined that the voyage could not be a success without Bjorn.

Rorik had slept uneasily with his wife in one of the huts on sacking brought from the ship. His men had killed all of the family except the daughter. Bjorn had taken her as a slave. A frightened scrap of flesh, barely a woman, she was now on board the *Sea Bear*. "Dried fish and a slave girl." Rorik lifted his wool shirt and scratched ferociously about his chest. "If, when we meet them, Irish warriors in these parts are as fierce as the fleas they breed here," he thought, "then we are in for some rare fights."

The *Sea Bear* lurched violently as the ocean rose in high winds. Soon after leaving the shore, they had raised the great mainsail and felt the firm slap-slap of a steady breeze, but now Rorik called for it to be lowered and the oars manned before the ship capsized or the mast snapped again. In their wake, the *Sea Serpent* did likewise. The storm had blown up so quickly it had almost caught him unawares. This was his third voyage to Ireland but he had never experienced such unpredictable weather before.

Bjorn joined him at the prow of the ship. His long, fair hair, soaked by the rain and sea spray, clung to his face. A wood and metal amulet, a miniature of Thor's hammer, dangled from his neck outside his leather jerkin. He shouted to make himself heard. "Our ally is one of the Ui Neill's who are powerful chieftains, you say."

"That is what Gudrod told me," answered Rorik. He was sure his cousin was fomenting treachery but uncharacteristically unsure how to stop him. Usually Rorik would have acted quickly and decisively at the first hint of mutiny, but found himself hesitant and unable to act against Bjorn. Oddrun was the reason. Rorik did not believe her fortune-telling but many of his crew gaped open-mouthed and believing when she went into a trance and screamed her predictions. Any move against her or Bjorn would have to be planned carefully. He had been stupid to let her on board.

"And yet he is willing to help us attack their kingdom?"

---

[9] A female seer who would go into a trance and, it was believed, predict the future.

"He is intent on revenge. He believes he has been wronged by his family over the death of a cousin. And he wants power which he thinks we can give him. Like many a fool, he has grand schemes in his head."

"Do you trust him?"

"I do not know him. Gudrod's ship, the *Sea Eater*, was forced to shelter on one of the western islands and he met this man. These shores have been touched lightly by Viking feet and there must be great wealth here. The Irishman can lead us to it. No, I do not think I shall trust him. There are times when I cannot be sure of my own people, Bjorn, so why should I race to trust foreigners?" Rorik looked his young cousin full in the face as he said this and Bjorn returned a steady gaze. He pulled wet strands of hair from in front of his eyes.

"You want Gunnar's body to be put over the side?"

"See that it is done." Such a funeral will not be taken well, Rorik. Guddrun has highbred connections and was well-respected"

Rorik was dismissive. "Put his axe to a sharpening stone and then fasten it to his side. Get Oddrun to say prayers. It will be enough to guarantee him a happy life in the next world."

Rorik did not reveal any information concerning the Chalice. Bjorn and the others were bound to question the purpose of searching for a glass cup. The Chalices they wanted were of gold and were locked away in the western monasteries of Ireland. Rorik hoped for a shipload of that precious metal, but he had also become obsessed by a dream of the power that the Glass Chalice could bring him. The discontented Irish nobleman had told Gudrod that all Egypt was looking for this mysterious Chalice. It had special, magical powers with which the holder could define that country's destiny and in so doing shape a future of wealth and power for himself. Rorik knew of that distant country. Swedish Vikings, sailing to Byzantium and beyond, spoke of Arab lands in the warm south which had incomparable riches. It is true that he and Gudrod had drunk enough ale to satisfy a village but Rorik's senses had remained sharp throughout and Gudrod was a man he respected, an outstanding *hersir*[10] and one not given to exaggeration. The news that his fellow-captain had brought from

---

[10] Title for a local leader, a man who owned land and who commanded other men in the area when they were called to do battle.

Ireland showed Rorik a door which, when opened, would reveal those riches. The key to the door was the Glass Chalice. The Arab rulers of Egypt would fill his ships ten times over if he could give them the sacred Chalice of St. Mark.

Escape

Ruadhan had learned patience during the long winter months. He waited and watched. Mist continued to shroud the island and Fiacc kept to his usual pattern of going and coming until the evening of the third day after Ruadhan had found the encampment. He did not return to the ledge and was not there the following day when Ruadhan woke to a bright morning full of early spring softness. Like a frown that goes from the forehead of an anxious man who hears good news, the mist had left the island. Ruadhan headed down to the shore with his bundles of dry grass.

They were not the most reliable of materials. He knew that but was desperate and so for one very long day he worked twisting the grass and reeds into makeshift ropes and tying the wood of the raft. The work was hard and frustrating. The ropes were frail and frequently snapped when he tried to bind them tightly around the boughs. He strengthened them by carefully tearing strips off his tunic and twining them with the grasses and with lengths of bark. When finished, the raft was barely seaworthy but Ruadhan was determined to use it. It gave him a chance of reaching the mainland. If it broke, if it sank, Ruadhan did not care. He had to get off the island and was ready to die in doing so. He drank from several runnels of water that trailed down the cliff face and for food, gathered mussels, periwinkles and cockles and ate them raw. A fire would draw attention. There was never enough and he always felt hungry, but it gave him energy to carry on. Confident that Fiacc had left for Clonmacnoise and aware that Ungorn may be hunting him, he slept that night on the beach under an overhanging rock in the cliff face.

Ungorn visited the clifftop above the two cells early on that fourth evening and waited until darkness gripped the island. When Ruadhan did not return to his cell, he scrambled down the cliff steps to the beach. Ruadhan was working outside the cave by the light of the moon and did not hear the little man edging along the bottom of the cliff. Ungorn decided not to kill him right away, not just yet. The stupid one was sensing freedom. Let him stretch and almost touch it a while longer, and then pull him back violently. Yes, that would be much more satisfying.

Long before dawn, like a stoat searching out its prey, Ungorn slipped noiselessly past the sleeping Ruadhan to the shore. It was an ebb tide on a calm night and the waves washed quietly, steadily against the land. He dragged Ruadhan's makeshift craft from the back of the cave over one of the great slabs of rock to the edge of the water. There, he cut the crude ropes, separated the boughs and set them adrift in the bay.

All Ruadhan's huge hopes for the new day drained from him when he saw what had been done. He knew there was only one person who could have wrecked his raft. He sat dejectedly for half the morning, fighting back the thought that he would never leave the island and waiting for Ungorn to return. The sea was as calm as he had ever seen it. The raft, flimsy as it was, would have taken him to the mainland. *The Word must be preserved... The forest will have kept you safe... you must retrieve the book and take it to the great monastery of Clonmacnoise.* Tulchán. Brooding and doing nothing would not help: on the contrary, it would let Ungorn keep the upper hand. Eventually, this thought claimed supremacy over others and Ruadhan became very active. Firstly, using kindling he had stored, he made a fire just outside the cave. It took him a long time to start but once the first strands of grass were burning, it was only a few moments before he had a fine blaze. He was amazed at how good it felt. It was his own blaze and an act of defiance. All through the harsh winter, he had begged for fuel but Fiacc had never allowed him to light a fire on the ledge. "Reject such comforts, Ruadhan, and kindle the spiritual fire within."

Ruadhan piled his shore fire high with the branches left in the cave and then quartered the beach and the rocks collecting driftwood. Of course, Ungorn would see the fire but Ruadhan did not care. It was a message saying that he might look weak and easy prey but that appearance was not all.

Eat: he had to eat, and not let hunger make him more vulnerable than he already was. Cooked in the fire, sea molluscs tasted better and satisfied him more than when he had eaten them raw. He also found several large crabs and put these in the embers at the fire's edge until their carapaces blackened and cracked. He burnt his fingers lifting them from the fire and forcing their shells back, but the meat tasted better than anything he had ever eaten before. The meal did not fill him and he knew that the contentment the fire and the food had brought would not last long. He also knew that the beach was a trap. He did not want to die there. He had to climb the cliff one more time and face Ungorn. Before he left the shore, Ruadhan pulled a partly burnt branch from the fire. *You will need a good weapon. You cannot travel that far without a weapon.* In two minds, he looked at it for a long time before dashing it on a stone nearby and breaking off most of the scorched end. It was not *a good weapon* but what remained of the branch felt the right weight and size in his hand, a heavy club with which he could defend himself and perhaps even inflict hurt on another.

In the mid-evening, Ruadhan made one final ascent of the steps to his cell. As he climbed, the gulls, their days full of nesting preparations, were noisier than ever and threw tantrums, shrieking in groups and scudding dementedly along the cliff face as if their nests, still unbuilt, had been invaded. If they had laid their eggs, Ruadhan could have eaten. He fought back pangs of hunger with thoughts of his escape and of reaching Clonmacnoise. Ungorn was not at the ledge and Ruadhan could not see him on the clifftop. The light was fading fast and when he heard scuffling above, his resolve to go further waned along with it. He crawled into his cell. The small entrance would be easy to defend.

The regular clatter of stones on the cell walls and his name called from above punctuated the early hours of darkness. Ungorn was in no hurry. He wanted the boy to know he was there and to torment himself with thoughts of what might happen; to be the terrified rabbit paralysed by the stoat's deadly approach. He had heard that the rabbit dies of fright moments before teeth part fur and muscle at the back of its neck. Perhaps it would be that way with the boy.

At first, although he was very tired, Ruadhan found it easy to stay awake. He rolled two heavy stones into place behind the reed door and then squatted facing it, with the club in his lap, waiting for the little man to attack. Time passed slowly. Ruadhan strained to hear every sound, expecting the next one to define itself clearly as a footfall. That sound never came and Ruadhan became very drowsy. To sleep would be so pleasant; to curl up on the straw, draw the blanket over himself, and fall into the deep, happy, healing peace of sleep.

Ruadhan's head lolled suddenly and he shook himself to alertness once more. He had to do something. To sit waiting in his cell was to play along with Ungorn; to do exactly what the malignant creature wanted him to do. He shifted the door slightly to look outside. A cloud moved across the moon and Ruadhan pushed the door back and slipped from his cell as noiselessly as he could. Far below, the incoming tide rushed between the rocks and scrabbled at the beach with urgent fingers. The clifftop was faintly outlined but there was no sign of Ungorn. Ruadhan replaced the door and then crawled along the seaward side of his cell to the furthest edge of the recess in the cliff face. Above him was twenty metres of sheer but badly fissured rock. Ungorn had to be at the head of the steps, since he would think there was no other way Ruadhan could leave the ledge. If Ruadhan could climb the rock face to the clifftop, he had a chance of escaping.

He did not give himself time to think about it. If he waited, his fears would make him colder than he already was and his hands would not grip properly. Reluctantly, Ruadhan abandoned his club and started the climb, moving steadily, not rushing, inching his toes and fingertips into new holds in the cracked wall of rock. The cloud passed the moon and by the renewed light, Ruadhan saw a route to the top. A metre to his right, a huge crack started and ran diagonally almost to the crest where it disappeared under a large clump of soil and grass that overhung the rock face. Provided there were handholds, he was sure he could reach there. He shuffled his feet slowly along the crack, stopping frequently to search with his hands for the slightest deformity: a cleft or knob, which would give him a new grip. Several times, there was only the finest of interruptions to the rock's smoothness to hold on to and Ruadhan's fingertips became numb and torn with the effort of trying to scrape a decent purchase for themselves.

Until he reached it, he had not thought the overhang would be a problem. He rested for a moment, breathing heavily. The night air was so still he thought Ungorn was bound to hear him, but there was no movement above. The crumbling sod of earth stuck well out from the rock face and overcoming it was going to be the most dangerous part of the climb. Ruadhan reached for a handhold in the short grass and, before shifting his stance, pulled to see how firmly bedded the whole clump was. It moved but not enough to make him lose his confidence. He edged that hand as far out and over the jutting earth as he could stretch without losing his balance, and then took a deep breath to prepare himself for what was to follow. He felt with his right foot for a higher toehold but found none. He would have to rely on his hands alone; grip the sod with both of them and pull himself up and over it. For a second that right hand was going to be his only hold, and as soon as he released his left hand from the rock, his body would fall backwards.

Ruadhan tried not to think of what would happen if his left hand did not find a grip or if the clump of earth came away when his weight pulled on it. He clenched his right hand on the grass and let go with his left. The moon disappeared again. He brought his left hand as quickly as he could to the overhang and burrowed into the soil beneath the layer of grass with his fingers. A shower of fine soil spattered his face. His legs swung free of the rock and he started to pull himself upwards, moving each hand in turn to gain a better hold. Only thin, rangy roots and loose stone held this piece of earth to the grass on the clifftop. Ruadhan heard roots ripping; more sandy dirt spilled in his face and the sod shifted slightly but held. By swinging one leg over the side of the overhang on to the firm clifftop, he was able to clamber free of the terror of the rock face.

Ruadhan's tunic was soaked in sweat and his heart was racing. For a few moments while he recovered from the ordeal, he could do nothing but lie on his back panting and gaze at the cold stars, hoping Ungorn had not heard him.

Ungorn, the stoat, had become impatient with his own tactics. He moved in for the kill. Just as Ruadhan made the final effort to reach the clifftop, Ungorn dropped stealthily down the steps to the ledge. When Ruadhan rolled over on to his stomach and began to look for his enemy, he did not see him but he heard his own name being called once more. He crawled on his elbows back to the edge of the cliff and was just able to make out Ungorn crouching outside the door of the cell. In a soft, wheedling voice, he was calling Ruadhan, and inviting him to come outside. Ruadhan jumped to his feet and ran as fast as he could. He stumbled and fell, stumbled and fell, but kept picking himself up and running onwards. He did not realise he was moving towards the headland and the dun until he saw the beacon. It had served its first purpose and drawn the seafarers to the island but still blazed in the clear night and now led Ruadhan to the encampment. He did not know what to do, where else to go. There he might find answers, a solution to his quandary of how to flee the island.

The old fort was crowded. Newcomers had arrived and from his vantage point on the tall rock, Ruadhan realised that these were the ones Fiacc had spoken of, the ones the beacon had been lit for. From their dress and weapons, he knew they were Northmen. A feast was being prepared and women busied themselves about several cooking fires. The men stood in separate groups, suspicious of each other. All still had their weapons girded to them. Some of the Irish had encountered Viking raiders before and bore scars and bitter memories. Others had heard stories that had gained a lot in the telling and so were surprised to see how human, how ordinary these men were. More Northmen entered the dun from the far side, carrying boxes and sacks. Out of one box came gifts for their Irish hosts, the spoils of raids: a length of silk; four strange animals carved in ivory; a large, silver brooch, and a heavy, keen-bladed sword with an ornately carved bone handle. Morann with his awkward gait stepped from the crowd of Irishmen, asserted his leadership, and accepted the gifts from Rorik. In return, he ushered the Viking leader to be the first to sit and eat meat and drink ale by one of many fires. Oddrun and Bjorn joined them. Almost immediately, with guttural shouts and simple gestures, the two groups began to make themselves understood. Everyone, especially Old Harald, knew stomach language and was delighted by the roasted and boiled meat they were given. Suspicions faded, and among the Northmen, disloyal thoughts against their leader were put to one side as they satisfied ravenous appetites.

Ruadhan's loneliness became more intense than ever. He was hungry, yes, but his hunger for company was greater at that moment than hunger for food. He wanted so much to slip down from the rock, run to one of the fires and sit in the middle of the boisterous crowd, happy to say nothing, but just to sit and listen; listen to the simple attempts to make conversation, to the stupidity, the crudity, the banality. He wanted to be a child again and feel the comfort and security of adult noise and movement. As the new allies ate and drank their way through what remained of the night, Ruadhan lay on the cold rock and tried to decide what to do. When the first glimmerings of the new day seeped out of the eastern sky, his anxiety increased. He had been stupid. He should not have stayed where he was. But where could he go? He was trapped. If Ungorn and others searched the island, they were bound to capture him.

Below Ruadhan most of the men slept by the fires. A few from each group stood or sat alert since they had been given orders to keep a clear head, stay on guard and be mindful of their new allies. One feast does not get rid of suspicions and neither group wanted to give the other the opportunity for treachery. The women were still active, feeding the fires and preparing oatmeal porridge for when the men woke up. Ruadhan watched them in their weary, unchanging pace as they bent and lifted, carried and put down. One was younger than the rest and Ruadhan in his tiredness had been looking at her for several minutes before he realised who she was. It was Samthann, the timid daughter of the fisherfolk who had been so hospitable. As she fetched water, she kept her head down and refused to meet the gaze of any man, Irish or Norse, she passed. She looked frail and frightened and overburdened by the wooden buckets which she lowered to the ground by the shelters not far from the foot of Ruadhan's rock. She clenched and unclenched her hands to rid them of the pull of the buckets' ropes, and then, as if compelled, she raised her head and looked at Ruadhan. Ruadhan stayed still and the only sign she gave of having seen him was a slight, quizzical tilt of her head before she lifted the buckets again and crossed to the other side of the encampment.

The realisation that Samthann had been captured and that the others in her family were probably dead shook Ruadhan out of his self-pity and irresolution. To lie and wait for something, as if by magic, to transform his situation, was childish. He was not a child. He had to get away from the camp and do it quickly. If he was caught, he, Ruadhan, the one who had humiliated the bully, Ruarcc, would put up a fight. His raft had been destroyed but a simple deduction, which he had not made before, told him that there must be other boats on the island, boats that had brought the Irish and the Northmen to the place.

The Northmen carrying the gifts had entered the camp from a point almost directly opposite Ruadhan by a track that led to a sheltered beach south-east of the headland. Ruadhan slipped quietly down from his rock and climbed over the low boundary wall. He walked back the way he had come, and then moved in a long semi-circle to the other side of the dun where he found the track and, in the twilight, saw the small sand and pebble beach at the end of a wide and shallow gulley. Keeping to the gorse at the side of the path, he headed cautiously for the beach. The Viking longships had been pulled well up from the water and close to the gulley entrance. Two currachs, larger than any Ruadhan had seen, almost as long as the *snekkjas*, stood next to it, and two smaller ones and a coracle lay upturned further along the beach. Ruadhan stepped as quietly as he could over a narrow band of pebbles at the top of the beach and crossed on sand to the smaller vessels. He stroked the hide coverings on one and allowed himself a smile. They could do with a new coating of wool grease.

He chose one of the currachs and bent to turn it upright. It was much bigger than his coracle but normally Ruadhan would have been able to turn the boat right side up with ease. Now, every time he gripped the gunwales and tried to lift, he felt dizzy and sick. He had had little to eat and the frightening, exhausting events of the night had drained him. Five times he tried before he succeeded in righting the boat. Several oars lay on the pebbles underneath. When he had recovered his breath and energy, he grabbed them and laid them in the boat. The boat slithered easily off the stones, down the sandy beach and soon Ruadhan heard the happy sound of waves licking the leather of the prow. It was a simple action now to push the boat out a short way, climb into it and leave the hell that this island had been to him. Now his body was surging with vigour and his mind with optimism. Facing the sea, he did not notice the second currach rising. It lifted and Ungorn stepped out from under it. Screaming triumphantly, and drawing his short sword, he ran into the water alongside Ruadhan. With his weapon, he pricked the young man under the chin.

"I pull you from the sea again, boy, but this time, no mercy."

Ruadhan said nothing. If he was going to die, he did not want to waste thoughts and words on Ungorn. His fickle body was weary again, weary beyond all telling. Tulchán had known when the time for his death had come and accepted it; Ruadhan should do likewise. He closed his eyes and focused his mind once more on the illustration to Psalm 46, the first page he had seen in the Psalter. He recited the psalm to himself, and imagined discovering his parents after death.

The sword thrust did not come. "A final torture he wants me to suffer," thought Ruadhan, but kept his eyes closed. "If I open them, he will see fear and that will give him satisfaction." His body tensed itself for Ungorn's blade to enter and he hoped death would cross the threshold swiftly after it. Another prick under the chin. One more. But that final thrust did not come. Ruadhan swallowed hard. There was a surging in his ears; a numbness came over them. His head spun. The tip of the blade did not press on his skin any more. He opened his eyes: Ungorn still gripped his sword but his arm hung by his side and he was staggering backwards, away from Ruadhan and out of the water. The little man's free hand lifted to try to stop blood flowing from a wound to his temple. His fingers fluttered about the side of his head, frantically searching for the source of the blood. They found it and Ungorn fell heavily. Samthann reloaded the sling but cast the stone aside when she saw Ungorn lying still on the sand. The sea busily erased his shallow footprints and lapped about his legs. She ran to Ruadhan who stood paralysed by the closeness of death and helped him into the currach. With ease, she pushed the boat out of the shallows and beyond the breaking waves. Ruadhan was powerless to help her. He lay flat on the bottom of the boat and the noises increased in volume and the inside of his head roared and the weird pictures flashed vividly as Samthann climbed on board and rowed them steadily from the island.

CLONMACNOISE

On Little Bone I Lie

As Abbot Ronan used a bone needle to scrape a speckle of dirt from under the nail of his left hand index finger, he smiled. He was particularly pleased. He had been right about Fiacc. The man had great potential. He would make an excellent monk and this finding of the Psalter was nothing short of a miracle and evidence that this man was to be showered with very special graces. So solemn; not given to levity and foolish witticisms like some he could think of. Perhaps he would turn out to be another Cronan the Hermit.

Abbot Ronan thought that it was quite in order for him to relax his Lenten fast because a guest had arrived. He had eaten with Fiacc after mid-afternoon prayers. Their meal had not been excessive: bread, milk, vegetables and herbs, food that the great Columban told us does not burden the stomach and suffocate the soul. They had prayed beforehand and eaten in silence. Fiacc had eaten very little, as Ronan expected. Self-denial was shaping a special soul.

Following the meal, the two walked about the monastery enclosure and Abbot Ronan questioned Fiacc about his prayerful isolation on the island. At first, Fiacc was reluctant to speak about his hermitage, and Ronan was impressed once more by the man's self-effacement; no, it was nothing less than humility. However, the abbot wanted to hear about it since the experience could be a light to guide others. Ronan ordered Fiacc to tell him and listened for a full hour to a harrowing story of suffering and demonic torment that Fiacc had accepted in Christ's name. They then prayed together once more and Ronan insisted that Fiacc spend his time at Clonmacnoise in the comfort of the guesthouse, the *tech n-oiged*. A big fire was lit; water carried and stones heated for a bath, and a leather couch prepared for his sleeping. All his meals would be brought to him. Ronan would send a monk to record Fiacc's experiences. Fiacc protested, as the Abbot had expected.

Was it a smile or a smirk? Brecc was loathe to give him the benefit of the doubt.

"Tell me, Brother Brecc, why are you so anxious to labour for the food that perishes."

206

Brecc could hardly contain himself. Who did this young man think he was fooling other than poor Abbot Ronan whose knees were as leathery as a camel's from praying but who could not tell the difference between a loaf and a stone when it came to judging people? Brecc dropped weeds he had pulled and shifted his stance to face his visitor square on. He placed both hands on his hips. "Don't look down upon "the food that perishes", Fiacc, or upon those who toil in the fields. And don't tell me I should be more concerned with the things of the spirit or, when the hour to eat comes, you'll find nothing in your bowl except your prayers."

His own sarcasm made Brecc feel uncomfortable but had little effect upon Fiacc who stared coldly at the monk. Brecc's tone became less abrasive: "If I thought you were serious about prayer, Fiacc, then I would not speak in this harsh manner to you but in all the time we passed together in foreign lands, you showed very little interest in the spiritual."

Brecc could have said more, a lot more, but stopped suddenly and wondered why he was wasting words on this strange man. He took a hoe, pushed it towards his visitor but only then realised that he was carrying the Psalter that the whole monastery was talking about. Fiacc remained silent. "It must have been a huge fish, Fiacc, to hold that in its stomach."

"It was."

"And it threw itself on to the shore at your feet."

"That is the way of it."

Brecc wanted to laugh in his face. With this man as his companion, he had travelled as far as any Roman soldier had and although he still could not say that he knew him closely, he thought he knew him well enough to be sceptical about this tale. He stared hard at Fiacc but the cold eyes gave nothing away. "That is truly a marvel."

Fiacc had found Brecc alone in the vegetable garden clearing the first weeds from among his leeks. The morning had warmed early and the valley was full of sound and movement. Boats were already on the river and *manaigh* hard at work in the fields which extended well beyond the monastery enclosure.

Brecc knew he was becoming more selfish with age. He wanted his garden and his prayers and that was all. He avoided company. Now Fiacc was back, had invaded the garden and wanted to talk. He looked strong and healthy, thought Brecc, with plenty of flesh on his big bones - a bull of a man. No doubt, Abbot Ronan saw this as another sure sign of severe fasting and holiness. Tut, tut, uncharitable thoughts piling one on top of the other, as usual. It has to stop.

"Why have you brought the book here, Fiacc? I am no scholar."

"No, but you were a most respected one. Abbot Ronan says that your knowledge of the styles and techniques of our scribes is great and you may know the one who made this psalter, if it comes from human hands."

Brecc laughed. Fiacc's final words made his mind up. He would help him if only to prove that it was indeed the work of *human* hands. Without any ceremony, Brecc dropped the hoe, wiped his hands on his casula and took the Psalter from Fiacc. A brief glance was all he needed to know it was the work of Tulchán of Cillebairre but he did not hand the book back to Fiacc immediately. He wanted to answer Fiacc and then be done with the book and with him, but the beauty of the pages stopped him and reminded him of days spent in the scriptorium when he was younger and when reading seemed to answer all his questions.

"Look here, see that red? It has an intensity which only Tulchán could produce, and look, see the delicacy of that curve, like a plump dove's breast. That's Tulchán. He could paint that without pricked and inked guidelines. This is his work, perhaps the last before he was martyred."

Fiacc did not look where the monk's finger was pointing. "He is the one who knew the whereabouts of the Chalice of St. Mark, isn't he?"

"Well, that is what we were told," Brecc replied, uninterested. "Look, see that blue. Incomparable! Lapis lazuli of the highest quality. He was a master of his art; such a gentle touch, like a dragon-fly on water."

"Have you found the Chalice?"

Brecc did not hear. He was surprised by the thoughts and memories Tulchán's Psalter had stirred. He turned the pages slowly to the final one. It was a beautiful work of art, a fitting presentation of the songs of the Israelites to the one true God, all one hundred and fifty one of them. One hundred and fifty one? From his student past, Brecc dredged up knowledge. The early Greek *Septuagint* translation of the bible contained one hundred and fifty-one psalms, one digit higher than the Hebrew numbering, and a Syriac version added more, but Tulchán would never have adverted to those. Surely not. What would be the point? Brecc looked hard at the last psalm. How strange. It was one completely unknown to him and completely out of step with the final chorus of praise that preceded it. It had to be Tulchán's own invention.

"This is odd; very odd. There is a short, extra psalm, one that is in no Bible I have seen. Why should Tulchán have done this?" Brecc was talking to himself and failed to notice that Fiacc had moved closer and was now standing alongside of him staring intently at the page. Brecc read the Latin:

> Like a stream, your life pours from me
> And brings joy to all the nations,
> But I have so many enemies, Lord.
> In haste I run and hide from them,
> Like a frightened young deer on the hills.
> My own defile the temple and the graves.
> Under stones I cower. I quake at the enemies' shouts.
> They have destroyed everything in the sanctuary.
> Wretched, I am plunged into a dark place, a pit;
> With bones I lie and on little bone I lie.
> Hear me as I cry for help!
> Listen to my prayer!
> Lead me, Lord, from this dark place
> And let your life pour from me once more!

The puzzle that this "psalm" presented brushed aside the plans Brecc had for his morning's work in the garden. It even softened his attitude to Fiacc, and he began to share his understanding of what the page could mean. Fiacc's knowledge of Latin was weak and so Brecc translated into Irish.

"Tulchán would not write such verses in imitation of Holy Scripture unless he had a very good reason and I am puzzled by the fact that this is a poor imitation with strange inconsistencies. That first line, *Your life pours from me*, is questionable, and look here, in the third verse: what are these clumsy references to *bones* meant to signify: *ossis* and *ossiculo*?" Brecc frowned and turned to another page in the Psalter. "Perhaps poor Tulchán was tired and unsure of what he was writing, for they are odd lines and it is a poorly drawn page. It looks as if it has been done by a young scholar whose hand was cramped with deep-winter frost. It is very strange."

Fiacc's face had a new alertness. "*Your life pours from me*: God's blood, God's life is poured from the sacred Chalice at the Eucharist."

Brecc looked at him disdainfully. "Yes, of course it is, but what has that to do with the psalm?" he snapped in reply.

"Perhaps Tulchán is telling us where the Chalice of St. Mark is hidden."

Brecc dismissed the suggestion: "The Chalice, the Chalice: why are you so concerned with the Chalice? God lives in his people in spite of this or that chalice and our friends in Egypt must learn this. I shall keep the Psalter for today, Fiacc, and go to the scriptorium where I shall study the furrows that Tulchán has ploughed and sown on this vellum to see if any greenery is pushing up among them. There is a lot for me to do right here but I am intrigued by what he has written."

Fiacc bowed to the old monk. He was alarmed by Brecc's plans but did not let the monk see. If Tulchán had written about the Chalice, he did not want the whole monastery to know. "I would be grateful, Brother, to know what you find out, as soon as you do, because I am also intrigued by this riddle."

Brecc experienced a slight dizziness and swayed slightly. To his surprise, this business had excited him. The Psalter suddenly felt very heavy. The pains in the arm would follow soon. Perhaps a day in the scriptorium would be sensible. What was it Fiacc had said? Was he misjudging the man? Could it be that his exile on the lonely island *had* changed him? "Oh, yes, yes, of course. But do not be hopeful that it has anything to do with the Chalice. It is probably some playful little puzzle Tulchán has left us. I don't think we shall ever find the Chalice."

Fiacc bowed once more. Brecc turned and walked quickly trying to disguise the faintness he was experiencing. He tottered slightly. Fiacc watched the old man head towards the scriptorium, and, uncharacteristically, felt a twinge of affection for him. He liked the way Brecc always questioned what was put before him and was seldom taken in by appearances, and he liked the stubborn, independent streak in the old monk. Fiacc shook his head slightly as if to rid himself of such wasteful emotion. If Brecc stood in his way, then Brecc would have to be cut down.

Brecc did not make any sense of Tulchán's conundrum on that day and regretted the time spent in the scriptorium. Using a simple concordance he himself had compiled in his student days, he looked up references elsewhere in the Book of Psalms to the major nouns that Tulchán used: *stream, temple, deer, graves, sanctuary, pit, bones,* but had not been able to draw any conclusions from what had been a very long exercise. He tried to decipher a message from the initial letters of every line, but that had been impossible and he had also tried in vain to make sense out of some words that seemed out of place. *Bones* and *little bone* troubled him: *With bones I lie and on little bone I lie*. They troubled him but he could not come up with any solution and so had decided that the exercise was pointless and that he would not sit at a desk any longer. Brecc wanted the feel of the earth beneath his feet and not the stone floor of the scriptorium. The soil in his garden had stirred with the sun's early spring warmth and he still had seed to sow.

The scribes of Clonmacnoise were pleased to see Brecc leave the scriptorium and library. He had been a noisy, disturbing intruder, muttering, grunting and, at times shouting out loud as he worked at a desk. He had not been able to sit for long and had frequently left the desk and stridden about the scriptorium as if he was crossing a ploughed field. It had been most distracting and one scribe, a pale, self-effacing monk called Servan had risen to protest but had met Brecc's angry gaze as he passed by on another of his frenzied circuits and had decided to sit down again. Brother Brecc had good qualities, of that there was no doubt, but, in the wrong mood, he had a very sharp tongue and Servan did not want to feel the edge of it.

Seven days later, two young people walked falteringly along the road from the west to the great settlement of Clonmacnoise. The track followed a ridge along a number of low hills that ran almost in a straight line. To the north lay a huge expanse of bog, while south lay the broad river, marshes and more bogland. The gentle slopes of several of the hills had been cleared of woodland and were speckled with dozens of wooden houses. On the highest hillock and close to the great river stood the *vallum*, the monastery enclosure. Once he had reached there, Ruadhan's journey would be over. It had been a long, hard, fast trek from the coast. In spite of Ruadhan's pleadings when the fit was over, Samthann had rowed from the island to the nearest point on the mainland where they had left the boat and walked to Clonmacnoise. Ruadhan had wanted to return to his original route and find the huge river Conal had told him about, but Samthann argued that the Northmen were as familiar with the sea as fish were and would find them easily on water, but never on land. And it was Samthann who gave great urgency to the task of reaching the monastery since it was one of the places the Grey Wolves and Northmen spoke of sacking. Ruadhan found it hard to express his gratitude to her. She was the exhausted one now, but it was her strength and clear-headedness that had brought them to Clonmacnoise.

Ruadhan was amazed at the size and the bustle of the settlement. The river, wide and slow, was dotted with coracles and people fishing from them. At the quay beneath the monastery enclosure, several large currachs were tied up. A masted one raised its sail. Next to it, monastic students from Clonfert disembarked from a smaller vessel. One path led directly from the quay to the enclosure while another crossed below it and wound, along the foot of the hills through fertile fields and clusters of houses.

Children ran and hid when they saw the two strangers coming and edged out of their hiding places to study them as they passed. One little boy was in such haste that he ran into the stalk ends of the thatch on a low roof and cut his face badly. Samthann moved to help him but he ran further away whenever she got near him. The adults paused in their work to look at them. Women's fingers stopped deft movements over narrow looms, and a group of men sawing, cutting and splitting a huge tree trunk lowered their tools and turned to watch. Their gazes were neither threatening nor welcoming, but simply curious.

Ruadhan was captivated by his first sight of Clonmacnoise, the place Tulchán had sent him to; his new, exciting home, the city at the crossroads of Ireland, a place of kings and saints. His tiredness and any fear that Fiacc might be waiting like a spider at the centre of its web, fell away from him. When he reached the ditch surrounding the vallum, he speeded his steps. The monastery had to be alerted without any delay to the terrible threat that was lurking. Ruadhan would find the Abbot and tell him everything that had happened: tell him about Tulchán; the Psalter; Fiacc; the island and the Northmen. Shoulders sagging and feet dragging, Samthann followed Ruadhan into the enclosure.

Later that same day, and one week after his unsuccessful attempt to become a scholar again, Brecc found a young man, not much more than a youth, sitting at the edge of his garden. His knees were drawn up to his chin and he looked both dejected and angry. Brecc's first reaction was to get rid of him quickly. There had been too many interruptions recently. The peace of his garden had been broken daily by visits from Fiacc who was very anxious to know if the psalm had yielded meaning.

"I am certain there is some message there concerning my spiritual journey, brother. Why else should that book be presented to me in such a marvellous way, in the belly of a fish?"

Brecc's patience had been frayed by these visits and the day before he had told Fiacc that he should go back and ask the fish what the meaning of it all was and stop pestering him.

The old monk gathered up his tunic and walked in a very determined way through the planted rows of leeks towards the ragged, dirty youth. He would scatter him like he scattered the birds at his seed. The young man saw him coming and looked right through him. Ruadhan did not care what happened to him now. Perhaps he should return to the forest he had come from and live with wild animals. He had been through so much and for what? It seemed to be for nothing. He could not be hurt any more than he had been already. Brecc stopped five metres from the trespasser, his resolution waning. There had been a commotion earlier in the day over two strangers, a young man and a young woman who had come into the enclosure. This must be the male. His obvious dejection touched Brecc's heart and a scrap of verse from the psalms he had pored over in the scriptorium came into the old monk's head:

Do not hide your face from me

when I am in trouble;

bend down to listen to me.

Brecc told himself off: why should he be angry with this young man? Get rid of the anger and show him God's face. And so, neglecting his garden once more, he sat with Ruadhan. Ruadhan was wary but for the second time that day, related his story from the time Tulchán had entrusted him with the Psalter to his arrival at Clonmacnoise. Brecc listened patiently and spoke cautiously. "I have travelled through many lands with Fiacc but still do not know the man. I have always felt uneasy with him."

Ruadhan was relieved to be with someone who did not dismiss his story out of hand but clearly anxious. "Now, I will lose my soul," he told the monk.

Brecc could not help himself. The words seemed so unsuited to the youth. He smiled. "Why do you say that?"

"I have told you things I should not have. Abbot Ronan forbade me to speak of the island or of Fiacc ever again. He told me my soul would be in mortal danger if I did. He also said I must leave Clonmacnoise, but where can I go? Tulchán sent me here. He said I would be welcomed."

"And so you shall be even... even if it means punishment for me."

"What will happen to Samthann? The Abbot was furious when he saw her."

"You were wrong to bring her into the *vallum*. Women are not allowed to enter lest, like Eve, they cause weak-willed men to fall again."

Ruadhan could not judge the old monk's tone and was not sure how sternly he was reprimanding him. "I came to Clonmacnoise to be taught. There are many things I have to learn."

Brecc felt ashamed. He had meant the comment to be taken lightly because he could not understand the great fear of women that some of his fellow-monks had. Temptation will come to everyone, even the hermit in his cave, especially the hermit in his cave, and he who falls has only himself to blame. Brecc looked at Ruadhan. He was dirty from head to toe, half-starved and worn out and a fine coating of sweat on his forehead suggested that he might have a fever of some sort. He had no cloak and his covering was hardly recognisable as a tunic. As the monk gazed, he recalled a story told of St. Moling who was visited in his cell by a youth dressed in purple. The youth asked why Moling did not salute him since he was Christ, the Son of God. Moling replied that that was not possible because when Christ comes it is not in purple but in forms of the wretched of the earth: the poor; the sick and the lepers.

"Rules, Ruadhan: we monks are the worst people imaginable for adding rules upon rules until we lose sight of *the* rules we have to follow, the Gospel rules Our Lord gave us. Do not worry about Samthann. She has been sent to work for a family of tenant farmers an easy walk from here. They will take care of her."

Brecc paused, let out a long sigh, grinned broadly and said, "You will have to be hidden until I decide what is best to do. There's nothing else to be done, my young fugitive, for, if all that you have told me is correct..." He saw Ruadhan's face fall at this qualification and quickly added, "and I believe it is, then you are in great danger. Fiacc is a dangerous man. Follow me." Brecc got awkwardly to his feet and for a moment, tried to ease the stiffness from his limbs. He took a couple of steps and stopped. He turned to Ruadhan. "Oh, and I should assure you that I have made a quick but authoritative assessment and I can say that your soul is one of few within this enclosure that is not in mortal danger."

A path led from the vegetable garden to the back door of the monastery kitchen. They met no one until they were inside and there they saw a monk at a rough wooden table rubbing the ash from burnt seaweed into a huge cut of beef. Brecc introduced Ruadhan to his younger brother, Eidnen, who was the cellarer of Clonmacnoise monastery. He was short like Brecc but much rounder in the body and the face, and it was his face that held Ruadhan's attention. Eidnen had only one eye. Where his right eye had been there was a knot of puckered skin which had knitted over the socket. Ruadhan could not help staring but Eidnen did not mind. He smiled, stopped what he was doing, rubbed his hands on a large piece of sacking tied about his waist and placed them on Ruadhan's shoulders. "Go on, look all you want. I'm used to it. I lost it as a child - a poke with a sharpened stick from another child - and now, I don't miss it. I see twice as well with the one I have left so don't try to steal any food!"

"And what is said of Odin, the great God of the Northmen, can be said of my brother. Losing one eye has brought an increase in wisdom," added Brecc.

Eidnen was happy to join Brecc's conspiracy and hide Ruadhan in the kitchen. At night, he could sleep on the long stone baking flag which would still be warm from the day's work but during the day, they would have to be more careful. The kitchen was a busy place, with people fetching and carrying most hours. The only place he would be safe was in the meat larder, which had been added to the main kitchen area and which could only be entered by an interior door. Joints of salted beef, pork and some mutton hung from the roof ready for the feast days when the monks ate meat. No meat would be eaten in the monastery until Easter and so it was very unlikely that anyone other than Eidnen or a thief would go into the larder. Sometimes, if all was quiet, Ruadhan could go to Brecc's garden.

Alone in his cell, Brecc knew he had to pray hard for guidance in this matter. He prostrated himself on the clay floor. Brecc believed that the youth was telling the truth, but had to keep reminding himself that he was young and had come to Clonmacnoise hungry and exhausted and, for these reasons, could be mistaken in his interpretation of what he had seen and heard. Hunger, cold and tiredness can fill the mind with all kinds of unreal images and lack of charity on his own part towards Fiacc could do the

215

same. However, Brecc was certain that Ruadhan could not have made up the whole story and that Fiacc was intent on some evil. Abbot Ronan had to be told; had to be convinced.

In charity, Brecc thought hard about Fiacc and tried to understand the man. He recalled incidents on their journey to Egypt: the murder in Alexandria; the skirmish in the desert. His hard exterior seemed unyielding and yet, one must always hope for change, for signs that God's light would flood into such dark souls. Brecc reflected on the parable of the workers in the vineyard and how even those who came late to work were welcomed and received the same payment as those who had worked all day. Perhaps Fiacc was waiting just outside the vineyard to be hired. "Perhaps I should have made him take that hoe," thought Brecc, and smiled to himself.

Two strange dreams filled Brecc's mind that night. In one, St. Michael was weighing the souls of the dead. In his left hand, he held the scales of judgement and in the other a staff. Crouched on the ground beneath him trying to drag down the empty scale was the Devil. St. Michael pushed at the Devil with his staff and at times, the Devil released the scale with one hand, and looked as if he was going to fall. However, the saint could never dislodge him completely. The second dream brought Brecc the answer to the puzzling riddle that Tulchán had posed with his Psalm one hundred and fifty-one.

The following morning, he found Fiacc at the guesthouse and, as promised and before addressing more serious matters, explained the psalm to him. "It is a simple play on words. I don't know why it was not apparent to me right away. Perhaps I expected a deeper riddle from Tulchán. The answer is in that line about bones: "With bones I lie and on little bone I lie". Whatever or whoever is being written about is in a grave. "Little bone" suggests it is in the grave of Ossene, a bishop and abbot of Clonmacnoise who lived a hundred years before us. His name, *Ossene* means *little deer* which we find in the fifth line, but in the eleventh line, Tulchán makes a play upon the bishop's name by mixing the Latin and the Irish, and suggesting the meaning, *little bone*."

"The Chalice of St. Mark could be buried there."

"The Chalice. The Chalice. Always the Chalice. It may be. The rest of Tulchán's psalm suggests that whatever it is, it was placed in the grave during a time of great disturbance, when Clonmacnoise was constantly under attack."

"Our Egyptian friends will be pleased."

"Yes, if it is the Chalice, but also disappointed since I do not think Abbot Ronan will grant anyone permission to disturb the grave of one of his predecessors."

"May I carry this news to the Abbot, Brother Brecc?"

"Well, yes, of course, if that's what you want. Tulchán's little field has been harvested. I have no further interest in it."

A bell started to toll, calling them to the divine office of *tiert*. Brecc turned immediately from Fiacc: his disquiet in the man's presence would make him punctual at communal prayer for once. Then he stopped himself as he realised he was evading the *serious matters*, the responsibility which Ruadhan's tale of the island had placed upon him. The monk turned back. Fiacc had not moved.

"I want to talk to you of other things, Fiacc, more important things. We must do so soon. We must talk and pray. St. Anthony told us that not speaking of your sins to another is the Devil's best way of keeping you in his power. Remember, it is never too late to repent."

Confrontation

Later that same day, Brecc entered the kitchen very agitated. He had tried as diplomatically as he could to speak to the Abbot about Fiacc, but as soon as the Abbot realised why Brecc had asked to see him, he had become very angry and had ordered him to be silent. He had then spoken to him severely and at length on the sin of envy and on the beauty of what he called Fiacc's *desert experience*, his prayerful isolation on a desolate island. For his punishment, Brecc was ordered to prostrate himself, to recite fifty psalms in addition to those everyone said, and to make one hundred genuflections. He was to do this every time the monks gathered for prayer and for one week.

The right side of Brecc's face twitched as it did when he was irritated and anxious and his tunic was still tucked up in his belt from working in the garden. Eidnen kneaded bread dough in a large wooden trough. He knew his brother's moods well and kept his head down, concentrating on the work. Ruadhan measured out more flour.

"There is far too much of this *desert* thinking if you ask me; it fills our heads with sand. So, Ruadhan, Tulchán sent you here for an education. I have a question for you, an important one." He stopped abruptly, and pushed the hem of his tunic more firmly into his belt. "The famous Brother Cronan is held in great esteem, Cronan the Hermit. Like Fiacc, but not with that man's pretence, he has cut himself off from the world. He spends his days praying in a cell high in the Devil's Bit Mountains to the south. He fasts for six days at a time and only breaks that fast to take a *bochtan*[11] of milk and water and a small bowl of gruel. He sleeps only one hour each night on the hard ground without any covering but his tunic..."

The twitching quickened and Brecc hesitated wondering if he should be speaking in this way to the young man. The bell calling the monks to prayer began to ring. Eidnen wiped his hands and took his apron off. Brecc did not respond. "And I don't say all this is wrong, the way Brother Cronan orders his spiritual life. Don't think that. Don't misunderstand me." He paused. Should he really be saying this, talking so much, as garrulous as a jackdaw? Did these speeches make any difference to anyone? Brecc could not answer his own question but knew he had to

---

[11] A liquid measure; twelve eggfuls

carry on if only for his own self-satisfaction. Oh, what an unrepentant sinner he was! "Tell me, have you heard of Brother Cainnech?"

Ruadhan shook his head.

"Of course, you haven't. Few have. It's all Cronan the Hermit and yet poor Cainnech *na m'bocht*[12] spends his days looking after the sick and the poor; and his nights. Many's the time I have seen him barely able to keep standing at our *midnocht* prayers. He was punished last week for yawning - extra psalms to recite with five genuflections between each. He was lucky the Abbot did not order him to be beaten. Cainnech's a good man and it isn't right."

Brecc stopped abruptly again, his face full of question marks. Eidnen slipped quietly out of the kitchen. Ruadhan stood still and silent, waiting for the question. His Clonmacnoise education had started.

"Tell me, whose work is more pleasing to God, young man?" asked Brecc as he pushed his tunic end down into his belt once more. "Answer me that."

"You mean Cronan's or Cainnech's? I... I..."

"Yes I do, but, no, don't answer. I shall tell you and that will put an end to all this. I should go. It is Cainnech's. If Cronan who fasts so much were to hang himself up by the nose for seven days out of seven, he could not equal the other who looks after the poor. So there you have it, and may God forgive me, and may Cronan forgive me, and the abbot forgive me for speaking out in such a forthright manner, even though it was only to Ruadhan and he barely a man. I must go to my *anam chara*[13] immediately. No, not immediately. Prayer, prayer with the others. I have been called. But see him I will and demand he gives me harsh penance. As this kitchen floor is swept every day or oftener, so must the soul be cleansed. Yes, I must go under the hands. And I should get rid of my tongue. If my foolish words were food, no one would ever go hungry in this land."

Being with Brecc brought comfort to Ruadhan even though the monk was angry and flustered. The two men were very different but he was reminded of talks with Tulchán in the quiet fields around Cillebairre. Out of the corner of his eye, Ruadhan studied Brecc. Physically, he was not like Tulchán at all. The dead monk was tall and thin while Brecc was short with

---

[12] Cainnech of the paupers

[13] Soul friend; the one to whom Brecc confessed his sins

signs of plumpness. Tulchán's fingers were long and delicate, toughened only where quill and paintbrush had made regular, firm contact during long hours in the scriptorium. At times, the inks and paints stained them, but he had been scrupulous about keeping them clean. Brecc's fingers were stubby, criss-crossed by old cuts, and callused. Soil was ingrained and they always looked dirty. Tulchán stayed calm whatever was happening and seldom showed extremes of emotion. His long face always had a shade of sadness in it and he smiled more with his eyes than his mouth. Brecc's face could rummage through a bag of emotions in a moment and still not come up with the one it wanted, but his smiles, when they came, filled a field.

The monk was not smiling when he turned and with short, fast steps left the kitchen and went towards the garden completely forgetting that the bell had called him to *noin*, the mid-afternoon time of communal prayer which commemorated the hour of Christ's death. He muttered to himself as he left: "*Fructus autem spiritus est caritas, pax, patientia, longanimitas, bonitas, benignatis, mansuetudo, fides, modestia, continentia, castitas.*" He would remember the call in a little while when he heard his fellow-monks reciting the office and would dash to the church, hands dirty and tunic still turned up and stuck in his belt, convinced that he was the biggest sinner in the monastery but also certain that his monastery world was as full of injustices as the world outside its enclosure. His mind was like a beehive. Work, work in the garden would bring some peace to it. The idea was appealing but Brecc frowned as he thought of it for he knew that his garden was his hiding place. With his tools, his fruits and his vegetables, Brecc had created a little space apart from so many of the realities of human weakness and evil. The boy had come to remind him that he had responsibilities in the world beyond his garden. He had no alternative now but to confront Fiacc directly.

Brecc called Fiacc to the garden late in the afternoon of the following day, a Sunday. It was not the right day to face the man with the evil he had done and the evil he was planning to do, but, if Ruadhan's tale was true, Brecc had wasted enough time already. He was not looking forward to the meeting and felt quite ill. As he waited, he experienced shooting pains in his left arm. He encouraged himself by thinking that since Fiacc had confessed and received the Body and Blood that morning, he might be ready to call a halt to his plans and become a true member of the community. He also consoled himself with the knowledge that he himself had also gone under the hands and received communion and so was well prepared should Fiacc become violent.

The days were lengthening considerably. The sun was still high and the monk was enjoying a simple walk about the place he loved best. A *walk* in the garden, that is all. He was always tempted but one rule he would never break was that of resting from work on the Lord's special day. The sun gave of real warmth and for the first time that year, Brecc saw a huge swarm of midges under an apple tree. He was sweating but in spite of that and in spite of his anxiety over what he had to do, he was happy. His world about Clonmacnoise was at its best; alert, vivacious, and straining to produce new life. To him, the unassertive hills, the tilled land, the isolated trees and bushes and the somnolent river were all strident calls for his attention and each looked as if it had been outlined sharply by a scribe's new pen. It would not be long to the great feast and the promise of the Resurrection. How could Brecc fail to be happy?

In spite of the spring warmth, Fiacc came to the garden with his capa over his head. "He shuts out the beauty, the goodness that is all around us," thought Brecc as he watched the younger man steadily approaching. They both nodded a greeting and then, in one long, breathless outburst which was punctuated throughout by stronger pains in his arm, Brecc told Fiacc what he knew and asked him to repent, telling him it was never too late and reminding him of the thief who died alongside Jesus. Fiacc listened and never took his eyes off Brecc's.

When the old man had finished, Fiacc asked him if he would like to pray. Without another word, Brecc knelt down on the broken soil and held his arms out wide. Fiacc came between him and the sun. Brecc closed his eyes, asked for peace in his mind but was visited by fretful thoughts about the boy and his own stupidity. What would Fiacc do to Ruadhan now if he found him? How could Brecc help him now? He was a foolish old monk who ought to have acted more decisively, who should not have given this evil man another chance, but people do change, don't they? They turn, like the thief to Christ, believe, and are redeemed, aren't they, dear God?

Not in his arm at first but in his chest remaining there and then back to his arm; one long pain that seemed to fill all of him; pain like a huge tree root erupting from the earth. His arms fell and Brecc slumped sideways, giving thanks that Fiacc had not added another murder to those he had already committed.

Fiacc made his way to the cemetery not long before midnight prayers. Usually, it was the time of deepest sleep for the monks but on that night, many kept a vigil by their dead brother's body that was now wrapped in linen cloths and lying in his cell. Thick cloud had placed a lid on the land, cutting off light from moon and stars. Fiacc had located Ossene's grave while there was daylight; a simple limestone slab with a small cross and his name carved on it. It was well away from the main church and surrounded by other graves, some with upright memorial stones. If the monks came to pray while he was still at work, he would be well hidden.

He lifted the slab with ease, and let it fall away from the grave. It hit the neighbouring stone and cracked. With a short handled spade, Fiacc dug quickly but carefully in the dry, flattened earth. Only ten centimetres below the surface, he came up against an odd lump in the soil. He scraped the remaining dirt off the top with his hands and then scrabbled at the sides. At first, he thought it was only a large stone, but as his hands cleared more soil, he was able to discern a distinct shape and make out a softer material wrapped around something firm. It had to be the Chalice. After a few moments more of digging, Fiacc felt the earth's hold on the object loosen and his anticipation of seeing the Chalice at last began to grow. He pushed his hands deep into the earth at its sides and the fingers on one struck a large stone. He winced with pain and pulled his hands back. Behind him, he heard movement.

The first monks were on their way to the church and would ring the bell to summon the others. Fiacc stood up quickly. He was close to holding the precious Chalice he had learned about in that strange church so far away, the Chalice that would give him power to take revenge on the family that had sent him to Clonmacnoise and, with Viking help, the power to rule his own corner of Ireland. He was very close and must take care not to let his eagerness ruin his plans. He stepped behind one of the tall gravestones.

A young monk, Murgal, left the path to the church. He had the responsibility of praying at the grave of the last abbot each time the monks gathered. Murgal shouldered this duty gladly especially so since the dead abbot was from his own home area just east of Loch Corrib and had led Clonmacnoise well. However, that night he felt ill with fever and even though his body shook with cold in the night air, his woollen tunic was sticking to him. The great St. Jerome had said that those who had devoted their lives to God should be like the cicada which is most alive and noisy at night. However, Murgal told himself, neither Jerome nor the cicada had experienced the Irish climate. He pulled his cowl about his head and tried to quicken his step towards the abbot's grave, but stumbled.

It was dark, very dark, but this was the first time that Murgal had walked into a gravestone when visiting the cemetery at night. He sat down on the grass and took deep breaths. "Who was it knocked me down?" he wondered, and reached up the side of the gravestone to feel the lettering. His fingers only needed to trace three letters for Murgal to know who his assailant was. He had walked into Forbasach's gravestone, a memorial to one of the Ui Briuin royal family of Connacht. He told himself that had anyone of lower status knocked him down, he would have protested, but seeing it was royalty, he would accept the blow meekly. Making apologies to Abbot Forbasach, Murgal used the gravestone to pull himself back on to his feet. What was he doing? He should be nowhere near that place. It was at least eighty metres east of the grave he should be alongside, that of Abbot Suibne, son of Cuanu. The fever was worse than he had thought and was confusing him greatly. With a parting pat on Forbasach's shoulder, Murgal started to search for Suibne, but the gravestones were moving before his eyes. He walked four paces and fell on top of Ossene. Murgal felt wretched. His head was like the inside of the monastery forge, but sick as he was, he told himself off for abusing the graves of holy men. This was consecrated ground. With a great effort, he picked himself up, but when he was in a kneeling position, he realised something was very wrong. He ran his hands over the grave. This was Ossene's burial place. He was sure of that. It had been marked by a stone laid flat. Now there was only bare soil; bare, disturbed soil. His hand closed round the handle of a spade. The horror broke like a flood into Murgal's mind and dashed the torpor of the fever out. Someone had removed the stone and had been digging in the soil. He felt about him. The stone lay broken, a metre away.

When, in the gloom, it became obvious that Murgal knew the grave had been disturbed, Fiacc stepped out from his hiding place. The young monk's back was to him and he was still on his knees, feeling around the gravestone. Fiacc had little time for any of the Clonmacnoise monks, and none at all for Murgal. The monk's meekness appalled him; a "first to pray, last to sleep" monk; a waste of a man. To Fiacc, life was a struggle to dominate or be dominated; like the trees in the forest that take the most sun and rain, it was the strongest who flourished. The weak, stunted trees, men like Murgal, cluttered the earth at the base of the great trees, and robbed them of the soil's goodness. Clearing them was a sensible thing to do. Fiacc stepped towards the young monk.

Murgal could not get up. His illness and the terror of the knowledge that he was kneeling on the desecrated grave and remains of Ossene paralysed him. He released a scream that was heard well beyond the monastery enclosure. As Murgal's fellow-monks took torches and came in search of him, Fiacc moved silently away, out of the cemetery, and took a tortuous route towards the guesthouse. When he reached it, he did not enter but turned and ran by a direct route back to the cemetery, joining others who were responding to Murgal's harrowing cries.

"What next?" thought Abbot Ronan. The monastery had not known such upset for several years. Brother Brecc's death had been sudden and had been a shock, but it did not pose questions for the community. Death is always near in a busy place such as Clonmacnoise and the ending of their earthly life was an occurrence the monks contemplated daily. Brecc's body, wrapped carefully in linen cloths, had been laid out in his cell and for three days, his fellow monks had recited the Office for the Dead. God was praised through many psalms and the brothers rejoiced because Brecc had been born to a new and better life. On the third day, marking the length of Christ's stay in the tomb, Brecc was buried in the sacred earth of Clonmacnoise cemetery not far from the desecrated grave of Bishop Ossene. A cold wind drove in from the west and brought rain which fell in large drops throughout the burial. It dashed new blossom from the orchard trees and carried petals, pink and white, to the grave's freshly turned earth.

The desecration of Ossene's grave and posed many questions. Why should someone commit such a profane act? Whoever it was had been digging for something, and, in fact, Murgal had felt an object wrapped in hide. Before the monks entered the church that night, Ronan ordered three of them to smooth the disturbed soil and replace the broken gravestone. Ossene and whatever else was there had to be allowed to rest in peace. When they had done that, they were to stay and pray by the grave in case someone attempted the sacrilegious act once more. The following day he sent for the few remaining members the monastery's militia and told them to organise a guard on the cemetery throughout the day and night.

The serious way Fiacc had acted in all of this impressed Abbot Ronan. In contrast, Brecc had been foolish and intemperate and had tried to speak ill of Fiacc but it was that man who had been exemplary in all that was required after the old monk's death. It was Fiacc who had found Brecc prostrate in his beloved garden. It was Fiacc who had carried him gently to his cell, and then had informed the other monks. Ronan saw that Fiacc was, in his own quiet, undemonstrative way, deeply upset by what had happened. Although he was anxious to return to his island hermitage and its deprivations, Fiacc had stayed at Clonmacnoise for the full time of the mourning until his friend's body had been buried with all the dignity of the Church's ceremonies. Only then, late on that third day, had he asked and been granted the Abbot's permission to leave for the island.

THE ISLAND
The Trials

The feasting had satisfied them for a while and the clouds of treachery among his crew had thinned, but Rorik knew it would not last. The restlessness was beginning to show itself once more in short temper and bickering and Bjorn and Oddrun were, without doubt, encouraging it. Rorik had to act against them soon otherwise he would lose all the respect of his warriors.

For fifteen days they had waited for the return of the Irishmen's leader, Fiacc, the one who dressed as a monk and who knew of the Chalice. Crooked Leg, who spoke for the Grey Wolves, knew nothing, except that he and the others were to fight alongside the Northmen and that the spoils, the great spoils, would be shared. Fiacc was the hub around which the wheel would turn. Everything depended on him.

Morann knew nothing and did not trust his guests. The Irish had not shed tears over the dwarf, but blamed his death on the Northmen. Uncomfortable as allies, both groups watched each other closely across the encampment. Only the bold Bjorn crossed the divide: he went among the Irish with no weapon, sat, ate and drank with them and learned their language until he spoke it as well as Rorik. On one day, he even challenged the Grey Wolves to climb with him up the face of one of the huge rocks about the camp. Several had fallen and bruised themselves badly, but all had enjoyed the sport.

Believing the idler the men were, the greater discontentment would grow, Rorik had given them tasks to do every day since they had arrived. First, shelters had to be built and when they were completed, he put everyone to work overhauling the *longships*. On that fifteenth day, most of the Northmen were busy at the ships, recaulking strakes with wool-yarn and tar or refitting wooden covers to the oar-holes. Yngvar, the ship's carpenter, although he could find nothing wrong with the old one, had been ordered to cut a new steering oar for the *Sea Bear*, and when he saw Rorik and Adils at the top of the gulley, was augering a hole to fasten it to the starboard side.

Rorik was not interested in the work that day but in checking on Bjorn who was meant to be supervising it. The young cousin was testing his uncle with disobedient and disrespectful behaviour, edging him into a confrontation. Some thought Bjorn was stupid and wrong to do this, but others admired his courage and were content to see him bait a leader who had led them to nothing but hard work and misery a long way from home. Rorik had slept fitfully. He felt and looked uneasy. Even his baldric and sword, which he had worn every day on the island, seemed heavier than usual and more cumbersome and his clothes felt as if they had been made for a much bigger man. As he walked towards the *Sea Bear*, he speeded up and lengthened his stride, attempting a manner becoming one who led. He cursed as he tripped and almost fell on the uneven path down the gulley. Adils spoke words of reassurance quietly. "Your strength will soon be made evident to all when we go into battle and reap great rewards. Rorik nodded but was full of uncertainty. He felt as if he were the king piece in a game of *hnefatafl*[14] with few other whites about him and no strategy to defend him. The boy's loyalty would remain constant no matter what happened; Adils would do anything for him.

There was no sign of Bjorn. Yngvar saw Rorik looking about and shouted: "He's with the Irishman, Blackbeard. They're getting to know each other better with the help of some strong barley brew."

Rorik's anger rose but he hid it well as he went up the gangplank on to the deck of the *Sea Bear* and cursorily inspected the men's work. He forced himself to find the odd shoddy piece of workmanship - a nail not hammered truly home; a slightly ill-fitting plank - but his mind was on Bjorn. He was furious that his cousin was not there but through the murk of his anger, a thin shaft of light began to shine. Bjorn was not so clever. His new friendship would be his downfall. If he wanted to walk in Rorik's shoes, he should first learn to walk in his own without stumbling.

A shout of pain brought him out of his reverie. Agnar, the smallest man in the party, a fisherman who had trekked south from his home in Hålogaland to join the ship, had crushed a finger with his hammer. He was shaking his hand as if trying to throw the pain away. Rorik laughed: "I hope you can do better when a weapon is in your hand, Agnar. As long as you don't do this to yourself in the middle of a battle, I shall continue to laugh."

The others joined in his laughter and Rorik experienced a fulfilling swell of confidence. He raised his voice and told all that soon they could let their tools rust and pick up their weapons. A great cheer went up and with

---

14 King's Table, a board game.

it, Rorik's spirits soared. As he left the ship and walked back towards the gulley with Adils by his side, he saw Bjorn and the Irishman walking uncertainly towards them from the far end of the beach. Bjorn was carrying a skin filled with ale which he raised in a mocking salute before he fell on to the sand. Blackbeard sat down heavily alongside him and pulled the skin from his grasp. Rorik gazed hard at them and a plan made itself clear. "Yes, yes, you are stumbling," thought Rorik. He smiled, clapped Adils on the back and said, "Come, my loyal son, we have work to do, important work which cannot wait."

Bjorn did not return for the night-meal that evening. At first, the Vikings joked about the missing man's drinking habits, but as the evening progressed, their laughter diminished. Rorik ordered Yngvar to take torches and lead a search party to find him. "Tell him I am angry that he does not eat with us," he said.

It had not taken Yngvar long to find Bjorn and his Irish friend. They were still on the beach not far from where Rorik had seen them. The Northman was in a drunken sleep and Blackbeard was dead. Yngvar looked all over the big Irishman's body by the light of his torch and found knife wounds under his ribs on his left side. Close by, he found Bjorn's bone-handled knife with a bloodied blade. He sent someone to fetch Rorik.

When Rorik and Adils arrived, Yngvar suggested that Blackbeard's body be taken to the top of a cliff and thrown over. They were both drunk, he argued, and accidents can happen. Rorik stared at the two still forms lying on the beach. He pushed Bjorn with his foot and the young man moaned quietly. He shook his head at Yngvar's suggestion and solemnly ordered that Bjorn and the murdered man be taken to the camp. "The Irish will be told the truth. They are our allies. In the morning, we will show them Viking justice."

A scrap of burning material fell from the end of Yngvar's torch on to his bare arm. He dashed it off and spat on the blistered skin. To his mind, this was asking for trouble. It did not make sense to Yngvar. Loyalty to your own came before all else. Northmen should keep together. "Punish Bjorn, Rorik, by all means but do it quietly, within the family. There's going to be trouble when this bear of a man does not turn up but why make it worse by telling them all that he was murdered by one of us."

Rorik ignored him and had Adils bind Bjorn's hands and pull him to his feet. He told Yngvar and his search party to get the longships into the water with all but one of their anchor ropes raised.

"I've not finished the repairs!"

"Both are seaworthy! Have it ready at all times to sail! Do as I say and stay all night with the ships. Guard them well."

Finally, with a great effort, Rorik raised the dead Irishman over his shoulder and returned to the camp.

When the other Northmen saw the solemn procession coming from the beach, they grabbed weapons and surrounded their leader. Sure that he was well guarded with Adils on one side and Horik, a young giant from Hordaland on the other and sure that, if fighting started, they could retreat to a defensible place among the rocks, Rorik walked into the firelight on the Irish side of the camp and gave them Blackbeard's corpse.

Morann, his crooked leg extended awkwardly to one side, knelt to examine Blackbeard's body. When he had finished, he slowly got back to his feet. "This is very different, Rorik, from the gifts you bore when you arrived on this island."

"We will talk in the morning, Morann, and, I assure you, justice will be done."

Morann, also guarded with a Grey Wolf at each shoulder, walked very close to the Northman almost, because of his gait, stumbling into him. "He did not *fall* on a knife several times, Rorik."

"You must trust me in this."

"You ask a lot of me, Northman."

"I know and when we fight alongside each other, I shall ask more."

Rorik doubled the watch that night and told all that anyone on guard found dozing would be killed on the spot. From suspicion and some superstition that she could influence matters, he slept apart from Oddrun. Throughout the night, a huge, baleful silence raged at the Irish end of the encampment, broken intermittently by formal speeches. The speakers called for action. If the *Finngaill* did not give them the killer, they should go and take him. What kind of men were they to sit helplessly like this? They had all known Blackbeard, had eaten, drunk, and fought with him. His cowardly killer had murdered him while he was happy with drink and while he wore his sins for all, especially God, to see. Were they going to take revenge or were they satisfied with the whining words of the Northmen's leader who said that he would see that justice was done?

The following day opened slowly as if it were still struggling with a deep winter stupor. To the Northmen on guard in the final hours before dawn, it seemed as if the sun had forgotten the island completely and was never going to rise. Adils had wrapped himself in three woollen cloaks but still felt numb with cold and the memory of what had happened. He had expected that the first time he took a life would be in the heat and confusion of battle when you have no time to think and when you have to kill or be killed. The beach had not been like that at all. Rorik had made him drink ale before he had gone back to find Bjorn and the Irishman, but it had not helped. His mind had stayed clear and his senses alert. Bjorn and Blackbeard were both in a drunken sleep as Rorik had said they would be. The fierce-looking Irishman had been muttering and chuckling as he slept. Adils' hand shook so much he almost dropped the knife and only stopped shaking after the first thrust through the Irishman's leather vest and into his flesh. The shaking had been so bad he almost left the beach without carrying out his father's order.

At first light, he was pleased to see his father emerge from his shelter looking rested and, in a strange way, bigger than he had the day before. A raven settled on a rock above Rorik and gave one harsh croak. A good omen, Adils thought. Odin speaks. He watched Rorik splash his face with cold water and walk confidently to where other guards were standing. He patted one on a shoulder, playfully drove his fist into the chest of another and then, pointing to the mainland, shared some comment with them. This was a Rorik Adils had not seen for many weeks, a Rorik who knew how to lead and who could outwit, or brush aside all opposition. Odin was speaking out loud! Following Rorik's lead, the Viking half of the camp came alive quickly and the day-meal was prepared and eaten. The Irish, still gathered about the body of their comrade, continued to watch them. A few now wore the whole skin, from skull to tail, of a grey wolf.

All of the Vikings on the voyage were free men and had the right to take part in the *thing*, the assembly that would judge Bjorn's case. They gathered round the main fire and sat in silence, each placing a weapon on the ground with the blade or spearhead pointing towards the centre of the burning pile. The fire was low and no one made a move to make it blaze once more. Before the assembly started, a dispute over procedure broke out. Harald argued that Oddrun should be called and, as one of her duties as a priestess, she should offer a sacrifice to the gods. "In that manner, this ground where we gather for this assembly will be made holy."

Rorik dismissed Harald's protest. "Oddrun refuses, old man, to have anything to do with this assembly, but like you, she is trying to tell the gods their business, while I, like a good Viking, invite them to do with us whatever they choose. The verdict will be theirs."

Most of the band of Irishmen wanted to take matters into their own hands and kill the accused man before anyone could stop them for they believed the Northmen would never act against one of their own. To them the so-called trial was a sham, a defence which the foreigners were building to shield their man. They were sceptical that justice would be done but edged closer curious to see what was going to happen. Rorik crossed the encampment, pushed his way through them and asked Morann to join with the Vikings as they sat in judgement of their countryman. Morann nodded his consent and when two Grey Wolves moved to escort him, waved them away.

Rorik was the first to speak. He pointed at Bjorn: "I have feasted with this man's father many times. His father and I are brothers. The blood-knot is strong and yet I say to you that this must not make me or any of us weaken in the cause of justice. Our laws defend us and our way of life. Our laws are like our swords: the making of them took a long time, their keenness has been tested by experience and they should always be bound to our side. Bjorn killed the Irishman. He has to be punished. There can be no argument against this."

After a pause, Old Harald rose. He stumbled slightly and one of his feet scattered the cooling embers at the edge of the fire. He spoke wearily, as if he had to, but believed there was no point in doing so. He suspected Rorik was behind the Irishman's death but had no evidence. "No one saw what happened on the beach, Rorik *hersir*. Bjorn may have been attacked by the Irishman. That one was quarrelsome. There have been times since we came here when I have wanted to sharpen my sword on his bones."

Some of the Northmen laughed for they loved to hear the old man speak in this aggressive way. He might have many years behind him but such words were not empty; he was still a good man in a fight.

"No witnesses have come forward, Harald, to say that the Irishman attacked Bjorn."

Old Harald looked anxious. He was straining to hear. He tilted his head so that his right ear, the one working ear, was toward Rorik. "No witness, you say?"

Rorik nodded.

"And no witness has come forward to say that Bjorn was the aggressor. When that is the case, it is always said that the one who is dead is the one who started the fight. In my home village, my brothers witnessed a terrible struggle across the fiord. They could not see exactly what happened, but one of the men was killed. Because the witnesses could not say who started the quarrel, the judgement was that the dead man was to blame. The one alive could not be touched even by the dead man's relatives who, naturally, wanted revenge."

A few others nodded their heads. They knew of similar judgements. Rorik shook his. "The dead man must have had fewer relatives in your village than his killer, Harald, for that is why the judgement went against him. If there are no witnesses, you bring a judgement that what will cause the least trouble in the village. That is what is just."

"We carry our village wherever we go, Rorik, and I say that what is best for peace in this village is to free Bjorn."

"Old age clouds the judgement. You forget, old man, that our village is the whole of this encampment. You will not bring peace to it by cloudy thinking and pretending he has done no wrong."

Harald's anger began to rise. Rorik had come close to insulting him in front of the whole assembly with that last remark, and even though he was their leader, he was not permitted to do that without just cause. Every free man in their society had a right to be treated fairly and civilly. "My judgement is as sound as yours, Rorik, and my memory reaches back further than yours into the history of our law-making, but I do not need it to tell me that our laws are for Northmen. Those people over there are not Northmen and the dead man was not a Northman."

"As long as they are ready to fight with us, then I say they are Northmen and the laws apply."

Harald looked around the assembly and then slowly lowered himself to the ground. He had said what he had to say and could do no more. In turn, other Northmen stood and put their points. A few sided with Harald, but an equal number spoke against him. They thought that there was nothing to gain by fighting the Irish on this island: Bjorn had raised his sail in a headwind by behaving as he had done towards his uncle and now he had to face the consequences. If he had to be sacrificed so that the voyage was successful, then that was how it must be.

Nearly half of the assembly did not speak. Some had been ready to break the bonds of loyalty to their leader and follow Bjorn, but this turn of events had made them think again. The silent, compliant Bjorn before them now did not look a man who could lead them.

Without rising, Harald shouted that Bjorn should speak for himself. Rorik nodded his agreement and all eyes turned to the young man. At first, it seemed as if Bjorn would not respond at all, but then he shook his head and remained silent. When, in his drunkenness, he had seen the Irishman's body by the light of the search party's torches, he had also seen the end of his own life and had accepted his fate.

One of the Northmen who had not uttered a word suddenly shouted: "*Vapnatak!*" a call to lift up weapons and end the assembly. He stood and brandished his spear, a sign that he had decided against Bjorn. Others joined him and clashed weapons to signify that they agreed. Rorik started to pronounce a judgement upon his cousin but Harald got to his feet and screamed that the number was not enough; as many were seated as were standing. The others rose, gripping their weapons but did not thrust them into the air. They kept them low to indicate that they had decided in favour of Bjorn and went to stand near Harald. As they did, they were jostled, and one of them was pushed to the ground. This was not what Rorik wanted. If it continued, there would be bloodshed and he would lose men. He ran quickly to the place and with his fist clubbed the man, his own supporter, who had done this. Adils followed and protected his back. The man went down on one knee. Before any more fighting could break out Rorik shouted for everyone to listen to him: "There is one way in which we can solve this beyond dispute! Bjorn must submit to a trial by ordeal. That way, the gods will judge him without our help!"

The bar of iron had been in the fire since midday. One Northman placed a pair of tongs nearby and two others watched Bjorn while he washed his hands in preparation for the ordeal.

"He must clean them and dry them and come straight to the fire! Make sure that it is done properly!" shouted Rorik.

Bjorn walked to the fire with a guard on either side of him. He quickly gripped his amulet and let it go. His heart was racing but he hoped his face and his actions did not reveal this to anyone. Rorik ordered Harald to take the bar from the fire and the old man did this as if it were going to cause him more pain than Bjorn. "One voyage too many," he said to himself. "I could have stayed at home with a slave or two to do the farmwork, and done nothing myself but eat, drink and tell tales to my grandchildren." Twice he let the bar fall back into the fire and as he was trying to retrieve it a third time, Rorik pushed him brusquely aside and took the tongs from him.

"I can tell your heart's not in this, Old Harald. You're not losing respect for our laws in your old age are you?"

"We are a long way from home. Too harsh an application of the law may weaken us in the midst of our enemies. Besides, this *jarnburor* is new and not accepted by all. It was never part of the old ways."

"The assembly has agreed to accept the judgement of the iron-bearing, Harald. You must be ruled by it too. Your actions have weakened us enough in front of these foreigners. Do not think I have not read the treachery in your heart, old man, and do not think that Rorik is one who respects grey hairs wherever they grow."

Harald's face showed no response. He stood up from the fire and walked out of its light and into the crowd of Northmen that stood waiting for the trial to commence. Rorik lifted the red-hot bar at his first attempt and thrust it towards Bjorn. The young man hesitated and kept his arms by his side. A guard grabbed one of his arms and started to force it upwards but Bjorn pulled it out of his grip and offered both hands, palm upwards to Rorik. Rorik placed the bar on them and stared into Bjorn's face looking for signs of fear and failure. Bjorn breathed in sharply and closed his eyes at the vicious touch of the bar. He started to walk forward. One ... Two ... Nine paces: that was the law. He had to take nine paces at a steady walk. Don't rush. Three ... Four ... Don't rush. Five ... Six ... Think of ice cold water bathing your hands when this is all over. Seven ... His bones! It had seared through to his bones! He knew it had and a deep forest darkness filled his mind with the thought of his maimed hands, scorched beyond healing. Eight ... a scream from that forest darkness begged him to let go and Bjorn threw the bar to the ground and knew he was condemned.

The Alliance

Fiacc pulled his currach quietly on to the beach close to the *Sea Bear*. Only two longships. Gudrod had promised more. The night was thickening quickly but fifty metres from the shore he had been able to distinguish the shape of the *ships* and felt a surge of excitement as he anticipated meeting the Northmen. Their boats, like well-aimed arrows, were beginning to pierce the bays and rivers of Ireland, and their warriors fought in such a way that Irish resistance had seldom been able to hinder them. He wanted their discipline and ferocity at his side and not the blundering savagery of the Grey Wolves. Only two. It would be enough.

He ran his hands along the *Sea Bear's* overlapping oak strakes and admired the workmanship. Each length of wood had been cut and smoothed with great skill and was firmly clenched to the next to build a strong hull. Fiacc believed the events in his life were similar: the visit to Egypt and the news of the Chalice; the banishment to the island and the meeting with Gudrod; the finding of the Chalice, and now, the arrival of the Northmen. They all fitted neatly together to build a powerful vessel which would carry him to revenge on his family and power in Ireland.

The Northmen guarding the *longships* let Fiacc start towards the gulley before they challenged him and took him to Rorik. Fiacc was angry but not surprised that Morann's wild band did not control the beach. However, even if the Grey Wolves had been defeated and slaughtered, he was not going to worry. His confidence was so great that only death could stop him believing that he would fulfil his plans.

The quarrels over Blackbeard's murder and Bjorn's trial were still simmering in both the Irish and Viking camps when Fiacc was brought from the beach and it did not take him long to sense the hostility. Too many men were bearing weapons and shields for it to be a peaceful scene. The Irishmen stood beyond their fire waiting for Bjorn's execution. The way he had been tried was confusing but they knew the iron bar had found him guilty. The light from the fire shaped their shadows into a huge, constantly changing phantasmagoria on the rocks behind them. Among the Northmen, Old Harald and his supporters were also unsettled by what had happened. Some accepted the verdict of the ordeal but others said that they had never experienced such a trial and could not accept its validity.

Fiacc was brought to stand a metre from the Viking leader. Rorik realised who it was and ushered the guards away. For a moment, both men remained silent. Rorik studied Fiacc's firm, composed features by the light of the fire's flames and felt both drawn to him and repelled by him. The attraction was to a man like himself, someone who, although he wore the clothes of the Christian's Godmen, was unlikely to waste words, a man strong both in body and in determination to have his own way. The repulsion came from the inevitable conclusion that, having rid himself of one threat to his leadership, he now faced a more formidable one.

Fiacc spoke first, identifying himself as the person Gudrod had met. "It is deeply insulting to be held a prisoner in my own encampment. This is not the way I expected to meet you. If you wish to succeed in what you have set out to do here in Ireland, then let me go immediately to my people and hear what they have to say. If you continue to hold me captive, they will not stand off for much longer and this quiet island will become a cemetery for most of us."

As Rorik had thought, the man was direct and fearless: "You are not our prisoner, Fiacc. Go to hear what winds stir the tempers of the Irishmen. However, if you wish us to be friends, do not leave both ears with them when you return to us, for I am the one who shall tell the truth about what has happened on this island since we arrived."

Fiacc strode from the light of one fire, through the central darkness of the encampment to stand by the Irishmen's blaze. Everyone, except Morann, talked at once, insisting that they act against the foreigners. Fiacc let them rant for a while and then demanded that they listen to him. The blood that ran in their veins ran in his. The deaths of Blackbeard and Ungorn would be avenged but to make the camp a battlefield was not the way. The shouting stopped but discontented murmuring began.

Morann spoke. "All we have had from you is words and promises. Where are these treasures you have spoken of: the gold, and the fat cattle that will feed us all next winter?"

"I bring news of that, believe me, Morann, and will speak to *you* of it. But for now, Grey Wolves, reign in your temper, your understandable anger. Do not measure swords with these Northmen. I will speak once more to their leader..."

Morann interrupted. "*We* will speak with him."

Fiacc nodded agreement. "If you are not content with what Morann and I bring to you after we speak with him, then we shall sheathe our words and start talking with our weapons. And if it comes to that, you will see, especially those among you who question my right to talk like this, that for every thrust and slash you give, I shall give three."

The leaders of both factions ordered a new fire to be built, *bigger than the others*, midway between their two stations. Irishmen and Northmen carried kindling and boughs to the place and, Rorik insisted, lit the pile at the same time with burning brands taken from their own fires. A great blaze flared quickly and Rorik and Fiacc announced that it was a symbol of the new unity between them. They would sit by this fire, strengthen the bonds of their friendship and plan the raids that would bring them all great wealth. Drink was passed around. Morann gave his assent with a slight nod but said nothing.

Adils joined his father in the discussions with Fiacc and Morann. They separated themselves from the crowd. Morann told Rorik that, before any alliance could be truly sealed, his own people would have to be satisfied in the matter of Blackbeard's murder.

"I will not execute Bjorn. That would prompt rebellion among my people," Rorik answered.

"Nothing less will satisfy us."

"I will not execute him but the sentence will pronounce him a *niding*, an outcast from the society." Rorik knew that this would be regarded as fair by those still grumbling on his own side even Old Harold since it gave Bjorn a faint chance of survival.

Morann repeated that only his death would satisfy the Irish. Rorik nodded and smiled as the Irishman spoke but there was more than a hint of impatience in his response: "Perhaps I am not explaining myself well. Listen closely. The *niding* has no rights at all. His life may be taken by anyone, even a slave, at any time..." He looked directly at Fiacc and then at Morann. Morann was unsure. "*Anyone* may take his life... Am I expressing myself clearly enough? *Anyone*, and no one will question what has happened."

Fiacc saw immediately what Rorik was suggesting, a solution that would keep everyone happy. Fiacc smiled back at his new ally, a man as deceitful and scheming as himself: someone to admire, but also someone to fear. "We will accept that, Morann," he said. Morann nodded his reply.

Not long before midnight, Bjorn the *niding* was pushed from the island in a coracle along a path the moon laid for him on a calm sea. Everyone gathered to witness his going. No one spoke and Bjorn was given no food or weapons and not even a blanket. The Northmen who favoured him argued with themselves that he could survive and, begrudgingly, accepted what was happening as a just sentence. The solitary figure of Oddrun stood on the headland where the beacon had been and, as the outcast, his maimed hands lapped with rough cloths, made his first painful strokes with the oar, she released a deep, unearthly scream and denounced all those who had played a part in Bjorn's banishment. Some of the Northmen shrugged their shoulders: if the gods were against you, then they were against you and it did not matter whether the priestess confirmed or denied this.

In spite of the lateness, Fiacc ordered the women to prepare food. The Irishmen and Northmen would ease their enmity and dismiss Oddrun's threats by drinking more alcohol and stuffing themselves with fatty meat. This was to be the first feast of many because soon they would raid the richest settlement in Ireland.

Rorik and Fiacc sat and ate together with their backs against one of the great rocks. They talked of many things. Firstly, the Viking wanted to know why his ally dressed as he did and was told that it suited Fiacc's plans to wear the tunic of a monk, but that he had no time for prayers and church-going. "People understand strength and ferocity and will never be led by love. These men, the Grey Wolves, know that as well. That is what they worship. Some will speak of Christ and bend their knee but believe more in the old ways. They bow to the sun, the moon and the trees as well as to the cross."

Rorik was pleased to hear him say that. He could not comprehend how anyone could follow such an insignificant man. "Yngvar is our carpenter. He can shave wood until it is as smooth as the surface of a bowl of water, but he cannot lead men. Carpenters are carpenters, and kings are kings. Mind you, Yngvar can fight like a devil and would not let himself be so easily taken and put to death as that Jesus was."

"And what of your gods, Rorik?"

Rorik straightened his right leg which had been angled under the other. It had stiffened and he rubbed it vigorously. "Of course, there are times," he replied, "such as when the sea becomes a monster, or when some oracle of Oddrun's seems to be proved true, that I shake from fear of a greater power, but those times are rare. We waste our life fearing the strength of the gods and denying our own."

Much to the Irishman's pleasure, Rorik wanted above all to hear about the Chalice. It soon became clear that nothing else really mattered and that the treasures he wanted, the ones he believed the Chalice could bring him, were not in Ireland, but lands far away in the Levant. Fiacc told him the Chalice was at Clonmacnoise but did not reveal its hiding place. They would take that settlement, he said, and then, recruiting more numbers as they progressed, move on to Durrow where his family had other interests. He spread some of the fine wood ash by the side of the fire and, with a stick, drew a crude map of the Irish midlands. Attacks on outlying farms would draw his family's soldiers from their dun to defend their lands and they could be defeated in open battle. Rorik listened attentively and gestured agreement but had no intention of letting Fiacc dictate a campaign. They would take Clonmacnoise, certainly, because it held the Chalice and, no doubt, many other treasures, but Rorik's plans did not include putting Fiacc upon the throne of a petty Irish kingdom. It was an impossible, foolhardy plan. While Fiacc was useful; that is, until the Chalice was found, Rorik would allow the Irishman his say, but once that task was completed, the alliance would end.

In her shelter among the rocks, Oddrun squatted and moved her head quickly, rhythmically in circles until she fell into a trance. Her howling and prophecies of doom were heard but not heeded by those who were feasting.

Not long after Bjorn's small craft had bobbed away from the island, a currach was rushed into the waters of a bay just south of the beach. Six heavily armed Irishmen clambered into it. They returned before daybreak, and slipped, unseen by any Northmen, into their shelters.

CLONMACNOISE
A Journey and a Vigil

"Our patience is running out," said the old woman by the door. "An extra pair of hands, we thought, would make our work easier, but she does not lighten our burden; she adds to it. She knows little of cooking and nothing of farming. And she stinks of fish."

Ruadhan looked inside the hut. The fire was out, and a young, heavily pregnant woman was blowing on charred brands and dry grass to relight it. Smoke and dust rose about her face. Ashes and the remains of many meals were strewn about the mud floor. Ants swarmed over half-chewed gobbets of meat and an infant sucked at a piece of oatmeal cake she had found. In one corner, a baby bundled in rough cloths, lay sleeping on a bed of rushes.

"Where is she?"

"Gathering wood. That's about all she's good for. Cross the ford and follow the path by the river south until you sight an oak tree, a noble tree. It stands on its own up the slope, well back from the water. It would shelter five hundred men. The priests of the old religion made sacrifices under its leaves and no one has ever cleared it or would. Go there. It's a good walk. Take the path to the right over the small hills to the heath. If you get to the bog, you've gone too far. Beyond you'll see woodland. It spreads itself back down the slope to meet the river after the bend. She will be gathering at the edge of it. Not many go into that wood. There are stories. Hunters, yes, but even the bravest among them never goes alone."

The young woman lifted her head and Ruadhan saw the flames licking about the sticks. She was panting and her face was very red from the effort. She sat back on her haunches, joined her hands over her abdomen, and, staring at the fire she had made, rocked to and fro.

"Tell the fishergirl she's been there long enough. Our woodpile is low," the old woman told him.

Samthann was fastening her bundle of branches with rope when Ruadhan found her. She was delighted to see him again. She felt different in his presence; a gentle flow of happiness began to stream through her body and mind. She stood and smiled shyly as he walked towards her. The only people she had ever known were her parents and brothers and the last distinctive and happy memory she had of them was the night of Ruadhan's visit. The boy with the book. She had not spoken to him that night, but in her heart, had made him part of her family. Now he was its only living member. She searched his face for signs of contentment, but was disappointed to find only anxiety.

She ran and took the sack he was carrying from his shoulder. As she touched his arm, that gentle flow became a surge. Samthann wanted to be with him. They sat beneath one of the hawthorn trees that fringed the forest. On its branches, a few sparks of white blossom hinted at the incandescence that would follow. As they ate one of the *paxeamata*, the small loaves Eidnen had packed the sack with, Ruadhan told Samthann all that had happened since she had been taken from the monastery enclosure and given to the family. "Eidnen has been good to me, but says he can hide me no longer. He witnessed Fiacc's vigils and prayers by his brother Brecc's dead body and doubts whether such a man could be so evil and so doubts me. Now, there is no one among the monks to whom I can turn, no one I can convince..." Ruadhan faltered as an unnerving thought entered his mind. "Tulchán first, and now Brecc: death stalks the monks that I befriend."

Samthann answered him calmly and directly: "Then we must leave, Ruadhan. The book is here. Your mission is ended."

Ruadhan shook his head. There had to be more. Tulchán's insistence and all that had happened to him, the pain, loneliness and near-despair shouted out that there had to be more to his mission than the simple handing over of the Psalter. It would be revealed slowly and perhaps with more pain, but he believed that his adult life and the future of the settlement at Clonmacnoise were to make a complex weave. Besides, there was the immediate concern of defending Clonmacnoise from the Vikings and the Grey Wolves.

"No, Samthann, I must stay close, keep watch on the river and do what I can to stop Fiacc and the Northmen. But you must go, go to Cillebairre. Alert Conal and bring him here with all the soldiers he can muster. He knows the Northmen and how they fight. Go and tell him what has happened to me. He will come. I know he will come."

Now it was Samthann's turn to look troubled. The journey from the island to Clonmacnoise had not whetted her appetite for more travelling. She would do what Ruadhan asked even though it meant leaving him and fostering doubts over whether she ever would see him again. The small bay where her family fished had been her world for fifteen years and, until the

241

Northmen came, she thought she would never have to venture from it. Now, in less than a month, she had stretched her legs over a fair number of Ireland's valleys, hills and plains, and met more people than her imagination had let her believe lived on earth. Not many of those she had met made her want to travel and meet more. But this was what *he* wanted and she wanted more than anything else to please him. "I will do it, Ruadhan."

"Eidnen says that a poet and his servant are leaving in that direction at first light tomorrow, travelling on a chariot. The poet is sheltering in the monastery. He was to stay longer in these parts but one of his poems has offended a local chieftain, a quibble over the true meaning of a word, and he is being hunted. Eidnen thinks I am going and told me to meet the poet beyond Clonmacnoise and travel with them as far as mountains known as the Heights of the Saints. From there, a track runs west through a pass in the hills and on to Cillebairre. You must take my place. In three or perhaps four days, perhaps less, you will be there."

"But what about you? What will you do?"

Ruadhan smiled for he saw the concern behind the calmly delivered question. It pleased him, but he was not sure how to respond to it. They had slept apart on the journey to Clonmacnoise but had grown much closer. Ruadhan regarded Samthann with a mixture of awe and puzzlement. The silent, cowering fisherman's daughter of their first meeting was also the resourceful woman who had saved his life and brought him to Clonmacnoise. As he looked at her now, he realised that as Ite had been taken from him, Samthann had been given to him. Samthann had Ite's determination but whereas Ite would never retreat from whatever faced her, Samthann's firmness was qualified by a mildness and timidity that Ruadhan found beguiling and confusing. "In an odd way, the family you served has told me what to do. They say this wood is seldom entered except by bands of hunters. It is protected by many superstitions none of which I know and none of which would daunt me. The forest was my first home, remember. It will welcome me and I shall hide among its branches until you return with Conal. The land slopes gently upwards here and I should be able to find a good vantage point on the ridge for watching the river. This is the way Fiacc will lead the Northmen."

On the River

Fiacc and Rorik's men disembarked and camped at the northern extreme of a great lake south of Clonmacnoise. Thick forest edged most of the water but they found a landing place where the bank was a patchwork of gorse bushes and fast growing young ferns. There they would take food and sleep early in order to rise well before dawn. It had been agreed that they would travel the final distance on the river in the darkness of the first hours of the new day.

"Catch the monks while they are at their prayers," argued Fiacc.

With Rorik and Morann, he discussed the attack once more. Behind them, the trees, which had their own ragged individuality in daylight, merged into one mass and the forest lay like a huge black sword with its unevenly serrated upper edge silhouetted by the paler darkness of the evening sky. Fiacc had cast aside his monk's tunic and sandals. He now wore shoes, trews banded from ankle to knee, a leather vest and a short madder-red brat fastened beneath his chin by a bronze and glass kite brooch favoured by his family. As he sat down by a small fire with the other two, he felt confident. "Clonmacnoise is poorly defended. The monastery enclosure, Rorik. That is where the treasures will be found."

"And this Chalice, the Chalice of St. Mark, where is it kept?

"Most likely it will be with the other objects of great value: gold and silver vessels, patens and reliquaries, in the great church, the *damliag*. It is the stone building that dominates the enclosure."

"Then I will lead a select group of my men to force a way to that place. That will be my priority. Do you agree?"

Fiacc, feigned reluctance and argued against Rorik's plan: "I am the one who knows the place. I should be the one to lead such a group."

Until then, Morann had been silent. He sniffed loudly and ran both hands slowly down his deeply lined face. "I will choose some of my men, the best of my Grey Wolves, to join you, Northman, in that foray. We also like gold chalices."

Rorik nodded. Grey Wolves would join the band that would secure the monastery's treasures. "They will be subject to my command."

Morann shifted his damaged leg, articulated disconcertingly like a spider's, slowly back from the fire. He looked directly at Rorik. "Don't worry. They will do what they are told to do."

"Told by me," emphasised Rorik.

"Told by *us*," retorted Morann.

"It never makes sense to pass command to and fro especially in the heat of battle."

"We shall see," was all Morann replied.

Before settling to sleep, Fiacc walked with Morann about the makeshift camp and discussed further who among the Grey Wolves should go with Rorik into the *damlaig*. Fiacc suggested that since this action had to be swift and decisive and Morann was hindered by his deformity, Aed, a short, red-haired, straggly bearded Connachtman, should lead that group. "I have noted that he is feared by the others and so they may respect him in battle. Put him in charge."

Morann laughed. His experience taught him that the Grey Wolves had little understanding of *respect* on or off the battlefield. He had been in many melees with them and had not made the acquaintance of *respect*. And anyway, what in the name of Christ, Odin and Cú Chulainn was this man talking about? *Respect* was dumped at the wayside by all combatants long before the battlefield was reached. Aed? Fine. Aed would do. He was indeed feared by the others. "He is the one *I* choose," answered Morann, "the one *I* assign to this task.".

"Tell him to watch Rorik closely throughout the fight and to see that he acts as a true ally should."

Morann nodded his agreement. "He knows to do that already. We all do."

Fiacc lay down apart from the other Irishmen on soft ferns he stamped to the ground. He unfastened his brat, wrapped it fully around him and as he fell into a deep, undisturbed sleep, reminded himself once more to keep an eye and a weapon for *all* his allies when they reached Clonmacnoise. With Morann and the Grey Wolves, the politics were simple. There would be plunder enough to satisfy them. With the foreigners, it was different. He had no illusions about the alliance with Rorik. It was frail and most likely would be short-lived. The Northman would keep to the agreement only as long as it served his interests. The Glass Chalice fastened them to each other. Like Fiacc, Rorik was fascinated by the Chalice and its potential to grant the holder power. The Irishman knew that if he allowed Rorik to have the Chalice, their alliance would have no external buckle but would depend upon fickle integrity and trust.

Rorik sat away from the river at the edge of the clearing and scratched every part of his torso that his hands could reach. He still had not got rid of the fishermen's fleas. That was an unlucky place. Some said alder bark was the answer; some said elder leaves: some said holly berries and others said an infusion of all three. He had not had time to put any of the cures to the test. There were other things to think about and that's what he was doing. He was not anxious. Rorik had no doubts that the raid would be successful and that its harvest would place him high in everyone's esteem when the *Sea Bear* returned home. Swedes would carry news of the Chalice to Byzantium and to the Caliphate and they would return with offers the Arabs made for its purchase. Rorik wanted immediate gains from any deal, something to convince doubters that the glass cup was of great value: gold, silver were preferable, and the Caliph of Baghdad must have plenty of those. However, he also wanted long-term benefits to strengthen his political power in Trøndelag; perhaps a trading monopoly over some of the Arabs' goods such as silks or ivory. Yes, that would be very satisfactory. The leader of the Northmen rolled a blanket tightly round his body and legs but kept his arms free and his sword close. Before sleeping, he pushed his back up against a tree. Bjorn had been dealt with, but caution was still the best policy. The following day was going to be a triumphant one in spite of Oddrun's mutterings. On board the *Sea Bear* she had distanced herself from him and passed most of the journey rocking backwards and forwards and chanting cryptically. As he wondered where she was and what she was doing, a small tremor of uncertainty passed through his mind. Her behaviour could still unsettle the men and weaken them in battle. He calmed his anxiety by recalling that, since Bjorn's death, she had been alone in her discontentment. The others, including Old Harald, were caught up in anticipation of the fight and the spoils that it would bring. Still, it was a grievous offense. She should have slept with him before the battle to show that there was unity and as a sign that the gods were pleased with Rorik's preparations.

Oddrun had no intention of lying with Rorik that night. She left the clearing, went deep into the forest and before sleeping, took a flat, black stone she had carried from Trøndelag out of a leather pouch. On it, she had scratched several runes. She made deep cuts in her cheeks and let the blood drip upon the stone held in the bowl she made with her hands. As it fell, Oddrun called upon Odin to help her take revenge for Bjorn.

Old Harald sat closer to the fire than usual that night and saw many past battles in flames that reddened his face fiercely. When he lay down, he prayed that his bladder and the rest of him slept deeply that night. He always lay on his right side but that night an aching in his sword arm made him turn on to his left. He had never had such a pain before and wondered what it meant. Before he slept, he ran his hand over some of the scars thirty years of fighting had brought him. The new day was bound to bring him some more. As long as it brought him plenty of meat and, who knows, perhaps a woman, he did not mind the cuts.

Adils could not sleep. His mind filled with what might happen during the raid. Some said it would be a brawl, nothing more, and that scratches from the monk's cats were the only wounds they would finish the day with. To Adils, whatever the resistance, it was going to be a battle; his first. He wondered if, by the end of the following day, he would have killed in hot blood. The only regret he had about killing the Irishman on the beach was that it had not been a fair fight. He wondered if he would be killed and what the killing blow would feel like. He might be wounded: would he bear the pain as a Viking should? If wounded badly, would he be able to stand the humiliation of being maimed for life? Adils dug his fingers sharply into his stomach and tried to imagine what a sword thrust felt like. He did it again and then a third time, tensing his muscles before every blow, something he would not be able to do in the heat of a fight.

Adils could not chase such unnerving thoughts from his head no matter how hard he tried. Mother: he strained to remember his mother. A Frankish slave, they said she was. Long dark hair and an oval face to which he could put no features. "Mother, please push these fears from my mind." Singing! She used to sing to him, but not one tune had stayed in his head, or if it had, it was behind a wall which his fears had built and would not let him climb. Swedish Vikings killed her, they said, in a raid. And probably raped her beforehand, they said. And perhaps afterwards, they said. Adils listened to the night. What were normally soothing sounds: comrades shifting and murmuring in their sleep; an otter slipping from the bank and blending with the water; an owl hooting; a breeze stroking leaves, became the screams of fighting men and the clash of their shields and swords. Lines from Oddrun's oracles crowded his mind and his nostrils filled with the rank smell of his sweat.In spite of his terror, Adils dozed a short while before the camp roused itself to travel the last stretch of the river and attack Clonmacnoise. Yngvar shook his shoulder and joked that young Adils slept late like an old campaigner. The camp broke up quickly. Stew left over from the night before and hard bread provided their breakfast. Bleary-eyed and numb-fingered men brushed past each other in the sharp cold of the morning darkness, trying to fix axes and swords into girdles and muttering curses when they failed. As they readied themselves for battle, some of the Irish called upon the old gods to give them the speed and ferocity of the wolves whose skins they wore. Everyone, even Adils, became eager to stir their muscles into life, to be on the river and to start the attack. A disorderly crowd heaved towards the *boats* and the Irish and Vikings came close to fighting before they had even seen Clonmacnoise.

Rorik, in mail-shirt and iron helmet, took his position at the prow of the *Sea Bear* and shouted for torches to be fastened to its gunwales and to those of the other boats. He forbade Oddrun to join him and banished her to the *Sea Serpent*. On board that vessel, Old Harold shook his head. Having that woman on board on such a day would most likely be a curse.

The race that had started in the island bay and been sustained along the sea coast and up the river, continued now, as Irishmen and Vikings struggled to steer and row their boat into the lead position. The foreigners were the more experienced sailors but the Grey Wolves with Morann in one of the lighter and more manoeuvrable currachs quickly put a distance of thirty metres between their vessel and the *Sea Bear* and *Sea Serpent*. Fiacc gripped an arm of the lead oarsman. The Grey Wolf tried to wrest himself free but Fiacc held firm. He would not join the race and held his currach back. He was in no hurry to shed blood or to be the first to meet the unexpected.

The Ambush

From the front of the company, Conal raised an arm to signal they could rest for a while. Makarius offered thanks, sighed heavily and slumped over his ride's neck. The horses' hooves padded quietly to a halt on pine needles, and the supply wagon's wheels stopped creaking. The only sounds were the rustling of a breeze in the treetops and the rhythmical running tread of the foot soldiers following well behind. Conal had pushed himself, his band and the horses to the extremes of physical endurance on the trek to Clonmacnoise. The journey from Cillebairre had been a hard, exacting one, with the girl urging them onwards every time they rested. They had lost the way twice but searched doggedly until their direction was true again. The noise of their passing brought the people of isolated farms warily to their doors. Occasionally they stopped to take water, to eat and to relieve themselves but never for long.

At the Máenmaige rath, Fearghal had given them a change of horses, the aid of six soldiers and the promise that news of the Northmen would be carried to the king. He also added food, weapons and medical provisions to their supplies. Fearghal himself had said he would join them, but, deeply intoxicated, had been unable to mount. Six was not a great number but Conal saw that they were hardened fighters. Donnchadh, in particular, impressed Conal: a small dark man with sinewy limbs and the strength of two twice his size.

Riding horses on the rough tracks of Ireland for three days and nights with hardly a rest had left Makarius bruised and aching. Their gait was very different from a camel's and their backs much more uncomfortable. He was quickly convinced that the tough little Irish horses enjoyed inflicting pain on their riders and looked for the hardest routes to follow. It was penitential. Illness had afflicted him long before leaving Cillebairre, and, as the journey to Clonmacnoise neared its end, he felt close to death itself. He had managed to sustain himself by continuously reciting a text he had discovered in Cillebairre's library, words from the Antiphonary of Bangor:

Domus deliciis plena... Super petram constructa... Necnon vinea vera... Ex Aegypto transducta...

A house full of delight... built on the rock... and indeed true vine... translated from Egypt.

It had been his choice to travel. He insisted on accompanying Conal in the hope that the great monastic settlement of Clonmacnoise might help him rediscover the sense of purpose he had lost during the long, dark winter months at Cillebairre; might bring him to that *house full of delight... translated from Egypt*; might grant him the Glass Chalice.

The cold he could stand since he had endured many bitter desert nights. The rain and damp were something completely different, a hostile force that he found hard to fight. He never knew rain could come down in so many different ways. One day it would be like fierce stinging insects that reddened one's face, the next, like mysterious smoke that hid every feature of one's surroundings. The sun locked itself away from these people day after day after day. When he heard the terrible news of Tulchán and then watched Georgis' body swell hideously before his tormented death, Makarius suffered deep dejection and lost sight of his reason for being in Ireland. Nothing at Cillebairre could cheer him. He spent whole days, regardless of the weather, sitting or walking alone by the river and in the hills. The ancient Fathers wisely taught that a busy monk is besieged by one devil, but countless wicked spirits attack an idle one. Makarius knew the teaching well but did not heed it. The devils found him defenceless during that Irish winter. He watched the people of Cillebairre about their work but never felt inclined to help them. Occasionally, his conscience tried to pull him out of his sloth and despondency but it had always failed. He knew he should be active and should mix: some days saw him longing for company and yet, when he was with monks such as Nuadu or Mochan or with Conal, he found it hard to disguise the contempt he had for them, for their ways, their food, their language, for the land they inhabited. He even resented their hospitality because it stirred his conscience into suppressing this resentment. With Tulchán gone, Makarius felt his presence in Ireland was losing all purpose, and with Georgis gone, he felt no real fellowship with anyone. Some news from Brother Brecc of Clonmacnoise might have brought relief, but none had ever come. Brother Brecc had his garden to attend to.

During that restless time in Cillebairre, Makarius began to wonder if the Chalice could make any difference, if one glass cup made by his own people hundreds of years ago at Natroun, a glass cup that could be broken, shattered, ground into a million particles, scattered irretrievably and returned to sand, could unite his people and make them immovable in

249

their faith. He doubted whether it could help them at all. He recalled the Irish monk's angry words at the desert monastery of Baramus: "Faith in God should not depend on a drinking cup, no matter whose hands have held it!" Was it right for him to place his hope for his people in this Chalice? Such thoughts had shocked him but he could not still them. He told himself repeatedly that his people were calling for the return of this blessed cup and that they were placing their hopes in it. During Advent with its fast, he had tried to find relief in readings from the prophet Isaiah, words that had comforted and strengthened a people who, like his own, had been invaded and subjugated by a foreign power: they too suffered *anguish, gloom, the confusion of night, swirling darkness.* His brothers and sisters believed the Chalice would restore them to their rightful place in Egypt; bring them salvation in this world and the next. The Most Holy Pope and Patriarch of the Great City of Alexandria and of all the Land of Egypt, of Jerusalem the Holy City, of Nubia, Abyssinia and Pentapolis, and of all the Preaching of St. Mark had ordered him to retrieve it. It followed that his doubts were irrelevant, but they would not go away. The demons were at work, as active here in Ireland's greenery as in the desert's browns. In the firm belief that Clonmacnoise might shake him from this *accidie,* Makarius had insisted on riding with Conal, his warriors and Samthann.

Conal had been reluctant - the Egyptian was not well, could slow them down - but had acceded. It was foolish of him probably but he believed it would bring no real harm since there had been many auspicious signs since his return from *Sliabh Naofa*: the round tower was rising again albeit slowly; *bolgach,* the terrible skin disease had raged through the neighbouring valleys but had but not visited Cillebairre; his permanent militia had grown to be a compact fighting force of twenty men under the loyal and effective leadership of Eoin and Corraidhín and, the most propitious sign of them all, Carnait was pregnant again. Signs, all good signs. Bréanainn the priest had joined them at the muster on the clearing and had given their mission a blessing.

Conal was wary. A short distance ahead, the track widened and left the forest and they would travel in the open. They were not far south of the great settlement of Clonmacnoise. He trotted his horse to the edge of the trees and surveyed the land. With only a half-moon showing occasionally to help him, Conal discerned below him a wide expanse of cleared land sloping gently to the river and on the water saw the lights of the enemy flotilla. He backed the horse into the forest and waited until clouds fully covered the moon before commanding his band onwards. As they started, Donnchadh suggested trying to halt the boats before they reached Clonmacnoise and proposed a strategy. The next twenty miles were undertaken in a deep, early morning dark with Conal forcing the weary horses, men and woman into even greater exertions.

Samthann led them to the edge of the wood where she had last seen Ruadhan. When the horses were tied, Conal dispatched Donnchadh and a handful of warriors under Eoin to the riverside: "Harry them! Do what you can to slow them down."

The rest he ordered to go ahead under Corraidhín's leadership, alert Clonmacnoise and organise a defence of the place. "Get them from their prayers! We will be with you soon." Then he went in search of his young friend.

"Somewhere on the ridge of the low hills that run away from the river. Find the highest lookout point. He will be there or in the wood near there," Samthann had told him.

Exhaustion quickly closed Makarius' eyes, rested his mind and he slept deeply beneath the may trees.

*****

The smell of horse was so strong that Ruadhan thought it had woken him and not the rough hand pressed to his mouth. He started to squirm free of the grasp but the intruder held him firmly. Dawn had not yet touched the land and only the faintest glimmering of moonlight penetrated the forest's interior. It was a few moments before Ruadhan saw, to his great relief, that the strong hands were Conal's. The older man smiled down at him and whispered. "I thought you had learned lessons, Ruadhan, but this time, there was nothing to deceive me. Your camp was easy to find and it was easy to surprise you. However, there is no time for more lessons now. This day promises to be busy enough."

Ruadhan wanted to shout with delight but Conal gestured, warning him not to. "You have neglected your duty as watchman, Ruadhan. The Northmen and their Irish friends are on the river not far from this place. We are doing what we can to slow them down."

"Is Samthann with you?"

Conal grinned: "Here we are about to have the fight of our lives and you are worried about that young woman, as worried, I would say, as you

251

were about Ite. Do you remember? It was the last time we were together. I can understand why you are anxious, Ruadhan. She's strong willed, confident, resourceful and beneath the grime of travel, there's a beauty to catch the eye. Yes, she is with us. She led us here. I had no hope of finding you without her."

"We must warn the monastery, Conal."

"Corraidhín is raising the alarm, but from what I hear, I doubt if that Abbot will move before he feels Viking steel trimming his tonsure. But enough of talking until we are settled by a quiet fireside, Ruadhan. I have some sailors to attend to." Conal, his mind surging with thoughts of the ambush that was planned helped Ruadhan to his feet. "I have not sent many into the wood since we have not the means to engage them here. I want to sting them and assess their numbers. I am going down to the riverbank. Samthann is by the hawthorn trees on the edge of the wood. She said you would know the place. Someone is with her; a priest from a foreign land who speaks of your friend, Tulchán, and who is searching for a special Chalice. His path has not been smooth since he came to our land. His companion and fellow-priest died of a fever in Cillebairre and he himself is now weak from some similar ailment. Ireland has not welcomed them. Will you go there and let the forest be your protector for another day or will you come with me and fight?"

"You trained me, Conal, taught me many a warrior's ways, but I do not want to kill."

"And I do? You should know by now that I would avoid any fight but what is before us this day cannot be flinched from and once you step towards a foe, all thoughts of choosing other than mortal battle, have no place. I repeat, Ruadhan, I would deflect this fight if I could but I cannot and I tell you this: already the anticipation is transforming me and will transform you. I would like you by my side. I could force you and there is an active spirit inside me that wants to do that, but I will keep that sword sheathed and leave you to choose. Join me, Ruadhan, and discover how the fight stimulates, thickens your blood and brings new colours to the day and how, joined in battle and fighting for your life, those colours intensify and your body shapes itself for feats you never thought possible. I watched you fight that cur, Ruarcc. You are more than ready. I know you are not a coward. Come with me."

Ruadhan did not reply. He searched Conal's features to try to understand how his silence was being judged. It was obvious. Conal could not hide his disappointment. "Go then, go to where Samthann and the Egyptian are. Join us at Clonmacnoise when the rest of us have won victory for you."

"Will you meet me by this wood if you fail, Conal?"

Conal snorted. "I fought with the Northmen, Ruadhan. Whatever the outcome, I will not leave the battlefield."

Conal moved agilely and soft-footedly away from Ruadhan and was quickly cloaked by the wood. He half ran, half slithered down the wood slope through a thinning corridor of trees to the riverbank. With the anticipation of battle, the heavy weight of tiredness that had stooped his shoulders fell away and the frustration of near failure at Cillebairre, of a still unsettled community, and a half-built tower, was forgotten. The tactical cunning and the almost animal instinct for danger and self-preservation that had grown during his long years of exile with the Northmen resurrected themselves and were ready to be put to a severe test. He knew they could not stop the invaders at this place but they would slow them down. Conal reached the others hidden along the banks. Most of the net Donnchadh had taken from local river fishermen was just below the water's surface, but the ropes holding it were visible at the river's edges. On his side, they led out of the water and into the trees and dense bushes that came close to the verge of the river. On the far side, a grassy bank bare of trees, his men had secured the ropes under heavy stones. The trap was set. They waited in silence.

As soon as Morann in the leading currach realised what the obstruction was, he ordered his men to pull on their right oars to steer to the bank. It would be easier to sever the net where it was tied to a tree rather than hack at it from the boat. Rorik saw what was happening and it confirmed him in his belief that he had allied himself to fools. He shouted from the *Sea Bear* warning them to be cautious but the distance was too great for him to be understood. The Grey Wolves rowed swiftly to a muddy landing place a short distance back from the net. Before Morann could give more orders, two of their number grabbed torches and jumped from the boat, laughing and fighting for the privilege of being the one to cut the ropes. Art pushed Angin out of the way but when he ran forward was tripped by Angin's outstretched foot and fell heavily. They were like boys playing a game and completely guileless of any danger that might prowl around them. Angin scrambled to his feet, jumped over his friend and crashed into the dense undergrowth. Art got up, rubbing his knee, picked up his torch and followed at a slower pace. Angin was well named. He could run as fast as a hare. In the boat, the other Grey Wolves leaned on their oars, arm muscles twitching uncontrollably from the hard rowing.

The *Sea Bear* drew level but Rorik ordered his men to douse the torches, raise their shields from the ship's side and to stay in midstream. He gazed intently through the darkness at the stretch of wood the two men had disappeared into and a sardonic smile came to his face. When Fiacc, in the second currach, saw what taking place, he told his oarsmen to double their stroke and head for the beach.

Angin half ran, half crawled to the tree where the net was fastened, still laughing from his play-fight with Art and unable to catch his breath. He heard rustling in the bushes close to the tree and thrust his torch towards the sound. "Art, are you ready to eat the dirt again, my friend?"

Young Colman was the first to engage the enemy. He moved quickly into the circle of light and knocked the torch from Angin's hand. At the same time, Donnchadh grabbed the Grey Wolf from behind and drove a knife with much-practised skill up under his ribs. He twisted it to the right and then the left and then pulled it free. With only a low moan, Angin slumped to the ground.

Art's torch had been damaged when he had fallen and almost snuffed out. Its meagre light illuminated only the closest branches. He thought he heard a muffled call from up ahead. He did hear shouts from the river but could not make them out. He stopped pushing forward through the undergrowth and listened. At first, his own panting filled his ears, but then was overcome by the distinct sound of shuffling in the bushes. His torch flickered out. Art cast Angin's name before him into the darkness but it was not taken. He turned and ran but lost the path they had trampled from the river and headed deeper into the wood. He wove his way clumsily among the trees. Saplings whipped at his face. His name was being called but he could not be certain from which direction and careered on until he tripped over a fallen tree. He had risen to his knees when Eoin's first blow hit his neck just below the ear. He shouted for help repeatedly as he was beaten to death.

254

Morann struggled to stand and stop them but more Grey Wolves scrambled from the currach in response to the calls. Two had already stumbled into the forest's dark, dense mass when Fiacc's boat pulled alongside. Fiacc stood and screamed at the others not to be so foolish. "Don't you see what they are doing? They want to lure more of us into their trap! Go there and you will never see Clonmacnoise! Go in there and you will not see tomorrow!"

It was clear reasoning that made the Grey Wolves hesitate but they were reluctant to accept it; one of their number was being tortured. Morann added his voice. "He is right! This is foolish," and self-interest triumphed over crude loyalty to their four friends swallowed by the forest. Those who had stepped from the boat on to the bank clambered aboard once more.

Rorik knew from their tactics and failure to launch an attack on the boats, that not many men were hidden in the trees. His crew eased the *Sea Bear* forward until it nudged the net and then Horik swam to where the ropes entered the water. As the sky was lightening gradually, Rorik ordered five of his men to train their bows on the foliage above the swimmer. They were not needed. Horik cut the ropes without interference from anyone on the bank and swam back to the longship. The *Sea Bear* moved on and had cleared the drifting net when it was targeted with slingshot. A small, ineffective volley rattled against the boat's sides and the shields followed by a solitary spear that hit its mark, an oarsman's shoulder. The wounded man was pulled quickly from his bench and laid flat on the deck. His replacement settled his rhythm as quickly as he could to the new frantic pace of rowing and soon the *Sea Bear* was out of range. Fiacc's currach followed the *Sea Bear* swiftly past the net, then the *Sea Serpent*. Fifty metres behind, the unsatisfactory skirmish had left the other Grey Wolves frustrated and angry. They argued over new rowing positions and jostled each other. Their vessel drifted in the gentle current and teetered dangerously as they rearranged themselves. "That Viking priestess has us all cursed!" one of them shouted as he sat heavily on his bench and grabbed an oar. He heard a faint *whoosh* like a sudden breeze stirring leaves the instant before a spear pierced his neck. He pulled the weapon free and blood gushed from the wound. He collapsed forward. When the others saw him dead over his oar, the clamour subsided. Morann ordered two Grey Wolves to pull him roughly from his spot and another to replace

255

him at the oar. "Be quick!" The boat stuttered forward erratically until the remaining crew of the second currach settled to a rhythm and rowed as fast as they could up the river to join the others for the assault on Clonmacnoise.

Desecration

Abbot Ronan dashed from his cell to the library. He had ordered the reliquaries and other treasures be removed from the main church but had anyone thought of the precious books? Had he told Servan to see to them? Some had gone, but not many. Ronan did not know which way to turn: the Gospels, of course, and at least one Missal; perhaps the one brought from Iona by monks who also fled these Northmen. But what of the others? What of all that learning, the Christian heritage that God had seen fit to ask Ireland to preserve: the sacred scriptures in Hebrew, Greek and Latin; the writings of Jerome, Irenaeus, and Augustine? Ronan scanned the walls of the library. Like heavy fruit ready to fall, over one hundred leather satchels holding books hung there.

Sounds of fighting by the quay broke into the library's quiet. Ronan grabbed the three nearest satchels, put their straps around his neck and left for the main church to see that his orders had been obeyed. People who had never entered the enclosure before were rushing in all directions carrying a few of their belongings. They were like ants scattered by a burning brand thrust into their nest. Fields, herds and homes were forgotten in the wild rush to get away from the attackers. An elderly, hunch-backed man, leaning heavily on a staff, hobbled past him. A mother, with a screaming baby in her arms and two other children at her heels, almost knocked him over. Ronan wanted to tell them to stop; to remember who he was and where they were; remind them that the enclosure was a special place set aside for men who dedicated their lives to the service of God; a sanctuary of peace, of prayer and humble work. He was on the point of shouting at them when he saw a knot of fighting men by the guesthouse. The Northmen were inside the enclosure. The church. The door was ajar. Ronan entered and closed it behind him. Inside, he knelt and prayed briefly before checking that important items had been cleared. Had anything been left? The thurible wrought in the shape of a bird hung by long ropes at the side of the sanctuary. Its sides were still warm and, stirred by Ronan's touch, faint fumes rose from the incense. What was it made of? Silver? It was heavy; far too heavy, and would have to be abandoned. The sacred cloths and vestments were behind the altar. He must take as many as he could. The book satchels were very heavy. Perhaps he would leave one. There was so little time.

The door crashed open and the first raider ran towards him screaming obscenely. Ronan was at the altar. He turned to face the man and saw three others had barged in with him, winners of a race to reach what they thought would be the treasure trove. The Abbot had no means of resisting them. Even if he had, he would not do so, for that would be to join with them in profaning the Lord's House. All he could do was place his body in their way; a poor sacrifice at God's altar. Ronan fell to his knees, an Onias mildly defending the Temple from its defilers. He kept his eyes open and waited for the blows which his Heliodorus would deliver.

They never came, for just as in the passage from scripture which had entered Ronan's mind, a horse and fearsome rider appeared. They came in fury through the door of the church scattering the raiders and running down the Viking about to strike the kneeling Abbot. Even with death so close, Ronan searched his mind frantically for the lines of the passage. He realised that the horse was not "richly caparisoned" and neither was the rider "accoutred entirely in gold", but the similarity in circumstances had to be more than coincidence. God had shown his power. Ronan collapsed unconscious.

Conal wheeled the horse violently to face the rest of the band. His entrance had startled them and he still had the advantage. There was not enough room to work up a gallop but he charged as best he could and slashed right and left with his sword dealing savage wounds to two of them. The charge, however, was too wild: his horse took several fierce blows and beyond the raiders, collided with the wall and threw its rider. Conal was stunned but recovered quickly and faced his opponents. All three were still standing although the two he had hit had little fight left in them. He breathed in deeply and felt great strength flooding his muscles. Conal knew he was their match. To show his supreme confidence, he dropped his shield and drew a dagger. Some of his blood, but not his life, would be spilled in the church. To let them know that he had been trained in the same school as they had, he held his sword high and in a loud voice named it "*Vikingbitr*.[15]" Then, without any thought of stratagems, he ran towards the raiders screaming. Hacking with his sword in his right hand

---

[15] Vikings often gave their swords names. Two examples are Gramr (Fierce) and Langhvass (Long and Sharp). Conal names his Viking-Biter.

and stabbing with a dagger in his left, Conal quickly inflicted terrible wounds upon the three who faced him. For two, they were fatal. The third ran, bleeding from the head, out of the church and Conal raced after him.

Old Harald had not been able to keep up with his comrades and his bladder had begged him successfully to stop. He was groaning and relieving himself outside the church when he heard the call of death in that one Norse word and now as the Irishman rushed outside like a true *berserkir* who could never be stopped, he knew that call would not go unanswered. The last of his piss dribbled down his leg. The strange ache in his sword arm had been a warning he should have heeded. The die had been thrown. There was little point in resisting.

In his frenzy, Conal had felt none of the Northmen's blows, but now, as a calm and sadness suddenly began to settle on him, he noticed two deep cuts on his arms and sensed the metallic taste of blood in his mouth. In the middle of the fight, he must have bitten his tongue. Carnait, his loved one with that cruel imperfection, filled his mind for the first time since he had left Cillebairre. Conal shivered involuntarily, shook himself and spat. It was not the time to dwell upon thoughts of her beauty or to indulge in the remorse that always came to him after a fight; the weariness brought by exhaustion and the terrible understanding that the killing would go on and on. He had to keep his head as clear as possible and he had to rejoin his men. He should not have allowed himself to be distracted by the attack on the church especially so early in the fight. With the others, he should have kept a tight formation. He went back inside quickly, retrieved his buckler and then led his horse to the altar and lifted the conscious but dazed Ronan on to its back. "They have not finished with your church. Go from here as quickly as you can. Go and hide. Clonmacnoise will need you when this is over."

Ronan acknowledged that he had heard what Conal had said and gently spurred the horse forward through the door of the church.

*****

Ruadhan had no intention of spending the day under the hawthorn trees. The Psalter had been brought to Clonmacnoise but was now under threat once more. He was determined to go to the enclosure and find it. Samthann did not understand but would not leave his side.

All along the narrow path to the noble tree and from there on the road back to Clonmacnoise, they met families fleeing from the raiders,

259

adults carrying small ones, older children pulling carts. Some brandished clubs and hurried quickly by, frightened now of any strangers, but many urged the young people to turn and go with them to find safety away from the monastery. They pointed to the smoke rising from burning houses and told Samthann and Ruadhan that they would be killed or worse, be taken as slaves. Nothing they said shook Ruadhan from his resolve. He and Samthann ran most of the way and even when they came across bloody evidence of the Northmen's attack, they did not falter.

*****

There was a brief lull in the fighting. Crouching close to the church wall, Conal assessed what was happening. He was pleased with what he saw. Almost all the families running from the invaders had fled the enclosure and its immediate surroundings leaving it as the battlefield for the armed men to fight over. Dondchadh, Corraidhín and Eoin had regrouped their men and remnants of the Clonmacnoise militia by the side of the refectory. All were now on foot. They had kept themselves in a tight knot and looked as if they had suffered few casualties. At the quay and all the way up the slope to the enclosure, they had harassed the Grey Wolves and Northmen, following Conal's orders to stay together and to strike quickly and withdraw quickly. Even though they had been stung severely, the raiders had not united in an effort to defeat the defenders. They had broken into small, separate gangs that were ransacking the buildings within the enclosure. It was obvious they were led poorly and were in disarray. Conal knew he could not hold the enclosure but also knew he had not lost the day.

He was about to leave the church, go through the cemetery and join Donnchadh when two Grey Wolves came around the corner of the building. Both were running but one dragged a twisted leg behind him. They stopped when they saw Conal and brought their swords and bucklers into fighting positions. The taller of the two rushed at Conal but stumbled over a stone as he neared him. He recovered from his stagger into a half kneeling position but before he could defend himself, Conal slashed at his neck. Blood gushed and ran over his shoulder and down his arm. He looked up at Conal as if beseeching the quietus, swayed for a moment, tried to draw breath strongly through his mouth and then fell sideways to the ground writhing.

260

The second Grey Wolf moved towards Conal more warily. Conal started! The man's odd, lurching gait prompted a distant memory of children sharpening lengths of ash to try to spear fish. It couldn't be! Conal backed off and looked down at the man's severely deformed leg and then back to the face and familial likenesses, the high-boned red cheeks, the broad forehead, the black hair. Recognition came to the Grey Wolf at the same time as he caught sight of the distinctive scar on Conal's forehead.

"My brother," he asked, "can it be you?"

"Morann?"

Morann nodded.

"You fight with the *Finngaill*. Why is this?"

"I fight alongside whoever will give me an advantage, Conal, but I will not fight my brother."

Conal laughed scornfully, "Your hatred branded me, Morann, and almost claimed my life."

Morann shook his head, "Long gone is the time when, little more than a child, a foolish child, embittered by my deformity, I wished you dead." Carefully, keeping his eyes on Conal all the time, Morann laid down his battle-axe and shield. "I will not fight you."

Conal gripped his sword firmly. The warrior within him struggled with this strange lull and with long-buried fraternal feelings.

Morann smiled, nodded understanding and then deepened Conal's puzzlement by what he did next. With both hands, he tore frantically at his leine until his almost hairless breast was bare. Conal gazed transfixed at the conspicuously white flesh and its blue tracery of veins. Why in the midst of battle was he making himself so naked and vulnerable?

"What are you doing?"

"We are of the same blood and have been separate for too long, enemies because of one terrible mistake I made. Forgive me." Morann put one hand to a breast and squeezed it gently so that the nipple became more prominent. He beckoned Conal with his other hand and its long, thin fingers. Only then did Conal realise what his brother was doing. It was the old way among men of bringing about reconciliation and attesting affection. Morann was inviting him to suck at his breast. Conal's mind was in turmoil. He knew this gesture, knew it well, an old way, a Celtic way of healing wounds in a relationship. At first every part of him, body and soul, recoiled from committing this act. He almost felt nauseous at the thought.

It did not belong here on the battlefield or anywhere else. It was not of their generation. It belonged to the past. Its innocence had been defiled and the priests and chiefs had outlawed it as a scandalous incitement to impurity between males. Conal knew that what was happening was outrageous, abnormal, and yet, at the same time, something central to his being told him that this was right; that this was a wondrous gesture on his stranger-brother's part, a stunning contradiction to the hatred and violence that raged about them and one that he should acknowledge and reciprocate. Hardly aware of what he was doing, Conal placed his shield and sword on the ground, tore open his garments and advanced towards his brother. Neither spoke. Conal put a hand high on his brother's free arm. Morann removed his other hand from his chest, gripped the back of Conal's head, and moved it gently forward and down towards his bared breast with its sprouting of hair and the nipple in its dark brown halo. There had to be sounds and yet all Conal experienced at that moment was silence... and stillness. Once again... stillness. Conal was transported to *Sliabh Naofa*, his last morning there and that *stillness*. Was this God making Himself present here in the midst of chaos and death? With reverence, Conal opened his mouth and placed his lips on his brother's nipple. With reverence, he sucked, tasted the salt on Morann's flesh but as he did, he also discerned a tensing of the arm his hand rested on followed by a deft movement and the stillness and silence were shattered as Conal, feeling the tip of a blade entering flesh beneath his ribs, screamed in anger, gripped the arm firmly and recoiled before Morann could push the knife further into him.

"Brotherly love? Cain's blood still races in your veins!"

Morann broke away and moved swiftly to retrieve his axe. The wound to Conal's side was slight but in an effort to deny what had happened, his head still spun. He made no effort to reach his weapon. He pointed to the scar on his forehead. "You do not need to better this, Morann. Turn. Flee. More are coming. You will not win."

"Time has changed nothing, Conal. Don't ask me why. You would think that as the sea wears down the stones it washes over that my hatred would have dimmed, but it has not. I have dreamt many times of our meeting again, *special one*, and each time, in my dreams, I have cut you down. You may not believe me, but I am sad that I found you at this place. I wish it had been otherwise and I had been left with my dreams. But we have met and I have to do this!" On those words, he rushed towards his brother at a pace Conal would not have thought possible. Conal did not move, still suffering the strange paralysis of will this discomforting encounter had inflicted upon him. He did not need to move. Dondchadh had become anxious waiting for his leader and with two others had crossed to the great church. He arced his axe fiercely into the back of Morann's head before he reached Conal.

Dondchadh was puzzled. Why had Conal looked so defenceless before the Grey Wolf? Exhaustion perhaps. Dondchadh felt weary too. The tough little man slumped against the wall of the church. He breathed heavily but his eyes scanned the enclosure, watchful for any new move their enemies might make. Conal gripped his arm briefly in a simple gesture of praise, thanks and encouragement similar to the one he had given his brother a moment before. The taste of Morann was still on his lips. He ran his tongue over them and spat. The fighting was not over. Conal would not let this extraordinary interlude shake his resolution. He shuddered and picked up his sword and shield. Both he and Dondchadh knew that the enclosure could become a trap. It was time to leave it, reform and consider new tactics.

*****

An angry Rorik tried to stay in control of his emotions. "Search every building again for a Chalice made of glass! It has value beyond its looks! Then set fire to them!"

Bands of Grey Wolves and Northmen charged once more into the churches, the school, the refectory, the infirmary, the scriptorium and library, and the monks' cells, crossing and recrossing with each other and becoming frustrated and angry when they found little of the treasure they had been told to expect. Even the granaries were despoiled in the search for plunder. They argued and fought with each other, lost the little discipline they had. There was no one to give clear orders. The only gratification came when they discovered the kitchen had a larder packed with salted meat and a good supply of ale. It was clear that the monastery had been warned, but, some maintained, unlikely that the monks had had time to carry the treasures far. Without waiting for any orders, individuals and small groups of raiders raced from the enclosure to search for riches in the woods and bogland about Clonmacnoise.

From the highest point on a gently rising ridge east of the monastery, Conal watched this development with great satisfaction and rallied his small band to harry and kill the attackers who were so disordered and were behaving in such a rash and impetuous manner.

*****

As he led Samthann into the monastery enclosure for the second time, Ruadhan remembered Ronan's anger on the first occasion. Now, the enclosure's peace and exclusiveness had been shattered in a way that could not be matched by the arrival of a young woman. Not even Ronan would have protested this time. The morning was old when they entered and they found only a few Grey Wolves and Vikings. Several wore priests' vestments looted from the great church. Some were wounded and all wandered listlessly about the enclosure in the aftermath of the fight, still hoping to find well-hidden treasure or more of the ale they had already supped in large quantities. The main church was ablaze but the library looked as if none of the raiders had been near it.

Ruadhan was wrong. The floor of the library was littered with the satchels and their books. Adils was there. With his sword, he slashed at the straps of another satchel until it fell from the wall spilling its contents. He idly turned the vellum pages of the book with the tip of his sword. The marks made by the pens looked like the cracks in the bark of an oak tree, but otherwise meant nothing to him. He stopped turning the pages when he came to one that was illuminated. The central figure in the painting that took up most of the page was a man - or was this their God? - in long, colourful robes and with his hands extended from his side. Two smaller men who looked like soldiers gripped his arms. The large eyes of the central figure were simply drawn but they fixed Adils in their gaze. He moved his head to try to avoid them. This man was barefooted, had no weapons and he was held a prisoner by those other two. He could not be a god, thought Adils.

Where was his father? They should have remained close but as the raiding party made its way from the boat into the enclosure, its battle-formation had been broken. Adils' mind had spun so violently with the sudden onrush of combat and with primal thoughts of self-preservation that he was quickly separated from Rorik. Small groups and individuals fought apart and in order to try to regain a hold on what was happening, Adils had sought refuge from the skirmishes in the library. He had not

264

deserted. He was not a coward. He had fought, fought well, he believed, and may have killed. He could not be sure. Was it going their way? Adils did not know. He was about to leave the library to fetch fire when Samthann and Ruadhan rushed in. Adils recognised the slave the foolish Bjorn had taken from the fishing settlement. He lifted his sword high. They were both breathless but the young man spoke rapidly in Irish.

"It must be here! I have to find it! I will find it! Help me!"

Adils was confused. Screams and curses were the language of battles, not this prattling. Did the boy think words could stop Viking steel? Ruadhan edged forward and Adils stretched his sword arm higher, but as he did so he realised he was going to find it hard to kill these two. Why? Perhaps the fact that they were not armed stirred the guilt that remained from his murder of the Grey Wolf; perhaps his battle-stirred blood had cooled for too long looking at the Irish books; perhaps those eyes staring from the page meant that their God was exerting some power; perhaps Oddrun had placed a curse on everything to do with this voyage; perhaps it was the fact that they were young like him.

Ruadhan got down on the floor and crawled among the books. He did not care that his life was in danger. He had to find Tulchán's book. Samthann stared intently at Adils. Slowly, the Northman lowered his sword and looked quizzically back at their acquiescent god on the page. Ruadhan frantically pulled books from satchels and turned their pages and the pages of those that had already tumbled into the open. Some were too small; some too big; some had different binding. When a brightly illuminated page caught his eye, his heart rose, but each time, closer inspection told him the book was not the Psalter.

"He told me to protect it! Protect the Word!" He crossed the floor on his knees glancing at some books and looking hard at others. Not once did he look up from his search to see what the Northman was doing. One book lay open. A Psalter? An angel, a tree! Was it that page, the first he had ever seen? Ruadhan looked for the blaze of many colours which would not die down, blues, golds and reds shaping the figure of an angel half-seated with its back to a slender tree. He looked for the finely drawn branches and leaves that arched over the angel's head. He looked for intricate pattern that claimed the edges of the page and in it, those soft folds of a mother's cloak wrapped around her child. They were not there in the crude representations he found as he turned pages and scattered books. Nothing of Tulchán's art was there. Still he would not give up and started to work through the books again. Samthann call his name softly but insistently. "Ruadhan, Ruadhan, come. Get up."

Adils angrily gestured for them to leave and threatened them with his sword once more. To Ruadhan's surprise, Samthann bent down as if she too was looking for the Psalter or perhaps, going to help him to his feet. Neither was the case. Certain she and Ruadhan were being taken as slaves by a foreign devil, one of the band that had slaughtered her family, Samthann grabbed the strap of a satchel still heavily packed with its book, rose slowly but then stepped agilely towards the Northman, swinging her improvised club at his sword arm. This took Adils completely by surprise when his grip was relaxed and his sword clattered from his hand. Quickly, hardly knowing what he was doing, Ruadhan picked it up and stood, a reluctant warrior on the battlefield.

Adils laughed. He was not afraid and thought of rushing Ruadhan. He had a slight advantage in height and weight and the Irishman seemed uncertain, hesitant. A flesh wound, Adils thought, would be all he would suffer. He doubted if his enemy had the strength or the will to kill him. But what would the girl do? She had already shown that she would not stand by while he and the Irishman struggled. Adils stared at Ruadhan. Ruadhan looked back at him, and kept the sword hanging innocently at his side. To Adils there was something in the Irishman's gaze; something in the place; something in that picture that usurped his battle spirit, told him thoughts of fighting were foolish and should be banished.

Ruadhan reminded himself that the young man in front of him was one of a breed that had killed Tulchán, taken his step-mother and destroyed the only place he had been able to call home. Horrific memories flared in his mind. In the days immediately after the raid on Cillebairre, hiding in the forest, Ruadhan had gone over and over how he would take revenge. Part of him wanted those thoughts to return, to storm into his mind and make him act; make him step forward and cut at this man until he was dead. The thoughts returned, but the red rage did not. He had come to the library for Tulchán's Psalter. Such hatred was not a part of any lesson Tulchán had taught him and was not within him.

Adils was puzzled by the strangeness of the encounter and particularly by his own indecisiveness and unease. Perhaps it was a curse. As Ruadhan and Samthann watched closely, the young Northman went down on his knees and found his book once more and the illuminated page that had enthralled him, the picture of the soldiers and their prisoner. He took a dagger from his belt, and carefully cut the painting of Christ free from its binding and, keeping it flat, pushed it under the front of his leather jerkin. Suddenly, sounds of fighting stuttered into their sanctuary. Adils looked alarmed. Grey Wolves, not Northmen, were close by. He gestured for Ruadhan and Samthann to leave.

Ruadhan threw the sword away and it clanked loudly against the stone wall. He and Adils stared at each other for a moment longer, both of them expressing bewilderment. Samthann grabbed Ruadhan's hand, "We have to go now! More are coming!" Outside, as they ran from the library, Ruadhan tripped and, looking down, was sure he recognised the body of the young man he had watched wearily turning the spit that night on the island. Clouds now moved rapidly over Clonmacnoise bringing rain in short, heavy showers. Gusts of wind stirred small waves on the surface of the great river.

*****

It was mid-afternoon on the day of the battle when Makarius stirred. The deep sleep had refreshed him but he was still very weak. He sat up, knelt and tried to pray. After a few moments, when he felt strong enough, he struggled on to his feet, pulled off the rain-soaked, heavy woollen brat the monks at Cillebairre had given him, and stood in his thin cotton Coptic tunic. He felt cold but pleased that with this simple gesture he was making an important declaration and emerging from the deep melancholy and torpor that had afflicted him. The spiritual disease had brought physical illness in its wake and at Cillebairre, Makarius had seldom been free of headaches, fevers and fainting fits. But now, standing uncertainly and shivering in just his cotton tunic, he felt renewed in vigour and any doubts he had had began to fall away. He was a Coptic monk wearing his uniform for Christ and he was on a mission for his Church. The Chalice had to be found and returned.

The young woman, the one who had called them from Cillebairre, and a young man had stayed with him at the edge of the wood. He remembered that she had wiped his face with a wet cloth from time to time. Both sat close by him and Makarius had made sense of some of their talk through his broken understanding of Irish. They had talked about him. He smiled at the boy's clumsy attempt to pronounce *Makarius*. The

267

boy had also mentioned something precious that had to be saved. Had they spoken of the Chalice? It is possible. Perhaps Brother Brecc had told the boy about it. It was here at Clonmacnoise! Yes, the boy had said that. The precious Chalice of St. Mark was here! Makarius raised his thin arms upwards and gave thanks to the God who had directed his poor servant to that place. A heavy shower began to fall. The drops spat off the leaves into Makarius' face. With his arms still held heavenwards, he stumbled out of the forest and onto the path towards Clonmacnoise.

By late afternoon, Makarius had reached the monastery enclosure. He had very little recollection of how he had succeeded in getting that far. A sea flowed and ebbed, flowed and ebbed in his head and with it a terrible ache. His vision was distorted so that the route, the buildings that still stood, and the people who pushed and prodded him or cowered from him, were glimpsed as in a thick fog. At the guesthouse gate, he was challenged and beaten by guards, Northmen and Grey Wolves, united now in drink. They mocked Makarius. His strange speech and dress amused them until someone suggested that he was insane and should be killed or avoided completely. "Touch him and you too will go mad," said one Northman. "The Devil is in him and he will cast a spell on you," said a Grey Wolf. "That's the Devil's language he speaks." One of them swung his axe, but stumbled as he did so and hit Makarius' shoulder with the haft and not the blade. The axe rebounded. He tried to regain his balance and strike again but another restrained him and told him to leave the madman with his devils and to enjoy another drink before the ale ran out. The rain lashed down once more. Makarius had hardly flinched with the blow and, in awe, his persecutors backed away from him. From then on, their superstitious respect for the mad allowed Makarius to stagger half-blind through the enclosure, until he stumbled into the cemetery.

In an act of desecration which a few of the Grey Wolves had refused to take part in, the Northmen had driven cattle into the burial area. Standing memorial stones had been toppled and graves soiled with animal deposits. Large areas had been churned into a morass. When Makarius arrived, a few cattle were still inside cropping the grass steadily, the tumult of the attack only a faint twitch in their memories. Makarius knew he should find the church. The Chalice – the Precious Blood – the altar – the church. Find the main church. He lurched from gravestone to gravestone asking each of the dead interred there where the church was. He was certain that having been brought so far, so close, he would be guided to the Chalice even if it was by the dead.

The rain stopped as abruptly as it had begun. Makarius slipped in the mud and fell into a drainage ditch which carried rainwater away from the cemetery. The level of water in the ditch was rising rapidly. Makarius attempted to pull himself out several times but kept slithering back until he no longer had the energy to try. He lay still and felt his back and legs sink slowly into the leaves and mud that had accumulated in the bottom of the ditch. He prayed that his strength would return soon but before he had finished his prayer, lapsed into unconsciousness.

*****

Before Fiacc entered the cemetery, he looked about him at the devastated monastery enclosure and experienced a slight feeling of regret, not for the dead Clonmacnoise monks or their religion, but for the work, achievement, and organisation that the settlement had represented. From here, the monks had controlled a large area of land and all the people who lived on it. Fiacc could not help but admire and envy that.

All along the hills, in spite of the dousing rain, thin trails of smoke rose lazily from the ruins of houses and hung, reluctant to disperse, in the still, warm, early evening air. "Viking incense," he thought, and a grim smile forced itself from his hard features. To the south-west, a faint rainbow arched over the broad river.

Ossene's grave was as it was before Fiacc had returned to the island, with the two parts of the broken slab pushed clumsily together. Fiacc lifted and dropped them to one side of the grave. The soil underneath was still loose from his first attempt to disinter the Chalice, and it was not long before he had the precious object in his hands. He peeled the layers of hide from the Chalice and gazed quizzically at it. The glass was thick and cloudy with a slight blue tint. The base was large and flat, no doubt to lessen the chances of spilling its precious contents. The fluted stem was a mere six centimetres in height and was topped by a wide, shallow bowl that had two handles affixed to its side. Engraved on the base of the bowl was the Gethsemane scene with, at the edge, the naked figure of a young man, little more than a boy, running away. Fiacc felt strangely light-headed and had to sit down in the grass. Finding the Chalice of St. Mark had come to mean so much to him, had become *the* purpose of his life, the reason why he rose in the morning, ate, drank, moved his limbs, and slept;

the reason why he had endured life on the island. To have it and use it to gain revenge, wealth and power was everything to him; it explained why he was alive. He gazed intently at what his hands held half-expecting some manifestation of the power it could release; perhaps it would glow in a spectacular way, or perhaps he would feel a burning sensation where he was touching it. There had been stories. Nothing happened. He noticed for the first time that it was grimy in spite of its heavy wrappings, and that the engraving was scratchy and uneven. He had thought the Chalice would be grander; that it would, through beautiful design and ornamentation, blazon the fascination it had for so many. Fiacc fought against disappointment.

"Surely, you would rather have gold than a glass chalice, Fiacc?" Rorik stood on the other side of Ossene's grave, with his sword unsheathed. He was filthy and blood-spattered and his speech was quickened by the intoxication of battle. Sweat streamed down his face and cut channels through the grime.

Fiacc shuddered slightly and pushed foolish emotion well away from him. "Rorik, like you, I know the real worth of this cup lies not in its glass or even in its history, but in the power it can give some people over others: you over Arab traders in the Levant; the Copts over their oppressors in Egypt; me over my enemies in this country."

"You are forgetting that the Chalice alone does not bring you power, Fiacc, but the Chalice and the promise of Viking strength. Once that Chalice is in my hands, you have only the promise."

These two had come to know each other well in a very short time. No more words needed to be said. Once Rorik had the Chalice, he would renege upon the agreement to help Fiacc secure control of a large area of the midlands. Fiacc looked for Aed and saw him moving stealthily and quickly from the direction of the church. He congratulated himself on his foresight but his pride did not let him rely upon Aed. He lowered the Chalice gently to the ground.

"I could kill you now, but out of respect, I shall let you die standing," said Rorik.

"Let me draw my sword and we shall have an honourable fight: surely that is the only way for honourable men like ourselves."

Rorik laughed. "I have overestimated you, Fiacc. I thought you were as double-tongued and lacking in belief as I, but now find you are a

270

fledgling in deceit and understanding. You should have listened to your teachers when they told you not to place your trust in this world."

As Fiacc started to get up from his sitting position, he pretended to stumble forward, came closer to the Northman and, rising the second time, lunged and pushed him up against one of the remaining gravestones. Rorik tried to bring the hilt of his sword down upon the Irishman's head but before he could, Fiacc grabbed his sword arm with both hands, forced it over the top of the stone and, with a swift downward movement, broke it. Rorik dropped his sword, howled and fell to his knees. He pulled the smashed arm to his body and cradled it. Fiacc drew his own sword and was about to end Rorik's life when the sight of Oddrun climbing the low cemetery wall made him stop. By that time, Aed was at the scene and he too had his sword ready to hack at the Northman. Fiacc stopped him and pointed to Oddrun.

As she leapt down from the wall, Oddrun screamed and ran towards the combatants brandishing an axe. Fiacc could not understand what she was shouting. It was something similar to her cries from the headland when Bjorn had been pushed out to sea. Fiacc slashed once at Rorik's legs and decided to leave him to the woman and her Viking gods. He picked up the Northman's sword and threw it as far away as he could. Aed looked curiously at the disturbed grave and the glass Chalice.

"He was a suspicious man, Aed, sure that I was out to cheat him. Look what that has led him too."

Aed took heed of Fiacc's warning and watched in puzzlement as he retrieved and wrapped the Chalice. He made sure Fiacc walked in front of him out of the cemetery. As he passed the ruined church, he looked back and saw Rorik limping in search of his sword as Oddrun closed on him.

*****

Makarius' lapsed in and out of consciousness. When he first came round, he saw a figure not too far away by one of the graves. Praying? Someone had said Mass each day standing by his predecessor's grave and alongside his own open grave. Who was it? Marianus, it was; Marianus, a blessed man and someone with whom Makarius had a distant familial relationship. The Irish Marianus was moving. Makarius was just able to make out that the person was bending, and moving his arms. The picture was blurred but the Irish Marianus was digging. Then nothing was clear any more. Two gravestones became one and then became four and then became blackness.

Conscious once more, his head full of devils, Makarius saw that someone else had come to the cemetery and was by that grave. Two men were talking. Words came to him not in a steady flight that a hunter could shoot, reload his bow and shoot, but from all directions like birds scattered from a wheat field. He could only bring down the odd one: "Fiacc", yes, yes, "Fiacc", and "Chalice", yes, yes, yes, "Chalice"! That must be the sacred Chalice he had come to secure for his people! They had the Chalice and he had been granted the opportunity to fulfil the mission entrusted to him. For months he had felt unworthy, a failure, but now, by a miracle of sorts, by the intervention of Marianus, he was being offered a chance to redeem himself. Paul and Barnabas had quarrelled bitterly over the question of Mark's fitness for missionary life. Mark, the one who brought knowledge of the Saviour to Egypt! Perhaps Makarius had judged himself wrongly; he could retrieve the Chalice. Marianus had come to tell him this. He had to act and pulled himself halfway up the side of the ditch. He scrabbled in the mud to get further but it was no use. He was exhausted. He slithered back to the bottom of the ditch. *You have shown me much misery and hardship, but you will give me life again. You will raise me up again from the depths of the earth.* Makarius lost even the will or energy to pray. At first, he was sure the dense cloud was outside of his head; a low, heavy accumulation bringing more rain, more Irish rain to cool him down, and he could not understand why he felt so hot. He fell into insensibility once more.

The Enclosure Retaken

Corraidhín lay on sheepskins in the makeshift hospital, a simple shelter of hides fastened to several bushes. Part of his bowel had spilled through the wound the spear made. Conal examined it closely and nodded, "That is the proper colour. It can be repaired if we are quick." Colman and Eoin lifted Corraidhín carefully and, to raise the wounded man's hips, Conal placed a folded blanket under him. The two others lowered their comrade and then pinned his arms and legs. Conal stepped back. Samthann poured wine freely over the wound and using a small knife extended the tear at both ends. Bright new blood flowed down Corraidhín's skin. His breathing quickened and became stentorious. Eoin looked questioningly at Conal.

"She needs to do this. The intestine would not return easily through the original wound," responded his leader.

Samthann used two dulled kitchen hooks brought from a nearby farmhouse to draw the lips of the wound apart. Corraidhín groaned. Conal knelt and held the hooks in place with the wound gaping. Then, starting with the part closest to the lesion and in the hope that it would refind its former order, Samthann carefully, deftly, pressed the length of bowel through the cavity and held it in place for a moment. "Release the hooks." She splashed more wine on the wound. Corraidhín winced and struggled. "Don't let him move!" Eoin and Colman strengthened their grips. Corraidhín passed out.

"He has lost a lot of blood," said Eoin.

"Bring the edges of the wound close together. Hold them there!" Samthann told Conal sharply. "Pinch them! He can't feel anything now."

As Conal did that, she threaded a needle with the horsehair he had given her.

"I saw it used in the Round City," Conal said. "Make the stitches deep and tight, otherwise his guts will be in his lap again." Slowly, cautiously, Samthann pushed the needle into and out of Corraidhín's flesh sealing the wound. When she had finished the sutures, she knotted and trimmed the horsehair. Conal nodded his thanks to her. Without speaking, head down, Samthann left the shelter to look for Ruadhan.

"She did well, the fishergirl. She has saved him. I don't doubt it. Eoin, Colman, mix honey and wild garlic and apply it to the wound. Then bind him with strips of clean linen but not tightly. And stay with him. When he comes around, give him what's left of the wine to dull the pain."

After inspecting the sentries, Conal joined the others and sat down heavily. The scar on his forehead itched. It became sensitive at times of great agitation. He rubbed it hard and brooded on the day and the killing. He dwelt particularly on the encounter with Morann but not with any sadness arising from a residue of familial feelings. Time, absence, conflict and anger at Morann's battlefield treachery had eliminated the last faint traces of such sentiment. What was harder to come to terms with was how quickly he had lowered his defences on that battlefield and how he owed his life to Donnchadh. Conal shivered and looked about him to assess their position. He doubted that it would be tested that night but the ridge to the east where they were encamped was a good position to defend. He released the fastening on his braided hair and teased it out. It fell about the sides of his face in long dark curls streaked with grey. Looking towards the monastery, he saw that several fires burned brightly in the enclosure but intuition and experience told him that the celebrations among the enemy would be subdued. Conal breathed deeply and told himself that the day had been won. He had trained his small force well. His men had fought with discipline: only four had been killed and three unaccounted for but it angered Conal that Clonmacnoise had not been better defended by its own people; all but two of the small, ill-trained militia, along with most of the monks, had been slaughtered. The raiding force was not the largest he had known: two *snekkjas* with perhaps seventy Northmen and the currachs with perhaps thirty Irish renegades. A few monks had fought well but he wondered if most of them and the *manaigh* of Clonmacnoise were all like young Ruadhan who would not carry a sword. Conal could not see how any settlement would survive unless its men took weapons in their hands and defended it. But dwelling on what had happened would not help: he had to hone his mind for the day that would follow. The survivors around him were exhausted, bruised and wounded, but in a richly happy mood, celebrating quietly with a few of the Clonmacnoise families that had fled the dawn attack but stayed close to the settlement. Ruadhan and Samthann sat apart from the rest, doleful. Donnchadh lay closest to the main fire, aching from his efforts but content. Conal spoke: "They see our flames but will not come near us. They have suffered more dead and more wounds than we have and they have no clear knowledge of our numbers."

274

The others murmured their agreement and in turn, voiced their particular memories of the day. They were tales that had grown well away from the facts in the few hours since the fighting had stopped: one opponent became two; a stocky Northman became a giant; a clumsy, fortunate blow became a well-aimed, lightning-like sword thrust. Nevertheless, they could claim a victory of sorts. They had not stopped the raiders from entering the inner sanctum of Clonmacnoise but they had frustrated them in their intention to seize the treasures and they had inflicted serious losses upon them. The storytelling and the blazing fire began to heal the Irishmen to the marrow of their bones.

Conal spoke once more: "I have been among the Northmen when the pickings have been poor, and am glad I am not with them now. Drink will rule their heads and they will fight among themselves. If the help we expect comes from the Ui Maine, we can rout them completely."

Ruadhan recounted his own story. The others found it hard to understand his concern for the book. One of the soldiers laughed and said that the tale was exaggerated or that Ruadhan had been lucky enough in the library to meet a Viking who was sick in the head. Another said he believed Ruadhan. God had been watching over him and Samthann.

"Even without the book, you still have its words in your head," said Conal. Ruadhan was annoyed with Conal for trying to console him in this way. What did he know of the book? Several times at Cillebairre he had admitted his ignorance of what was written in the scriptures. "Tell me some of those words you learnt from Tulchán; the psalm."

Ruadhan remained silent, but Conal persisted: "Tell us them. They will be good to hear after this long day of bloodshed."

Begrudgingly, Ruadhan recited psalm forty-six.

"They are not lost. They are in your mind and in your heart."

*****

The Northmen had lost their leader and twenty-six warriors and, apart from livestock, had found little to loot. They drank and ate well into the night but the feasting which should have dulled their rage, sharpened it and did nothing to quell their frustration. The remaining men of the Grey Wolves were also angry and confused. Most had spent their day searching the land around Clonmacnoise, occasionally fighting with quick, elusive opponents as difficult to engage and kill as shadows. More than half their number had not returned and they too had lost their leader. The other one,

275

the mysterious one who had dressed as a monk was missing. Individuals had seen him in the enclosure during the day but no one could remember him being active in the attack. Aed had also disappeared along with one of the currachs. Bitter quarrelling racked both groups throughout the night.

Adils saw great danger in what was happening. They had to stay united and leave quickly with the few spoils they had. Nothing could be gained by lingering in that place. The small band of Irishmen that had harried them so successfully was probably reinforcing itself and preparing an assault on the enclosure at first light. As he walked through the camp, the huge fires that the men feasted around did nothing to dispel his fears since their light was dwarfed by the great serpent darkness that lay coiled about the enclosure hill, a brooding, threatening darkness.

Adils began to give orders and to look after his own. The Grey Wolves were not his responsibility and besides, he did not trust them and did not think they would take orders from him. He doubled the guard about the enclosure and told Yngvar to take several men and make sure the *Sea Bear* and *Sea Serpent* were ready to embark at daybreak. He also told the carpenter to hole every other vessel tied up at the quay including the Grey Wolves' remaining currach. Finally, he ordered him to take Rorik's body to the ship. Yngvar had witnessed Rorik's ignominious death. "She cut his face making strange markings, Adils. It is to forbid him from entering Valhalla."

"Her scratchings mean nothing, Yngvar. His entry is assured. Now, go, take him and place him gently where no one will bruise him further with their rough comings and goings."

As Yngvar left, Oddrun stepped out of the darkness. "I do not come to mourn, Adils. Rorik brought it on himself. The gods were perturbed and demanded to be recompensed."

"They are not alone in seeking such," was all Adils said.

Although some questioned his right to lead, several of the older ones saw the sense in the orders Adils was giving and were content to accept his authority. Adils was uncertain that all the men would follow him but knew they would unite and act purposefully if all could agree why the attack had failed; if their anger and frustration could be poured into one reason which answered all their questions about the day's events; if they could find a scapegoat. Once the idea entered his head, Adils knew where to point the finger and knew all would point with him.

Oddrun was to blame. She had cursed their mission and a witness had seen her kill their leader. While the fire still blazed and the ale was still plentiful, Adils denounced her and she did not deny the accusations. She lowered her head as if in shame and did not speak. As their priestess, she mediated between the gods and humans. When the gods favoured her people with prosperity and health, and victory in battle, then it was clear to all that she had done her job properly. When disaster came their way, it was equally clear that she had neglected her work and had to be punished. There could be only one punishment in this case and it would serve as a sacrifice which the Northmen hoped would bring the gods once more to their side. All, including the Grey Wolves who realised what was happening, roared their agreement. Oddrun's head moved slightly as if she too was assenting. She had accepted this logic all her life and did not struggle against it. Of all the Vikings who had survived, she was the only one who was content with the outcome of the day. Adils, the son of the slave girl, was enjoying his triumph, but Oddrun was sure it would be short-lived. Rorik was dead, marked for Niflhel, and his voyage was doomed: the gods *had* listened to her. Oddrun smiled slightly as Adils fulminated and as he put a length of strong rope about her neck. Two men, each gripping an end of the rope, led her outside the enclosure wall in the steadily falling rain.

*****

Cathal, King of the Ui Maine of South Galway moved his force the final few miles just before dawn. Thirty of his men rode and were followed by over seventy on foot. The call to rid Clonmacnoise of the Northmen and the Irish bandits was one Cathal had responded to eagerly. It would make amends for his own terrible profanation of the monastery not long in the past when he had thrown the newly elected *secnabb*[16] into the Shannon and the poor man had drowned. He was only a Munsterman, Flann, son of Flaithbhertach of the Ui Forga, and the monks had no business electing him, but his death had troubled Cathal ever since. He had sent Abbot Ronan many cattle in reparation for what had happened but his conscience had not rested. Perhaps it would when this day was over.

---

[16] vice-abbot; second-in-charge of the monastery

The Irish attacked at daybreak and in spite of Adils' precautions, his men and the Grey Wolves were soon in disarray. The Ui Maine horsemen spurred their mounts up the slope and forced their way easily inside the enclosure while a strong party of their foot soldiers cut off the path down the slope to the quay. If the Irish attacked the longships, Adils knew that Yngvar and the few guards could not hold them for long. He mustered all his men by the guesthouse gate and they moved out of the enclosure. A few Grey Wolves joined them. A third of the way down the slope, those who still carried spears hurled them at the Irish foot soldiers, and then the whole group formed itself into a wedge and charged ferociously into hand-to-hand combat. Their charge took a few of them through the Irish line and on down to the *Sea Bear*, but Adils at the centre of the wedge and those to the side and back of him were halted.

Looking down from the enclosure, Cathal ordered foot soldiers held in reserve to close on the Northmen from behind. The Northmen tried to keep together and fight back to back but as the Irish steel slashed and thrust and men fell, their formation broke and individuals were isolated. Adils never rested his sword arm; he hacked to his right and then, under his shield, to his left. Horik succeeded in staying close to his new leader and deflected many blows aimed at him. "Go, Adils! Run to the *Sea Bear* before it's too late!"

Adils heard the advice and started to scream and whirl his sword furiously. Horik hurled himself at the terrible wall of Ui Maine soldiers that blocked their path to the quay. The wall gave slightly but then quickly reformed around him and Adils glimpsed one of the Irishmen grab Horik's lank black hair and repeatedly stab at his side with a dagger. Great badges of blood formed on his leather vest, but still Horik stood tall, screaming in defiance and pain, and his determined resistance drew more of the Ui Maine to him. Adils saw what Horik was doing. A gap had appeared in the wall. He was sacrificing himself for his leader. Adils knew there was nothing he could do to rescue Horik. If he waited a moment longer, he too would be trapped. He ran full tilt at the gap Horik had created. As he dashed through it, a spear tore at his shoulder and the hands of someone on the ground tried to pull him down, but he kept running, stumbling, almost falling on the slippery slope down to the river with the victory cries and insults of the Irish filling his ears.

Yngvar moved the *Sea Bear* into the middle of the river and ordered those on board the *Sea Serpent* to hole that longship and abandon it. The slaughter on land would not leave survivors enough to manoeuvre and power two *snekkjas* to safety. With its anchor raised, the *Sea Bear* shifted nervously in the water. Adils crashed through the reeds at the river's edge, waded as far as he could and then swam to the ship's side. Once on board, he surveyed the hillside to assess how badly his men had fared. As if to lie in the mud of the battlefield was undignified, Horik knelt in death with his body arched forward and his head on the ground. A few other Northmen fought on near him but could not hope to escape. Agnar, the fisherman, was one of them. Adils saw the Ui Maine soldiers wrestle his axe from him and force him to the ground. One, two, three, four Northmen were in the water heading for the *Sea Bear*. With those already safely on board, they would make a crew of only fourteen. Adils tested the air: it was still after its restless night and there was no point in trying to raise the sail. The long retreat back down the river and from Ireland would be slow and painful.

When the last man had been pulled on board, all the survivors except Yngvar at the steering oar and Adils at the prow, crouched on the middle benches behind fixed shields and started to row. In spite of the spears that were hitting the *Sea Bear*, Adils stood erect, determined that some Viking pride would be salvaged from the disaster at Clonmacnoise. His father lay in the open hold amongst the provisions and their miserable plunder. At the quay, angry Ui Maine soldiers searched in vain for a boat in which they could follow and then, frustrated, watched the *Sea Bear* move slowly from them. Adils feared what lay ahead. Blind courage had carried him through the night and through the morning's battle, but now his mind became a riot of uncertainty. The river surface was calm; the oarsmen established a rhythm, and the sleek sides of the *Sea Bear* cleaved the water with confidence, but young Adils was a long way from rest. His body began to shake. The wound in his shoulder seeped blood steadily. Out of all the chaos of the day before, his memory showed him the encounter with the young Irish man and woman in the library. He reached inside his jerkin and pulled out the page he had cut from the book. The barefoot God held him in his gaze once more.

That morning, Conal was oddly content to rest his men. It had been agreed that they would join the Ui Maine attack only if necessary. From

279

their encampment, he watched the *Sea Bear* leave. He knew that such a small crew, spirits embittered by a humiliating defeat, was unlikely to be able to take the longship over huge lengths of sea and through the many dangers that would come its way. Other boats and different crews would take their place. There was a restlessness among the Northmen that was like a heart trying to thrust through its chest; a need to travel, to explore, to conquer. At mid-morning, he led his band from the ridge back to the monastery, on the way dealing ruthlessly with three Grey Wolves who had deserted the battlefield. As they neared the devastated settlement, they met families returning from hiding and taking paths to the charred ruins of their homes. On the hillside beneath the enclosure, the Ui Maine soldiers were gathering and laying out the dead in a ragged line. Nearby, the first monks to return were tending to the wounded. There was bustle and clear intent to restore Clonmacnoise but Conal's thoughts were on Cillebairre. He would return as soon as possible to his home. That community had to learn to save itself from such attacks. He would return to his wife and the son she carried. Her beauty had grown with this pregnancy and convinced Conal there was another male within her. This was a child he would ring with a stockade from his first day in the world. Cillebairre was Conal's destiny and it would be his child's. The sun shone in a clear sky and the wet grass steamed.

In the enclosure, only the guesthouse was left intact. Abbot Ronan was considering if it would be right for him to stay in it, when he recalled who had occupied it last. He wondered if he could forgive himself for being so credulous. He had listened to Fiacc and not the boy. He had forgotten how strong evil could be and how active the Devil is in this world. But that was the past. He would do penance and a lot of it but, for the time being, had to put his mind to other matters. There was a great deal of work to do burying the dead, attending the wounded, rebuilding the churches and the cells and healing bruised spirits. Cathal of the Ui Maine was to be thanked for his intervention. It was reparation on Cathal's part, no doubt, and the strengthening of a relationship that could be of great advantage to Clonmacnoise. The Egyptian: he must not forget him. What a state he was in and all for the sake of a glass chalice! Using a glass chalice for the great sacrament! A strange practice and certainly not one Ronan would follow. *What was it that Brother Brecc, may his soul rest in peace, quoted concerning chalices made of different materials? Had it come from*

Boniface? Holy Week and Easter were almost upon them; preparations had to be made. Their faith was being tested. Clonmacnoise was suffering like the Lord its monks followed, and it, like him, would rise. Matters could be much worse, Ronan told himself, and resolved that before the day was out, he and his fellow monks would celebrate a special Mass of thanksgiving. He walked from the guesthouse to gather the *sruithi*[17] who had survived and enlist their help. As he passed the ruined library, he saw a woman carrying water. Ronan went to her and gently, but firmly led her from the enclosure. The attack had caused serious disruption, of course, but the right order had to be restored at Clonmacnoise as soon as possible.

Ruadhan searched for Fiacc among the dead. Where was he? Ruadhan needed to know. The long, cold, winter months on the island cliff face had seared a deep, fearful impression on his mind. Even the reassuring presences of Conal and Samthann did not dispel his anxiety. Piece by piece, from what captured Grey Wolves told them, the story was assembled: the alliance; the Chalice; the desecrated grave; Fiacc and Aed's disappearance. In the evening, a Ui Maine scouting party reported that a currach had been abandoned ten miles south of the settlement and under it, they had found the body of a short, red-haired man with a thin beard. His neck had been broken. They also found discarded clothing.

Ruadhan's mind was too full for words or sleep. When night came to an exhausted settlement, he walked through the Ui Maine camp and into the enclosure. The guards let him pass unchallenged. He looked into the darkness about Clonmacnoise. The night breathed contentedly. A hundred fires bespangled the low hills and on the great plain that slumbered to the south, Ruadhan saw, mere sparks in the blackness, a hundred more. Tulchán had said that Ruadhan's destiny was at the monastery of Clonmacnoise. What was there for him here? About him lay the stricken heart of the monastery. Only scorched beams and tumbled stones remained of its churches, school, library and scriptorium. Would that heart slow its beat until there was no hope of recovery? Ruadhan wished he could see his future clearly. He wished he could quieten his thoughts, and not be anxious about what lay ahead; he wished he could accept and understand what had happened but that was not easy. His life had been like the sea that had thrown him on to Fiacc's island: harsh,

[17] elders; advisers

uncompromising and vindictive. Would he find understanding, peace and contentment this side of death? Someone was walking up the slope towards him. It was Samthann, the girl, the woman who, like Clonmacnoise, had become a fixed point in his life. She did not speak but came and stood close by him. She touched his arm. Together they looked over the dark plain. Behind them, they heard the first stirrings as the monks of Clonmacnoise began to gather in the ruins of the great church to chant their midnight office, songs praising God's creation of the world.

GALWAY - NANTES

Nantes first, and then Marseilles once more, and from there to Alexandria. Who knows, perhaps Nantes will be far enough. It is a busy port. Traders from many nations conduct business there, including the Northmen. And there may be Arabs.

Like a stoat on a rabbit's neck, the Chalice had a hold on Fiacc's life. Even if he had wanted, he could not shake it off. It had possessed him from the moment it had first been mentioned in that Alexandrian backstreet. The search for the Chalice had advanced his bitterness and promised him sweet revenge on his relations. It had given his life purpose. And in spite of the setback at Clonmacnoise, he could not shake the intense belief that ownership of the Chalice would bring him power and wealth that he would be granted such by those who knew the radical change this object could bring to the peoples of Egypt and beyond.

The ship lurched viciously in the high sea and prompted Fiacc to give his thoughts to more immediate concerns. The shelter of Galway Bay was now well astern, and the vessel, with a light cargo of hides and wool, was feeling every move the water made. He renewed his tight hold on the Chalice and looked about the deck at the Bretons. One of them, a sombre-featured man with tightly curling jet-black hair answered his stare. Fiacc wondered how long they would keep their curiosity in check.

The captain looked at the sky, cursed, and wondered if he had made the right decision to put sail. Of course, they had. He and his crew had been too long in Galway and there had been too many arguments over payment for the iron ore and wine they had carried from Nantes. Trading ought to be simpler and everyone ought to benefit, but it seemed it could never be like that. Someone always wanted to press your price down, question the quality of your goods, make a bigger profit. He hawked violently and spat over the side of the ship. Ireland always paid him with chills, a thickened throat and fever. He looked along the deck at his passenger sitting huddled against the gunwale, and recalled how the monk had come to the Galway quayside insisting that he had to travel with them since he had important business at the court of the Emperor. The captain had been reluctant, but a curiosity about the man and, he had to admit, fear of him, had persuaded him to agree. It had been the eyes, which had unnerved the captain; cold, still eyes that he was sure had never shed tears. He laughed at his foolishness and also at the idea that someone who mixed with Emperors would board his ship. But, who knows, the holy man might have influence with high-ranking moneyed ones who could help salve the wounds of the loss he had most likely made on this voyage. *A monk, a harmless monk. Monks from France to Ireland, and Ireland to France. Sometimes I think I am captain of a floating monastery and not a trading ship. And all he'll pay me with is his prayers ... unless ... unless he will part with that precious parcel he clings to so fiercely.* The captain gazed ahead. Rain was not far off. A few prayers might be necessary.

Later that day the captain agreed with his crew that the monk should reveal what was wrapped in the hides. It should not be kept secret, they argued, for it might be an object that would bring ill luck to the voyage. If that was so, it must be taken from the monk and jettisoned. This crew, like most others the captain had sailed with, carried a full hold of superstitions about appropriate behaviour and about what should and should not be brought on board. They feared the oddest of items: clothing made from certain animal skins, red-headed women, fresh flowers or blossom, the feathers of a seabird, an unused cooking pot, and many more. Not one of them could have told you the reasons why these items were forbidden, but each man believed that if they were allowed on board they could sink a ship in the time it took you to wink. The members of the crew felt aggrieved. The monk was abusing their hospitality, they claimed. It was only right that they should know what he was carrying. The captain agreed although he knew that their self-righteousness was a thin curtain behind which stood greed. Like himself, they hoped the Irishman was carrying, not something that would curse the ship, but an object of great value, a treasure that would make the journey profitable. The monk had to be persuaded to share it with them. After long, grey days in Galway haggling over a miserable cargo around damp smoky fires, the sailors from Nantes wanted to look on something precious, something that glittered; jewels, silver or gold, something that would make the days less grey when they reached home.

As the rain fell gently and as the light dimmed, Fiacc studied the Munster coast which was still visible on the port side. One of the crew bent alongside him to adjust a shroud. He was a short, barrel-shaped man with features which had been severely disfigured from birth. One side of his face looked as if a great hand had pulled the flesh upwards crumpling the cheek and the skin about his eye and mouth. He finished adjusting the rope and while turning from his work, bent and grabbed at the Chalice. Not for a second had Fiacc let his guard drop and, as the man laid his hands on the package, he brought his fist down heavily once, twice on the side of his head. The sailor fell to the deck and crawled away moaning.

Several others had been watching and Fiacc's blow acted as a signal for them to advance steadily towards him. The broad-shouldered, swarthy sailor with the inky curls led them. He brandished an axe and another Breton behind him carried a heavy club. Fiacc looked to the captain who was standing at the prow, but was answered with a shake of the head. The captain then averted his gaze and pretended to give his attention to the forestay. The dark-skinned sailor halted the advance an axe-blow from Fiacc. He lowered the weapon. "Hand over this treasure that you hug so fondly, Irishman, or this axe will kiss your head."

Fiacc stood up slowly, and calmly stared the sailor in the face. "Your axe does not frighten me, but before you do anything more, I must tell you that you abuse a priest and do so for something which you will not value and which you will not be able to exchange. Take this from me by force and you will have wasted your energy and, more importantly, damned your soul for no profit."

Some of the crew muttered their reluctance to continue. The man was not just a monk but a priest who repeated the Lord's words and actions at the altar. Their leader was not daunted. "If it carries no value in the marketplace, there's no harm in showing us what you have, is there?"

"There is nothing here for you. It is a relic of the Holy Church which I am returning to its place of origin."

The sailor had heard enough. "Show it to us, monk!" he shouted angrily. "You could have brought some accursed thing which will put us all beneath the waves!"

Fiacc unwrapped the Chalice to their curious gazes. Glass? They were puzzled and disappointed. The dark-skinned one let his axe fall to the deck and thrust both hands forward, demanding to inspect the Chalice. Fiacc almost gave it to him but stopped himself and shook his head. The sailor stepped towards him and grabbed one of the handles. Fiacc tried to keep a hold on the rim of the Chalice with one hand, but when two other sailors grappled his other arm and forced him back, he had to let go.

Once it was in his hands, their dark, leathery-complexioned leader crossed the deck and held the Chalice up to inspect it in the light that was fast fading. The monk was right. There was little he found of interest, little to excite his greed further. The engraving caught his eye. Perhaps that was important. He looked at it carefully: soldiers seizing a man; others standing nearby; a naked boy running away. The rest of the crew became curious as well and crowded close to him. The two holding Fiacc released him and also traversed the deck to have a closer look.

Fiacc knew there was little he could do, except wait for the Breton to abandon the Chalice as worthless, but he could not control the rage that had risen within him. The Chalice was his. The Chalice was his future. The Chalice held his destiny. He wanted it back in his hands and he wanted to hurt those who had taken it from him so roughly. He drew a dagger from inside his tunic and pushed his way through the sailors. From the prow the captain saw the dagger and shouted a warning. The one holding the Chalice turned and Fiacc slashed viciously at his wrist. The sailor let out a shocked cry but kept a grip on the handle and tried to fend Fiacc off with his other arm. Fiacc grabbed a handful of the man's thick, oily hair and forced his head backwards. The man swung his injured arm and the Chalice over the side of the ship and screamed for the others to seize the Irishman. Fiacc had to save the Chalice. He dropped the dagger and reached for it. The other sailors pulled him back and Fiacc felt a short knife striking into his side, thrust after thrust, one, two, three. The dark sailor watched in satisfaction. His painful grimace turned into a smile and he released his hold on the Chalice.

With a great effort, Fiacc lashed out furiously at the sailors, scattering them. Before they could attack again, he climbed on to the gunwale and followed the Chalice into the turbulent, icy waters. The crew watched to see him come to the surface. They thought they glimpsed him on two occasions but concluded that the shifting patterns in the greyness that was now all around had deceived them.

"We're well rid of them both!" shouted the captain. "Now, to work! This weather holds nothing for us but discomfort. Get this ship to a quiet bay for the night."

OTHER BOOKS BY THIS AUTHOR

THE DEAD ARE LISTENING

Three teenagers, out on the moors working on a school project find Leo, an old man who has been beaten badly. They help him and unwittingly become the target of a Nazi-style group. Leo is a holocaust survivor with crucial information. The story weaves together the teenagers' experiences of the 1990s and Leo's painful memories of the 1940s moving all the time towards its terrifying final confrontation. This is a novel full of humour – but with serious intent – and it is very much of our times.

... a stunner of a book... one of the most intelligent teenage stories to be published for some time. (Financial Times)

Here is a powerful, passionate, deeply disturbing novel which deserves to find an audience among readers of all ages up to the oldest... Best read at a sitting and then returned to later to savour the details. Certainly not a book to be ignored. (Junior Bookshelf)

THE WARREN

... is set in the not too distant future. Genome mapping is complete but extensive genome therapy is still a long way in the future. Faced with war, global viral diseases, a failing economy and collapsing Health Service, the government encourages alternatives. Pressure is brought to bear on "Defectives" to "do the right thing", opt for sterilisation or suicide/euthanasia. The Regulators, a secret para-military organisation force Defectives to comply. To avoid sterilisation, the young narrator leaves home and finds a network of underground tunnels that is home to a hybrid community of resisters. Among them is Sarah. When their efforts fail, it becomes clear that there is a traitor in the Warren. The story reaches its climax as the Warren is attacked. The narrator has to make vital decisions concerning his relationship with Sarah and is faced with startling new knowledge of those who have been hunting them.

... slow, detailed scenes are absolutely superb... Brilliant stuff... so much detail and observation. They complement the action wonderfully.
Charlie Sheppard, Editor, Random House Children's Books

SACRIFICE

Teenager Claire Cullen's grandfather has died in odd circumstances. Claire and her friends go to stay at his isolated house in the in the north-west of England. A terror gang occupies the house and holds them captive. The terrorists' mission fails and the house is besieged by the SAS. Garry, the youngest member of the gang, is ordered to kill and maim. It should be easy, like in the films, with him not feeling anything, off-camera like those who shoot Harvey Keitel at the end of *Reservoir Dogs*. It isn't. *SACRIFICE* is crossover fiction, a thriller for young adults that will appeal beyond that age. It moves swiftly and contains a lot of action. However, the changing relationships of the three teenagers, Claire, James and the terrorist, Garry Glennon are at the story's heart.

Sacrifice is a complex and often powerful novel, which by its conclusion develops into a strong, exciting and heart-stopping thriller.
Rebecca McNally, editor, MacMillan Books

i

EXPATS

November, 1972. The location is Karanuba, a Central African state and one time British colony, now independent under the Peerless One and his secret police, the Fut Fut. The rains are late and a five-year insurrection led by General Gabriel Guevara Malanga is reaching its anti-climax with the occupation of a mission village and school in the remote Northern Region. A dinner party at St. John's Secondary School brings a group of expatriates together, all with different motives for being in Karanuba. As they dine and analyse Africa and Africans, they are surrounded by the rebels at the commencement of what many believe is the decisive move in the protracted civil war but what the cynical Malanga calls his "swan song". The rebel leader could advance sound military reasons for occupying the mission but the truth is he has taken it because St. John's has the only marching band in the country. The occupation is meant to bring the war to an end without loss of face but the Peerless One reneges on a secret agreement made with Malanga and the mission is attacked.

Wow!

The Karanuba Bastion

WHATEVER

Late evening on the first day of the school holidays, teenager Ben Hamilton and his brother lie in a hedge spying on the owner of the mill house as he conducts an odd nightly ritual. Ben is fascinated but his mind is more occupied by thoughts of Holly Gates. He has to find ways of meeting her. Not even the World Cup or the mill house will distract him.

Ben is not the only person with Holly on his mind. John, the owner of the mill house, single, alone, devoted to the Virgin Mary and to the memory of his mother, is also obsessed with Holly Gates. He stalks her and as England take the lead in one of their group matches, he kidnaps Holly Gates and imprisons her in a room that is a candlelit shrine to the Blessed Virgin. An extensive police search begins. Holly lives in terror. However, her understanding of her captivity and her captive's motives change and we learn that the mill house is not the only home that holds deep secrets.

Ben dreams of rescuing Holly and comes close by accident to doing that. Ben and his friends rampage through what they thing is an empty building. All Holly has to do is call out and they will find her. She makes her choice.

THE AGE OF REASON

The year is 1958: satellites are launched; atom bombs tested; the aeroplane carrying Manchester United's Busby Babes crashes in Munich; ITV, with programmes such as *Double Your Money*, tops the ratings and ten year old Martin Doran, nursing an injustice done to him by his mother, climbs a tree and surveys the small town world he is growing up in. From the tree, he introduces us to himself, his family and some of his colourful neighbours especially those who live in the Black Bungalow. He has to confront the fact that his little sister is dying. He also has to come to terms with the breaking of a promise he made to an ex-prisoner of war, an act that he believes may lead to his own death. Martin is greedy for knowledge and explanations. He has reached the age of reason and made his First Communion. He should be able to work out why things are as they are.

THE AGE OF REASON is a sensitive, humorous and, at times, tense, first person narrative that recreates vividly the changing culture of late 50s Britain though the eyes of a precocious child confronting the ageless challenges of growing up.

THAT CANYON PRESS

thatcanyon@gmail.com

Printed in Great Britain
by Amazon